Diana DeRicci

Purple Sword Publications, LLC
www.PurpleSword.com

WOLF'S SEDUCTION
Copyright © 2010 DIANA DERICCI
ISBN 978-1-936165-57-5
ISBN 10: 1-936165-57-0
Cover Art Designed by Anastasia Rabiyah
Photographs Copyright Jimmy Thomas, RomanceNovelsCovers.com
Silver Lining in the Clouds, KenjiImages, Dreamstime.com
Intense Timber Wolf, Hkuchera, Dreamstime.com
Edited by D. Thomas Jerlo and Traci Markou

Published by Purple Sword Publications, LLC
Tucson, Arizona, USA
www.PurpleSword.com

CONTENTS:

WATCHING
HER EVERY
MOVE

*Dedicated to my writing buddies
on Royal Blush Authors.*

CHAPTER ONE

STACEE palmed her receipt from the girl at the register, and with a final smile, strode out of the gold-gilded boutique doors into the calm spring sunshine. Swinging her black and white striped purchase bags in obvious victory, she paused on the broad sidewalk, waiting for her best friend Kay to catch up. Six sweaters and two outfits, all designer labels, were a hell of an after-season find. The better dressed she was, the better the impression made on her buyers. She didn't play in the small leagues anymore. She had to look the part. Dressing for business made sense.

"I know that smile," Kay said with a matching grin, joining her. She'd made some great finds too, carrying several plastic and paper bags, her little purse on her shoulder by a thin black spaghetti strap. She pulled it off and dropped it in the bag of the last store she'd been to, so she'd always know where it was. Kind of an odd habit, but Stacee knew she'd done it since Junior High.

"I scored. Was there any doubt?" Stacee arched a fine eyebrow questioningly. The sunshine felt wonderful beating down on them, winter beginning to feel like a much forgotten song—lovely to hear, not missed until it's heard drifted out from a radio that can't be found.

Kay laughed in triumph, holding her own bags up to show off the names of the stores. "None."

She had barely said those words when the unexpected wall of a man slammed into Stacee, smacking her into the pavement with a startled cry. Her head cracked painfully against pavement, the impact sounding like a gun had been fired right next to her ear. Stars exploded. She couldn't breathe! She felt like a gasping fish, trying to suck in air. Weight bore down on her as someone scrabbled against her, flattening her chest to the sidewalk making finding air next to impossible. Sharp pain flared outward from the side of her head when the first shallow breath filled her screaming lungs. Her world faded to gray then blacked out.

JONAS leapt at the man as his prey tried to scramble over the poor woman he'd crashed into.

"Freeze," he snarled, shackling the man's collar in a relentless grip. He yanked at the young man, almost a boy really, practically jerking him to his feet in his rush of anger, forgetting to watch his strength for a brief moment. Jonas would have caught him. No one could outrun him. The poor woman had just made it a shorter chase. The young man lurched off of the woman he'd collided with, flailing and clawing to wrench himself free.

"Stacee." The woman who had blocked any other avenue of his guy's getaway dropped to her knees, shopping bags scattered in colorful disarray around the pair. Staring at her unmoving friend in numb shock, her features paled. Jonas couldn't spare either more than a glance. His attention was on the guy in his fist, but it bothered him that she still lay prone on the ground.

The youth twisted and fought against the steel of Jonas's grip but there was no way in Hell he'd let him get away now. Not after months of surveillance and tracking. Too much was at stake in this investigation. "Where is the packet?" Yanking uncooperative hands behind his back, Jonas snapped handcuffs on his captive. Deep draughts filled his lungs after his three block chase.

"I don't have anything!" he shouted.

Jonas shook him and the youth's light black jacket shimmied and swayed with the force behind Jonas's tugs. He bucked his shoulders trying to dislodge Jonas. It didn't work. He shoved him against glass, pressing him into the storefront with no remorse. Jonas was oblivious to the gathering crowd gawking and murmuring amongst themselves. His attention was on one person only. He searched the young man's pockets and along his waistband for anything. He scowled when he came up empty on all counts.

"Where is it?" Jonas demanded, leaning in close to make sure his growl of anger wasn't missed. Or misunderstood. Stupidly, the young man showed no fear at the threat right behind him.

All Jonas got in answer was a smug, arrogant smirk over a shoulder.

"That isn't going to work on the judge," he warned quietly, leaning in to make sure the point wasn't lost on his quarry. Sirens wailed. The street cops were arriving along with his department. There was no mistaking the two different types of vehicles. People began to crush in, wanting to see more. *Damn 'bloody wreck' gawkers!* Of course, no one had stopped to help the poor woman out cold on the pavement. He had moments when he just hated the human race.

"Step back!" Jonas shouted over the crowd. "Police business." Most ignored him, stopping like statues rather than dispersing. They were smart enough to create an invisible line and not cross it. Good to know his snarl still worked. No sense in escalating the free drama into a full blown riot.

"Stacee," the other woman whimpered, brushing away a tangle of auburn red hair from her friend's face. Only about two minutes had passed since she'd been hit, but she still wasn't moving.

He couldn't let go of the blonde guy in his grip, but spared the unconscious woman a quick studying look. Shoulder length hair spilled across her back, where he did a quick inventory down to a tapered waist and a very nice rear, showcased by designer's intuition in form-fitting jeans. "Is she breathing?"

4

Her friend snapped up at his question, her eyes full of worry, then nodded from her side on the ground.

"Make way!" an authoritative voice shouted, splitting the crowd. Several uniformed police officers, and a few who weren't, poured into the little drama central unfolding on the sidewalk.

Jonas shoved the young man toward one of the plains-clothes guys with a nod. The officers in blue began crowd control. Jonas knelt by the injured woman.

"What's her name?" He lifted his face fleetingly to make eye contact, but dropped his gaze again to pay attention to the lady as he checked for her pulse.

"Stacee. With two e's," she replied in a shaken voice. The two women must have been good friends for her to explain that to him.

Jonas looked over his shoulder. "Thompson. Call me an ambulance." The man did so without hesitation.

The woman chose that moment to try to move beneath his touch. She moaned, shaken and fighting to get her bearings. "Easy," he cautioned. "Don't move yet. The EMTs will take you to the hospital."

"No." She groaned, trying to turn over. His hand stayed her with gentle pressure, proving she wasn't ready to move yet. A sudden shudder rocked her frame, worrying him. What if something more had happened to the poor woman than being knocked out cold when she'd been hit?

"Miss, you've been hurt."

"She hates hospitals," her friend explained to him. Worry shadowed her gaze.

"She doesn't have much of a choice," Jonas stated. His hand settled on the woman's back only to hold her still. "She was knocked unconscious. She needs an x-ray at the least."

A near silent moan of dismay reached his ears from beneath his fingertips, carrying up his arm. She shuddered once more then slackened. It only took a few minutes for the ambulance to arrive and a gurney to carry her away.

Jonas studied the crowd as it began to disperse, searching for what, he didn't know, but hoped he'd see it. He didn't after several minutes of searching, and his brow furrowed. He knew he felt it. Someone was watching the activity on the street and sidewalk. There were too many scents in the air to try to find just one, and even if he did, he wouldn't recognize it in the morass of city life. The larger problem was: where was the packet? Those memory chips had to be found! He cursed silently under his breath. The young man hadn't had the package on him. Had he lost it? Had he ditched it somewhere on the run after the handoff? Where? The chase had been short and swift. It wasn't as though there were a lot of places he could have just tossed the brown envelope on the street.

He spun when the slam of a door pulled him back to the scene. Strobing red and blue lights snapped his focus to the moment at hand. "What hospital?" he asked, seeing the EMT lock the doors to the rear, hiding the woman on the gurney strapped in for the ride. Unaware of what prompted his need to know, he waited for the answer.

"Southern Memorial."

He nodded then watched the lights disappear down the block, turning right at the next intersection. Downtown city streets were a bitch. One ways and nothing but traffic.

The woman's friend had gathered their shopping bags and was standing, looking around rather stunned.

"Would you like someone to walk you to your car?" he asked her. The brunette seemed a bit shocked and he wanted her to breathe a while before she got behind the wheel.

When she nodded, he signaled for one of the guys on his team to walk with her to her car. He then retraced his steps to his own vehicle, searching for any possible hiding places along the way where the courier could've tossed the memory chips to come back for them later. Ledges, drains, planters. Anything that could be obscure from passing view but reachable. He didn't see a single helpful thing on his way. Those three chips had sensitive information on them. Security sensitive. National security sensitive. They had to be found.

Jonas uncovered the right delivery point to confiscate the stolen chips just that morning from his network. Talk about moving fast when good fortune landed in his lap. Except the damn jerk hadn't had them on his person when he'd crashed into the poor woman. He was positive he hadn't missed the hand off either. That was today. He knew he wasn't wrong about that. The courier was his mark. There hadn't been anyone else in the informant's tip. He even had the guy's description. The delivery to the second. The chips were due to go to the buyer today, so the courier had to have them on him somewhere. Only...Jonas didn't know who the buyer was, or where this silent buyer was from. And now the chips were missing.

Not the most auspicious day in his career.

He let out a snarled sigh. Eight months of work and now a dead end to report back to the DOD.

Gripping the steering wheel in clenched fists, aggravation rode his failure like an eight second bull ride up and down his nerves. A not in the least bit pleasant feeling. Out of habit of covering all the angles and possibilities, he drove to the hospital. He couldn't pinpoint any deeper need to check on the woman or why she was on his to-do list now. That unanswered oddity wasn't helping his aggravation level in the least.

He parked on one of the multi-level garage floors and headed through the automatic doors, instantly feeling the temperature change and the array of scents in the air. He avoided hospitals like the plague. Working like any other fed, the anonymity made what he was hard to distinguish outside of his own kind. Being one of a very highly respected pack, he had ways of avoiding random drug tests from the city and department, piss tests that would make for some very uncomfortable conversations if he should ever have his secret discovered. Could explain his deep dislike for all things medical and nosy.

At the nurse's station, he gave a description and the injured woman's first name, explaining her situation briefly. When the duty nurse frowned, he showed his badge and offered a toothy grin. "It's private business," he intoned coolly. The nurse gave him an arched look for throwing his weight around but divulged the room number after only a moment of searching. Must not have been too many Stacee's that afternoon with head trauma.

He found the room with S. Hales on the temporary door plaque. The door was cracked and he heard conversation. He paused to listen. His investigation was one thing, privacy was another. He could claim either for standing just outside the door.

"Just a headache right now. I don't think they're going to make me stay for long."

"Well, that's good. You didn't look so hot coming in. I know how your blood pressure rockets when they start getting pokey and proddy on you."

An amused chuckle was the answer. "You are a master of understatement. That's why the floor nurse wants me to be watched for a few hours. My blood pressure did a Mount Vesuvius impression."

Confident he wasn't interrupting anything dire, he tapped on the door. A quick, "Yes?" drew him through into the room. The injured woman's voice was rich and full, like the dark eyes that found his. She didn't seem to have suffered too greatly from her mishap on the sidewalk.

"Sorry to bother you," he explained, apologizing for the interruption.

The woman at her side was the same friend from earlier, looking much more in charge of herself. She stood to leave.

"I'll see you later, Stacee. Call me when you get home so I know you're okay, okay?"

Stacee nodded in answer then lifted a hand to the bandage on her head with a combined wince. Watching every detail, it wasn't hard to guess the movement didn't help any. The door drifted closed behind her friend's departure.

He spotted the shopping bags at the end of the bed. "Special delivery?" he asked kindly as an opener, nodding at the brightly colored bags. He walked closer, around the end of the bed to stand at her side. He didn't sit down.

"Work clothes. I probably won't see her until after next week, so better now than naked."

Her humor made him smile. She seemed to be completely relaxed. Even with a bandage the size of a dinner plate on her head, she was lovely. Soft skin that was pale but reminded him of summer peaches. Rich, auburn hair, with streaks of red that flowed around her shoulders. Thick. The kind of hair he could bury his hands into. He briefly remembered the feel of it when he'd sought her pulse earlier. The beguiling scent of her skin filled the room, and he drew a deep breath without thinking about why he did. An aromatic, like a lotion mixed with her own feminine scent. Alluring, yet unique.

He dragged his thoughts back from his appraisal, returning to his purpose. It took a few heartbeats to clear his thoughts to get that far. Then he frowned, and fought it. It wasn't her fault that his day had gone to Hell before lunch.

"I owe you an apology and thanks." Best to get it said, get what he needed then get the hell out of that room. Now that he knew that unique attraction of her scent, he found himself wanting more of it, and of her.

"Oh?" she inquired. He felt the weight of her steady stare studying him. He knew the look. He'd just done the same thing to her. And he had to admit, he didn't hate the feeling.

"For being the wall that stopped my guy from getting away. He hit you a lot harder than I think any of us had originally thought. People getting hurt has never sat well with me."

"That's kind of you..." she replied expectantly.

"Jonas. Agent Dreyer."

"Jonas Dreyer?" He nodded in the affirmative. "Stacee Hales, but I guess you knew that already."

He shrugged but smiled to soften it. He had to check all happenstance. He didn't think this woman was in any way part of the chip theft, just an unfortunate bystander, but it never hurt to ask a few questions. Falling back on training was a safety net too, for being there, in her room. He wasn't sure he could pin any other reasoning to it. He knew he didn't want to think about the attraction that he felt standing so close to her in that bed. She was at a disadvantage for one. Vulnerable. He forced his expression to a placid blankness when he caught her gaze once more.

"Do you think you could answer a couple questions?"

It was her turn to shrug. At least it wasn't a full 'get the hell out of here'. He'd half expected it. He let out a slow breath, ignoring why the thought of her tossing him out on his rear bothered him.

"I won't keep you long." He asked the basics, pulling out a short notepad and pen. Name and private information. Where she'd been that day, what her next destination had been.

"Saturday shopping with a girlfriend," she explained. "I got a bonus and was helping stimulate the economy."

He coughed to hide his chuckle. Her wicked grin was infectious. She had a sweet bottom lip that drew his attention with her laughter. Full and curved with a delicious taunt that crept up whenever those eyes glowed with laughter or teasing. It was the first time he'd ever liked someone on the spot. That was definitely a plus, considering.

He snapped the cover of his notepad closed, stunned at the direction of his thoughts. He did *not* need a female complication in his life. Bachelorhood worked just fine. He pulled out a card. "In case you have any questions," he volunteered, not caring if it sounded lame. He was *not* asking for her phone number. He couldn't remember the last time he'd asked for a girl's number anyway. Probably high school. He'd gone straight to the Army and then onto the force afterward. Even though he had hers, she hadn't given it to *him*. He made sure his subconscious was aware of that fact.

"Agent Dreyer?" She palmed the card and relaxed back onto the bed. "Why all the caution?"

Now that he could answer, just not to her. A gut instinct? A precaution? Something that hadn't sat well since she'd been hit, at the least. He knew someone had been watching the entire time they'd been putting on Drama Downtown for the crowd. Whether it was the next connection, the buyer, or the hand off to the courier he'd caught, he couldn't say. And that uncertainty had every warning bell going off. With an internal smack, he knew why he'd been set on checking on her. He needed to make contact with her. Meet her. Know her. She was going to need his protection.

He never questioned those primal instincts either. This time, he was pretty sure he was going to enjoy his watch.

"Nothing too serious," he replied, smoothing the little white lie. "Just following through on details."

"Well, thank you then," she replied.

He left her room feeling the light, breathy sound of her goodbye on his skin for the rest of the day.

CHAPTER TWO

STACEE dropped the shopping bags and her purse on the counter as soon as she was in her house. Then the first thing she did was hunt for the scissors in the kitchen drawer. She cut the information band off of her wrist with a sense of freedom, then tossed it in the trash. She *hated* hospitals. She'd spent enough time in them when her father passed away. She didn't need the reminders. At least she was able to convince them it was their constant poking making her do the blood pressure mambo. There was no telling how long they would've wanted her to stay otherwise.

She leaned over to stretch and immediately regretted it when she went woozy trying to stand straight again. She just needed to eat. It was late, well past eight now after her little sojourn to the hospital for head x-rays. At least the next day was Sunday. A full day to regroup before work on Monday, and to lose the bandage. She didn't need that at the office.

Scrounging through the fridge, she thought back over the crazy day she'd spent. Her back was stiff from being pummeled by a locomotive in the form of a full speed male. Setting the salad bits on the counter next to her, she began to make something light for dinner. She'd regret anything heavier at that hour. Especially since there was a new headache oozing to sit between her ears. She just didn't have it in her to cook over a stove.

She'd been surprised by the agent's concern, silently warmed by it in fact. Agent Dreyer was not a slouch by any

11

means. He had to be close to six foot, and had the cutest dimple in his cheek when he was trying to hold his smile in check. She wondered what it would be like if he let it loose on the unsuspecting feminine world. He had assessing eyes that warmed and froze at intervals. The man had a natural poker face, but she'd seen him relax a time or two while they'd talked. Almost as if he had to remind himself to keep the cool façade while they'd talked. Working in the volatile real estate market for the last ten years had given her quite the insight to human nature and expression, and Jonas Dreyer was a work of art to study. In constant flux. In constant thought. She wondered what kind of thoughts went through that mind of his to make those expressions. She was willing to bet he was a hell of a conversationalist.

She palmed two ibuprofens to take for the impending headache to take with her salad and a tall tea, and settled at the table to eat. Once she slowed down, it didn't take long for fatigue from her day to crawl in and get comfy with her body, probably the aftereffects of the collision combined with the ache in her brain. She'd be the last to argue with it.

With a sigh, she decided to call Kay in the morning. Right now, a hot shower and the rest of her tea was about all she wanted.

THE beginning of her week went by rather uneventfully, making meetings, showing houses and going over contracts. It was almost normal enough to make her forget about the bruise on her forehead except for the occasional, almost tactful, worried comment. There was very little she could do to hide the mark in her hairline. Just had to wait for it to fade enough to not be a center of attention.

It was Thursday before she began to suspect something wasn't right on her street. The Neville's, her neighbors several houses down on the opposite side, had a well maintained Cadillac that they kept in the garage, but for three days she'd seen a car sitting right in front of Mr. Neville's pride and joy, their pristine yard. Same car. Same spot. Same time. *Same bat channel* she mused, lowering her eyes to study it as she strode to her own car in front of the garage. Not that she was knocking Mr. Neville's enjoyment in his yard, but his entire retirement now was his riding lawnmower. Looking at the sleek model, she knew his oldest son who lived in town did *not* drive that kind of car.

Was it a visiting friend? She doubted it. The elderly couple's full stretch of friends were limited to the senior center variety. Not to mention that the car was there at seven-thirty every morning. That car looked way too fast and too new for their generation. Especially in her neighborhood, where being over fifty was more the norm than the oddity.

She'd loved the house she owned when it had come onto the market. The neighborhood had been well established and stable. The house had needed very little in repairs, which worked well for her. She could wield a mean hammer and miss her thumb while she was at it, but more than that and she'd be walking the yellow pages for a handyman. There was also stability. Namely, the incoming buyers, when there were, weren't interested in redeveloping the lots, so the market and the neighborhood were safe. It wasn't unusual for new home builders to come in and tear down older homes, rebuild and mess up the entire neighborhood by raising land values and taxes and causing headaches on a palatial scale. Stacee would take safety over new and sparkly any day.

She slid behind the leather strapped steering wheel, the auto seat adjusting as she settled in, trying to get a better look at the strange car without being too blatant about it. Was that a person behind the wheel? As far away as the car was, it was just too hard to be positive. The idea that someone was in the car at that hour of the morning, someone she didn't know, possibly watching *her* gave her a chill, making the hair on her arms rise uncomfortably.

Her father had taught her to always be aware of her surroundings, to take a mental picture if she could. Grab enough detail to make a short list of facts if asked. She did that as she pulled away from her house, in the opposite direction from the parked car. Safe driving habits and attention to those details paid off when she looked up to check her rearview and spotted the dark car. She frowned. Had she been followed all week? Was the car, and the driver, following her? It seemed far too likely as the vehicle kept an even pace with her.

She took an unplanned exit ahead of schedule.

"Damn," she muttered when the car not only followed her, but kept an exact distance from her, even through several stop lights. The only reason she suspected she was being followed was because it wasn't all that rare for clients to follow her to a house to show. Except those instances were ones where she didn't want to lose her tail.

This time, it felt imperative to her to lose this one. And fast.

She clicked a button on her console. "Office," she stated firmly, paying attention to her driving. It would suck to run a red light now.

"Hales Prop—"

She cut off her secretary without an ounce of apology. "Rebecca, I won't be in right away. Cancel my planner for the day and reschedule everything."

"Stacee! What's wrong? You sound completely stressed."

She drew a breath to calm herself, not in the least surprised. She drove, thinking at the same time and praying doing both wouldn't make her have an accident. Breathing seemed to help calm her. "I'm not sure," she replied, not wanting to worry her secretary for nothing. She hoped it was nothing. She spotted a coffeehouse ahead and decided to make a detour. "I'll call you when I get a chance." Then she hung up.

Stacee made a beeline for the drive-thru, digging through her purse for Agent Dreyer's card. She didn't even hesitate when his face and voice appeared in her memory. Not that he was the kind of man she could forget. She was very glad of that fact, and that he'd left her a card.

She dialed with trembling fingers while making her order, glad for probably the first time ever how slow the coffee drive-thrus really were.

"Dreyer," he answered on the second ring. The timbre of his voice was at once comforting.

"Agent Dreyer. Stacee Hales. I'm sorry to call out of the blue, but I think I'm being followed."

"Where are you?"

No pandering. No condescension. Crisp and business-like in a heartbeat. His absolute calm fed into her. She wanted to believe in it and latched onto his voice like a lifeline. She felt her lungs relax for the first time since she'd spotted the car. She told him her location and where she was headed. Although she wasn't going to her office now, she had no better solution.

"No. Don't go to your office. Where can I meet you?"

Inspiration slapped her when she realized what street she had turned onto. "I have an open model on Avian." And the keys were in her briefcase. She'd shown the house just the day before. It was only a few subdivisions away from where she was sitting. Minutes to get her to the house. And to him.

She repeated the address, and he told her he'd meet her there. Everything would be okay. By the time she got back on the street, she'd almost convinced herself she was overreacting and that she'd have to apologize for disturbing him by the time she saw him.

Stacee took her time driving in an unhurried way. She tried to drive like any other person, on any other morning. Not trying to run stale yellow lights as many drivers do. She lost her sense of ease when she spotted the dark car behind her without a problem. Even though she felt scared out of her mind, she didn't want it to show. The coffee stop hadn't deterred the other car in the least. "Just like I'm going to show the house," she whispered. "Nothing to it. Just another day."

Yeah, she'd believe that when she got through her morning.

⚋⚋ ⚋⚋ ⚋⚋

JONAS traded his coffee for his holster and jogged out to his Explorer Sport, sliding on his jacket on the way. He activated his GPS and found the exact house he needed. He was on the highway in less than three minutes. Time and traffic seemed to drag against him no matter how hard he cursed it.

The memory chip trail had gone cold, and now Stacee was calling him. Twice this week he'd almost called her to make sure she was still safe and sound. Stacee Hales had been like a constant buzz in his brain. A burr he couldn't shake. Now he was glad he hadn't. Something about this woman was connected to the chips. And he had to find them. Apparently, he wasn't the only one who thought she had something to do with their disappearance.

He'd had that niggle on his conscience since he'd met her. Something that appealed, and drew him to her. But right now, her safety was the only thing on his mind. He hadn't had the freedom to dwell on the rest of it.

Jonas clutched at his phone when it rang.

"I'm trying to look nonchalant, but it would help a hell of a lot if you were here," she told him, her voice gritty and forced.

"I'm almost there," he replied, watching traffic fly past as he sped toward the house. He kept his own voice even to try to keep her calm. She wasn't used to this kind of drama. He ate it for breakfast. "Tell me what the car looks like."

"A dark blue foreign. Expensive. I can't make a model from here. A Mercedes maybe. They're more than a block away. They just turned around the corner." Her voice was strong, surprisingly calm. She sounded more relieved when the car disappeared out of her sight. Her voice was doing funny things to his nerves too. He shook it off. He had to keep his focus.

"Stay in the car until I get there."

"Like I was going to move?" She made a crude noise. It made him smile. She wasn't scared. She seemed almost angry by the sound of things. He could forgive her that. It wasn't everyday people were just out of the blue followed on their morning commute.

"I see you."

He pulled up behind her, ending the phone call, and parked his truck. She got out, slipping out of the door like her legs were made for those red carpet style entrances. He felt his tongue push against his teeth, not to mention his cock as it woke up in appreciation. The ache was fast and hard. And he couldn't look away.

The woman had legs to die for. That waist he'd seen in her jeans wasn't bee sized either. It flowed into feminine rounded hips that swayed oh-so-gently when she walked in her heels. A striding sensuality that some women were born into. Stacee had gotten that gene in excess. He watched every single step she took with a growing desire to see more. He couldn't even blink.

He loved heels on a woman, and she walked like she was made for them, as though she owned the ground she walked on. A slow rolling saunter that made him swallow. Hard.

Her hair swayed in loose waves around her shoulders and face. The colors in the sunlight reminded him of chocolate covered cherries from Christmas. Those boxes of red that he saw in stores everywhere every year. Now he knew what they looked like on the inside.

"Hey," she said in greeting, rolling a shoulder. She leaned closer as his window came down. "Thanks for taking the call. It's probably nothing, but it freaked me out."

He almost reached out and caressed her cheek to comfort her, but caught himself at the last second before indulging in the pleasure. He *needed* to see if her skin was as soft as it looked. He clenched his fist against his thigh instead. He was glad he was sitting down. He'd never be able to hide his arousal from her. Having her so close, her light perfume on the air between them, was making him throb like a horny teenager in the uncomfortable confines of his slacks.

He was surprised his voice worked on the first try. His tongue sure didn't feel like his own. "You did the right thing. The guy who rammed you didn't have the stolen property on him. I think the next link in the chain thinks you might have it somehow." He'd actually been dreading this moment for that very reason, but couldn't really hate it because it brought her back to him. Even he was man enough to admit he had wanted to see her again. It was actually all male thinking behind that want, but he'd do what was necessary first.

She shook her head, consternation and deep thought bringing her brows together. "Not likely. Unless it was part of the dirt I swallowed when I kissed pavement, I know nothing."

His lips twitched, even in the seriousness of the moment. He noticed she still had a sizeable fading blue splotch in her hairline, but makeup had covered it fairly well. "I bet that caused all kinds of questions at work," he sympathized, nodding at the bruise.

She sniffed. "You don't want to know. Let's go inside. I feel exposed out here."

He wasn't about to argue.

She released the lock and promptly shut the door behind them. A sigh of relief was loud in the empty house as bolts clicked into place. She wasn't taking any chances. "How long do you think they'll sit there?"

"Probably all day."

She groaned in answer, searching the ceiling, probably looking for a quick miracle. "What am I going to do? I can't have a following entourage in my day to day."

He took her measure in a swift, calculated glance as she paced, peeking out a side window then dropping it to pace some more. He couldn't lie to himself. What he saw, he really liked.

"I don't think you'll be a real target. The package that was supposed to be handed off between the first courier, my guy, and the collision with you is missing." He flexed his fingers, annoyed with the events of that day even though he couldn't have done it any other way. The package was missing. He just had to be the first to find it.

"So what? I'll be a pretend target?" she asked tartly. She tilted her chin up, challenging him. All he could think of was how badly he wanted to kiss the path of skin beneath her ear.

He cleared his throat. Why couldn't he think straight around this woman? "No. Not exactly."

She crossed her arms beneath her chest and narrowed her beautiful speckled eyes to slits. The woman was a stunner. She'd stunned him at first glance, prone in a hospital bed and he still hadn't recovered.

"Explain 'not exactly' to me Agent Dreyer," she stated, a sheer chill in her words that made him want to stuff his hands into his pockets.

"Well," he began, searching for the best way without divulging too much, but it was as far as he got.

Bullets shattered the window she stood next to and two more into a sparkled fall of deadly shards and ice-like glitter.

CHAPTER THREE

STACEE squealed, hit for the second time by the solid body of a guy like she was interviewing for the tackling dummy position of an entire football squad.

"This has got to stop," she muttered, disregarding the fact that she was hiding in his shoulder, shaking. His hand and body cradled and covered her with his protective breadth as the last of the window fragments settled around the pair on the floor.

"Which part? The bullets or the drama?"

She chuckled into his shoulder. Damn, she liked his humor. "Getting laid out like a pancake. It's hard on a girl's body."

He made a sound of admiration. He held her close, one palm wrapped around her head to protect her from falling glass, his other on her hip as he covered her entire body with his length. He flexed his hand on her hip and she couldn't help but feel every single movement. Searing heat pressed against her possessively now that she had enough air in her lungs to feel his body. The hard wall of his chest covered her completely and she couldn't help but notice just how solid that wall was against her. His weight pressed into her, forming against her. The tender sensation of his hand against her scalp belied the strength she felt everywhere else. A wild flutter hit her stomach and sank lower as her nerves reported back every little detail about his body against hers.

"Depends on who the girl is, in my mind," he replied against the shell of her ear in a low growl that was anything but professional. His breath bathed her nerves with a zinging shock as he whispered those slow words into her ear. The rumbled sensual depth of it made her blood run hot. That flutter intensified into its own earthquake and a shiver rocketed down her length. Her heart jumped and tripped for a completely different reason than being shot at. She could feel every inch of his tensed length and even in the most inappropriate of moments, it was hard *not* to take notice. Where he lay above her, the hard outline of his cock was pressed deliciously against her thigh. She felt herself begin to smolder with desire.

"Don't move," he warned her, his voice neutral again. Thankfully popping her lust-filled bubble. She had to be out of her mind to be thinking about him like that at a time like this!

He reached behind his back, and she saw a handgun appear from beneath his light charcoal jacket. He rolled off of her body, glass dropping with a tinkling sound to the wood covered floor. Shattered bits crunched beneath his feet as he crab walked along the wall and peeked out between blind gaps. She watched as he followed something outside with his gaze. A second later the sharp scream of tires told her the shooters weren't sticking around to see if the job was done.

He stood slowly at the wall, fixated as the sound disappeared. A moment later, he reached down and offered a hand.

"What, might I ask, was the point of that?" she demanded.

"It's a mind game. They know you are involved and are warning you."

"Really? A strong email would have done just as well." She carefully shook her body to remove lingering glass slivers, trying to not do the natural thing and brush her hands down her suit.

He produced a handkerchief and helped dust her off, carefully lifting the ends of her hair away from her collar and brushing anything harmful free. She noticed his lips were twitching.

"What?" She didn't want to have to deal with a smart-aleck agent next.

"I'm glad you're not the type who falls back on hysterics."

"Hysterics?" *He was kidding right?* She did have every right to, but being the daughter of a policeman she'd kind of had the trait trained out of her.

A solid brown eyebrow rose over his green and blue melded eyes as he paused, his hand hovering over her shoulder. She'd never seen such an artfully constructed color in her life. He dusted her off on both sides. She felt the heat from his hand against her neck and the throb of her pulse quickened. It wasn't the only thing to start throbbing either.

"Hysterics," he murmured. Then he smiled. A real smile, pleasured and content. The dimple she'd only seen hinted at, appeared. The urge to press a single kiss to the sexy facial marker made her heart hitch against her ribs. He was a gorgeous guy, several inches taller than herself, with laugh lines around his eyes. He had a slightly short nose and a sexy mouth. Kind of a darker version of Keifer, and she wasn't the kind of woman who'd turn him out of her bed.

It was obvious Jonas shaved regularly. His skin was nearly smooth with a taut suppleness, his face full of character but firm. She spotted only a few grays peeking from the full bodied brown of his trimmed hair. Late thirties was her best guess, and fit and solid if her recent introduction to the world of Agent Hard Bodies was any indication. At thirty-six, she wasn't any kind of spring chicken either, but something about him, his smile, that dimple, made her want to see just what the rest of him would feel like pressed against her body, without the glass and definitely without clothes. The idea of it sent another warming tingle to between her legs.

Slowly the air in the house changed, became charged between them. It swirled around them with something awakening. Something wicked and taunting and hungry. And she wanted it. Her pulse ticked, beating harder against her ears as his eyes met hers and stayed. A shiver rocked her spine when the lightest touch of his fingers stroked beneath her ear where he'd been clearing her hair of glass fragments. The rough feel of his tips forced a light gasp of shock and pleasure all wrapped together from between her lips. She'd forgotten he was helping to dust her off when she'd become absorbed in her study of him. A delicious study she really wanted to continue. The indistinct scrape of his touch jolted her back to the room.

And the most intense, drugging stare in a pair of eyes she'd ever encountered.

They stood less than a step apart. A single movement, from either, would bring them body to body.

Just a little closer, she willed him. She wanted to taste him. She wanted to feel the strength of his kiss, to caress his lips and have it returned.

Jonas made the move before she did. All she could see was the heat in his gaze, the tanned warmth of his skin, the way his lashes lowered over his eyes just enough to make them sizzle when he moved closer. She inhaled and found the warmed scent of something woody, a light cologne maybe, heated by his skin and it made her tremble within as he hovered over her lips. Her breasts grew sensitive, desire making them, her, throb. Her nipples hardened and she ached. She couldn't remember the last time she'd had such a deep and needing reaction after hardly more than a few words.

"Beautiful," he whispered, his breath a bath of heat and hunger against her lips. Then he closed the gap completely. Her eyes fluttered closed as sensations hit her with the shock of a steamroller. Zings of heat coursed through her body and she quivered, feeling the sudden dampness between her legs. She was falling, but he held her as her legs dared to quake. His fingers threaded completely into her hair and held her steady, captured, but not with harsh strength. With a gentleness that shook her to her core. With nothing but the mere strength of his kiss, he held her to him. He brushed against her and she hungered. Her fingers rose and clutched as though seeking a lifeline at his waist in answer. She had to hold on or be pulled in too hard and too fast into the searing heat that enveloped her. Then she stopped worrying about it.

So long... It had been so long since her last kiss. Her divorce was a long six years in the past. A few failed dates afterward and she'd laid her sex life on the back burner to concentrate on her business. She remembered now what she'd been missing out on. She moaned as the seductive whip of his tongue stroked her bottom lip and opened for him eagerly.

She knew she felt the earth shift when something deep and hungry rose from him, a growl, a groan, she wasn't sure, but it enveloped her as completely as a cocoon of velvet. The trailing tease of his tongue dared her and she answered, kissing him back with a reawakened desire that scorched her from the inside out.

A shrill tone, a song jingle sliced through her bliss with little welcome.

Calmly, he sipped once, twice, releasing her slowly. She wanted to cry out in denial, but knew it had to end. That was her phone cutting into her moment of heaven. Her office to be exact.

Warm fingers slid from her hair, caressing her tenderly in their retreat. She pressed the button on her Bluetooth when he stepped back then watched as Jonas reached for his own phone. Likely doing the same thing she was doing. Explaining why shots had been fired.

"No, I'm fine," she answered once Rebecca had calmed down. The perimeter company had called the office when the windows had been shattered, disrupting a field of protection. Stacee's gaze followed the man a few feet away as he spoke calmly into his own phone. She heard snatches of his conversation, giving details about the car and answering questions.

"Stacee?" came the worried query. "Is everything okay now?"

She smiled at her secretary's concern. A sweet girl, younger, newly married and sharp as a tack. "I'm fine, really," she went on. "There's been a misunderstanding. I have an agent here with me now."

"Oh, that's good!"

Stacee thought so too, her gaze following him hungrily. "I'll call as soon as I can. Hopefully, things will be back to normal soon."

"Okay." Then she went on to rattle off the changes that had been made for the day, and Stacee nodded or made suggestions as her day was rescheduled.

"I'll call later if tomorrow is bad too." A final note and then she hung up. Jonas was done only a moment after her.

"Everything okay?" she asked him. He seemed troubled, his gaze far away and thoughtful.

He spun on a heel and prowled back to her. She couldn't think of any other way to describe his walk. It was more than a swagger and twice as dangerous. "I'm not sure. I need to get back to the office and check on a new lead." He lifted a hand to her face, cradling her with a tender awareness that made her heart beat like crazy all over again. She almost whimpered. "You all right?"

She nodded, having a hard time finding her voice. Her lids closed as sensations bombarded her again. The rough but tender comfort of his hand, the strength she'd felt in his body, the undeniable urge to feel him against her. All of that was nothing compared to the piercing sharpness of his eyes. She felt powerless beneath his stare. Her heart was pounding.

She instantly craved his touch again when he let it slide free. What she craved she couldn't put into words and prayed it wasn't so obvious in her expression. Every touch added fuel to the hunger.

"If you see anything out of the ordinary, don't hesitate. Call me. I don't care how unusual. Okay?" he pressed.

She blinked and nodded, barely able to breathe and talk. It was one or the other, and breathing took precedence.

"The local boys will be here in a couple minutes to take a report on the shooting." He handed her an extra card, standing so close she was able to see the rise and roll of his chest as he breathed. "Just tell them to contact me. I have to get back to my database. They know where to find me."

"Why?" she asked, not wanting him to go, knowing there was more here than simply the need to follow through on his case. She palmed the card and waited.

"I caught the license plate on the car. They're getting careless, which means they're getting desperate."

"What was the stolen property?" If people looking for it were getting desperate... It was enough to freeze the unending lust into a block of ice.

Jonas frowned, obviously debating on how much to share with her. His prolonged silence wasn't easing her worries any. His eyes gave away nothing as he debated. Finally he told her, "Three memory chips. National security sensitive information. They were stolen a few days before you had this," he tenderly brushed hair away from her forehead, exposing the still tender spot, "happen. We tried to stop them before they actually got the chips, but something went wrong. They had a decoy and slipped out of the noose."

She caught a ripple cross his shoulders. It could only be frustration. "There was someone on the inside, wasn't there? Your inside guy gave it away, didn't he?"

He snapped up, blinked at her suggestion, then laughed a mirthless sound. "Too many drama shows," he retorted flatly.

She shook her head, sure her next answer was going to throw him for a loop. "No, my dad was a cop too. He died in the line of duty. I even took the first year of academy training thinking it was the right thing to do, but it wasn't. I wasn't being a cop for me."

"Shit, Stacee. I'm sorry." He seemed genuinely apologetic.

She shrugged. His sincerity was appreciated, but not necessary. "He would talk to me about the cases he was working, or the stories going around the precinct and we'd work out the angles. I liked pretending I could be a cop at that point in my life. He said I was deviant enough to see it from both sides." A reminiscent smile flitted over her mouth as she remembered her father and those discussions. That ability to see more than the obvious was what made her a good realtor now. She could read buyers like her father used to read liars and crooks.

Jonas's chest rocked with a hard chuckle, shaking his head as though in surprise, then all humor left him again.

He neared her. She felt the tingle of his gaze on her skin, touching her, searching her. "You're something else," he said, an unknown meaning to the words. A meaning she didn't understand at all. But the heat in those marine colored eyes made her want, more than she had in a very long time.

His lips were hot, catching her by surprise, claiming her kiss. Staking his claim. Desire and want wrapped into the single action, and she felt herself sink into it instantly. It was over before she'd realized it had begun, and then he was gone.

Chapter Four

Six hours later, Jonas still tasted her kiss. Nearly strawberry but something much, much sweeter. Tantalizing. And a sexy bottom lip that he'd wanted to kiss since the moment she was close enough to smell her perfume. He'd seen the way desire had darkened her speckled hazel eyes. He knew he was going to kiss her. Like breathing, it wasn't conscious. It just was.

He dropped his head, cinching his scalp between tightening fingers in frustration. Sexually and otherwise, Stacee was killing him. He ached in so many places, in ways he'd never touched on. That was why he'd left her. He'd run. No lying to himself. He should've stayed and given his half of the incident report. He had to leave or the urge to do more than kiss that mouth would have become a reality. One kiss and he'd almost forgotten everything—including his own name. He wasn't sure what he was doing about any of it yet, either.

Marriage had never been a thought because of his lupine tendencies. It still wasn't. Instead he'd opted to go into the Army, using the underground channels to smooth his enlistment. Secrecy came with a price, and modern times were making it more and more of a challenge but there were those in the pack who thrived in that kind of subterfuge. Hidden from the world in plain sight. It helped that the pack had connections all over the world, in all societies. He had to admit, he'd tasted the adrenaline rush himself. It was part of why he worked for the DOD. Couldn't be much more entrenched in the wheels than working with the damn government.

26

But Stacee was creating a wrinkle in his world. He'd been told he was too cold, too untouchable by more than one female. They were right. They'd also likely run screaming if they learned why that was the case. But Stacee didn't seem to know that, or care if she had any idea. He knew she didn't have any clue to his nature. It wasn't possible for a human to tell the difference. Only his own kind could, and he knew most of them in his region. Regardless, he hadn't been able to forget her since that first moment, and it was driving him up a wall. He was ready to howl he was so wound up over the woman.

He almost snorted as his thoughts sank deeper into an unknown territory of lust, imagining her the way he'd seen her that morning, forceful, demanding answers then pliant beneath his kiss. He could easily see her in much more arousing ways too. Naked, beneath him, or riding him, taking in every solid inch of his cock. Lush, silky skin slick with passion, her heat enveloping him as he sank deep into her welcoming body. He could imagine quite a lot, as he quickly discovered. He shuddered as the images sliced his control like that horror movie character Jason and his knives.

She even spelled her name like some pep squad cheerleader girl. That same girl had grown into one hell of a woman. His body was only too willing to point that out. Savvy, unshakeable and intelligent were just a few things he'd noticed since meeting her. Curvy and luscious with a scent that made him want to pull her against him and never let her go, and all that hair. If he'd been alone, he probably would've howled for quite a long while.

He thought for a brief instant about slackening his body's hunger but just the idea made him tremble with the urge to hurl. And grown men did not hurl. Not at work. Not at their desks. *God, I have this bad.* He rubbed at his temples a little harder but it had no effect. The last stress relief he'd had in the name of a roll in the hay, because he knew he'd never remember the girl's name, had been longer in his history than he cared to remember. The less he'd had as he'd matured, the less he'd missed it. Until now. And damn, what he wanted, he wanted *bad*. He growled in his throat at the admission. The noise of the office surrounded him, thankfully hiding his turmoil.

"Here's your car info," Randy announced, dropping the file at Jonas's elbow, yanking him back to the chaos of the offices surrounding him.

He snapped around to look up at Randy. The interruption was a touch of relief with the latest news. And a relief to be out of his own thoughts for five seconds. "Thanks for being fast."

Randy shrugged. "There were only so many possibilities with what you gave me, and I didn't think the eighty-two Dodge was going to be it."

Jonas grinned. Randy was thorough besides being fast. He flipped the file open and read the car specs. "Did you put out the APB on it yet?" he asked as he read the details.

"First thing," Randy confirmed, leaning on the edge of Jonas's desk. "You think they are the buyer?" He flipped a look toward the file beneath Jonas's fingers.

"Or the next courier." He glanced at the vehicle owner information on the paperwork. A business entity, one he recognized from months of reconnaissance. He let out a slow breath. They were getting closer. Finally. Unfortunately, seeing how close they were gave his stomach a twist that he really didn't like. He knew who would be next if they were searching from their end if he thought about it. It didn't take very long at all to figure it out either. Hell, they'd just shot at her that morning.

What was he waiting for?

"Thanks again." He stood from his chair and grabbed his jacket, shrugging it over his shoulders to hide his holster. No sense in lying. He was going to check on Stacee. The real lie was that his only motivation was to make sure she was still safe and sound.

STACEE left her office ahead of schedule as a precaution. What difference could it make? She hadn't even walked through the door until after two in the afternoon. She checked her mirror every time she'd gone somewhere, whether it was down the block or to show a house. After leaving the house with the shot out windows, she'd specifically bought a fresh coffee and sat in her car in the shade of a large tree next to one of the downtown parks. She wasn't about to get out and make herself a target again, but she couldn't go to work with gallons of adrenaline pumping through her system either. She'd practically jumped right out of her shoes because a cat howled as she approached her car. She needed a few minutes to put her head back in order, to rationalize the shots and her place in this new mini-series of her life. She needed to try to forget those incredible kisses, along with the feel of his hard length against her, pressing into her in all the right places. In ways that made her tremble and yearn. Maybe it was time to start dating again if these chance encounters with a near stranger were turning her insides to Silly Putty.

By the time she'd hit the bottom of her cup, she had fixed her rattled nerves and went to work. Now, gratefully, it was time to go home. She took every precaution she could, using an alternate route, hiding amongst the large tractor-trailers when she could. A little common sense and her father's sage advice came in handy. Sporadic checks in her mirror showed her to be tail-less, which gave her a sense of relief.

Once she was parked and in her own home, she breathed another sigh of relief. She could use as much as she could get after the morning she'd had. A knock at her door barely ten minutes later took her by surprise.

"Who is it?"

"Meter reader," came the brusque reply.

Her brow furrowed. Since when did they come to the front door? She leaned closer to the door. "What do you want?"

A throat cleared. "Your meter box has been damaged. Looks like a kid hit it with a baseball. Just wanted to show it to you. If you can't find out who did it, it'll show up on your bill."

"Really?" she wondered. When did it happen? No telling since she wasn't home during the day.

"You better have ID," she warned them even though she knew she had no choice but to see if her house had been whacked carelessly. Her eyes widened when they landed on the men on the other side.

JONAS drove to her home with a sense of dread. She hadn't answered her cell phone and her secretary said she'd left nearly an hour before. His only thought was she had better have been in the shower when he called and she hadn't picked up. When he approached and spotted the dark Mercedes, he knew his answer.

He called in for reinforcements, parking in the neighbor's driveway without remorse. Drawing his weapon, he crawled along the side of the house, listening as shouts and crashes echoed through the cream colored walls. He breathed, keeping his head cool when he wanted to rush in and beat the shit out of them for coming here. He couldn't think of Stacee being hurt. The idea of her hurt and bleeding or worse, made him see red. He sucked air in through his nose to calm his racing heart. Patience and training soothed his rattled nerves back to ice.

Rising on his feet, he looked over the pane of one of the front windows and spotted two men, tearing her living room apart.

"...bedroom." He heard it as a muffled order with a gesture and one of them spun and left his field of vision. He couldn't see Stacee in the front room but prayed she was all right. He waited until the second moved out of sight deeper in the house away from the only door he knew would likely be open then slunk his way to it, opening it with a stealthy slow twist.

His entrance went unnoticed, closing the door without snicking the mechanism. He doubted they would have heard it anyway with the racket they were making in their search. They were a loud couple of pricks. Sneaking up on the joker in the kitchen wasn't hard. He wasn't expecting to be interrupted. The butt of Jonas's gun against his head solved that problem. He sank to the floor unconscious in a heap. Sparing a brief moment, he locked one of his hands to a cabinet handle with his handcuffs, searching him for a weapon and finding two. He slid them underneath his belt, safety on, then he skimmed the floor for the bedroom.

He found the second asshole on his toes pulling stuff off the top shelf of her closet when Jonas looked around the corner of the door into the room. Stacee lay splayed out on the bed. His heart tripped painfully at the bruise on her chin. *Bastards*. They were going to pay for that. Her room was already trashed, drawers pulled out and clothes all over the place. His gaze narrowed at a flash of white against dark black denim. Was that lace trim in his front pocket?

Jonas snarled at the sight, no doubt in his mind what this guy's trophy was. He straightened to his full height and gripped his gun, imagining every little thing he wanted to do to the intruder for payment. He'd settle for putting his ass in jail for the moment.

"Hey asshole," he barked, whipping around the door with his gun already aimed at the man's head. "Don't move."

Sweat popped out on the other guy's brow at his appearance. He lifted wild, searching eyes beyond Jonas.

"He isn't coming," he taunted coolly. He motioned for him to raise his hands. "Kneel." He looked like he was only waiting for the right chance to dive for Jonas. It never came.

Swearing when it proved Jonas wasn't lying, he knelt and dropped his hands behind his back. A few minutes later he heard the arrival of booted steps through the front door and knew backup had arrived.

Once the one before him was in handcuffs and he could holster his own weapon, he handed over the guns he'd confiscated then quickly went to Stacee's side.

"Hey, baby, you in there?" he questioned softly, crouched by the bed caressing the hair away from her face where she lay on her side. The warmth of her skin against his fingers alone made him feel so much better, knowing she was okay, just beat up. Again. Poor girl. What a craptastic week for her.

"I don't know. Are they gone?" she whispered back, without moving a muscle. Or opening her eyes.

He stroked her hair to soothe her. "Yeah. Both of them, though your place will need a week's worth of maid service."

She huffed a short breath, but didn't say anything about that. "I was praying if I stayed still and didn't move, they might leave me alone."

"How long have you been awake?"

"I don't know. I know one of them came in here twice before they started seriously searching." Her eyes opened and speared Jonas to the quick with the meaning of what she was getting at. She shivered in reaction. "I think he was thinking about it but they had priorities. And I was no fun if I wasn't fighting back."

He shook his head at her level of cool, well aware what she meant. Now he wished he had done more than just arrest their sorry asses for putting their slimy hands on her. He put a hand under her arms and stood, bringing her up with them until she was on her knees on the bed. Wrapping his arms around her and holding her tight seemed the most natural thing to do. Her arms curved around his neck and nothing had felt more natural in his life.

A funny tumult hit his heart at the thought, making it worse because he didn't want to let go. So he didn't. He didn't think about it either. Just the here and now. That was something he could deal with.

He leaned back and inspected her face. "You're getting quite the collection," he murmured teasingly.

She lifted a hand to her jaw. "Wasn't expecting it, that's for sure. Gave me some line then popped me. I thought guys didn't hit girls."

He smiled watching her work her jaw back and forth, consternation coloring her cheeks. "The good guys don't."

She stopped moving and caught his stare, something so deep, so hungry in the depths of her eyes, he felt swept up into their dark swirls.

"I like the good guys," she said, sounding almost breathless.

He was lowering to her lips before he could stop himself. He had to taste her. Had to know she was okay. Had to feel her the way he'd been craving since that morning. Her breasts were pushed against his chest, warm and giving. His hands cradled her, holding her at her waist with a firm but tender weight.

The brush of her fingers in his hair sent another shot of lightning into his blood stream. His hold tightened, finally giving in to the feeling. She welcomed him, devouring his kiss passion for passion.

Sweetness soaked into him as he suckled on her tongue. She shimmied closer, and he felt the teasing heat of her against his cock. He groaned. *So good*, he thought. Then he stopped thinking altogether when she brought them even closer. He couldn't remember the last time a kiss had been this good, this consuming.

A throat clearing jerked him back to his senses. He relinquished her lips with slow enjoyment, but he left his hands right where they were. He couldn't give a rat's ass if rumors had started flying five seconds ago. He wasn't letting her go.

He looked behind her as she leaned to rest against his shoulder for support.

"Yes?"

"They are heading down to lockup, sir, if you would like to come make your statements."

"We'll follow you in a few minutes," he stated, brooking no argument from the officer at the doorway. He turned and left the pair in the bedroom. "I'll take you with me." He rubbed his cheek against the top of her head. He couldn't seem to stop touching her. There was only one way he'd ever get enough, and even then he wasn't sure it would be *enough*. It gave him pause, but the argument didn't convince him to let go.

"You don't have to do that," she replied, sounding extremely content right where she was.

"I do if I'm taking you out tonight."

She laughed, burying herself into his neck to hide it. Her warm breath soaked into him just like her kiss had. He'd never felt so hungry for a woman's touch or her kiss in his life.

He fought with himself to sound normal, because he sure didn't feel normal. He felt hot, overheated, hungry, ready to gorge himself on the wonders of her luscious body. She wasn't making it easy for him either.

The sight of her in her business suit was hot. He liked a confident woman, and she dressed to shout that confidence to the world. Sexy sharp skirts. Heels to make his mouth water. She was a total package kind of woman. The idea of her in something like her jeans—the ones he hadn't forgotten—were enough to send him into a lusting tailspin too.

"Why don't you get into something relaxing?"

"Because I don't have a Jacuzzi," she retorted playfully.

He almost groaned as he sucked in air, envisioning her soaked and naked, or naked and soaked, he didn't care. "Do you hurt?" he asked, fighting to keep himself in check. He didn't like the idea that she was still aching from her misadventures.

"Only a little, but right this minute, I feel wonderful." She sighed in pure contentment.

"Stacee, if I don't let you go, it'll be hours before we leave this room," he warned her, albeit regretfully.

"I'd be fine with that," she replied, running her tongue up the side of his neck. His eyes slammed shut in reaction. He stretched, giving her room to play, and she didn't disappoint. The slight scrape of her nails against his scalp was just the precursor to the delicious torment he was about to receive. He couldn't find the strength to tell her to stop.

Daring lips and a wicked tongue painted a heated trail from his shoulder to his ear. Tender and wanton, she nipped and scraped against his nerves with her teeth, causing heat and lust to harden his cock until he thought he'd died and gone to heaven. He felt his entire body tighten like steel in answer. His groans deepened into hard growls of need.

The sexy minx was seducing him. And he was almost ready to let her. God, what he'd give to feel himself buried inside of her heat. To feel the slide of his cock inching slowly into her pussy, the soft squeals of pleasure he knew she'd make scorching his nerves with every caress. The taste of her skin on his tongue, the heat of her touch burning him like she already was. He shuddered with sexual longing when she nipped at his earlobe, drawing on it to suckle like he'd played with her tongue just a moment before.

He lifted a hand and swept it through the wave of hair down her back, thrilled at the silky feeling, the richness of it on his skin.

"Sweetheart," he tried, sounding like he'd run a ten mile marathon as he gasped beneath her touch. "We're not alone yet."

"Mmm..." she breathed against his flesh. Hot pants of breath wove over his neck, as she stopped her attack on his nerves. He shuddered with a long lost desire that she'd unerringly awakened with that wicked pouting mouth and eyes the color of the most artistically blended brown and gray marble. "Kiss me, Jonas. Kiss me like I need you to, and I'll let you go."

His heart went right through his ribs. He'd never been needed with that breathless intensity before. He'd never been on the receiving end for that deep of a hunger in a woman's touch before.

"Baby." He swallowed his own groan as he lifted his head to stare down into her eyes. Fringed in dark chocolate lashes, lit from within with what she was feeling, with what she desired. Him. Open and trusting, believing in him. And craving just as much as he was, but able to give him what he needed, space and time if he wanted.

If he could give her what she needed to let her know it wasn't one-sided.

He could. In spades.

He lowered to her lips and felt the earth move.

Chapter Five

Jonas spread the blanket on the ground, trying not to gape at her bared legs beneath her summer dress as he did so. She wore a cream sweater over her shoulders but those legs... He had to remind himself there were other things to look at in the park.

"This was a wonderful idea," she told him, sitting after he'd sufficiently spread out the blanket. He placed the second one nearby for when the temperatures cooled, with the basket dinner he'd brought at arm's reach.

With the sun setting, the bruises she'd collected that week would be harder to see, but the bruises were the last thing he found himself staring at.

Jonas shrugged. He'd brought girls from his pack to the park to listen to the music in past years. The season was just starting. Every Friday night until mid-September. This was the first time he'd brought an actual date though.

"I'm glad you're not disappointed it's not the usual restaurant thing."

She smiled when he looked down at her. "Oh, not in the least. I love being outdoors." He had to sit. Her words had the effect of knocking his legs right out from underneath him. He stretched out next to her, his legs in front of them as he leaned on an elbow. Safer to already be on the ground in case she said anything else that he had that kind of reaction to.

He glanced at her, catching her profile as she studied the layout of the stage and the couples scattered thinly on the grounds. It was early in the season. In a few weeks, it would look like a New Jersey seashore with towels, blankets and people.

Stacee seemed perfectly at ease, very relaxed considering the week she'd had. He'd postponed the offered date to tonight when he remembered the concerts were just starting up again. Stacee hadn't argued, saying a day to relax from the break-in and start the dreaded cleaning of her house should be faced.

She absently pushed a wave of hair away from her face, and he followed the entire motion like it was a 'must see' movie clip. He wanted to bury his nose in the crook of her shoulder and just stay there.

He drew a hard breath and faced forward to listen, or at least look like he was.

What was it about Stacee that drove him so hard up that wall of lust? That made him hunger? He dropped his attention to the stage as the first sounds of a guitar soared up to them on the hill incline. Was she the one? The 'mate' that many of his male brothers had already found? Jonas knew the right woman for him didn't have to be pack. She could just as easily be human. The genetic ability he carried was male dominant. The women who found their loves among the packs were no different than most, just better adaptable. And devotional to the extreme. Pack couples never strayed, never divorced.

The idea that she could be that one woman for him struck him with terror and lust at the same time. There wasn't any point in fooling himself. He wanted her. Just laying there as she swayed and smiled to the music flowing around them, he wanted her. Yet if she was the one, taking her to his bed would make her irresistible to him forever. He almost snorted. Like she was resistible *now*? She was also the first woman to completely distract him from a working case. Ever.

Not good, he mocked himself.

He didn't have the freedom to lose his focus. Those memory chips held the entire nation's safety on them. Bank codes. Security codes. Access to classified government information. They had to be found.

"You don't like the song?" she asked, a glint of humor in her gaze.

He relaxed, realizing his shoulders had gone tense with his thoughts. "No, it's fine. I come here usually once or twice a year."

"Then?" she asked, lifting a hand to run through his hair. He lifted himself into the caress as though compelled to answer.

"Just thinking about work." He rarely gave out details. Stacee was the first—the only—to know just what he did.

"This isn't on the clock tonight," she reminded him. She leaned over and pressed a kiss to his mouth, soft, warm, giving, flipping his world yet again because there was absolutely no demand in it. It was simply a kiss. For him. "Relax." Devilish lights rose in her eyes and her lips twitched. "Or I'll make you forget in front of everyone."

"Is that a dare, woman?" he asked her, heat coursing through him like lava flow. Damn, would he ever stop wanting her? Somehow, he doubted it.

"Try me and find out." She arched an eyebrow in challenge, and he couldn't resist.

Weaving his hand through her fall of hair, he pulled her closer until her lips were just above his. "Never dare when you can't see the challenge through." Then he kissed her deeply and learned just what it was she'd dared.

Of all the kisses they'd shared, this one burned his brain, would forever be in his memories as *the* kiss that melted him. Suddenly, his jeans were tight in the worst place, and the light denim jacket was too hot. He thrust his tongue into her, claiming her in a way he'd never expected to know. She dueled, meeting his pace, nipping and welcoming him at turns. It was hard as hell to show restraint and not tumble her beneath him with them in very open view of everyone who cared to look.

Thankfully, the next closest couple was several dozen yards away and hardly any more interested in the activities going on around them than he was in them. The only person who had his undivided attention was the woman in his hands.

The sweet scent of her skin filled his lungs with every breath. The deliciousness of her arousal wove around him, making him want more than just the kisses, more than he'd ever wanted before. There'd always been a definite lack of *something* when he'd had sex with the other women in his life. With Stacee, there was an abundance of that missing element, of passion, of fire and desire, and he knew this would be the woman who would stay with him always if she accepted his nature.

If he was ready to show her.

He withdrew from the kiss, his thoughts in ever growing circles of turmoil. With a seeking thumb, he brushed against her bottom lip, noting the blush swollen warmth. He didn't have that freedom. Not with her in danger and possibly a target for the ones seeking the lost chips. She panted against him. She wasn't fairing any better than he was if her heavy lidded looks and flushed pink cheeks were any indication. He took the prudent road and didn't say one word about that kiss. One word would be all it would take to fall headlong into those eyes and shout at the world to leave them both alone.

"Hungry?"

She nodded. The wanting expression on her face told him food wasn't even on the list, but it was the only thing he could offer her.

※ ※ ※

HE dropped her back off at her house that evening, walking her to the door like any gentleman would have, except the thoughts he had were anything but gentlemanly. They were ravenous and demanding. Every cell in his body craved ripping that dress from her body to see the treasures hidden beneath. The goodbye kiss was much more reserved, gentle. He didn't have the strength for another assault like he'd received in the park. Another one of her kisses like that and he'd be walking with her right into her bedroom. And he couldn't. God, how he wanted to, but he couldn't. Not yet. There was always the possibility of not ever, but he didn't like the idea of not having her in his life, or the picture it created.

Somehow he'd gone from questioning to nearly accepting in one night. He needed to clear his head. It was happening so fast. He should call one of the others in the pack. He couldn't. Most of the men were solitary and didn't do the 'male bonding' thing the way human males did. Males of the pack had higher than average alpha tendencies. Most couldn't stand to be around others for very long without challenging each other in some way. Bloodshed between the pack males was strictly forbidden because of that male dominance trait. It had happened in the past and was punishable in archaic ways.

That only left one choice. He'd have to ride it out. With a final sipped kiss he waited for the sound of her door lock then strode to his vehicle, escaping the hunger that blazed his trail before him.

Once home, he stripped with a vengeance, leaving the back light of his home on when he rushed from the porch, landing on four feet easily. With a bounding leap, he was over the rear fence and into the woods behind his property on the outskirts of town. If it couldn't help his thoughts, running until exhaustion forced his mind blank seemed the next best thing.

Chapter Six

"You're kidding, right?" Kay teased over coffee late Saturday afternoon, her smile as wide as her eyes with her playfulness. "He's kissed you into a coma and hasn't made one grope?"

"Nope," Stacee answered. "He's been an incredible gentleman about it." She felt the blush on her cheeks and didn't even bother to try to hide it. She loved the tender way Jonas treated her, as if she were precious to him. He hadn't even tried to caress a boob or grab her ass. She'd have to remedy that and soon. She was melting from the inside out with wanting him. She could still turn and find his scent on her skin from where he'd cuddled with her beneath the blanket the night before, or lick her lips and discover the memory of his taste from his kiss. He was driving her crazy with deep desiring lust, and he wasn't even there. It was crazy how much she missed him.

The two women sat in the warming spring afternoon on the patio of their favorite caffeine hangout, just enjoying the light breeze and the scudding shadows from the racing clouds overhead.

"Wow," was Kay's awed reply. She sipped, drawing a thoughtful look. Her next words were subdued. "Your mom isn't going to like this."

"Again, nope."

Stacee played with her straw to her iced coffee, well aware of how her mother was going to react to Jonas.

If she even deigned to speak to him, or her daughter, once she found out he was in law enforcement. Like her father.

"She's going to have cow."

"You are such a brilliant wealth of understatement," she replied dryly.

"Well, you know me best. And still love me, I might add," she said with a playful laughing wink. "Where is wonder guy today?"

"Probably working. He's been on this one case for months. I'm just glad it looks like they've finally pulled me out of the 'she knows something' equation." She rubbed at her arms, dislodging the chill she got for mentioning it.

"Who? The cops or the bad guys?"

"Both." At least she hoped so. "I look like a Laila Ali loser because of all of this."

"It'll fade."

Stacee waved a hand in dismissal. "It's just been a hassle at work, trying to talk to someone looking like an abused wife."

"True, true."

"But it's temporary. The damage those goons did to my house..." She curled a lip in a rare flare of anger. "That wasn't cool. The upholstery bill alone is a nightmare. Every cushion in the living room." She'd spent the weekend making headway in cleaning her house and writing off damages for the insurance company. That had been oh-so-much fun. She still had a long way to go too.

"Ugh!" her friend groaned in sympathy. "But it's a good chance to redecorate." Kay tried to brighten the damage with her usual sense of optimism. It was one of those things that Stacee loved about her best friend, even if she was insane most of the time. Stacee rolled her eyes in silent answer.

Her cell phone rang, and her heart sped up at the ring tone. Only one person had that sound. Kay respectfully lowered her eyes to her drink, seeming to have way more interest in her straw than the coming conversation. Too bad she couldn't shove cotton in her ears too.

"Hello sweetheart," he purred when she answered. That melting sensation she felt whenever she thought of him grew with a fast boil that raged hotter at the sound of his voice. "Where are you?"

"At the Mocha Hut with Kay. Where are you?"

"About twenty feet behind you."

She gasped and whirled. She spotted him leaning against a tree at the farthest edge of the patio in the thicker shadows from the shade trees. He must have either just arrived or just showed himself if Kay hadn't seen him. He was so still she hadn't even noticed him at first against the tree. He snapped his phone shut and sauntered over, his eyes on her, and hotter than the sun with hungry desire in their swirling depths.

"How'd he do that?" she demanded gaping over Stacee's shoulder. That answered that question. Kay hadn't seen him at all.

"Were you spying on me?" she asked, slicing him a look from below lowered lashes, with no real offense in the demand. She liked the way he looked out for her.

"Keeping you safe," he replied, unrepentant. "I couldn't take any more voyeurism." His grin was lighthearted, but there was a weight in his expression and on his shoulders that hadn't been there the last time she'd seen him.

"Ha. Ha." She jabbed him with a stiff finger in the hip in punishment.

He grabbed a spare chair and swung it to their table, sitting at an angle to see outward while he sat next to her.

She lifted an eyebrow questioningly. "Why were you keeping me safe? I thought the connection to me was cleared."

One of his hands rose to the back of her chair and idly played with the ends of her loose hair. A frown on his sexy mouth made her fear his answer.

"Just a gut instinct." It was a slow, almost half-hearted reply, but immediately she knew it for what it was.

She knew something had happened. She was learning she could trust his sense of danger, and how to read him. He'd saved her twice. She also knew there was a lot he couldn't tell her with Kay there. He was playing with her hair to make their meeting seem nonchalant, relaxed, but his eyes never stopped roving the surrounding areas, never stopped scanning and searching. The beauty of it was no one could tell he was doing it just by watching him. The relaxed image was a lie. His subtlety was unbelievable.

Something had changed, or maybe nothing had changed at all. Maybe she'd let herself fall into a sense of safety with the

Goon Boys behind bars. How many more people could possibly think she had anything to do with the missing chips? Chocolate chips she'd vouch for, but computer chips? Not a chance in Hell. Absently she twitched her lower jaw, remembering the burst of pain on her face when they'd rushed her at her house.

A light touch on her spine jerked her back to the table and the sweetest aqua eyes she'd ever seen. "Don't worry, baby," he told her, his thumb stroking her between her shoulder blades tenderly. "It's fading fast."

"I told her the same thing," Kay remarked over her stirred coffee, clearly not upset over being ignored now that Jonas was there. She'd accepted him as a part of the friend circle in a way that warmed Stacee, which made him fair game to Kay's acerbic sense of humor. Luckily, he gave as good as he got and had won Kay over pretty quickly too. Their sparring matches would be the stories they'd share with their friends for years to come.

If Jonas was still there. Silently, she prayed she'd get the chance to find out.

JONAS tried not to lose his concentration to the naked legs beneath the table. Shorts. The woman had worn shorts. It was bad enough the tank top exposed some of the creamiest skin on her shoulders that he'd ever seen, dappled with sunlight and shadow. He shifted in his chair, forcing the surge from his lower extremities, focusing outward again. There was no such thing as relief around this woman.

He was there to protect her. That was, unfortunately, the truth. His network had picked up a call conversation between one of his marks and someone else looking for the chips. He was sure the someone else was the man behind it all. The man who was going to make the play the chips were intended for. This new development had completely overridden the sexual desire he'd been battling since Friday night.

The courier who'd started the whole chain reaction was just another pawn. The two in jail were a sacrifice. He knew that now. They weren't going to be bailed out anytime soon either. They'd screwed up and gotten caught without finding a single hint to the chips' location. The memory chips were still out there. That nugget of information worked in his favor too. If they didn't have them, he still had a chance at finding them first. He'd been hunting for them with a single-minded intent since the week before. Double checking every option he had, retracing every connection and step he'd made.

And now the man at the end of the rope had pinned all his attention on Stacee. He had a name for him now too. Gregory Lipton, a low-lying Senator in Washington. That wasn't much of a surprise. That's where the most effective deal would be made for something this combustible. The weight of the government on three little memory chips, boards smaller than the length of his stretched palm, but worth a fortune to the right seller.

Worth his country's safety for the wrong buyer. Every missile launch code, every single triple-threat password. He had no doubt it had taken a *lot* of hacking and under the table cash to get the chips loaded, and now they were a power play. And Stacee seemed to be the woman with the goods.

He glanced down and almost groaned at his own pun.

His eyes almost fell out of his head when he realized she wasn't wearing a bra. Her nipples were blatantly obvious, and begging for attention through her shirt. His tongue pushed against his teeth as his cock swelled in his pants. He'd become an unending hard-on around this woman. He wanted to taste their lush tips with a ferocity that stole his breath away. She was driving him insane in no slow order.

He swallowed, swiftly looking up, but not before Kay caught him red-handed, a knowing smirk on her face that went right over Stacee's head. He gave her an innocent look and went back to his surveillance.

The problem was this time, if she got him into her house, he wouldn't be leaving, and his nature be damned or not, he wasn't going to make himself leave her side again either. Not after the nights he'd spent dreaming about her legs wrapped around his waist like a vice. Not after the hours he'd spent with her taste on his lips, the heat of her skin on his tongue. He was a strong man, but even he had a limit to this kind of frustration.

He'd hit that limit Friday night when his run didn't do a damn thing to ease his frustration and was paying the price for it just by sitting next to her. And he was in no way a masochist. He hadn't come to terms with what all of that meant yet—there were still many variables in the damn way—but he knew what he had to have, who he had to claim and taste. And if he had to claim her before her feelings, or his, were realized, then so be it. It wouldn't be the first time. But he was done with the self-torture routine.

With his hand around her waist, he led her from the table when they were done with their drinks. Kay waved as she drove away.

"What's on the agenda?" he asked, striving for nonchalance. He almost achieved it.

"More house cleaning. I shoved things into the closet and picked up the drawers in my bedroom. It's all that's left really."

"That doesn't sound too bad."

She made a harrumphing sound in disagreement. He guessed he couldn't blame her. It wasn't his house that had been demolished in the searching. He leaned her against the fender of her car, blocking her from view, feeling her pressed against him in so many delicious ways, places that were begging for the contact. Getting her naked right that second wasn't likely going to happen sadly. He glanced down when he finished a perimeter sweep. *Damn sexy shorts,* he cursed silently after he'd made himself promise to not look. He might as well have stopped breathing.

"So tell me the truth." She wound her arms over his shoulders. "You didn't just happen to stop here and decide to hang out."

"Busted." He exhaled with a wry grin. "I've got the buyer's name."

"A breakthrough? That's great!"

He wished he could share her enthusiasm. "The problem is, they can't be charged until they have the chips, or at least attempt to get them."

She ran her teeth over her bottom lip in thought. That sexy bottom lip.

"Which leaves...me."

He nodded, meeting his eyes to hers when she lifted them. He felt the shiver that coursed over her body even as she snuggled closer to him, as if seeking his warmth. He folded her in tighter to his body. He nuzzled the side of her neck, well aware how much his body was enjoying the contact. He let out a slow breath. He was also very aware of the danger Stacee was in because of this whole mess. With him searching for the missing memory chips from his end, and the buyer in Washington doing the same, she was right in the middle. Somehow, he had to keep her safe.

Somehow, he would. He just didn't know how yet.

CHAPTER SEVEN

STACEE eased one of her hands into the rich brown of his hair, and his eyes glittered in the sunlight. "You have the most incredible eyes I've ever seen," she told him.

"Thank you."

With little warning she dragged her nails lightly from his scalp down his neck, mimicking scoring his skin. He arched and growled, throwing his head back as his eyes snapped shut. She'd never had the guts to come right out and tell a guy that she wanted to get as naked as possible and see what came next, but if Jonas couldn't understand *this*, then she really was reading him so very wrong. There was an almost animalist intensity to Jonas. Taking a chance, she dragged those same nails down his chest until she reached his last rib, and held on, digging through the cotton of his t-shirt. Muscles jumped and bunched in answer. He tensed from his shoulders to his knees, and she felt it all along her body. She wanted to see him react, not just feel it.

His jaw was tight. When his eyes popped open, the fire she found in them was rich and deep. "Be careful how you play," he warned her. She tilted, hearing a deeper entendre in the words, but too caught up in the spontaneous wildness of the seduction.

"I want to play," she informed him, pouting softly. She wanted more than that, and she was pretty sure he knew it.

He lowered until he was right next to her ear. His voice dropped a whole octave, sending shivers cascading down her spine. "Get in."

She didn't hesitate to ask why. She found the door handle and slid behind the wheel. He was in on the other side before she'd shut her door.

"Pull out and turn right at Oliver." She nodded at the crisp directions.

Oliver was a beautiful street with old-style buildings and huge storefronts. Many had historical markers and were kept up as part of the town's historical presence. He pointed to an alley that was lined on one side by trees. "Park there." She did. The thick canopy of trees shaded the street and parking between the trunks provided some protection. At least on a Saturday the alley wouldn't see much traffic.

He undid his belt buckle and moved his seat all the way back. "Come here if you want to play," he taunted her in a seductive tone.

"In the car?" She almost giggled, her eyes widening at the idea. She wasn't exactly seventeen anymore. She'd only done it twice in a car in college, and that sure hadn't been all that memorable.

"No. But you should know better than to taunt the big dog on the porch." He reached over and easily lifted her onto his lap when she undid her own belt. His strength surprised her. The way he just plucked her out of her seat and settled her onto his lap made her gasp. He sank down so she wouldn't hit her head on the roof. Her legs tangled with his, and then she couldn't move if she wanted to. She didn't.

She slid an arm around his neck. His hair was already mussed from her hands. What was a little more damage? "Who said I was taunting?" She twirled her fingers through the thick strands.

"Trust me, sweetheart. You're playing with fire." He kissed her, pressing into her firmly. There was no mistaking the hard length of his arousal beneath her, and she squirmed to rub against him. Hard and thick, the bulge dug into her rear. She wished they *could* do it in the car.

He licked at her lips, teasing them until she met him half-way, then there was no going back. With a hand behind her head, he slid his other beneath her tank. Her stomach fluttered and jumped at the heated touch of his fingers on her stomach.

Desire hit a new high when he cupped her breast, toying with her nipple. He teased the nub, twisting and raking his nails over it. She was panting and squirming in a heartbeat.

"Like that?" he breathed. "I bet you taste as good as you smell."

She wasn't used to having a guy talk during sex, or making out. She quickly found out it was a fast rush of a turn on.

Moans slipped free when he moved from her lips to the arch of her neck, nipping and running his teeth and tongue over nerves. Lightning zinged from the side of her neck to her breast, back and forth as he teased and licked. She arched and moaned shamelessly when he switched his teasing to her other breast.

"You should never wear a bra around me. I love being able to touch you, just like this." And he showed her, his hand cupping her, rubbing her, between the mounds and then back to the hard peaks he'd created. He shaped them, caressed them. Pinching to within a heartbeat of real pain, then soothing them within his palm. He worshipped her body. "You should see yourself. You're so damn beautiful," he murmured against her ear, licking at the shell then finding the lobe between his teeth. "I can't wait to see you completely lost, beneath my touch."

"Jonas," she whimpered. Her insides ached with all the teasing. Dampness slicked her core. Muscles were clenching in demand, in unfulfilled need. Craving pleasure she hadn't had in six long years.

"What baby? You know you want to tell me, to say it. I've seen it in your eyes every time I kissed you. You *want*, baby." She whimpered again. She did want. She wanted everything he was doing to never stop. She threw back her head and gasped as new shivers rocked her body. "I know what you want," he reassured her when insecurity seemed to have silenced her tongue.

And oh damn, but did he.

He bent down and licked at her breast with his wicked tongue. The shriek was a little louder.

"Shh. Can't have anyone calling the cops," he told her with a wolfish grin. He took a deep breath. "Damn, you smell so good, so hot." Then he ducked down again and suckled on her breast. He tipped her up and encircled her completely in his hot mouth. Drawing her deep with sharp pulls, he bit lightly at her breasts, and she writhed in answer. She clenched his head, her world spinning as her body tightened. He suckled and twirled her nipple until she shook in his hold. She knew she was wet. She hadn't felt this needy in years.

The snap came free on her shorts and she moved a hip, opening for his touch. She'd beg for it at this point. She ached and burned. A deep sound erupted from his chest when she felt his fingers toying with the curls above her sex. She actually quivered beneath his fingers.

Then he slid his fingers south, and it was all she could do to not scream in ecstasy.

He buried his lips beneath her ear, sucking hard on tender skin as he caressed her clit. "I knew you were wet," he said, his voice hoarse.

Shocks erupted when he manipulated her folds to give him better access into her heat. He rubbed his fingers slowly up and down, teasing her, spreading the slickness of her arousal over her heated flesh. She stretched out against his shoulder, hooking a leg over one of his knees.

"Yes. Just like that," he told her then swirled his thumb over her clit. "I'm going to make you come, Stacee. I want to feel you come, your pussy tight around me, feeling me."

She quaked. "Yesss," she moaned. "Please." She stopped caring about anything; her entire world was his hands and what they were doing to her body.

He slid one finger then two into the aching heat of her pussy. She clutched at anything within reach as he stroked her walls, easing his fingers in and out in a slow rhythm.

"Imagine my cock doing this to you." He drew out then pushed in, twisting a little to touch several places, then his thumb flicked at her clit. "You want to feel me filling you, don't you?"

"Yes!" she gasped, fighting hard to not shout.

"Take my cock, Stacee. I'm filling your pussy." His voice was a dark grinding in her ear, filled with delicious temptation and pleasure she'd never known. He pulled out and slammed his hand into her, ramming the heel of his palm against her sensitive skin. She whimpered. "You're slick and so tight." He did it again, twisting and touching as he mimicked the motion of his hard cock filling her body. Contractions raced down from her womb. "Yes, Stacee. You want to come. Let yourself go."

Somehow he wrapped his other arm around her and traced her mouth with a finger. Lost in the sea of desire, she wantonly sucked his digit into her mouth, suckling on him as he fucked her pussy.

"Shit Stacee," he groaned. Then he increased the tempo and she was lost. Her orgasm started as a whiteout, a blast of ecstasy that spilled stars into her eyes. She sucked harder on his finger and he didn't disappoint, pounding against her flesh in a rapid, intense rhythm. "Come sweetheart," he ordered. "Come now!"

And she did. Gasping for breath, her body bucked as she tightened around his hand. He ground against her mound. Shocks flared in all directions, up her body and down her legs. With her head tossed back, she sank into the orgasm, floating as her body clutched and milked the hand that filled her. She couldn't remember the last time she'd felt that good, felt that level of pleasure, if ever. It took a few minutes to finally begin to recognize the world surrounding her. And the very hard body of the man beneath her.

He was panting, resting against her shoulder.

"Jonas?" she whispered.

"Shh. Don't move. Just...don't move." He was gasping for breath the same as she. She shook when he twisted his fingers then pulled them away. What he did next was surprising and erotic. He drew each finger into his mouth and savored the flavor, licking away the slick sign of her pleasure with the utmost care and enjoyment.

"I knew you'd taste good," he told her, his expression calm even though she felt how tense he was beneath her. He had to be in pain. But he stopped her when she tried to move. "No. Don't move."

"But—"

"I'm fine." He swept his arms around her and tucked her against his shoulder, just holding her. He brushed her hair to the side and said, "You've got a new bruise, but your hair will cover this one."

She placed a hand over the sensitive spot and felt the way her pulse beat against it. He gave her a hickey? "I'm not complaining." She grinned at his apologetic blink. "About any of it."

He tipped her chin. "This wasn't a one time deal, Stacee. I want you; we both just need better timing."

"I think I can do something about that."

He smiled, those aqua eyes of his warming. She snuggled in closer to his shoulder, and he looped his arms around her. Her eyes drifted shut in satisfied bliss, while she enjoyed the feel of his arms wrapped around her.

A few minutes later, he told her, "There's something I have to tell you before that happens though."

Oh, that did not sound good. All kinds of serious problems came to mind. Diseases were at the top of the list. Was he married? He didn't act like the guilty, deceiving type. Was it something physical? He didn't seem to have an erectile problem. She had felt it more than once.

"What?" she queried when he seemed hesitant to explain more. Anxiety was running all kinds of worrisome problems through her thoughts now that he'd said that.

A buzz sounded beneath her hip. He reached into his pocket and answered his phone.

"Dreyer." He sat and listened for a brief moment. "Okay. I'm on my way." He snapped the phone shut. "Sorry sweetheart. Back to the grind."

"Just tell me you're not married," she demanded quickly, unable to hide the hurt frown.

He froze, then caught her gaze. He relaxed beneath her, snuggling her closer for a tender moment. "Not at all. Never have been."

Then that only left... "Okay, what is it then?"

"It's nothing life threatening or hideously awful." He pressed a kiss to her forehead. "I got ahead of myself. I'll explain it, but it's not an emergency."

"You promise? This isn't teasing to get even for me taunting the big dog, is it?" She slid from his lap, finding herself back in her own seat once more. She lifted her hips to button her shorts and straightened her tank top.

"Baby, you can taunt the big dog all you want. He'll never bite you. I promise you that," he assured her with a wink. "I want to explain it, and I will, but I need to get back to the office."

When she couldn't meet his stare, he lifted her chin with a gentle hand. "Sweetheart, you trust me with your life, don't you?" She nodded, swallowing hard. It wasn't fair when he looked at her that way, as though she was the most perfect woman on the planet, and she was his. "Trust me a little longer, and I'll tell you everything. Okay?"

She knew she had no choice to but see it through. She was falling. Falling hard for the agent, and the man.

Chapter Eight

THE last of her house was clean. *Hallelujah.* She didn't want to go through this again. *What a mess,* she thought with a derisive head shake. Her newly upholstered couch cushions were due by the end of the following week along with several smaller pieces that she'd had to special order to replace. A few knick-knacks she'd simply written off. The less hassle the better after the week she'd spent.

Her closet was mostly put back together, the last of her tossed possessions going back to where they belonged as she tidied up. She spotted the shopping bags on the floor, her latest finds that she'd all but forgotten about with people following her and breaking into her house.

After that glorious stolen interlude with Jonas, she'd come back home to work on her house, and he'd gone back to his office. It was something she would have to accept. It was his work, his job. She knew he wasn't in quite the same kind of danger her father had lived in everyday, but it still wasn't like working in an office everyday either.

Honestly, she didn't think she was lying to herself to admit that she could accept that his job was dangerous. Someone had to do it, and Jonas was damn good at it. He'd told her some of his background Friday night over thick hoagie sandwiches and wine while they listened to the music in the park. It had been the best date she'd had since her divorce. Even cuddled beneath a blanket, all he'd done was massage her thighs or arms. He never tried to push for something more. Although she'd found out today just what happened if she was the one who pushed for it. And she had no complaints. The smile she'd worn since he'd left her side was pretty self-explanatory.

She lifted the different store bags from the bottom of her now mostly clean closet, setting them on her bed to spread out and clip tags to disperse the new things through her wardrobe. There wasn't a rush to get to them. They were winter clothes, from last season on sale. Not that anyone else had to know that.

She pulled the long sweaters out and spread them on her bed, admiring the colors, feeling a bit victorious over finding the designer labels for a steal. She pulled the receipt from between two of them, remembering exactly how her day had gone after she'd first touched it, then folded the bag to toss.

A skittering sound inside of the coated paper bag stopped her. Curious, she opened it and looked.

And felt her heart slam to a dead stop.

A single small bubble package, less than an inch thick slid along the bottom of the paper bag. It was roughly as long as her hand when she pulled it out and held it.

"Oh shit," she choked out, feeling her stomach shoot into her throat then fall like a rock to her feet.

JONAS was rereading files on the Senator, trying to find his connection to pin him with the intelligence espionage when Randy stopped by his desk.

"Hey, Dreyer. Did you hear? Your courier boy was bailed out this morning."

He snapped up. "He was? When?"

"About ten." Jonas looked at his watch. It was well past six. He'd left Stacee over two hours ago.

"Who set his bail?" He was already rising from his chair. When things move, they moved fast and for the first time, he tasted real fear. Only it wasn't for him.

"He claimed it was a relative, but the money was wired in from D.C."

"And the other two?"

"Still sitting in their cells."

"Shit," he ground out. "He was the only one who may know where the memory boards are. Trace that money wire!" He started for the front doors of the ground floor nearly at a run. He knew that the courier was heading straight for Stacee. It wouldn't be hard to play connect the dots at this point for anyone and come up with Stacee Hales.

His phone rang just as he jumped into his vehicle.

"Dreyer."

"Um, Jonas. You know that certain thing you've been looking for?"

He winced at the violent tremor in her voice. "You found it, didn't you?"

"Uh huh."

"Lock your doors. I'm on my way."

"Thank you," she whispered, sounding completely relieved. "I—"

"Stacee!" He shouted her name. He didn't care that several heads had swung around to gape at him. The line had gone eerily dead.

He punched speed dial with his heart stuck between his ribs. "Randy. Stacee Hales found the boards. Her line just went dead."

"Rally the troops?" he asked.

Jonas narrowed his eyes as he hit the freeway well over the speed limit. "Bring who you can spare."

"On it."

He disconnected and tossed his phone to the seat, gripping the steering wheel until his knuckles popped. He counted the minutes as he floored the gas pedal, ticking off miles to Stacee's house.

STACEE'S hand shook. "Jonas?" she squeaked. Nothing. "Oh God. This is not funny." Dropping the cordless phone from her bedroom, she raced for the front door, making sure she had locked it. She lurched to a frozen stop. She heard footsteps outside her door and gulped air. Jonas couldn't possibly be there already.

Backpedaling for the kitchen, she opened the dishwasher and tossed the small package in the silverware basket, locked the door, and ran for her bedroom.

Someone jiggled the front doorknob behind her, and she slammed her bedroom door just before whoever was outside her front door shot the lock out of it. Her whole body flinched at the explosive sound and the ensuing crash as the door was shoved inward.

"I told you she would be easy to find," she heard someone say through the door, hearing far more bravado than a voice that young should have. He must have been the one with the gun. There was silence to his statement though. Was it one or two? How many were out there? She frowned when she heard steps, the intruders apparently unconcerned with being noticed. Definitely more than one. Why was her house the one getting all the assholes?

"Yeah, yeah. No, they haven't found the chips. She has to still have them."

Stacee gulped again and anxiously searched her room for something, anything, to protect herself with. The pillows off her bed? Not even. She refrained from cursing. She didn't even own a bat. Her mother had her father's remaining gear at her house. She had nothing. She heard a crash and winced at the shattered sound. Probably one of her large lamps or TV. Just that much more to clean up. Another loud crash. Her poor living room. She wanted to cry. It seemed they didn't know she was still in the house. She'd put her car in the garage since it was Sunday. Lucky her. The phone cord must have been a precaution.

Her gaze went to the open closet in desperation. One of the extension pipes from the vacuum cleaner? She dismissed it right away. Where was her mini tool kit? She did a mental search and discarded the idea with disappointment. The toolbox was in the hall storage closet. No hammers here.

Damn!

Okay, think Stacee! What do you have? She searched and got an idea, a trick her father once told her about when she had rented her first apartment. She only hoped it would work.

Unplugging her lamp she set her plan in action, thankful she still had the scissors on her bed from when she'd been snipping tags free from her clothes.

Wrapping the wires quickly, she twisted the ends together to hold bared copper flush against the knob then carefully plugged the cord in. Nothing happened, but she wasn't going to be the one to test the theory either.

She leapt for the other side of her bed, forcing open one of the side slide windows then shoved the screen free. It popped out with a wrenched crack. The loud thuds of footsteps were definitely heading in her bedroom's direction. They knew she was home now.

She swung a leg over the sill and shimmied herself out to the other side just as a loud scream filled her house to the rafters right before a solid crash on the other side of her door shook the walls. She didn't turn to look, falling to the ground and hugging the side of the house. Violent curses were echoing up and down the house. The sudden vacuum of no electricity hit her home.

She stilled with a stunned feeling. It had worked.

One toasted bad guy. The rank stench of melted wires and what was likely singed hair filled her nostrils from the window just above her with her next gasped breath. She shook it off, searching for the safest route.

She spun on a foot and raced for the front of the house. There was no sight more welcome than Jonas's Explorer pulling up to the curb on her side of the house. Hiding at the side of the house, she waved a hand to him from the shadows to get his attention, then held up two fingers, flipping them from herself then toward the house when he spotted her. He motioned for her to stay where she was and crept up to the house, drawing his gun as he neared.

Her heart was beating so hard, she wondered how it stayed in her chest.

Jonas inched through the door, and then she couldn't see him. She prayed like she never had in her life. Not when her father was dying in the hospital, no medical miracle saving him, not when she'd sold her first large commissioned house, not even when she'd divorced her ex and prayed his dick would fall off out of spite. No, this praying was deep, spiritual and aimed solely for Jonas.

She needed him to walk back out that door. Tense minutes passed, or maybe only seconds. She had no idea. Silence and agony of the unknown were all she had.

A gunshot rent the air with sickening sharpness.

She jumped, swallowing the scream. Her skin instantly iced over with fear. She slumped against the side of the house, tears filling her eyes as her greatest fear filled her heart and soul. She knew at least one of the thugs who'd broken in had a gun.

Silence.

She gasped a hard sob.

"Stacee?"

She snapped straight in a heartbeat. Lurching off of the wall, she barreled around the corner of the house and ran into his arms.

"It's over, baby."

She sobbed as his hands tucked her emotionally drained body into his.

CHAPTER NINE

NOT three minutes later, police cars began to pull up, circling and blocking her house and every way in or out of the neighborhood. Several were unmarked and had men in starched suits pour out of them. Doors cracked open up and down the street, and people gathered in pockets on the sidewalk to watch.

"Drama and bullets," she muttered, rocking her head against his chest.

He chuckled, running his hands up and down her spine in comfort. "You're the best drama around, sweetheart." His breath was warm against her ear as he kept her close, protecting her from staring eyes.

She thumped him on the shoulder with a limp fist, trying hard not to laugh, just too happy to express that it was Jonas who walked out that front door.

"Agent Dreyer." One of the suits addressed him when he approached. "The memory chips?"

He nodded and tipped down to press a kiss to her temple.

"Dishwasher," she breathed for him and him alone.

A rumble of surprised laughter shook his chest. "Do you want me to stay here?" he asked her, willing to stay if she wanted.

She blinked back the sudden heat of her tears at his offer, but shook her head. "No. This needs to end."

He drew a deep breath, and she felt as a heavy tension covered his frame as if he wanted to say something, but one more breath later, it was gone. He nodded and caressed her cheek.

"I'll be right back."

She realized, with no small shock, that she would willingly wait for him every day, forever, as he walked with the Secret Service guy into her house.

Silence. What an amazing sound. Blessed silence. A good silence, the quiet of nightfall at her home.

No more questions, no more strangers tromping through her house, over her yard, or a dozen cars parked like an automaker's fence line at the street. The moon was just rising beyond the row of houses across the street, somehow making the last hour or so seem very surreal. All she had to do was turn around to know it had all happened.

The front door was ajar behind her where she sat on the porch, watching the moths dance and flutter beneath the streetlamp over the sidewalk. It wouldn't close properly until it was repaired, and that would be tomorrow at the earliest. Her window screen would also need to be repaired. Thankfully, the medics who'd arrived to tend to the shot victim had also dealt with the guy who'd electrocuted himself into a numb stupor right outside her bedroom door. She hadn't seen any of the aftermath, but had received several impressed looks for the idea.

Silently, she sent a prayer to her dad. Her mother was still hurting for the brave, loving man who'd been shot in the line of duty doing what he loved outside of his family, and she couldn't blame her for her pain. As Stacee got older, she'd understood that pain better, but she would never forget the things he'd taught her.

Warm thighs pressed against hers as Jonas sat behind her on the porch, wrapping himself around her in a cocoon of warmth. The strength of his steeled arms circled her, and she never felt safer.

"You shouldn't stay here tonight," he said, leaning until his chin rested on her bare shoulder. "No power, a door that doesn't lock."

"It stinks inside," she added offhandedly.

His chest moved with a short laugh. "Is that why you're out here?" he asked, pulling her closer.

"Some of it."

She shivered when his hands found skin and massaged. "You're cold. It's still too cold at night to be out here in shorts, baby."

"I could call Kay," she told him absently, loving the feel of his palms on her thighs, rubbing warmth back into her. She arched back into his chest, and he dropped a kiss on her exposed throat. Warmth seeped into her quickly, her body recalling what had happened between them just a few hours before.

"I don't think so."

"Oh?" she breathed, quickly falling under the tease of his fingers and lips.

"Come with me," he beckoned in a seductive voice that sent a thrilling shiver down her spine.

Her hands landed on his, halting his rubbing, which had slowly been maneuvering toward the inner part of her thighs. A delicious sensation that she hated stopping. "You want me to come home with you?"

He sat in contemplative silence for a moment, then laced his fingers through hers. "Actually, I want you to come home and stay." Wicked heat flared when he taunted her earlobe with his tongue.

"Jonas?" This was moving fast between them, into territory she wasn't very familiar with. She'd been out of the dating game for a long time. Attraction was one thing, even lust. Taking it to the next level? She wasn't sure if she was that ready.

"Hm?" he answered, deeply engrossed in the slope of her neck and shoulder, dropping heated and seductive kisses where he could reach. He did that a lot, given the opportunity.

"I don't do one night stands."

He shrugged behind her. "I don't either. I told you earlier, it wasn't just that once. Not by a long shot."

Her mouth popped open, but he silenced her with a finger over her lips. "Just come home with me," he purred against her ear. "Let the rest sort itself out." He slid his hand with a teasing lightness down the front of her throat until he found the weight of her breast. She moaned as he circled sensitive skin and teased

63

her nipple to a hard point beneath her tank top. She shivered with renewed desire as he worked his magic over her, finally caressing her, arousing her only the way he could.

The warmth of his touch flowed until it rested on the top of her thigh, his fingers between her legs, just *there*. Not moving, not seducing, not inciting. They both knew what he was capable of, but he wasn't using that to force a decision. But the memory of the pleasure he'd given her was burned into her.

He was the devil reincarnate. She agreed completely, over-run with a delicious hunger for his touch, a passion only he could give her.

JONAS helped her while she packed a couple bags with clothes and womanly necessities. She locked her car in the garage, and he installed a heavy security lock on her front door to keep it as safe as possible when they left.

He didn't doubt what he was doing, but it still made him nervous. His future with this woman was hinged on two things. Whether or not she could accept him and his secret, and if she couldn't, if she'd ever forgive him for using the bonding of sex to keep her if she couldn't accept his nature. Because he wasn't going to let her go. Not now. Not ever.

He hadn't had a lot of time to assimilate that afternoon's tryst in her car, but it had driven home just who she was, and that she was meant to be with him. He'd never felt so compelled, consumed like he did like when he was with Stacee. The world could blow up and he wouldn't notice, and likely not care so long as he had her in his arms. Her scent, her flavor, the silkiness of her skin and the brush of her hair. All of it drove him wild, in a deep primal way. Even then, after hours of questions and telling and retelling of the facts, he couldn't remove the taste of her from his tongue. He craved to taste her heat for himself, to lap up the pure honey of her pleasure. If he was the big dog, she'd reduced him to a rub-my-belly puppy.

He knew the truth, what he was skirting around like a kid on hot concrete running around the pool on his toes with anxious skips, wanting the coolness of all that water, but terrified of the leap. He didn't fear it, but just the same, it left him tangled in knots to know what he was facing. That this could be the biggest change of his life, or the worst relationship he'd never escape. Give him a shoot-out in a dark alley any day. This was going to kill him without ever touching a gun.

"You know, my mom is going to love you," she said in a low distracted voice from her side of the vehicle.

"Oh?" he asked with an arched eyebrow, surprised that mentioning her mother was the next thing she'd bring up. It told him that he wasn't alone on this thoughtful train.

"Yeah." She fluttered a hand between them. "She'll love you until she learns you're a cop, then she'll hate you. She'll eventually learn to like you."

"I see. Would telling her I'm not a street cop help?"

"She won't see the difference between an agent and a cop. You carry a gun," she told him with a crooked smile. "Just thought I should warn you."

He nodded. "I understand."

"I thought you might."

"But her daughter, your father's daughter, is a woman to be proud of."

She lightly shrugged away the compliment, unable to hide the pleased smile in the small confines of the vehicle. "She still has some bitter moments."

"We'll smooth them over." He slowed and pulled into a long driveway. An electronic gate opened, and he rolled through, double checking in the mirrors as he moved past it that it locked in place.

"This is a very nice house," she said, sitting straight to take it all in. "I didn't picture you as living in the woods."

He was rather proud of the house himself. A large sprawling ranch house that he'd added the fence to. The trees were bountiful and towered over the yard, and reached for some distance from the rear where he preferred to run, unhindered and undisturbed.

"A house made for a family," she said almost whimsically.

For the first time, he saw it through her eyes and could agree. He also knew he had the right woman. If everything went well tonight. He felt that growing fist in his gut twist at the worrisome thought.

He glanced at her in the dim lights surrounding them. Her face glowed from the ambient lights, her attention elsewhere as she studied his home. His only thought was he'd never known a more beautiful, brave woman in his life. There was only one thing left to do.

He took the plunge, and the water felt incredible.

Chapter Ten

JONAS silenced the truck and turned to her. He brushed the thick hair away from her face, spotting the hickey. *His*. And he'd cherish and protect her for as long as she lived. "Are you sure you're okay?" He searched her.

She cupped a hand over his. "I'm fine. Now."

He swallowed when his heart danced. His physical response was keeping him off center, but he tried to keep it from showing. Between his body's crying need to possess her completely, his nature demanding he claim her as he should, and the worry he felt at all of the above, there was no center of gravity for him. He was teetering hard, deciding which direction to move in first. Claim and let it work itself out, or explain and pray. He wished he knew. The indecision, the worst of his life, was causing his stomach to take on a permanent pretzel feeling.

"What's wrong?" she asked him, tenderly swiping her thumb over his bottom lip.

He drew a breath, pulling in his wandering worries and let it all back out. "Nothing. Let's go in."

He palmed her bags while she carried her purse and he let her go in first. The first woman to stay with him. The first woman to walk into his den, into his home.

"Jonas, if you'd rather I stayed somewhere else, I can stay with Kay. She won't mind." He jerked up, aware he'd been frowning in the direction of her suitcase.

"No," he stated firmly. "This is just... I've never had a woman here before."

She nodded, as though unsurprised. "I can see that. You're very territorial."

That she'd read him that well, amazed him. "How do you know?" One thing he knew, was Stacee knew people, knew how to interpret silence, or looks. He realized he'd really have to work to keep things like Christmas presents a secret from her.

"You always put yourself between me and whoever else may be nearby, even Kay. Don't get me wrong, I don't mind it, but I know when you're being possessive. You have an assertive nature, or you wouldn't do what you do. You're an alpha. I know what that looks like."

He blinked, struck speechless at her choice of words. He swallowed, not daring to let himself touch her. Barely daring to breathe. He wasn't used to feeling fear. He refused to start now, even as it clashed with an unexpected hopeful elation. "And you don't care that I'm like that? Because I can't change it."

She shook her head. "Nope. Doesn't bother me in the least."

Relief swelled and he felt like a weight had been lifted from his shoulders. He could do this. He could tell her. He slid his jacket off his shoulders, exposing his holster. He reached for one of her hands and led her into his living room.

"Don't worry. We're going to talk first," he told her as he sat her down. He tossed his jacket over the back of a chair and unbuckled his weapon to hang on the tree with his denim jacket. "I told you earlier before we went further, there was something I had to tell you."

She sat on the edge of the chair, attentive. "I remember." She watched him as he paced.

Okay, not as easy as he'd believed. He sucked in another hard breath. "It's going to sound crazy."

"Well, if you're not sick, or have some disease, what could it be?" A perplexed frown had overtaken her brow.

His heart banged against his ribs as trepidation filled his body. He knelt next to her and reached for one of her hands, holding her in between his. He forced the four words from his mouth. The first time he'd ever told another of his nature. "I am a shifter."

He couldn't look up, dreading what he'd see. Disbelief, shock, astonishment, alarm. Fear.

Seconds grew thick with silence and that fear he refused to acknowledge returned.

"And I'm a natural blonde," she snipped, her words devoid of all humor. "Don't tease me, Jonas. You don't have to tell me some ridiculous lie if you don't want to see me again. It's not like we actually slept together." She yanked her hand free and pushed him away to stand. He blocked her, and she tumbled back down to the chair. "Although why the big show to get me to come home with you..." She trailed off and put more distance between them.

He growled. He did *not* like her losing her trust of him. "You trusted me until five minutes ago to not hurt you, to never lie, to protect you. Why would I lie about this?"

"Because shifters are a fictional thing!" She threw her arms up then around her body in protection. "You are sick. How they never found this on your psyche eval, I'll never know."

"I can prove it," he stated calmly, finally looking up at her. "I can prove it. The reason I brought you home with me is because I had a choice to make. I either trusted you enough to tell you before I took you to my bed, or took you first and hoped like hell you could live with the beast within the man, because there's no going back." He took a breath and stood before her. "I trusted you enough to tell you first."

She shook her head, trying to not laugh, the first sign of hysteria.

"I *cared* enough to tell you first," he added. "Will you at least let me prove it to you before you leave?"

Her melded eyes were dark, but glistening as her thoughts tumbled around behind them. He feared what they were, and hoped like hell he'd never have to find out. He wanted to dispel every doubt, every disbelieving glare.

He frowned. "I'm not going to hurt you, Stacee. You *do* know that. I would not, could not hurt you. This big dog never could."

"What are you?" she whispered in a thready voice, still watching him suspiciously.

The first taste of relief was impossible to ignore. Curiosity was a strong reaction. "Wolf. My pack is scattered through the city."

She nodded, as if trying to absorb it all. "Wolf," she repeated numbly.

He offered a hand. She stared at it. "Come with me, sweetheart. It will all make sense soon." When she hesitated, he knelt again. "Stacee, look at me." He waited until she did. "You know who I am. You know I would never hurt you." He almost blurted the three little words. They wouldn't help right now. It surprised him how easy they had risen into his throat. He guessed he should've listened to his father a little better. Once he'd given in, it all seemed so easy. It was just the execution that was killing him.

Hazel eyes watched him with suspicion. At least it wasn't the fear. He could battle suspicion and win. "Where are we going?"

She wanted information. Fair enough. "Just to the rear of the house. Claw marks are a bitch on hardwood."

Eyes widened, then blinked. "You're serious?"

"Never been more serious in my life. You wouldn't believe how much it cost to get them sanded and buffed the first time."

A nervous grin popped out with a chuckle. She reached for his hand. Together, they stood.

Stacee followed him as he walked through the house toward a room in the rear. The hallway wasn't very long on this end. The room he stopped in was wide and open with a closet filled with blankets and a single table, empty at the moment, at one side. There were a couple throw rugs, as though the room acted as a mudroom for the house. Glass doors showed a view into the dark shadows of the woods in the rear. She could make a clear view of the fence at one point, like it was purposely kept clean of vines and debris. The rest was buried within the encroaching forest.

Vertical blinds hung fully withdrawn to show the entire expanse of the entrance. He opened one glass door and flipped the switch for the lights outside. A porch fed off the rear of the house and a single chair.

He led her to the chair and asked her sit. "Just in case," he stated.

"Just in case?"

"You feel the need to collapse," he told her with a touch of his humor.

She eyed him. "You're really serious about this?" She knew she should be running as far and as fast as she could away from him and this house, but some morbid sense of curiosity was keeping her right where she was. Whether it was to call him a liar and be done with it or... And it was the 'or' that wouldn't let her just run. He was acting too serious about it, too sure of what he was trying to make her believe. There wasn't an ounce of deceit in his mood, words, or actions.

Either he wasn't lying or he deserved to be in Hollywood.

He had started to unbutton the work shirt he'd put on over the t-shirt she'd seen him in earlier in the day. Sinewy arms appeared out of the sleeves.

"I've never been more serious. See, I could've skipped this entirely. Made love to you first but then you'd have had no choice in the matter. I'm not that kind of evil," he admitted calmly, winking at her.

"No choice," she repeated in a dazed murmur. "Thank you, I think, for not going that route."

"You're very welcome." He'd shucked his shirts and had kicked off his shoes and socks and placed them on the table. His jeans went next and his underwear.

Her mouth went dry seeing him naked. He wasn't in the least bit shy about it. Her gaze started with what she knew and traveled his length in sheer womanly appreciation. His penis twitched and moved as her gaze caressed him. He wrapped a palm around the shaft, then stood proudly for her inspection.

He glanced down at his erection, and raised an eyebrow. "You think I do that for just anyone?"

She dropped her gaze immediately when she felt her cheeks heat. His laugh was kind, warm, and sultry.

He leaned over and stole a quick, gentle kiss then he walked off the porch. "Watch closely, because it goes pretty quick for someone my age."

"Does it hurt?" she asked. Was she believing this nonsense? *No. Firmly. Of course not.* She just never would've pegged Jonas for being unstable.

"No." He held up a hand, stalling any more interruptions. "You can ask to your heart's content when I know you believe me."

So, with that, she sat and watched, just waiting for the moment to call him a liar to his face and be done with him. She'd never been made a fool of. *First time for everything.* Except she didn't see what she was expecting. In less than a minute, she felt her jaw become unhinged as he seemed to fold in on himself.

The transformation was amazing, incredible, unbelievable, but there it—he—was. Legs bent as he fell to four legs instead of standing on two. Fur appeared on skin. His face grew longer and ears grew pointed. He was a rich brown pelted wolf with the wildest green-blue eyes she'd ever seen in an animal.

It was a good thing she'd already been sitting. She *would have* collapsed. Hell, she probably would've fainted if she'd been standing! He shook out his coat and ran a paw over his face, as though clearing his vision. Then he sat and cocked his head, waiting expectantly. She sat on her hands to hide their trembling.

"I think you better come back," she managed, sure she sounded weak. Lightheadedness swooped down on her with a swift strike, and the shadows tilted.

CHAPTER ELEVEN

JONAS watched her eyes roll into the back of her head and her body slump in the chair. The chair idea had been spot on. He shifted back, his body reabsorbing the teeth, tissue, and bones into his own shape until he stood straight again. Well, he guessed fainting was a step up from hysterical screaming, but he hadn't expected that reaction from Stacee to begin with.

Scooping her up, he carried her to the bedroom and laid her out next to him, curving his body around hers. He wished she weren't still completely dressed but better this than finding herself in the bed with a naked man *and* being naked herself. He was used to sleeping in the raw. And with clothes in the way, he sort of had to behave himself, when he really didn't want to. Not when he'd showed her and wanted her with every fiber of his body.

Hell, he still had the damn erection! He nuzzled her neck to not groan. Talk about torture. Instead, he covered them both with the blanket and wrapped an arm beneath her, cradling her head on the pillow, running a hand along her side with the other as she breathed unaware. Buried as he was against her throat, she smelled like vanilla and cherries today, and that sweet honeyed scent that was only her. That same ripe tantalizing scent that he'd found holding her in the car earlier when he'd been unable to *not* touch her somehow, especially after the invigorating sensation of her claws digging into him. That marking feeling had brought the wolf wide awake in an instant. Jonas had needed to have a taste, needed to know the truth.

He hadn't been at all prepared for the lust, the hunger or absolute pleasure he'd experienced with her in the car. There'd been no chance to fulfill his body's howling desires. Bringing Stacee to orgasm had been the closest thing to pleasure and pain he'd ever experienced. He'd do it again in a heartbeat too. Feeling her climax had been one of the most erotic moments in his life. He had a feeling his woman was an erotic dream just waiting to happen. He'd been playing back his hottest dreams for a week now, imagining her in every position possible. Like a porno reel. That in itself had been its own kind of torture.

He hoped before the end of the night, he'd have the chance to experience at least a few of those fantasy induced dreams. For the moment, he kept himself relaxed and gradually managed a light doze next to the woman who stirred him like no one else ever had.

Jonas was aware enough to feel her move and instantly snapped fully awake at the first sensation of her stretching next to him.

Glancing at the clock, a little less than an hour had passed. Good, she had probably needed a little rest after all the shocks she'd had earlier. No harm in a nap.

"Hey baby," he breathed against her shoulder.

"Hey," she answered. Still no screams. He took that as a good sign.

The weight of her hair played through his fingers when he brushed it. Moving it, he dropped a kiss to her shoulder. She fit snug into his shape, her ass pressed against his groin and his reawakening erection. He wouldn't rush this part. It almost killed him to not roll her over and indulge his fantasies.

"You said 'your pack' earlier."

"Mm hm." He nuzzled her, letting her talk, ask, decide.

"How many are there?"

He did a quick headcount. "In the south pack, about thirty. Last I knew, there were eight packs in the city."

"I see." Silence. "So the odds of people knowing you exist are slim."

"We protect our secrets, our kin, and our pack. We have for as long as I can remember."

"Are there others?"

"Shifters?"

She nodded.

"Yes."

"Wow," she breathed.

"I'm sorry I frightened you," he said moments later. "I never meant to."

She rolled over in his arms to find his gaze. God, he loved her. Those stone and chocolate eyes, lips that tasted of heaven and a body that he'd want until the day he died.

"You didn't frighten me. You shocked the living shit out of me," she retorted. "You. Do. Not. Exist."

His mouth popped open, but she covered it with gentle fingers. Was she denying him? Was she going to walk away after all? His stomach lurched. The sudden pierce of a knife sliced him from the inside out. Pain like he'd never known. His skin felt icy all of a sudden. He couldn't move. She was going to leave him. She was going to walk away from him. His worst nightmare was about to happen.

"Jonas. I'll keep your secret forever." It was a whispered promise, and one that crashed his entire world into a vacuum of pain.

His features froze. His entire being felt brittle, from his heart outward. Like he would shatter. He had to find a way to win her to him.

He couldn't believe he was the only male who'd failed.

He was so caught up in his misery he neglected to notice what Stacee was doing, oblivious to the movement when her fingers slipped from his mouth to trail over his ear.

The warmth of her hand on his face dragged him back to the bed in slow increments.

"But I do exist. You saw me," he challenged. The pounding in his ears was his breaking heart.

"Yes. But outside of this room, outside of this house, you can't. I know that. I'd never break that trust."

He shook himself. She was touching him. And had been. How long had she been doing that? Trailing her fingers around his ear, down his neck. *She's touching me. And she knows.* It took a second for that to sink in as well.

Shudders racked his body when she pressed her nails into his chest and dragged them down his body. A slow growl rumbled out of his chest at the sensation that left fiery trails in their wake. "Stacee," he cautioned. He wouldn't take her if she couldn't accept him. Fuck, she was killing him.

"So I take it, this isn't the kind of secret you share with just any girlfriend," she said, taunting his nipples with light flicks.

"No," he replied, although the one word felt torn from him as desire raged through his body. She didn't know what she was doing to him. The animal she was toying with.

She seemed to be studying her hand as it meandered and caressed across his chest. His stomach clenched when she traveled down the thin line of hair that led due south.

"That's good to know."

He snapped up from watching the hypnotic sway of her nails on his skin. What was good to know? Damn it!

"Stacee!" He clasped her hand, stilling it in a firm clutch. He couldn't follow even one conversation with her touching him that way.

"Jonas?"

He swallowed and drew a deep breath. "What?" He tried not to snarl it, but he was a wreck and she wasn't giving an ounce of mercy.

The glimmer of her eyes sparkled up at him as her lips twitched, her expression all innocence. She ran a foot up his calf, teasing him.

"Why am I still dressed?"

He fell silent for a solid three seconds. Then she squealed with laughter when he tossed her onto her back and ripped the tank from her body with a single tearing yank.

"Hey!" she shouted.

"I'll buy you five more," he said just before he ravished her mouth. Her hands plowed into his hair and held him captive as he thrust between her lips, no request in the motion.

It was sheer claiming.

Her nails scored his scalp and back, giving as much as he was, taking whatever he dished out and giving it right back to him, passion for passion. She lifted her hips and rubbed her center against hard flesh, and he groaned. Taut buds rubbed his chest with each breath.

Grabbing her hands, he pinned them in one grip over her head. Lavishing a trail, he drew his tongue from one wrist to the soft skin of her inner elbow, nipping until he reached her shoulder. Each kiss created a telling shiver on his travels. "You smell so good," he said, burying his nose into the crook of her shoulder.

She whimpered and arched into him. He didn't stop licking her there. He caressed her collarbone, then dipped into the shallow of her throat. He wanted to taste every inch of her skin on his tongue, and knew by the end of the night, it'd be close to accomplished.

He swirled around the tight tip of her breast and she lifted in answer, whimpering for more, pressing into the heat of his mouth. Tugging gently he felt her respond, her breast warm and soft in his hand. He cupped her, molding and gently kneading her body to his hand. Her skin was as sweet as summer wine, and just as heady. She quivered with each new pull on sensitive skin. He drew her deep, scraping his teeth and tongue over her sensitive nipple to heighten her arousal.

Releasing her, he dipped down to her belly button and unsnapped her shorts once more. So close to her sex, he found the proof of her arousal easily, and it only made him hungrier for her body. And this time, he would taste her the way he wanted to.

She lifted her hips with an impatient nudge to remove the offending shorts then he moved to lie between her thighs, brushing tender kisses to her trembling legs. He slowed down to savor her. Her body, her taste, her scent. He wanted to know her, all of her. Lifting her ass, he hooked her legs over his shoulders, tipping her treasure to his mouth. She shivered with anticipation and moaned when he brushed his fingers over the tight curls guarding her core. He drew a deep breath. There had always been something about a woman's arousal that had excited him. Now that he had Stacee, her pleasure, her scent was the only one he needed.

"Beautiful," he murmured, then he spread her labia and licked.

She moaned, long and deep. He blew a slow stream of air over her damp flesh. He saw the way she fisted the covers of the bed, felt the way she quivered with desire and pleasure. He loved that about her, that she gave all of herself over to his touch.

"Has anyone ever made you come this way?" he asked her.

"N-No. Why?" she managed on gasping pants of air.

"Relax, baby. I've wanted to do this so badly," he admitted. "Today almost killed me in the car, but I don't regret a second of it. Now, it's my turn."

Rolling her clit between his fingers, he licked at her pussy, lapping at the honey that glistened on her skin. He groaned as the sweet taste poured through his system, sending heat and fire through his body and straight to his groin. She thrashed and moaned in answer. The scent of her body swam all around him as he lashed at her pussy, long delving strokes that made her jump and push into him, seeking what he gave her until he reached the swollen sensitive nub of her clit. She quaked harder. He thrust his tongue as deep as he could to lap up the sweet juice of her desire.

Sliding two fingers into her channel, he deepened the pressure of his tongue and she moaned, a throaty sound that ricocheted off the bedroom walls. Sucking sensitive flesh into his mouth, he rolled his tongue over her, devouring her in increments. He'd never tasted a sweeter heat, a hotter pussy.

Pressure built as he stroked her inner walls, eliciting sharp moans and cries with his rhythm when he began to drive into her, pulsing against aroused flesh, using his thumb to stimulate her with each thrust. He felt her climax building, felt the way her pussy tightened around him as she neared that precipice.

No words were needed this time. He twisted his fingers to rub his knuckles against swollen flesh, thrusting them deeper with hard twists, finding the secret spots that were meant to be pleasured. She exploded, crying out as liquid silk coated his fingers. He buried his mouth against her, drinking in her juice like ambrosia. He lapped up every drop, lost in her passion, craving her satisfaction.

Lifting over her body, he pressed kisses of wonderment to her flesh, awed by the beauty he'd found, inside and out. The strength of this woman, his woman. Settling on an arm, he sipped at her lips as she floated, her cheeks flush with satisfaction. Reaching for the drawer of his nightstand, he withdrew a small box. Tearing into one of the foil packets, he covered himself quickly, feeling her fingers wandering along his back and hip.

Glancing to her, he caught her arched eyebrow.

Feeling busted, he explained, "It was an impulse thing after Thursday morning."

"I'm glad you thought of it," she replied, sounding genuinely relieved. Considering it had been more than three years since the last time he'd needed one, it had been very impulsive. Then he was fitting himself between the creamy softness of her thighs and thinking ceased to matter.

Air hissed from his lungs as he sank into her folds, feeling the shudder and quake of her tight body accepting him. She moaned and grasped at him, arching to take his full length. It only took a few moments to find that point, that perfect rhythm of pleasure between them. Sharp gasps escaped. Sweet pleasure rocketed up and down his body as her muscles held him, caressed him, and he was lost.

Fire spread as his strokes deepened. Her leg wound over his calf, pulling him tighter into her and he answered, driving in harder. She was close. Her entire body shook with the depth of her desire. Her hips lifted to meet his driving thrusts. He ground into her mound and she shouted, clawing and bucking. Her pussy clenched down on his cock, and he clenched his teeth, lost to her orgasm. Hot wetness bathed him and he threw back his head, shouting out his own release, a pleasure like he'd never known, soaring with brilliant bliss through him. He pushed himself deeper, wanting to feel this forever, this heat, her pussy wrapped around him in sated desire. The last spurts of his climax escaped.

Gasping for needed air, he collapsed to his elbows, his face comforted by the swell of her breast. Her arms wrapped over his back, holding him to her. He couldn't think of one other place he'd rather be.

79

She dozed beneath his weight, or maybe she had a brief moment of unconsciousness. Stacee wasn't sure. That had been the best orgasm of her life. Her entire body felt languid, loved. She'd never felt that before, sheer satiation. She prayed she'd get to feel it again. Jonas wasn't laying on her fully, supporting himself to not crush her, but she honestly didn't care. She didn't want him to move at all, loving the feeling of his skin next to hers.

She nuzzled his face, brushing little kisses to his temple, and he moved to give her better access.

Running her hands up and down his back, she felt the way the muscles bunched and moved beneath her touch. Something was bothering him.

"What's the matter?" she asked.

"I'm not sure," he replied. "Did I happen to tell you I love you yet?"

She smiled. "No, but I had an inkling."

He lifted to look into her eyes, the aquamarine of his, deep and adoring. "When?"

"When you told me you'd never told another your little furry secret." She stretched her arms over his back then resumed her meandering touching. "I had no idea shifters were real, but it explains a few things."

He rose onto his flat palms. "Oh?"

"Your strength, for one. The way you can go still as stone. That's not really a human trait. It's very hard to do and keep still. Models train years to accomplish that technique to mimic mannequins. I don't exactly see you as the model type," she told him with a soft chuckle.

"So, you've been watching me," he challenged playfully, nipping at her chin.

"Oh, I'd say I've been watching you a lot. I love what I see."

"After only a week?" he mused quietly, as though to himself.

"After only a week," she confirmed. She cupped his face and brought him down to her. "I love you, Jonas. Now, it's my turn to make you scream a time or two."

The wicked grin that appeared showed he was more than ready to be tested.

Alpha
Awakening

---

*Dedication: Selena, Michelle,
Cynnara, Leslie, Tim, Mina and JMo.*

CHAPTER ONE

Rush stood patiently in line waiting to make his coffee order. The Mocha Hut was nearly empty on a Saturday, mid-afternoon. The scents of coffee and different baked cakes permeated the air. He wasn't on duty, and he wasn't in a hurry to get home, either. His sister was moody because her boyfriend was out of town again. She was too much like their mother, and it drove him up a wall. Taking his time getting home was the least of his sins at this point.

Lost in his musings and lack of plans for the weekend, the dragged scrape of a metal chair behind him caught his attention, snapping him around.

A petite woman had leaped from her seat, glaring at her companion.

"Steven." Rush heard the hiss of the other man's name. "Let it go. Leave me alone."

When she tried to step out of reach, the man lunged for her. She squeaked with a hint of fear wound into her anger, now. Her evasiveness looked like something she'd become accustomed to.

"Kay, please. You're making a scene."

Rush frowned at the hidden threat in the lowered growl of a plea. The blond man made another dash for her that she barely managed to evade.

The woman flinched. "The hell I am."

Rush could swear by the man's posture she was about to be tackled.

He didn't know their story, but the blond trying to bulldoze over her was easily twice her size, probably early thirties. The only other two in the coffee shop had stopped to watch the free drama from the far side of the counter. Of course, neither of them thought to offer a moment's aid to a volatile situation.

Rush stepped into the blond's line of sight. "Is there a problem?"

"Butt out." Rush got a glaring, belligerent snarl for his effort.

Rush slid his hand into his back pocket. "Look, either go home and cool off or be arrested for public disturbance. Your choice." He kept his voice low, yet firm.

Dark brown eyes narrowed at the interruption. Rush didn't blink. He didn't know who this man was, and really didn't care, because Rush was used to being obeyed regardless.

"The lady asked you to leave her alone." He hadn't looked in her direction, but he sensed her move out of the other's line of sight. When the guy before him didn't budge, he withdrew and opened his wallet, showing his badge. "I'm not going to ask you again." The lowered warning was distinct. Leave or suffer the consequences.

Steven, if he'd heard right, shoved a chair out of his way, creating a new wave of racket when it bounced and clattered against the table. "We're not done Kay." He stormed out, slapping the door wide open on his way, making it bang against the outside hinges.

He waited a few minutes for Steven to return. When he didn't, Rush turned to find her. "You all right?"

She nodded, her arms around her slight body. "I wasn't expecting that."

"He's never been violent?"

"No. We weren't even dating that long when he broke it off."

Rush took a step closer to study her. Inky lashes surrounded thunderhead gray eyes. Rich, dark, black-brown hair swayed around her shoulders to not quite halfway down her back. There was no sign of old bruises, no wary glances to search her immediate space as though she were expecting retaliation for her earlier denial. Unfortunately, this woman made a perfect target for someone with a violent edge. She was petite and easy to overpower, beautiful and apparently able to stand up for herself. A heady mix of femininity and backbone. Glancing at the heeled boots she wore, he wondered if she even came to his chin.

"He broke if off?" he asked, remembering to find his voice before his mind *and* body wandered off on their own.

She nodded once. "He was getting persistent about getting together again, and I told him no." Her arms finally dropped and her chin came up, those dark eyes shooting defiant sparks as bright as lightning. "All he did was annoy me with his persistence. He didn't make me mad until he tried to grab me. That's not like him."

"If you hadn't dated that long, it might have been exactly like him, and you're just now seeing it," Rush cautioned. He'd seen enough abuse cases to know physical violence was hardly ever exposed in the early stages of a relationship.

"True. It never occurred to me. We broke up quite a while ago."

Quiet music wafted through hidden speakers, returning a calm to the interior of the shop. The sound of feet on tile and voices told him the rest of the customers and staff had already dismissed the little disturbance. "Would you like to share a coffee?" Rush offered, taking himself by surprise. He wasn't sure why he offered. His duty was done. She was safe, but he found he wasn't ready to say goodbye. *It wouldn't hurt anything to give her a chance to put this behind her,* he told himself. His offer had nothing to do with the color of her eyes, or the sweet slope of her bottom lip.

She reached and picked up the chair she'd knocked over in her own haste to avoid Steven's grasping. "I'd like that." Standing closer to him, she held out her hand. "Kaisha Noelles, but everyone calls me Kay."

He took her hand and felt the warmth of her skin all the way up his arm. Desire, raw and unexpected flashed over his senses, a brilliant burst dying down to a slow burning ember as quickly as it had appeared.

"Rush Donovan." Swallowing, he cleared his throat when he sounded husky. Her entire palm vanished within his own, delicate yet strong, and was he imagining it, or was there a scent of sunshine in her hair?

Rush caught himself before he leaned in to find out for sure. Releasing her, he eased her back down into the chair she'd claimed and strode to the counter to make an order.

Turning away was also the safest, fastest and least telling action to help him calm the raging case of wanting from her touch. He'd never felt anything like her softness beneath his fingers, or had so quick of a reaction. Taking her entire form in a glance was pure maleness—the appreciation was all his. Snug jeans that coated her legs like soft leather rounded her rear when she'd stooped to grab at the chair, her brown hair swaying with the movements over a simple filmy blouse with a chemise beneath it. Evocative yet sweet.

Giving the drink order, he tried to get a stern grip as his entire body woke up, aware of her like no one in his lifetime. As her remembered scent infiltrated his brain like a stamp of indelible ink on paper, he had a feeling that what had started as a simple need to help a lady in distress was going to turn into something a lot harder to walk away from when they hit the bottom of their drinks.

KAY watched him turn and speak to the barrister for their cups. Her mind was still spinning over the near attack from Steven. They'd broken up months ago. Why would he want to come back to her now, when he was the one to end it between them? It had been some story about a personal issue, and he didn't know how long it would take him. Rather than have her wait for him, he had politely ended their occasional dating. She'd moved on. Her heart hadn't been invested, which was probably for the best considering what she'd seen today. The last thing she needed or wanted was to find herself in *that* kind of a relationship.

"Here you go," he said in a warm as honey voice. How did a man with that rugged of a face get that kind of voice? The voice wasn't the only thing to appreciate about her knight in shining armor. He looked young, until she looked into his eyes. There was a calmness in them that spoke of maturity, a soul who had seen a lot and refused to let it weigh him down. The day's growth of dark beard gave him a rakish aura that added to the masculinity of his face. With slightly thick lips and broad cheekbones, she found the deepness of his eyes hard to resist. She also couldn't help but wonder how it would feel to slide her palm down one cheek, intrigued by the allure of the sensation. She hid the wondering question behind a tentative sip of her drink.

"That's good."

He smiled at her approval of his choice.

Rush sat across from her, palming his own drink between solid hands. Well-muscled arms were molded by a navy blue t-shirt, stretched across a very impressive chest, the strength hinted at beneath the molded cotton. He wasn't overly tall, which truth be told, Kay found intimidating at times. She didn't stand five-feet barefoot. Her size had been perfect for gymnastics, but not real life.

Watching him over her cup, she followed the planes of his face. Not exactly handsome. Maybe striking would be better. Definitely a man used to being in command. A quiet confidence rested all around him. Thick raven black hair looked finger combed into loose swirls over his head. She'd already decided his best asset was definitely his eyes. A deep-sea blue with a smattering of dove gray and brown throughout. How something that artistic could ever be simply labeled as hazel was beyond her. His eyes were as gorgeous as the rest of what she'd seen.

"So, you're really a cop?" she asked after he'd had a chance to sample his own drink.

"A detective, but yeah, for the records," he joked lightly. "You?"

"I work at Savrenson and Son."

"The jeweler downtown?"

She smiled, pleased he knew of the store. "That's the one. I work there part-time as an appraiser. I actually deal in antique jewelry."

"Is that a piece?" he asked, noting a ring on her hand with a glance.

"Yes, it is. This is a family heirloom, though," she explained, letting the light sparkle off the peanut-sized emerald and gold band.

"It's lovely," he said. Glancing up, she noted he was looking at her, not the ring when he said that.

Was he flirting with her? A rare warmth filled her face, and she dropped her gaze. "Thank you."

An hour flew by without notice as they talked. She couldn't remember when she'd sipped her last drop, or when she'd stopped caring if there was anyone but them in the shop. He told her stories about himself and his sister, and she regaled him with tales of growing up with her best friend Stacee. Laughter soon erased the ugly scene she'd been a part of before Rush's intervention.

"Can I ask you something?"

Kay shrugged, completely at ease with Rush. "Sure."

"Do you only do antiques or can you get a feel for something a little more modern?"

Her grin broadened. If there was one thing she knew, it was jewelry. "If it sparkles, I can tell you what it's worth."

"Mom had a few pieces that she wanted to hand down. I'd like to know what they are worth."

"Are you planning on selling them?" she asked, torn at having the chance to see them, but wondering why he'd want to sell something valuable to his family.

"Definitely not to sell. She'd come back and haunt me for even thinking it."

"Your parents are deceased?" she asked sympathetically, curling a hand over his where he rested them together on top of the table.

His gaze fell to where she held him with a wide-eyed stare, his thumb brushing her skin after a hesitant heartbeat then capturing her hand between the both of his. Warmth fluttered from her belly downward at the simple act. "Unfortunately. I became Sheridan's guardian at an early age."

Dark shadows dulled the life in his eyes as thoughts filled them. A few seconds later, he blinked them away, looking up at her again. "I have a few more responsibilities now, but she's still my younger sister, and I'm still her brother."

There was love in the gruff words, a light smile softening the harsher grimness his memories had brought to him.

"I'd be happy to look at them," she told him, bringing her attention back to the question. The heat of his hand over hers was growing. For some reason, the image of trailing her fingertips up his forearm to dance lightly until they reached a bare shoulder appeared before her, and her breath grew ragged.

"Good." Rush seemed genuinely pleased, his eyes catching the light to glint at the same time his lips lifted. "Can you come to the house to see them? They're in the safe there. Or, I can bring them to the store for you."

"You don't have to. I can look at them wherever. I have a kit that I can bring. If you want a certified appraisal, I have permission to use the store for that."

He lifted her hand still captured between his and held it to his lips as an absent gesture. She wasn't even sure if he knew he was doing it.

But she sure did. The instant he brushed her knuckle over his lower lip, her heart tripped over itself like it was falling down stairs. At some point in the last hour, he'd moved closer, almost at her side, and the ease and tender care of his fingers wrapped around her, while holding her hand, stole her breath. The languid strokes were causing sparks the size of lightning bolts to fly through her system.

"I don't think I need a certified declaration right now, but it wouldn't hurt to have it later for insurance."

Kay nodded, her voice lost beneath the tender swipe of his touch. The warmth of his breath as it flowed over her skin sent liquid tingles down her spine, a raw ache building deep inside as an answer to some call she didn't, or couldn't, hear.

Somehow, she managed to trade her information with him, thankful there were such things as muscle memory and autopilot, because her brain had officially checked out.

He walked her to her car and even held the door for her.

"Thanks," he said. "Buckle up."

She guessed it was as ingrained to say as 'hello', and smiled in answer.

Rush didn't move until she couldn't see him in her mirror any longer.

CHAPTER TWO

Rush walked into his house, hearing the television from the living room.

"Hi!" his sister shouted.

"Hey," he called back. He went to the kitchen and opened the refrigerator, but after several seconds, closed it, not finding what he wanted. He wasn't exactly sure what he wanted, either.

No, that wasn't true. Rush knew exactly *what* he wanted. Kay had officially set his world on fire, and he doubted she even knew it. He blew out a frustrated breath. His entire body had been a living ache since he let her drive away.

"What's that for?" Sheridan asked, slipping up behind him to sit on a bar stool, an eyebrow arched in question. "Have a hard day of nothing?"

Cool tile from the kitchen outward to the rest of the house kept that much from becoming a blistering inferno, but from the inside out, Rush couldn't tell if it was him burning hotter than a volcano or the summer sunshine heating the house through the windows.

He crossed his arms and leaned back on the hip high counter, not exactly ready to share his find with his sister yet. He was even less able to explain Kay to Sheridan. He couldn't explain something he didn't understand himself and do a good job of it, so staying quiet for a few minutes seemed to be the best idea he'd had all week. "Don't you have a boyfriend somewhere? Or two?"

"Ha. Ha. He's in Chicago hosting a client."

Rush knew Brant was in marketing. It was more than he needed to ever know about Sheridan's love life. The only thing he ever wanted to know was if her boytoys were pack and from whose territory, so when he's called out for some indiscretion, he knew how to handle it. Sheridan wasn't a player with young hearts, but an unsettled female could stir up trouble like a hornets' nest in a high wind.

"What happened to you?" She frowned, meeting his glare while resting her chin on a raised fist. "What's got your tail in a twist?"

He guffawed. "You would say that," he accused, foregoing a real answer.

Sheridan shrugged, grinning madly. "Younger sister privileges. Besides, someone has to harass the pack alpha every now and then."

He smirked. Rush knew his sister was good at it too, and not just because she was his second. "Nothing. There was a ruckus at the Hut. Some guy trying to intimidate his ex."

"Jerk," she muttered with a glowering frown.

He felt the same way. "He was."

Kay on the other hand... He crossed his ankles trying to restrain the pounding throb beneath his zipper. It had been a constant battle since the first sound of her velvet voice that afternoon. It wasn't a reaction he was used to. It was one reason he'd sat and talked for so long. He'd had a noticeable problem within two seconds after following her mouth on the edge of her cup. Supple, dusky lips that looked soft and delicious, slick with the whipped cream from the top of her coffee. He'd imagined every second of leaning over and licking her clean himself from that moment on. And he hadn't been limited in his imagination to her lips.

The thought of tasting her lips, the curve of her jaw, the delicate skin beneath her ear and even burying himself in the thick mass of her hair had kept his blood heated and racing through him all afternoon. Smooth skin had teased him, visible beneath the filmy blouse she'd worn. Lithe and delicate, he'd wanted to lick every visible inch, and then find out what wasn't. More than once, he'd had to forcefully bring himself back to what they were discussing because as much as he'd fought it, he couldn't ignore what she did to him. Now, after almost an hour and distance, the burn had mellowed, but it was there, like a hidden spark from a wildfire, waiting for the chance to burst into a rampaging blaze all over again.

At one time, he'd waited, prayed and hoped he'd find his mate, his match, the one woman who would stand by his side as a leader to his pack and a companion for him, but after watching his mother wither away following his father to the grave, falling in love had ceased to be that much of a necessity.

Rush had thrown himself into the pack, into raising Sheridan, and his work. At not quite fifteen, it was that or go into foster care for a year and be separated from Sheridan permanently. He refused to let that happen. He had no choice but to pick up the pieces, and with the help of the pack, tie their broken home back together. So far, he thought he'd done a decent job. He'd earned his detective badge the year before, after being on the street force since he was twenty-one. Sheridan was in college learning all that CGI art stuff that he had no hope of understanding. He couldn't lie, least of all to himself. He wanted Kaisha, but wanting sex and *wanting more* were different animals to him. One he refused to bend to, the other, his only choice, was to ignore because sex with Kay...

He drew a steadying breath, remembering not to groan with his sister so close. The sex would be incredible. It would be what he'd always craved.

It would be the end of everything he'd worked so hard for.

He ran a hand through his hair.

"You okay?" Sheridan asked quietly.

He looked up, becoming aware she'd been watching him like a bug on a windshield the whole time he'd been negotiating his sanity. "Yes. No." He stopped before he dug himself in deeper. "Yeah," he finally conceded.

"Which is it?"

"I'm fine."

"Uh huh. 'Lie To Me' is a TV show, not what you're supposed to do," she told him with a knowing glint in her gaze. It sucked when his sister was also his closest friend.

"Smart ass," he retorted, grinning because he should know better. His sister could ferret out a lie faster than a wolf could terrify a laying hen.

She stood and approached him around the kitchen bar, her eyes piercing his secrets. "Rush, are you okay? There's something different about you."

Ah hell. There was little chance she'd leave now. Could she tell? Should he admit to what he believed happened? Face the truth or hide it? He wasn't at all surprised when there were no quick answers and nothing was as easy as he'd believed it should be.

Whether he did anything or not about what happened with Kay, today was up to him. His first priority was to the pack, and Sheridan was his chosen second. Honestly, she had a right to know.

Then why did it twist his gut as though he were destroying a beautiful secret, something fragile and breathtaking, to tell her about Kay? He was unprepared for the slicing heat in his stomach, and it killed the tight throb he'd been fighting for more than two hours now, since that first touch, the first sound of her voice. Pack came first.

Resigned, he stood straight, dropping his arms to his sides and Sheridan paused a foot away, her worried eyes never leaving his. "I found her."

Sheridan's face paled. He nodded. That's exactly how he felt too.

———————

Kay's feet slowed as she neared her apartment door. Lying before it on the cement was a bundle, a paper-wrapped bunch of flowers, just like the ones in the display when you first walk into the local grocer. Nothing fancy. But the surprise of finding them there still gave her pause.

Looking around her, she was alone. The lot was clean, a few cars gone for the weekend, but otherwise it looked the same as it did every afternoon. The cheery chirp of the birds or the warmth of the sunlight did nothing to stop the chill that strolled too easily down her spine at finding her gift. She'd never had anyone do something like this, and after Steven's show of temper earlier, she wasn't thrilled to find them now. The thought that somehow Rush... She dismissed that almost immediately. He couldn't have beat her here from the coffeehouse.

She rolled the flowers with a toe, waiting, and then gingerly crouched to pick them up. There was a small card inside the colorful ensemble. Her heart tapped a solid rhythm against her ribs, unsure about what she'd find. They looked to be fresh, warmed from the sunlight, but not dried or wilted. How long had they been there? Obviously not that long. And from who? Looking around her, she couldn't see or hear anyone. Wary just the same, she lifted the card out of the center.

Kay, I'm sorry. Call me. S.

She huffed a disgusted breath. *Not likely*, was her first thought. The tightness across her forehead grew noticeable as she studied the card and the flowers. Was he being persistent for a reason? Why? Had he been there waiting for her after the argument at the Mocha Hut? If he had, for how long? She dragged her teeth over her lower lip. The idea that he had waited for her at all gave her a new chill. What did he want?

Steven had called that morning, wanting to meet to just talk. She hadn't seen anything wrong with a quiet conversation between them. They hadn't been lovers, and Kay hadn't seen Steven in almost three months, when he'd said he needed that time. He was the one who had told her not to wait for him. They hadn't reached that depth in their relationship where she'd pine away for him, heartbroken. She would have left long before then. Kay didn't do 'heartbroken' for anyone. They were no more than good friends who went out together, shared a few kisses. Steven had been a gentleman—until today. Frowning, Rush's warning echoed within her ears again and she had to agree. She hoped whomever Steven went to next didn't have to deal with his temper. Paper crunched beneath her fingers, reminding her of the flowers she held.

"You found them."

She whirled at Steven's low spoken voice, a gasp slipping out before she could stop it. "Steven!"

He lifted a hand, but dropped it quickly. "I'm sorry. I didn't mean to frighten you." He stuffed his fingers into his jean pockets and stood a few feet away. "Now or at the Hut."

Kay studied him with a new set of eyes. Was he playing her, using her emotions, or was he being honest? This was the Steven she'd known, the one she'd been to movies with, shared jokes and a few kisses. Sweet, thoughtful. *But it had been him earlier too,* she reminded herself, demanding she get back together with him, and then threatening her when she stayed firm in not wanting to.

She drew a breath. "Thank you, Steven." Holding out the flowers, she told him, "I don't need the flowers, though."

His expression darkened. "It's an honest apology," he snapped.

Kay blinked and drew another slow breath. This, *this,* was the guy she'd seen earlier. "And I accept the apology. I can't accept the flowers." It didn't feel right. She didn't want what the flowers meant. A connection. A reciprocation.

"Why?" he demanded. His hands were loose at his sides now, and he crowded her into the door at her back. "Why don't you want to get back with me?" Something dark and cruel heated his brown eyes. Stark jealousy. "It was that guy, wasn't it? I saw you talking with him before I left." Steven snarled lowly, as though his territory had been threatened.

Kay was no one's property.

Not for the first time, she hated being so short, but she refused to be treated like this.

"Back off," she ground out, shoving against his chest, the flowers crumpling within her fist. He knocked them out of her hold, scattering them like winter leaves across the thatch of grass that lined the front of her building. Her strength was nothing compared to his. He slammed her backward until she was flush with the door.

He curled a heavy hand over her windpipe, locking her immobile against the wooden panel. "Let me in," he ordered on a lowered growl, literally blanketing her form with his, glaring down at her.

She shook her head. She was dead if she did. A scream bubbled up into her throat, but his hold locked it in place. Air wheezed in and out of her lungs, her heart thudding as she fought to not panic.

Palming her keys between her fingers, she made a fist. They say go for the face, but she doubted she'd have more than one chance, and a face shot was too long and too high for her.

Pulling back her arm, she rammed her keys right into his ribs. She flinched when her knuckles dug into cotton, creating a deep score into his flesh. He howled, his hand clutching convulsively around her throat like a vise before falling slack. Slick blood covered her hand. When he jerked away, he ripped the keys out of place. Rivulets quickly created red lines in his shirt.

Blistering pain exploded across her face before the sight of his hand registered. Stars erupted then she hit pavement with a harsh cry.

"Bitch." He held a hand to his side, staunching the flow of blood. Shoveling stiff fingers into her hair, he yanked her from the ground. "Wrong thing to do," he breathed. "You should have just let me in."

He shook her by her hair, making her keys fall from her fingers. The jangle of her purse thudded to the ground when he shoved her flat against the door again, limp with shock and blistering, driving pain. Half of her face was somewhere between numb with pain and in so much agony, she wanted to scream with it. She couldn't focus. Her head felt heavy, and the pinching strength of his fingers digging into her scalp was the only thing holding her on her feet. Swallowing, she tasted blood on her tongue.

"Freeze!"

Kay barely heard anything anyone said over the harsh ringing and pounding in her ears. Her eye had shut, making the focusing worse for what she could see. A swelling she didn't want to think about tightened her jaw. She couldn't open or move it. Breathing alone was a nightmare of effort and pain. When the hand in her hair loosened, she collapsed to the ground for a second time. She was pretty sure that was where she wanted to stay for a while.

CHAPTER THREE

RUSH listened to the scanner in his pickup, carefully taking turns, fighting his instincts to crush everyone in his path to get to Kay's. He'd almost blanked out the call on the scanner at home, used to hearing its constant chatter when he was off, but when he'd heard Kay's address, nothing short of the apocalypse could've held him back.

With an almost sickening feeling, he knew what had happened. "Public disturbance, my ass," he muttered as he milked another yellow light. Ambulances aren't dispatched for public disturbances.

There were two cruisers, a gaggle of witnesses and onlookers, and the ambulance. Strobing lights gave everything an eerie cast of light: blue, red and flickering white. Steven was handcuffed and in the back of one of the patrol cars. Rush snarled, his hands curling into fists reflexively, recognizing the blond. Steven should be thankful Rush was on this side of that bulletproof door.

His next thought was finding Kay. Striding with purpose toward the front of the ambulance, he headed for the open doors at the rear.

"Sorry, sir." A hand lifted and stopped him, barely. He almost plowed right over the duty officer, but managed to control the urge. A rookie to the beat. Rush knew almost everyone on this side of the lake. He had his badge out faster than the cop could cry 'mama'.

"Where is she?" His tone was an 'answer me now' demand.

The rookie studied the badge then nodded. "Inside. She took a hard hit to the face."

Rush didn't let his anger show. Steven had just made a mortal enemy with that news. He didn't wait to be invited, but simply circled the uniform in front of him and climbed up into the cave.

"Hey," he said gently, discovering her propped up on the gurney. He sat down next to her, letting the EMT finish his job with a single nod.

"Rush?" she asked, confused and groggy. She turned, but didn't open her eyes. One was obviously incapable.

"Yeah." He cupped her hand, feeling the limp curl of her fingers around his palm. The simple connection shoved his heart into his throat.

"I gave her something for the pain," the tech across from him said. Rush heard, but didn't answer. Half her face was black and blue, a gnarled mess that had swollen her eye shut. The blood had been wiped away, but the damage was deep. That didn't even touch on the clearly marked ring of bruising around her throat. If he ever found Steven alone...

"Is she going to the hospital?" he asked, unable to tear himself away from watching her float in her drug-induced stupor.

"She said she didn't want to go. Asked for friends to be called. We're waiting for a response."

He hissed a low curse at her stubborn streak ready to override her request, knowing they wouldn't wait either way in her condition, then he took a closer look. She'd taken a beating, but looked to be mostly in one piece. Then the scent of blood filled his nostrils with his next breath. "Whose blood?" It was more of a growl than he'd intended, but the tech didn't seem to notice. There were splatters on her clothes and he found more signs of it on her other hand, like it had been wiped clean.

"That guy's. She tried to rekey his ribs."

Rush smiled, thinking, *That's my girl,* then quickly blinked, wondering where the thought had come from. She was unaware to the tumult of his thoughts, or his desires. The need to wrap himself around her and protect her was impossible to ignore now. His soul was crying because she was lying injured before him. It stole his air at how quickly, at how deeply those needs rifled him. He'd just found her, yet the immensity of how little time had passed since their meeting, of how little he knew about her, seemed to make no difference. She was there now, and that was that. He was going to have to deal with it, somehow. Lifting her limp hand, he brushed her fingers against his lips absently, unaware of the intimate contact.

KAY winced when she moved. Everything from her waist up hurt. Her head was killing her, and her mouth felt nailed shut. She tried to lick her lips, but could barely feel them. Her throat was dry and when she swallowed, raw heat burned her from her chin to her chest. Her eyes weren't in any better shape. She'd swear someone had locked them both closed. A low groan filled her ears and it took her a second or two to come to terms that it had been her making the sound.

"Easy," a soothing male voice said. A honey soaked voice that she'd thought she'd dreamed at some point.

"Rush?" she croaked.

"It's me." The sweep of tender fingers brushed over her forehead. "Where does it hurt?"

She thought for a moment, concentrating. "Almost everywhere." Her voice rasped painfully, and she tried again to swallow, wincing harder when it hurt like hell.

"Here, drink this." A firm hand beneath her head supported her and something liquid and cool touched her lips. She felt wetness as it ran everywhere but down her throat where she needed it. After a couple of tries, she managed a swallow or two. The tender swipe of a towel followed the tepid trails, confusing her more.

"Why can't I open my eyes? What's going on?" Her body felt absolutely leaden. At least she wasn't alone.

"Do you remember getting home this afternoon?"

Her brow creased. Flashes filtered through the fog. Steven. The flowers. His anger. The pain. She shrank down into the softness beneath her instinctively. "I remember." Her voice shrank too, sounding small and wounded, something she'd never believed herself to be.

"You're at the hospital for a thorough check." The wave of words was soothing in the lowered timbre.

"Why?" She tipped upward, searching for where she thought he was. The tender brush of his finger against her uninjured cheek proved her right.

"When he hit you, he did some damage to your eye. They applied a numbing agent to ease the worst of pain because the damage was pretty deep. It's covered and will heal, but for the moment, you're bandaged."

Well that explained why half her face felt frozen. "Why are you here?"

"I heard the call on my scanner. I wasn't that far away." The comforting wisp of his lips on her forehead took her by surprise. "Rest for a few minutes. I'll go get the doctor and let her know you're awake."

"Okay," she murmured. The sound of the door swooshing open then closed told her she was alone. She purposely flexed her fingers, legs and arms, cringing when she tried to find out just how extensive the damage was. Then she moved her jaw in a circle. That was a mistake; the agony was brutal. More aware, she could feel the swollen damage to her lip, the taut ache to her jaw. He'd belted her a good one. Half her face felt mauled. She probably looked it too.

Asshole.

"Hello, Miss Noelles." A cheerful, feminine voice filled the room. "How're you doing?"

"Feel like shit." A rough laugh made her tense. "Ah, hell. You're not alone, are you?"

A low, breathy chuckle told her what she couldn't see. Rush had come back with the doctor. "There goes my princess image." It was at worst, a mild complaint.

A chair was dragged to the other side of the bed. Warm fingers curved through hers. She completed the hold automatically, without thought. She knew who it was. The question was why, but she didn't want to ask that with a witness. She was simply grateful to have somebody there, wondering why Stacee hadn't come yet.

She let the doctor do the routine vitals before asking, "When do I get out of here?"

There was a pause and she felt Rush try to stand. "No. He can stay. He's a friend," she quickly assured the doctor. *Don't leave me alone,* she silently whimpered.

"In a couple of hours, at the most," she answered. "We've done an x-ray on your jaw and there's no permanent damage."

"There's a problem though," Rush stated. She focused on his voice, feeling the tender sweep of his thumb running over the back of her hand. It was warm and intense at the same time. "You're blind for the next week, or until you heal."

"What about my other eye?"

"Can't use it for forty-eight hours. It's only a precaution, to keep the injured eye from doing something negative in reaction with your working sight because of the trauma." That was the doctor again, crisp and direct.

"Well, crap," Kay muttered.

"You're doing fine, Miss Noelles." The sharp click of a pen seemed unnaturally loud in the room. "A few prescriptions to help with the swelling and pain and you'll be home by this evening."

"Thank you." She listened for more, then heard the repeat of the door opening and closing.

"There's something else." Rush's steeled tone made her tilt on her pillow toward him. "You said Steven had broken up with you a while back. How long ago?"

"About three months, I guess. He called and ended it over the phone, said he had personal problems."

"Honey," Rush said, making her tummy flutter at the sweet sound of the one word on his lips. "He broke up with you because he was in jail."

"Oh, shit," she breathed, not caring how tarnished her crown became.

CHAPTER FOUR

KAY nodded, albeit slowly, and no doubt with pain, physical and emotional. Rush watched her face and body for any sign of strain. The bruising on her jaw was darkening and there was little anyone could do about the finger-sized necklace of blue around her neck. Just looking at it created the need to pound Steven into something concrete, and Rush typically didn't have a violent bone in his body.

"How did you find out?" The lowered note of her voice was considerably clear, considering the shock that her latest boyfriend appeared to be a criminal.

"When they ran his background," Rush explained. "He has a rap sheet that's several years in the making. A long list of petty stuff, but in the last three years, he's gotten into some bigger things."

"How big?" Kay asked. Her fingers tightened on his, and he wondered if it was a conscious reaction. He rubbed her hand between his with a slow back and forth motion, wanting to warm her, to tell her she wasn't alone.

"Drugs."

She shuddered, drawing a slow breath. "That explains the erratic behavior."

"But it doesn't explain his attacks on you," Rush stated. "It doesn't explain much of anything." Rush was positive there was something more going on with Steven and Kay. He just couldn't put his finger on it. Being late in that realization had put Kay in the hospital. If he'd done his job better instead of watching the way her lips moved, or the sway of her hips, he might have been able to stop this from happening.

Her head tilted on the pillow, as though searching. "Where is Stacee? I know I told them to call her."

He cradled her hand closer. "She's at her mother's."

"Crap," Kay muttered, her body going slack with disappointment. "That was this weekend?"

"I talked to her while you rested. She made me swear to have you call as soon as you get settled, so she knows where to come when she gets back to town."

"Where am I going to go?" Her fingers clenched, tension stiffening her frame. "If I can't see..."

"Don't worry. I already have Sheridan cleaning out the cobwebs in our spare, if you don't have any other family you want me to call." He'd asked Stacee, but she'd been evasive about answering.

"You're kidding?"

The huskiness in her voice made her surprise sound throaty, and sexy, which it shouldn't, considering how much her injuries hurt her. It didn't seem to matter to his libido; everything about her made his body hum.

"I can't. You don't even know me."

He could see the thoughts as they flew through her mind. From coffee to sharing a roof, being in his care, was a leap for her. It didn't frighten her, but he could see she was uneasy about it.

"No, you don't know me either, but you need someone to help for a day or two. Is there someone else you can call?" he inquired, silently hoping there wasn't, but knowing if she did then he had to let her go. Sheridan thought he was insane as it was, bringing her home, a total stranger. An outsider who had no knowledge of his life, the one that revolved around his pack. Regardless of what she knew or didn't, he should have been there to help her, to protect her. He kept telling himself it was his job driving him, refusing to acknowledge that the reasoning could be something deeper. He couldn't deal with it yet.

With a slow motion, she rocked on the pillow. "No, no one."

Rush dropped his chin, the weight of the guilt of seeing her in the ambulance crushing him where he sat. Unconsciously, he ran her knuckles against his skin. He knew better than to let her go with a mad ex somewhere out there. Complacency had done this. His.

"Kay, let me do this for you."

"This isn't your fault," she murmured, her fingers firming over his in emphasis.

He didn't argue it with her; he knew they wouldn't agree. He'd been swept up, shocked at finding her, then running scared when he'd watched her drive away, practically leaving skid marks in the parking lot to go in the other direction to get home. If there was one thing Rush wouldn't do it was run from his duty. He could keep this impersonal.

Rush hadn't made up his mind over what the woman before him was supposed to mean to him. He'd been off balance since the first touch, the first sweet sound of her voice. It was telling that he hadn't been able to leave her side since he'd arrived at her apartment discovering her injuries for himself, but he refused to bow to it. Knowing *who* she was to him maybe gave him a foot up on dealing with it all, but it didn't ease his confusion any. If anything, the claw of confusion dug deeper because this woman was exactly the person he'd been avoiding finding most of his life. Watching his mother die after his father's accident had done more than scar him. The tragedy of watching her die before his eyes had molded his adult life.

When he should be running from Kay and everything she meant for him, he couldn't. That single admittance terrified him.

"I CAN walk, you know!"

"But this is fun," he joked. It sounded to Rush like Kay was about to choke on something, or maybe she was just imagining choking him. He didn't try to restrain the grin, knowing she couldn't see it.

"Has anyone ever told you, you're a nut?"

"Probably," he said, laughing at her disgruntled humor. It was late, almost eleven by the time he pulled into his driveway, but he'd never felt more awake. With Kay scooped into his arms, he easily carried her from the truck to the front door where the porch light was on. Sunshine enveloped his senses where he buried his nose in her hair, the first time he'd been able to really find out for sure. He wasn't disappointed in the least, the scent filling his bloodstream. The front door opened before he hit the steps, killing his rising euphoria. Sheridan was frowning, ignoring the woman in his arms. Rush wasn't surprised.

His sister turned on a stiff heel and left without saying a word, her silence speaking volumes to him. Her bedroom door closed quietly a moment later. He let out a slow breath. Kay wouldn't be staying long, and then everything would be back to normal. He hoped. That's what he continued to tell himself. Now, if he could only believe it.

He set Kay on her feet, closing the door behind them. Now that he had her there, he wasn't sure what to do. It wasn't typical for him to bring home women, for any reason.

"Is there anything I can do for you? Anything you need?" he asked, hesitant to make the next move.

"A change of clothes, if I could borrow something," she said. "I can get something from home tomorrow, if you don't mind taking me."

He mentally smacked his head, noticing what she'd changed into when they'd released her from the hospital. Damn it. She was in the clothes she'd been attacked in. Glancing down the hall, his first thought was asking Sheridan, but like any other intelligent male, he skipped that idea immediately. That was one fight he didn't want to have.

Linking his hand with hers, he pulled gently. "Come with me." He sat her down on his bed and pulled out drawers. "This should work." He turned to face her. And swallowed. Blood pooled below his zipper at the images bombarding him at an alarming rate. Pert breasts, strong, lean legs, gentle curves from her waist to her hips, in his shirt and nothing else. Lifting his gaze, all he could think was small mercies for her being blind. Clearing his throat, he stepped up. "Do you need help?" Part of him desperately wanted her to say yes, but he knew he needed to hear a no.

"What is it?"

"One of my shirts. It's long enough to cover you. I'll dig out my sweats tomorrow. They'll be long on you, but it's better than nothing. And yes, I'll take you home and you can get anything you need."

A small hand lifted, grasping the offering. "I can do that, I think." She tilted her chin as though looking up at him. "Why are you doing this, Rush?"

The rawness of her voice cut at him, but she seemed able to work around it. He kneeled on one leg in front of her, letting her know he'd changed positions by sliding his fingers into her hair. Damn the consequences, he needed to touch her.

"Do you know why I asked you to look at my mom's jewelry?"

"To get its value?" Her cute eyebrows crossed.

"It's a good thing you can't see my face," he told her, knowing he was grinning like an idiot. "I wanted to see you again."

"Really?" she asked with a breathless quality to her voice that hit him like a sledgehammer.

"Guilty." He massaged her scalp gently. "I am sorry though that this was how I got to do it. And whether you see it my way or not, I feel responsible for this happening to you. All I did was chase off the mean dog. I didn't make sure you were safe."

"Rush," she whispered, drawing out his name in slow frustration.

"Shh," he breathed, then leaned in and brushed a gentle kiss to the side of her mouth. Lightning electrified him at the merest touch. He jerked away before the wildness clawing through him demanded he take more. She was in no condition, and she should have been safe from everything in his home, himself included.

Taking a steadying breath, he stood. His intention had been to let her sleep in the spare, but if he waited another minute, or saw her in just that shirt, he was going to lose it. He reached for her hand. "Here, let me give you the lay of the land."

Explaining what she was feeling, he walked her around the room, letting her map the dresser, the bed and the location for the door to the bathroom. "You can tell this is the door out to the house by the wood." He let her hand run down the rough half plank that framed the doorway.

"Is this a cabin?"

"No, but I liked the accents when I had it built."

She smiled. "I do too. I bet they're lovely."

"Are you going to be okay?"

"I think so. Is there anything I can break?"

He glanced around the room. "Hardly." There wasn't much of anything in it at all. The alarm clock was indestructible, and beyond that, there just wasn't much lying around loose. Looking down at her, he realized she only came to his chest, making him feel like a skyscraper next to her. He wasn't sure if he was happy or not about it. Rush had never hit the six-feet mark. It didn't bother him, but she made him feel huge. *Aw hell.* He did like it. He swallowed his groan, something he'd been doing a lot since meeting her. "Go change," he told her in a gentle order, hoping the husky need in his voice wasn't as obvious to her as it was to him. "I'll get you water and your medications."

"Okay." She lifted her palm to cover her mouth, and a yawn cut short when her jaw refused to work. "I hope I don't look as bad as I feel," she muttered.

"Worse," he said, cutting through the ball of need with a teasing rejoinder, chuckling when she stuck her tongue out at him. The last thing he needed was her knowing he'd been standing with her for the last twenty minutes with a hard-on as thick as the trees outside, bruises be damned. He knew what she looked like without them, the sparkle of her gray eyes, the rich thickness of her hair. And her lips.

Shaking his head, he deliberately took a step back. "I'm shutting the door so you can change. Climb into bed and just say yes or no if you're not ready when I get back."

He was almost sweating at the possibility of finding her half-dressed, or worse, naked. Rush swore silently. He had this wanting problem bad.

He watched her turn and find the bed with easy steps. She must have counted or had an impeccable memory.

"I'll be done."

Leaving out the door, he dawdled in the kitchen, reading the prescription instructions no less than three times to ensure he had it right. She had been given the ones that needed to be taken with food at the hospital to monitor her reactions, so all she had to do was come home and go to bed. *In his bed.* Her scent was going to be all over his sheets, his pillow. Unable to hold in the groan of wanting any longer, a gusted breath eased the tension in his shoulders.

Bracing his hands on the counter, he bent at the waist, letting his body unravel for a few unrestrained minutes.

No one had ever told him finding his mate would make him feel like this. Rush wasn't stupid for being on his own with Sheridan for so long. He knew who Kay was to him. There just wasn't a handbook he could grab on the subject, and that sucked. He was a far cry from being a virgin. He knew what sex was and had enjoyed it when he could, though life in general hadn't made him a playboy. He knew the risks and refused to play the odds, but God have mercy, Kay was sinking claws into him that he knew she wasn't even aware of.

Every little thing about her turned him inside out with wanting. He knew she couldn't stay, knew nothing could come from actually meeting her, but he lost all reason around her. The term 'turned to mush' made complete sense now.

So far, he'd done nothing but touch her every chance he could. He'd even dared to steal a kiss. She should kick his ass for that. He'd do it for her, if he could. Everything he'd done had been reactionary, from the second he'd heard her address on the scanner. He needed to take back control of this situation.

Staring down the house and hall, he nodded. That's what he had to do, take back control. He had priorities. Pack came first. *Oh shit.* How long would it be before one of them heard about this? Would they come looking for her, testing his strength? Testing hers? A rock tumbled to his stomach and stayed there.

He dragged a stiff palm down his face. "Shit," he breathed. He was in no way ready for this to happen. There was no one to ask. His dad was gone. There were no real close friends, and he didn't know the other alphas in his region well enough. One or two, but to ask about finding a mate? He swallowed the sour heat rising into his throat.

He'd surprisingly earned the alpha position when, by some miracle, he'd bested the old alpha at the fun age of twenty-six. Now four years later, he still felt like a pup among the pack. He hadn't been trying to win the leadership, but fighting in form established a lot of things, and alpha was the big one. The pack didn't treat him that way, the insecurity was in his head. They respected him and knew he was young, but gave him credit for keeping himself and Sheridan going after the death of their parents. He'd made sure they both finished school, sold the old home to a pack member in need and when he could afford it, had this one built, better suited to them than the little forty year-old home his father had bought. Everything since that time had all been done with careful planning, each step studied and weighed. He wasn't a half-cocked kid anymore. He had matured out of necessity.

Up until now, it had just been him and Sheridan, and the pack.

Now... He swallowed then cursed again with a harder edge to it. With Kay, he was running on pure instinct and lust. A lot of lust. A mate threw everything he'd been working to keep sane into a whole new spectrum of imbalance.

Steady, deep breaths calmed a heart he didn't notice had been pounding. He'd take her the meds, see her through the next two days and *gladly* deposit her at home or with any friend she wanted.

It was the only, the safest, thing he could do.

CHAPTER FIVE

KAY waited for the audible click of the bedroom door closing then stripped as fast as her trembling hands could manage. At least she'd worn easy clothes, jeans and a lightweight blouse. God only knew what the shirt and chemise looked like now, and she didn't care. Kicking off her boots, she ripped off the jeans. She hoped everything landed in a pile where she was because if he came back and she wasn't ready... She whimpered and not out of fear.

She was so turned on, she knew she needed fresh underwear.

Damn it! She wished she could see. She wanted to see the way his eyes followed her like they had that afternoon, if they burned with the want she felt coming off of him with every stroke. There was no denying she wanted to return the caresses he'd been giving her almost non-stop. The husky roll of his voice had made her melt like butter more than once. Her heart had almost burst from her ribs at the touch of his lips on hers. It should have frightened her, but if anything, it had only left her craving more. He hadn't pushed, hadn't taken. If he had, she probably would have freaked like a screaming banshee. He'd given her the sweetest caress she'd ever received, completely cognizant of the pain and her injuries. Like a gift for her, a single touch of caring, it sent a jolt of heat straight through her system.

It was sad that even though she knew nada about him, she liked being with him, and loved being held like she mattered. She wanted him with a heated need that had been steadily growing since she'd met him that afternoon, but she honestly hadn't expected to see anything come of it; she still didn't. Desire wasn't unknown, but it had never been this... overpowering... before, either. She could barely stand with his warm fingers wrapped through hers, his every touch, word and motion attuned to her stuttered insecurity in her blindness. Kay felt absolutely safe with Rush, instinctively knowing he wouldn't lead her astray.

She could picture his face in her mind, the strength of his jaw with just the shadow of beard, like he hadn't shaved that morning. It had made him rakish and sexier than sin on a stick.

All she knew was her own face hurt everywhere, making anything she did painful, from smile to breathe. It was a wonder Rush hadn't run in the other direction. Kay was positive she looked like some horror movie makeup dummy.

"Damn you, Steven," she hissed. She hoped he rotted in jail for what he did to her. She wasn't a vindictive or blood thirsty type, but if he even dared to think she'd forgive him, he was more of an ass than she'd already labeled him.

Reaching behind her, she found the t-shirt on the bed where she'd laid it, and debated leaving her bra on or not. Listening, she heard nothing but her own breathing and no steps approaching, so she quickly stripped it off then yanked the t-shirt on. Running her fingers around the neck, she felt the tag stamp under her fingertips and turned it, slipping her arms into the sleeves.

She let out a grumbled sigh. Okay, at least she was decent. The hem reached her thighs easily, allowing her to relax a little more. She wasn't on display, thankfully. The bed was behind her. She'd been very careful to notice every tactile detail about the room she was in. From the feeling of the wood beneath her feet, to the area rug that was on the side in front of the door to the bathroom. Crouching, she picked up her things and laid them on the bed, ticking them off in her mind. Good, she had everything.

Walking the edge, she found the lip of the covers and slid under them, tugging them over her hips, then sat and waited. Rush was going above and beyond the call of duty. She frowned then winced with abrupt pain. Stacee was at her mother's this weekend. She and Jonas were officially informing her of their engagement, and Kay knew as well as her best friend did just how well that was going to go over.

Jonas was in law enforcement, the same as Stacee's dad had been. Stacee's mom had been devastated when he'd died in the line of duty. Saying she held a grudge was an understatement. Jonas had been winning her over in increments to make the truth a less bitter pill to swallow. The difficulties the girls each shared through their childhoods and through their parents was one of the reasons she and Stacee had been friends for so long.

Under the circumstances, Kay could forgive Stacee for not being there. Her hand flew to her mouth. "Crap," she muttered. She was supposed to call and tell Stacee where she was!

What time was it? Where was her purse? Where had she last seen it? She mentally rolled her eyes. She hadn't seen anything in over seven hours, at least. She didn't even know what time it was.

A light tap on her door had her letting Rush in with a quick, "Come in."

"Do you know what time it is?" she asked as soon as she heard his feet moving.

"Almost midnight."

"Rats." Her shoulders slumped. Make that ten hours.

"Why?"

God, his voice sent shivers down her arms and spine no matter what. It had to be because she couldn't see. Her senses were zeroing in on his voice. Had to be. Gathering her straying thoughts, she said, "I forgot to call Stacee."

"I told her to try here first in the morning if you hadn't called."

Following the sound of his steps and voice until he stood next to the bed, she crossed her arms and legs to hide the tightening response of her body beneath the shirt. It had little effect to help her reactions. Her belly quivered with him so close, relying on her hearing and surprisingly, the scent of his clothes and body to find him. He had a unique maleness to him. Not over doused with cologne, if he wore anything at all. Just a subtle spice that tingled her senses with awareness. The more time she spent with him, the more she found herself looking for it.

She made herself talk, because drooling was just not the image she wanted to give him. "Confident I'd come here, weren't you?"

"No, she agreed it was better, too. She knows roughly where I live, and I gave her everything from my phone number to how many baby teeth I lost."

Kay chuckled. "Okay. Where is my purse though? My cell phone is in it."

"It's probably still in the truck. I'll get it if you need it."

"No, tomorrow is good enough. Midnight is too late to call her mother's house." *Or mine*, she snorted in silent disgust. She wouldn't have called her mother anyway. There wasn't a point in it.

"Okay, time for your horse pills. I have broccoli green and something that I think is neon blue, but don't hold me to that."

She wished she could smile more. He made her want to laugh. His touch was gentle when he turned her palm to drop the two pills into it. "In the hatch," he ordered, the husky timbre sending shots down to her womb. She did the only thing she could do and ignored it and her body's response.

"God, this hurts," she muttered, trying to open her jaw enough. It was even harder to swallow water. He took the cup from her hand, and then she felt a dampened, warmed towel on the edge of her face. If she thought about it, she could almost feel tears at his thoughtfulness. She couldn't remember once when someone had taken so much time and effort in caring for her. Her mother could have used Rush's lessons. Kay pushed the bitterness away. The only reason she even wanted her mother was because she was familiar and Kay was alone and out of her element. Her mother had never wanted her, so it was an equal negative attraction. She refused to want or need anything from the woman.

"You'll sleep the night with those," he said, reminding her of his close presence. Like she could forget.

"Rush?" She listened for his breathing, turning toward him. "Thank you. I know you didn't have to do this, responsibility or not."

The sweep of fingers through her hair made her salivate. He was touching her again, combing through it with light strokes even though she could feel how the bandage restricted him. He never did anything too forward, always gentle and he seemed to know just what he could do without frightening her. It was hard to not relax into his palm and wallow like a happy pig in his kindness. It had to be the medications making her sappy. She did *not* act like this around guys!

"My pleasure, ma'am," he drawled with a hint of laughter. "Okay, time to rest. Don't worry about anything in the morning. We'll see how you're feeling then. Doctor Aimes said to report in if things changed drastically."

Kay nodded and lay down on her back. The covers were pulled up to her neck and patted down.

"Goodnight," he told her.

"'Night." She thought it would take a while for the pills to kick in, but she couldn't remember fighting to find sleep at all the next morning.

RUSH threw the covers off his body, frustrated with their heat, with anything he could name. He was too sensitive to anything and everything touching his skin.

The spare room had been cleaned up and Sheridan had put fresh sheets on the futon. It was as far as she seemed willing to go, though. The room was black with deep night, the window partially opened to clear the air.

After flipping for the last two hours to get comfortable, he finally tossed in the towel. Sitting up with his hands bracing his face, he rubbed his eyes. It was no surprise he couldn't sleep. He glared downward between his thighs with a distinct disgusted frown. Unable not to, he encircled his engorged length and groaned deeply, stretching his legs to give himself some room. He was so full, it was almost painful. Blood pumped into his cock, making him thicker, throbbing mercilessly. "How is she doing this?" he managed through gritted teeth as pleasure slammed into his body beneath his hand. He moaned when his fingers flexed, the sensations spiraling tighter. She wasn't even in the room with him, and he could smell every inch of her inside of his head.

He remembered walking into the bedroom after she'd changed into his shirt and had almost been knocked flat at the wall of desire in the air. She had been turned on and the headiness of her heat hit his senses with a sweetness that stole his breath, and nearly his capacity for rational thought. Flush with need and hungry for more, her body had been calling for his. It had taken all his willpower to follow through with his commands and just give her the pills and water. When he'd wanted to dive into bed and satisfy them both in a primal way that he was still feeling, he'd managed to walk out of the room with his sanity intact. He was still paying for that decision.

Sliding up and down his cock with a firm fist, he panted, needing more. Needing her. "Shit." He was teetering on the edge. With closed eyes, he imagined those lush lips of hers encircling the tip of his cock, and he groaned again, his heart pounding. If he could just reach release, he could forget how much he craved her. Could forget that it was her scent, her body, her voice that was making him feral with lust.

He leaned back, his hips thrusting into the ecstasy of his own making as dew drops glistened on the head of his shaft. "Yes," he breathed, his mind creating all the images he could ever imagine. He rubbed the moisture beneath his palm, slick against hot, sensitive skin, making him ache harder. The throbbing was building, heat gnawing right behind his balls. Her sweet body, the feel of her tongue lapping his flesh, teasing him with flicks and swirling to claim the moisture beads, the heat of her skin, the velvet feel of her riding him. *So good.* The strength of his need for her left his blood pounding like explosions against his ears.

A deep breath. *So close.* A low moan filled his chest as pleasure tightened his body.

Almost compelled, he released his flesh, exhaling a bitter growl of needy hunger that filled the room with an echo. No. The next time he reached completion, it would be with her. Period. Rush didn't know why, but he knew it was right. He knew no matter what he did now, he would never be satisfied. It would be like eating a spoonful of ice cream when the smothered in chocolate fudge and whipped cream sundae he was starved for was only two doors away.

His head jerked around. She was only two doors away. His blood raced through his body again, hotter. *Kaisha*. The sound of her name rocketed through his system.

Before he could think about it, much less understand the need, a sturdy wolf stood by the futon where he had just sat. Cautiously moving one foot in front of the other, he inched out of the spare, his gaze on his sister's door. He knew Kay was asleep. Sheridan catching him would see him getting his hide blistered by her tongue for what he was about to do.

Nosing his occupied bedroom door wider, he spotted her asleep just the way he'd left her, except she'd managed to kick the sheets off a little, exposing one small foot and a sleek, well-muscled calf. She may not be used to sleeping in different beds and had been restless before the pills kicked in.

Rush didn't care the reason. All that mattered was he could see her. He stood in the doorway and drank in his fill of her length. She looked small enough to still shop in the kid's department for heaven's sakes. The bandage across her forehead bothered him, and his lip lifted in objection. The wolf knew she had been harmed and it didn't like that fact one bit.

Carefully moving past the door, he prowled closer to the bed. Raising his nose, he tested the air, drew her into his senses, reveling at her sweetness, the warmth of sunshine and something so heady it made his entire body tremble with a renewed lusting hunger. It was *her*, her scent, her everything. His wolf knew it instantly. Rush wasn't ready, but arguing with the tunnel-visioned want of his wolf was a lost cause. Tentative steps moved him up the side of the bed.

He settled a paw on the edge and froze. She didn't move, her breathing deep and steady. *God, I'm going to Hell for this.* There was little doubt. His wolf couldn't have cared less.

Nudging beneath the edge of the covers, he inched along her thigh, licking with delicate learning sweeps, tasting her on his tongue, absorbing her scent and her taste to be forever twined with his.

What Rush would give to have her lost in the throes of passion, his hands cupping her hips as he licked her like a sweet confection all along the taut shape of her thigh to the very center of her being. He could imagine the tang of her juice, dripping over his tongue like ambrosia. Suckling on the plump edges of her sweet, pink pussy. He growled inside, the fantasy so real he could taste her when he licked his lips.

Lost in the wolf's presence, he let his desires run wild, his arousal hidden behind the animal's curiosity. Then he pressed his nose to the juncture of her legs and inhaled. He let out a sharp yip of satisfaction. She was ready for him. She was his. Before he could control the urge, he licked the crotch of her panties with a determined pass. Rush froze within the animal's conscience.

Stop it! Idiot!

She drew a deep breath in her sleep and twisted. The wolf waited for its mate to acknowledge him.

She's asleep. Leave her alone.

He knew he was literally yelling at himself, but apparently, no part of his rational mind was paying attention. The wolf hefted up on both paws and licked at her thigh and hip, nipping impatiently at the thin lace restricting him, wanting the treasure hidden beneath it, waiting for his female to come to him.

Well hell, Rush wanted her too, but not like this.

The wolf paused, then with a resigned sigh, clumped to the floor. Glad Rush had control, the wolf rubbed along the bed in compromise, leaving his scent, marking the bed and the occupant. It looked like his earlier decision to let her stay with friends, let her *go,* had been overruled.

He'd never experienced such an animalistic hunger in his wolf, and had never reacted like this to any female, pack or otherwise. He wondered if she would accept his wolf, and then shook himself before letting the idea become a real, aching want. Why would she accept something she'd never even known existed? This was new ground and there was no way he was going to hurry it or her.

He understood hierarchy and survival, but mating was new to Rush. Apparently, the wolf knew without a doubt. It was up to him to catch up.

Chapter Six

Kay lay in bed confused. She couldn't see, and it only took a few minutes of full awareness to remind her why.

Running a hand over her lower face, the pain was a dull throb now, the bandage a rough reminder of how the day before had gone for her. Sitting up at the edge of the bed, she hugged her arms around her. She didn't know what time it was, if the sun was up, anything. It was more than a little frightening to have no concept of her world aside from what she could physically touch at the end of her fingers. She kept telling herself it was temporary, half scared she'd start screaming because of the total and complete darkness swimming before her mind.

Carefully standing, she followed the room to the bathroom, managing to navigate the space without stubbing any toes, only cracking an elbow once on something more solid than herself. Running her hands along the walls, she found towels, then the sink. Good, she was going in the right direction.

Ah ha! She found her goal. A few moments later, she was fussing with the sink, trying to run the water when she jostled something. Running her fingers over it, she realized it was a razor. Moving cautiously, waving her fingers mid-air, she also found a can of shaving cream and a couple other things that wouldn't likely be in the spare room. A toothbrush and toothpaste. And hadn't he pulled a shirt out of a drawer in the bedroom?

Standing straight, she gasped lightly. Did he let her stay in his room? Why? She would have been fine in the spare. This felt so intimate. Without even trying, he'd managed to fluster her again. She could imagine him standing right where she was, a towel around his hips after a shower. Licking her lips, she shook her head, careful to not strain herself. Not good. No lusting after the knight in shining armor.

Too late.

He would stand right behind her, his shower-heated chest flush to her back, the thick, course sensation of his towel sliding along the backs of her thighs. The hard ridge of his cock would imprint her with his own need along her ass. Unhurried, simply enjoying the moment, he would play.

Imagining his hands on her body and the rough pads of his fingers caressing her, sent tingles up and down her spine. Her nipples budded into aching points beneath the t-shirt, rubbing beneath the soft cotton. Her head tipped, feeling the exploratory touch over her breasts to tweak and play with them before he cupped each to tug at the nipple with just a twist of pain. The shock sent a jolt of awareness straight down to land with a pulse between her legs. She moaned breathlessly, gripping the edge of the sink to stay standing. Her legs trembled and liquid heat dampened her pussy.

The warmth of his breath would flow over her neck, his lips and tongue teasing her the same way his fingers would, with flicks and nips of teeth and fingertips. The trail of his hand would linger on her stomach, tracing her bellybutton, making her squirm. Laving against her pulse with a slow, torturous tongue, his fingers would delve between her legs, gliding effortlessly into the moist folds of her sex. A shudder racked her frame as desire spilled into her bloodstream.

"Oh, God," she moaned. Shaking, she drew a breath, collecting herself. She was in his bathroom for heaven's sake, daydreaming. A sexual daydream! And if she'd had even another two minutes, she was sure she could have orgasmed imagining his touch alone. Another slow inhale and she released the sink, her insides still quivering and needy. She felt flushed from her cheeks to her knees, but with each breath, she trembled less with wanting.

Washing her hands as best as she could without seeing what she was doing, she blanked out the detailed pictures her imagination had kindly given her. She was only marginally successful.

Shaking the water off her hands, she carefully turned, reaching for the towel she knew was close by, and instead, bumped into a hard set of abs.

"Oh!" she squealed then stumbled a step, losing her balance at being taken by surprise, right into his arms. Warm and strong, he caught her. She swore she could feel herself melting from the surge of body heat between them. It went miles deeper than even his voice had gone the day before.

"Sorry. I wasn't trying to sneak up on you. I heard you moving around and wanted to make sure you were okay."

Her heart stuttered, and she fought to reset her equilibrium. Her brain was threatening to short circuit. She was pressed into the wall of his chest and stomach, her nose inhaling his scent of pure male and warmed cotton. A low purr formed in her throat. He felt so good. Without planning to, she rubbed her cheek against his chest, her arms winding around his waist naturally.

She'd never in her life reacted to a guy like she did to Rush. He made her feel absolutely wanton.

Horny, her mind supplied. Yeah, that too.

The weight of his fingers sweeping across her back sizzled against already sparking nerves, recreating the delicious desire she'd imagined only a few short minutes before. Molding herself against him, her blood raged. Good God! Was that his...? She licked her lips unconsciously. It wasn't small by any means, long and thick and... She knew she was drooling, drowning as her imagination and body left her restraint in the dust.

"Kay?" Her name sounded strained. The racing of his heart thundered beneath her ear.

Solid muscled thighs brushed against hers and her body went liquid. The urge to climb him like a tree and hang on blazed like a living need within her center.

A low groan vibrated his ribs and his arms tightened, encircling her. "Kay, you're killing me." She felt him move as he bent practically in half to bury his face against her neck. "Sweet hell. You feel good."

The ridge beneath his jeans pulsed against her stomach, and she swore her knees turned to water. Hot and panting, she clung tighter, swept up in the desire he created. She was so wet; she ached with the need to be filled.

Firm but gentle, his hands slid down her back and palmed her ass, squeezing lightly. A hummed sound of appreciation rose from him. "Damn, you're perfect. Freaking tiny, but so perfect."

"Gymnastics," she managed, nuzzling against him any way she could without causing herself pain.

A slow hiss was his answer. His next groan turned into a low growl and his hands braced her, lifted her and she naturally hooked her legs around his waist. He took two steps and sat on the bed, holding her over him, the movement pressing her pussy flush to the ridge of his cock. She couldn't hold back the whimpering moan. Sliding against him, she arched. The friction of his jeans to her underwear was sending her right out of her mind.

Stiff fingers slid upward into her hair, his other hand on her waist. "Do you want to come, baby?"

Did she! Her lips quivered and her pussy clenched, the hoarse words bitten off with his hunger right in front of her. She moaned low, wishing she could see, wishing she could kiss him. Instead, she simply nodded her head, rocking her hips over his pelvis in determined, obvious answer.

Rough as sandpaper, his voice filled her ears. "Then do it, Kaisha. Let me feel your pleasure."

Riding her hips against his body, she arched, her spine tightening like a crossbow being pulled to fire. The fingers gently massaging her scalp held her steady, holding her weight as she felt the slide of his other hand, caressing and learning. Fire spread in his wake. She almost screamed out loud when he inched fingers beneath the edge of her damp panties.

"Shit, you're soaked."

She trembled violently, a storm breaking over her when he found her hardened clit. Her world shrank to the ecstasy of his hand teasing her, the burning desire launching through her system as he stroked her.

"Oh, yeah, you like that. Ride it, baby. I want to taste you so bad," he told her gruffly.

Sensitive nipples stroked against his hard chest through the two shirts, sending a flurry of sparks into her brain. Sweeping across her nub with swift strokes, shocks stole her sanity. She couldn't help herself. Grinding against his cock, his fingers sliding up and down her slick pussy, the orgasm she craved came barreling down on her. The rise and fall of his hips urged her, pushed her closer and closer.

The pleasure of his fingers filling her channel sent her careening out of control. His groan became buried when he pressed his face into the crook of her neck. She snapped her arms around his shoulders, clutching at him. Sliding and pumping into her pussy, she milked the stiff digits, tightening around him with each stroke. Fireworks erupted behind her closed eyes at the pressure, the rough of his knuckles streaking fire through her veins. He was going to make her fly right out of his arms with the intense pleasure. The heat of his tongue sliding beneath her ear sent her to another level. Teeth, lips and tongue. It was too much.

Without warning, her entire body flared like a roman candle, hot, achy and hungry. The heated essence of her cream coated his hand in ecstasy. The liquid sensation against her own sensitive skin sent her plummeting over the edge again in a blast of euphoric light.

He panted her name, scissoring his fingers, demanding every last ounce of satisfaction from her body until he finally let them slide free of her sheath. He felt so good, his solid body holding her steady. Arms and chest cradling her protectively. She felt utterly relaxed within his embrace. Then he surprised her by pressing tender kisses to the side of her neck, as though relishing her. Kay almost sighed in contentment.

"I want to kiss you so bad right now," he told her. "I didn't hurt you, did I?"

Concern stilled his body until she was able to answer him. Gasping for breath, she shook her head. His solid frame supported her noodle-limp length beneath her unmoving hold. A pleased murmur was joined with a tightening of his arms. The warmth of his body aligned with hers felt so good, so right.

"Rush?"

If he was relaxed beneath her, the call of his name from somewhere in the house hardened him into a wall of concrete. A deep breath stretched his chest. Standing carefully, he placed

Kay on her feet, readjusted her shirt, making sure her hair was in place.

"Just a minute, Sheridan."

Shit! His sister! Flames crawled up Kay's face. She'd completely forgotten they weren't alone. And she'd practically jumped his bones! Was the door even closed? The heat in her cheeks spread.

A very light finger pressed to her lips. "Don't. I'm a big boy, and she's going to have to learn to deal with me being grown up."

She gulped, mortified. How could she do that? She almost lost total control. *Almost, nothing!* she scolded herself. Once he'd wrapped his arms around her, the entire world had disappeared. The heat of his body had stolen into her, and she'd been swept up into the moment. That wasn't like her at all. She'd never reacted like that to any other man. She'd had one long term relationship that fell apart and she didn't care to repeat it. That was before she met Steven, and being cautious hadn't pushed for more with him. She wasn't the kind to risk her heart. After yesterday, she was grateful for her own reticence. *Then what the hell just happened?* she inwardly shrieked at herself.

"Kaisha," he murmured. The petal soft press of his lips to hers froze her thoughts, reminding her where she stood, and with whom. "I can't wait to kiss you senseless, woman." It was a growled promise that totally belied the gentleness of his lips.

Kay knew she'd be anticipating that moment with barely controlled impatience now. She wanted his kiss and so much more, more that she shouldn't be wanting at all. No, it wasn't fair, and she knew it wasn't right.

Drawing a steadying breath, she didn't fight when he twined his fingers through hers. This was temporary. She would be going home soon or Stacee would get her. Kay didn't have a heart to offer him, and somehow letting things go further felt wrong because she couldn't love him.

Being wrong or right had little leeway though. She couldn't remember the last time her body had felt so satisfied, so complete. It was a dangerous lure. What she refused to admit fully was how much she did want Rush. How much she wanted the gentle man who made her feel whole and wanted. It was a temptation she couldn't succumb to, either the man or the feelings he generated.

CHAPTER SEVEN

RUSH held her hand in his, guiding her to the living room where he knew Sheridan waited. One glance at his sister and her frown deepened, her nostrils flaring at the scent he knew she'd find. He hadn't bothered to try to hide it. Rush didn't want to. For the longest time, Sheridan had acted the older sister to him, but from here on out, it stopped. He had no idea how to deal with Kay, but she was his. The wolf knew and now, without a doubt, he knew it. The remainder of the equation had no room for his sister's condescension. He was going to have a hard enough time from here on forward without his sister pressuring him.

Sheridan was six years younger than him and had taken a lot of the personal responsibility between them as he learned how to be alpha. Some were born, some were made. He was the latter. He was quieter, a thinker, and only aggressive when needed. Alphas he'd known had all been 'king of the mountain' men. The old alpha had been for decades. Rush had never asked for the position and hadn't seen himself as one, but his wolf was one hundred percent alpha and a bad ass in a fight. He was growing into the leadership and honestly hadn't ever planned on mating. It disturbed the balance he'd worked so hard to find and maintain.

He owed his sister a lot for that. It hit him hard suddenly. She didn't like Kay; not because she was another woman in his life, though that was huge, but because she feared Kay would take her place.

Damn. This was why Rush liked things a little more planned out. He could deal with upheavals, if he could prepare.

Unfortunately, nothing on this planet could have prepared him for Kay.

She halted at his side when he stopped walking. No sense in putting off the inevitable. "Sheridan, this is Kay Noelles."

His sister gave Rush a glacial stare, speaking to him. "It's nice to meet you, Kay."

And you lie like a rug, he thought, meeting her gaze without flinching. A shallow heat flickered to life in his gut when she refused to speak directly to Kay. He narrowed his gaze at his sister. If Kay was his mate, his sister would have to learn to respect her. Rush wasn't even aware of the bristling of his spine while he locked gazes with his sister.

"Hi," Kay replied, then a little stronger, added, "Thank you for letting me stay with you." Kay tipped her head as though in contemplation, her body relaxed at his side, but alert. "You don't want me here, do you?"

Sheridan blinked, apparently unprepared for her candor. "It's not my place to disagree with my brother." Sheridan crossed her arms, a cool dismissal on her face, telling him she didn't have to do anything—speak to or respect the woman at his side—if she didn't want to.

"Bullpuckey," Kay muttered. "If it's your house, you have a right, too." She tipped to essentially be looking at him. It was weird with the bandage over her eyes, but he was willing to bet she knew perfectly well where he was. Sadly, she let her hand slip from his. He wanted her warmth back. "I told you if it was a problem, I could go somewhere else, or even stay at home."

Sheridan rolled her eyes. Rush recognized her impatience. "Bullpuckey back at you. You're blinder than a bat."

Kay turned toward Sheridan's voice, a frown daring to twist those lips he'd barely tasted. They'd lost the puffy look and he swore he was counting the minutes to really taste them. Was it fair that after the pleasure he'd shared with her in his room, she made him feel like the horniest of teenagers? He sincerely didn't think so. He wanted her, too much, but keeping his sister from disrespecting her in front of him was keeping his attention divided.

"Worse. They at least can squeak at walls before splatting on them."

This was said with such a disgusted deadpan note that Rush had to hold his breath to not laugh out loud.

"That bad, huh?" Sheridan asked with a silent sneer.

"Until the turban comes off, then I'll have univision. I'll have a patch for about a week until the swelling and God only knows what else is healed. The bastard deserves meeting the grill of a Mack for this. Is there anything bigger than a Mack?" she mused, not at all repentant for wishing bodily harm on Steven.

"Wait." Sheridan's eyes pinned Rush from the other side of the coffee table where she'd stood from the couch at their entrance. "You're the girl that was roughed by the ex at the Hut? I didn't know this was what Rush meant."

Kay's hand lifted and gingerly cupped her jaw. "Yeah," she answered. "And my best friend is out of town on a mission, so Rush took in the stray."

Sheridan shook her head, her dark curls bouncing with her. When she lifted her eyes again, she looked apologetic, almost stricken with remorse and realization. "I'm sorry," she mouthed for his benefit, walking around the table. "Here, come sit down. Coffee okay?"

"Su-re," Kay replied, sounding confused. She wasn't alone. The abrupt disappearance of animosity from his sister made no sense. Rush had expected it to be a lot worse.

"I'll get some, too," he said, bewildered at his sister's sudden turn around.

Once Rush made sure Kay would be all right resting on the couch, he followed his sister into the kitchen. "Okay, explain what just happened." He leaned on the counter, watching his sister prep mugs and coffee.

"I owe you an apology. I thought the girl at the Hut and your find were two different people. When you told me about her yesterday, I was under the impression that Girl A had been hurt and you had found Girl B, who was...is...your mate." She spoke quietly, in a rush of guilty words. "You bring home injured Girl A and practically screw her in your r—"

His growl of warning cut her off and dark blue eyes swept to his, dropping quickly in deference. "Sorry. But now do you see why I was upset? I know you, Rush. You are as organized as the Library of Congress and here you are, playing with someone who you shouldn't be when—"

He lifted a hand to stop her rambling. "I get it. Sorry I confused you. One and the same." Sheridan had been studying when he'd left in such a hurry, hearing the dispatch call on the scanner the day before. She hadn't known a thing until he'd called and asked her to set up the spare room. "Right now, the bastard who hurt her is in jail, but I don't know for how long. He was arrested on assault charges, but had nothing else outstanding." Scumbag Steven's last stint behind bars had cleaned his latest crime slate.

Reaching for his cup, he said, "But I thought you were upset that I had found her. You weren't dancing in circles yesterday." He sipped, waiting.

It took her a minute to answer him as she stirred her coffee slowly. "You're right. I wasn't. I remember Mom, too," she said distantly. "I know that's why you live the way you do, but there's something about that woman out there." Glancing up, she asked, "Can I speak as pack, and not as your sister?"

"You know you can!" he answered quickly, surprised she'd think she had to ask.

She tipped her chin, a deeper deference than she'd shown all morning. "As your chosen second, you need more than me. You need your mate, and if she's the one, then don't screw it up."

Rush was pretty sure his mouth was swinging wide. He'd had no idea. This was his *sister*? "Do you mean that?"

Her touch on his arm was light. "I always knew you were a strong male, and an alpha, but you've hidden it. I think me being here has done that. You don't do anything without weighing how it will affect the both of us. You think you took Tays's place by default, but you didn't. Maybe a little sooner than anyone may have expected, but you are whole with the wolf. He's an alpha, because you are too, and vice versa. Whether you knew it or not, your wolf did, and that's why you challenged him so young. No one else was ready then, and they wouldn't think of challenging you now. You're not an animal, but you are intelligent, loyal and compassionate to those under you. She's living, breathing proof."

Suddenly she smirked and he wasn't sure he wanted to know why. But without asking, she was going to tell him.

"I've never heard you laugh like you do for her," she said. "I've never seen you *be* alpha like you are for her. You couldn't see your expression when you came into the room. You were prepared to fight for her, even against me," she finished calmly, with a total lack of tonal inflection.

He studied her, trying to wrap his mind around what she was telling him. "I knew you weren't happy."

"It was all over your face, too. And you had already decided who you would stand for," she told him without heat.

His hand paused on the rise with his cup. Had he? Was he already taking Kay over Sheridan? Had his loyalty shifted so quickly? His chest heaved with a drawn breath, eliminating a tightness he hadn't known existed. He couldn't deny the blatant truth behind what she said, not when it stood up and smacked him with a foot thick brick wall.

"You'll always be my sister," he said, his voice trying to crack.

"And you'll always be my brother," she returned, blinking hard. "It's time you became the alpha you were meant to be for this pack. I've always known you could do it and beating Tays was just the beginning."

"You're staying?" He didn't want to chase her out of his life, and he needed her to know that.

"Until you choose otherwise, I'm still your second."

He frowned, not sure if that was the answer he was honestly expecting from her. She rolled a shoulder, pretending unconcern that he knew wasn't entirely real. Then he had to think about it himself. What *was* he asking?

"Damn." He choked on the word.

"Love you, too," she whispered, not looking at him, giving him his pride. "Now go, before she thinks she's been abandoned."

She handed him the third cup in silence.

CHAPTER EIGHT

SHE called Stacee on the ride to her apartment. "Well, crap," Kay muttered, closing her cell phone after only a few minutes.

"What's wrong?" He slipped it from her hand, and she heard him flip the clasp on her purse, putting it away. The man was sweet on sweet.

Kay knew Rush probably had a good idea from her side of the conversation what the problem was. "She's not coming home. Well, she is, but she's going with Jonas somewhere and won't be home until late because of it." Her chin fell forward.

"Hey, I'm not going to dump you off at your door."

"I'm glad," she replied weakly. "I'm sorry I'm being so much trouble."

"Quit it. You are no trouble."

She harrumphed. "Your sister doesn't agree with you."

"Sheridan apologized."

"She left."

She heard Rush's exhale. His hand threaded through hers. "She was giving us privacy. She thought you were someone else and was royally pissed at her brother, not at you."

"Who is older?"

"I am, by six years."

Kay shook her head. "You'd never know it."

His laugh was warm. "I know. She pointed that out this morning too." She felt the truck slow down and then stop. "We're here."

Kay turned to find the door handle, but his hand stopped her. "Come here," he purred, that low, sexy rumble that had her melting from the inside out.

"Hm?" she asked, swiveling on the seat, though she hoped she knew.

She wasn't wrong. The warmth of his kisses started beneath her jaw, dropping heated surprises with every touch. Damn! She wanted to see. Her fingers inched upwards, memorizing the hardness of his muscles, the slope of his shoulders. A gentle tug brought them thigh to thigh on the seat. Her fingers delved into the loose curls she remembered.

"You taste so good." A shiver shot up her spine then rocketed goose bumps down her arms at the rough heat of his tongue gliding beneath her ear.

"Kiss me," she pleaded.

The swirl of his tongue paused. "I don't want to hurt you, baby."

"Please. Unless..." She ducked down, her forehead landing on his broad shoulder.

"Unless what?"

"The bandages. I know they've got to be the last thing anyone wants to see."

"I've dreamed of ripping them off. I want to see you again." The pulse of his breath against her skin, sliding through the strands of loose hair, warmed her. She felt safe in the circle of his arms.

"I want to see you too," she admitted.

A tender finger lifted her chin, the heat of his breath right in front of her on her lips. "Kiss me. You'll know when to stop, before it hurts."

Her heart pounded. Blood thundered against her ears. Lifting trembling fingers, she found his mouth. Caressing the shape of his lips with the tip of her fingers, she swore she could hear both heartbeats, his and hers, within the truck.

Easing herself forward, she found his lips. Kay had never explored the adventure of sex with a blindfold. The experience of kissing Rush without being able to see him was beyond anything she'd ever felt before, more titillating than any skin to skin caress that she could remember.

That morning had been explosive, both their desires so raw, so ripe she was surprised they didn't tear each other's clothes off and finish what they'd started, what they'd both so badly wanted. She wouldn't have said no. Rush did something to her, made her *want*; want sex, want his body, want him, period. He made her forget when he held her, touched her, kissed her.

Without being able to see him, the sensation of his lips, the male form of his mouth against hers, drove her right to the brink of no return. She craved to feel him naked beneath her hands, the solid shape of his chest beneath her palms as she caressed him, teased him. Yet the gentleness of the kiss was a sweet torture in its own way.

Cautious of her limits she pressed closer, her fingers holding herself steady in the thick curls of his hair. The taste of his kiss erupted on her senses when he let go, letting her take control of the moment. She felt it, the way he let her make every move, every step forward. Wanting spiraled through her, winding tighter like a coiled spring just waiting for the chance to explode into full desire.

Tentative caresses turned into a wanton seduction when she slid her tongue across his lip. Heat blossomed, filling her being with his scent, the feel of his lips against hers. The fingers holding her tight dug into her hip, screaming his own growing hunger held back in restraint. His chest rocked, fleetingly brushing against taut nipples in a give and take dance of breath. He played with her, stroking her tongue as she learned his shape, sucking lightly, giving her every chance to stop him or pull away.

She didn't want to. The twinges of discomfort were low, the pressure miniscule compared to the pleasure. A slow burn had taken root, and her only hope of surcease was the man tenderly worshipping her in a way she'd never once experienced.

Swept up into the rise of desire she went too far, wanted too much and gasped. He stopped instantly. "Kay?"

Breathing through the sharp pain, it began to recede almost as soon as it hit. Her hand caressed him, drifting over his ear to form to his cheek, her heart aching while her jaw reminded her why she needed to be careful. "I did that. Not you. I'm fine." She sensed his doubt and pressed a finger to his lips. "Heaven," she murmured, meaning it.

"Sweeter than candy," he replied. And she smiled halfheartedly, absolutely crushed that she'd had to stop, and worse that she knew he was blaming himself.

RUSH sat outside, watching the sunset behind his house, something he hadn't done in months. Except he couldn't tell anyone anything about the glory of the colors of the fading sun. His thoughts had kept him mired since they'd arrived back at his home after the stop at her place.

Kay was inside, resting in the spare this time, insisting she couldn't kick him out of his own room twice. The day had been long and tiring on her, and even though he was positive she hated taking the pills because they literally knocked her out, it was for the best. They both needed time. She needed time to heal; he needed time to think. The list on his mind was easily long enough to rival Santa's naughty and nice list.

Sheridan had still been gone when they'd returned and she wasn't back yet. Not a huge problem, but she usually told him where she was going. Taking advantage of her being gone, Rush had been camped out on one of the bleached Adirondack chairs in the quiet, trying to sort through the changes his life had taken on over the last twenty-four hours.

Amazing how much had changed in a day.

Twice today, Kay had literally bowled him over. He dragged a finger in memory over his lip, the essence of her body imbedded into his very pores now. If it weren't for the ramifications of a bonded mating, he'd have stripped her there on the bed and pleased her for hours. That was something he couldn't do without her knowledge. If instinct was going to bend his will to take a mate when he'd had no idea how he could, when he'd avoided it as much as catching the measles, the least he could do was give her the chance to refuse. Once she was his, there would be no others. The thought of loving her, tasting her body, caressing her soft skin for the rest of his life sent a hard shudder down his torso. A low heat boiled in his gut. Nothing he'd thought or done had eased it.

And then she'd kissed him. He shook his head mockingly. He'd told her to do it. What did he expect? Snorting at himself, he slouched a bit on the wooden seat, one leg bent on a slat at the knee. To be honest, he hadn't known what to expect, but any idea he may have held had been obliterated by the sweetest seduction she gave him. Her lips were more potent than any liquor, sweeter than any candy. If lightning had a source, she was it. He could still taste her, sweet as fall apples, and find her sunshine scent on every breath.

He shifted in the chair, adjusting his cock beneath his jeans, without an ounce of relief. If he didn't know it wasn't possible, he'd swear that his condition hadn't changed one iota since the first sound of her voice, the first glimpse of her thunderhead gray eyes, a sultry gaze that he longed to see again.

A rattle between the trees in front of him below the deck's edge dragged him to his bare feet, annoyingly hunting the growing shadows for the coming visitor. Wanting to relax as much as he could, he only wore his jeans, when he'd normally be in nothing if he'd been alone. Either way, he wasn't in the mood for interruptions, or visitors.

Not surprised to hear them nearing with the loud warning they'd offered, a pair of wolves loped from the trees. With his permission, they lost their skins, standing on two legs. He welcomed them with a nod. "Trevor, Zackary."

They both dropped their gazes in quiet respect. "Alpha," Trevor said.

"What brings you here?" He wasn't concerned with their nudity. Within the pack, it was normal, and he knew if either of these teenagers had shifted before being a hundred percent aware of their surroundings, they would pay their faults to him. They didn't know about Kay, but Rush knew she was out like a light, and thankfully, out of sight. He wasn't quite ready to share her with the pack.

"Zoe is lost. We were running and hoped she'd come this way." Trevor looked ready to puke he was so anxious as the words tumbled from him. His skin was waxen with exhaustion. They'd been running, and looking, for hours by the sight of the pair.

"Your sister?"

Trevor nodded.

"How long?"

"We came out this morning. Dad dropped us off and told us not to leave the Dale's land, but we all did and now we can't find her."

Rush frowned at that news. Mr. Dale was Zackary's uncle. He had a large wooded spread just east of Rush's property. It was prime real estate for the pack to kick up their heels. Their territory was wide spread, but individual wolf families had territory, too. Some were better suited for the wolf and were open to pack use. Rush knew Trevor and Zackary were out there often. This was the first he'd heard of his little sister running.

"Where did you last see her?" He studied both, hoping they had an idea of where to start. The Dale's property was huge and if they didn't stay on it, the odds weren't good they'd find her tonight.

"On the southern ridge. It's my fault," he admitted. "She wasn't up to the distance, and I got impatient with her." Shamefully, his entire body folded in, most likely wanting to crawl into the ground and stay there. "Zoe turned and ran back the way we'd come from, but she's not able to track scent yet. She never made it back to the house. She hasn't eaten since this morning."

Rush's impatience died a little for the youngster, his heart and tears in his eyes.

"I have to find her."

Zack rubbed shoulders in comfort with his best friend.

"We will. I want you and Zack to go back to the Dale's and wait. Do not leave once you are there. I'm not looking for two of you. I'm going to gather the trackers and start at the ridge. It may take time, but we will find her."

"Thank you, Alpha. I'll call Dad when we get there."

Rush didn't say anything to ease the fear he heard in the younger boy's wavering voice. There wasn't much he could do about how Trevor's father would handle his girl missing. "I know it won't be easy, but try to keep your dad at your uncle's. It's already sundown. Hopefully she found a hole to hide in."

Trevor nodded and with a shared look, both boys dropped to the ground, two wolves that spun and tore back into the trees.

"Shit," he breathed. He so didn't need this, but life and responsibility go hand in hand. With the evening's peace shattered, he spun to go inside.

Sitting on the side of the futon, he brushed the hair back from the dulling bandage wrapped around her forehead. He tested the edge and frowned when it moved a considerable amount. She'd been pulling it in her sleep. He'd have to do something about that when he got home. He'd already called Sheridan home and a few others to alert them to the emergency. He couldn't just leave her a note to tell Kay why he wasn't there, and it tore him apart that he had to leave her at all.

"I'm sorry, baby," he breathed, lowering to press a tender kiss to her mouth. "I'll come home as fast as I can." *Come home to you.* For the first time, he felt he was beginning to understand the relationship his parents had shared. The pain of his mother's decision was actually being explained a little at a time. Maybe she couldn't live on without their father. Maybe she hadn't wanted to die, maybe she'd been so lost she couldn't live on and saw no other way. Devastation and depression were powerful against a human body and mind. Rush didn't know. There was only one truth he was certain of at that moment. Leaving Kay, injured and alone, was killing him.

Her hand lifted and caressed his face then sank to her stomach, her breathing still deep. She'd known he was there, even in her sleep, and the belief that somehow she could, created a lump in his throat.

Hearing Sheridan's car outside dragged him back. Standing, he turned and left the smaller room, knowing he was leaving his heart behind this time.

CHAPTER NINE

KAY tossed in her sleep. She was sick and tired of sleeping, but the drugged abyss wouldn't let her go, not yet. She heard voices close by. Or was she dreaming? Rush's face appeared in her mind. That was his voice, she was sure of it. Centered on his voice for the last day and a half, she knew it was him without a doubt.

Alpha?

Kay frowned, trying to hear more, trying to understand the dream. Her body and mind felt disjointed, like she was drifting through time. She was aware, but it refused to connect to her body. Damn, he sounded sexy when he went serious like that. Husky and gruff. She fought to concentrate. Someone was missing. A child? That's how it sounded to her, his concern thick. But how could a child, any person, follow scent? Her frown deepened, fighting to comprehend what they were saying, to wake up.

"I have to find her."

"We will. I want you and Zack to go back to the Dale's and wait. Do not leave once you are there. I'm not looking for two of you. I'm going to gather the trackers and start at the ridge. It may take time, but we will find her."

"Thank you, Alpha. I'll call Dad when we get there."

This wasn't a dream! Panic was distinct in the lowered youthful tones. She tossed, grasping at consciousness, fighting the cloud over her mind, but being unable to force light into her senses with her eyes covered she couldn't do it. She felt weak, sluggish, lifting her hand to her head. If she could just see! The rough feel of the bandage across her forehead was foreign. Though she knew it was supposed to be there, she tried to remove it.

Then she heard him right there with her, felt his hand caressing her and her world calmed. Everything would be all right. The darkness pulled her down again.

RUSH, along with Tanner, who was Tays's youngest son and one of the best trackers in the pack, and Nicole, another who could find a flea on a ferret, managed to get within a mile of the ridge where Trevor said he'd lost Zoe's trail. There was no road, but the land was drivable. Now with the truck behind them and the sun long gone, the three wolves spread out. Time wasn't a concept to the three who scoured the ground for any scent, any sign that she'd passed.

Rush's focus was exact, but he couldn't help the stray thoughts, his worry for Kay, from flickering into his conscience. He'd been by her side since the incident with Steven, and now he couldn't imagine being without her. It was happening so fast, all the shocks and decisions. He knew he couldn't let her go.

The wolf snorted, disgusted at the notion. *Okay, I get it,* Rush groused back. He didn't know if the others talked to their wolf the way he did. It was something he'd done since he was a child, and when his mother died, he relied more and more on the quiet patience of the animal he shared souls with. They were one and the same, but different, symbiotic yet two entities within one shell.

A sharp bark snapped his attention to Nicole. She lifted her head and sniffed then whipped her tail up. She'd found something.

Jogging to her further down the ridge, Tanner joined them. Dropping his nose, Rush studied the ground and his body tightened on alert. She'd found Zoe's scent, but someone else had beaten them to tracking the young girl.

Zoe was being followed.

Shit. With a low growl, they began tracking the tracker and the prey.

KAY sat up and stretched. Rubbing her face, she refrained from rubbing her eyes. She'd done that once without thinking and the tenderness of her left eye had shot her with agony. The tips of her fingers ran along the bottom edge of the bandage. If it was night, then she had less than twelve hours to need the bandage. Her lips twisted as she debated.

It *had been* a precaution, not a necessity. She flexed her facial muscles and didn't feel faint at the pain to her left side. Her throat had lost the tight burn from being almost crushed, and though her mouth was tender, her lips didn't feel like swollen sausages any longer, not to herself and not to her fingers when she pressed against them, testing their healed state.

Standing from the edge of the futon, she placed herself in the map of the room. Turning, she walked the four paces to the bedroom, glad Rush had also walked her around this one, too. She found the bathroom easily enough. Now how did she get rid of the bandage?

Scissors would be best, but she doubted they'd appear because she needed them. Carefully, she slid her finger beneath the loosest edge and inched it upward with steady pressure. The tape gave easier than she'd thought it would. She didn't open either eye as the rough linen swathe slid upward. She peeled the remaining tape strips and the circle of linen cleared her crown.

She released a nervous breath. Her first instinct was to blink, but she remained calm. Turning on the faucets, she ran warm water and carefully patted her eyes, shuddering at the contact and relief of the moisture. She knew Doctor Aimes had prescribed eye drops for dryness. That would be next.

Patiently, though anxious, she wiped her hands and cheeks on the towel hanging behind her, disappointed when she didn't find the feel of muscular abs again. She'd barely breathed before, and Rush had been there, helping her. At least now, provided she wasn't seeing double, she'd be able to go look for him, not have to wait for him to come guide her around like a seeing-eye dog.

She turned on a bare heel, the familiarity of the natural hardwood beneath her feet. Standing straight she found the sink with her palm and cautiously cracked her eyes open. She stifled the cry of alarm, all but slapping her hand over her mouth to keep it from exploding into a wailing scream.

"Damn, you're a mess," she muttered when she could breathe beyond the shock. But she could see.

The undamaged eye was mostly clear, only a little foggy, which drops would likely fix, but the left... She sighed. Her left eye was blood red across the white, and she knew that it would take months for it to clear. At least another two weeks before her face would completely heal. Sonofabitch. *What did he hit me with?* She thought it had been a fist, but a fist wouldn't do this. It was lucky no bones had been broken. No wonder Rush had been all but waiting on her hand and foot. She'd been inches, if that much, from serious damaging harm. It's a wonder she didn't get a concussion.

Lifting her hair, she swept it back, noting the blue around her throat. Shaking her head, she realized that what she'd thought had been overkill on Rush's behalf had been a necessity for her. She couldn't have, shouldn't have, been left alone with this.

Stripping the bandage apart, she eked two strips of tape and a portion to cover her left eye again, knowing it was only temporary for the moment. The more she blinked, the clearer her vision became with her right.

"My, don't you look charming," she mocked her reflection with the make-do patch in place. *Princess image, hell.* She looked like a Tinkerbell pirate.

Leaving the bathroom, she meandered through the house, finally seeing the beauty of the home she'd been exploring with her fingers for the last two days. And he'd had this designed and built? It was gorgeous for a home.

The interior had a cocooning effect, solid with rough redwood accents. The scent permeated the air now that she could see the cause, like she walked through a sun-heated glade. It was cool inside, with large open rooms and several wall sized windows. The house wasn't dark. Although it was nighttime outside, a ceiling fan in the center showered the room in light.

"Gorgeous," she breathed. Glancing around, she wondered where everyone was. She walked toward the kitchen, but couldn't hear or see anything. Then she heard Sheridan's voice. She was outside in the back where a glass sliding door stood open.

"No, I'm sure Rush can find her, Emily. The boys didn't mean to leave her behind. You know how impulsive young pups are."

Kay slowed. She was on the phone, but before she could turn to leave her alone more of the conversation floated to her.

"Yes, he took two of the pack with him. Nicole and Tanner. It'll be okay, Emily. Even if she doesn't shift, she'll try to find a place to stay safe until morning."

Pack? Shift? Rooted to the spot now, she eavesdropped shamelessly.

"The Rysen pack? No, they're friendly on the south side. If they find her, they'll call someone."

Sheridan was trying hard to soothe an obviously distraught mother on the other end of the phone.

"Rush knows Thomas, their Alpha, fairly well. The territory dispute was solved not long after he took over Tays's place."

It was like a mini soap opera, but Kay was only catching half the on-screen dialogue.

"I couldn't go. We have a guest. Rush couldn't leave her alone, so I'm here." A light laugh broke some of the tension. "I'm not telling either. You'll have to meet her. She's pretty awesome. She'll make a good fem-alpha, I think."

Kay sank to a chair. They were talking about her. There were a few more words with a promise to call as soon as she heard anything, then silence.

Fem-alpha? What the hell was that? And why was she calling boys pups? Was it an endearment term between them?

Sheridan stepped up onto the risers that seemed to lead to the deck on the far side, freezing with a lurch in the doorway. "Oh, crap," she muttered.

"I know, I look hideous," she offered, latching on to the logical.

Sheridan shook her head. "Oh, honey," she demurred. Striding into the room, she sank down next to Kay. "You're fine. Colorful," she offered with a light tease.

"That's more complimentary than I could give." She hadn't turned to look at Sheridan yet. No sense in giving her the up close and ugly view. "What's happened?"

"A couple of boys were out in the woods and being impetuous idiots, left their little sister to find her own way home."

Kay gasped. "Are you serious? How old is she?" It was pitch dark outside. It was way too late for anyone to be left out there.

"She's eleven, but still too young to be out as far as they went."

"That's insane! Have search parties gone out?"

Sheridan nodded. "Rush has gone himself to find her."

Kay lifted a hand to rub her temple. "What is a fem-alpha? And who are the Rysen pack? Is it a motorcycle club or something?"

Sheridan's face paled. "Crap. Rush is going to kill me."

"Why?"

Sheridan's mouth popped open then snapped shut. Twisting her fingers together, she leaped from her seat.

"I don't know if I should—"

The phone rang, snapping both women to the sound.

CHAPTER TEN

Rush groaned, lifting his head to let it thud back to the ground, a dead weight that was just too much effort to lift. Everything ached. He was sure his nails would if they had nerves.

"Come on, buddy. You have to change, or move, or something."

Tanner was kneeling next to Rush. *Kneeling?* Why was he out of his skin?

Quiet whimpers reached him, the reassuring shush of a female comforting her sobs.

"Is he going to die?"

Zoe. Flashes of memory were beginning to register. A fight. A huge one. A shudder ruffled fur. He closed his eyes to breathe, uninterested in doing anything else. At least they'd found her. He could deal with the rest when he was ready.

"Rush? Not anytime soon, honey," Nicole soothed the young girl. "He'll heal. He's just tired."

"That's what happens when you take on five naturals," Tanner muttered.

"She didn't know," Nicole rebuked him. "It's not like we wear signs that we're shifters or naturals. She thought they were friendly." Nicole continued to wrap the terrified girl into her embrace, rocking her. As a female alone, she was prime for the plucking, age didn't matter.

"I'm not blaming her, Nic," Tanner stated evenly. "Although Trevor deserves anything his dad gives him for leaving her alone like this. She just hasn't learned enough to know how to tell the difference between us and them, or how to get home, but he didn't have to take them all on." Unaware of the mistake, Zoe had been happy to follow the pack who had found her, unfortunately being led right to their territory and lair.

Nicole snickered. "They took *him* on, remember? She's part of our pack. No alpha would just let her be stolen without a fight, natural or not." Nicole continued to brush her hand over Zoe's hair. Exhaustion was growing with the young thing, her body going limp. Rush managed to keep an eye on all of them through lids that just wanted to stay closed.

Somewhere overhead the sky and stars blinked down on him. He wished he were home, in bed, with his arms curled around Kay. The memory of sunshine in her hair soothed him the way Nicole's crooning eased Zoe. So long as he was breathing, he'd heal. He wished the other two would just take Zoe home. He was sure her mother was ready to rip heads off waiting for them.

"Come on, Rush." Arms wrapped around him, lifting him from the cool ground. "Just do me a favor, and don't shift until I tell you to, okay?"

He let out a low growl at being told what to do, but couldn't do much more as his body fell slack, the jarring movement causing blistering pain across his shoulder and back.

SHERIDAN drove in tense silence, her lips pinched tight, exacerbating the paleness of her face. She was stretched with concern and angst. Not that Kay could blame her. After hearing from Emily that Zoe had been found, nothing would have held either woman back, which put Sheridan in a real bind.

Because she'd had no choice but to try to explain to Kay something both were sure should have been left to Rush.

Short of strapping her to something solid, Kay wasn't about to be left behind. Rush had been injured looking for Zoe. They'd found her, but from the sounds of it, he'd been ripped to shreds extricating her from a pack of natural males.

Naturals? Shifters? Alphas? There was that word again. It was enough to make her head run in circles. This wasn't possible, whatever *this* was, but if Rush was hurt, she wasn't going to leave him.

When they arrived at the Dale's home, almost every light was on, even though it was well past two in the morning. Kay sat straighter as they neared and spotted Rush's pickup truck. The tailgate was down and a young girl was sitting in the bed with a large dog.

"There's Zoe," Sheridan said.

"Where's Rush? Inside?"

Sheridan twisted her hands over the wheel, her body taut. "No." Her unblinking eyes were locked on the animal in front of them. "Rush is going to kill me," she whispered again. "You shouldn't be here, not yet."

Slipping from the car, Kay didn't have a chance to ask her anything else. She followed behind the other woman, but instead of going inside, she went right up to Zoe and the dog. Only, the closer they got to the truck, the more Kay was convinced that wasn't a dog beside her leg.

"How are you, Zoe?" Sheridan asked gently.

Thick tears trickled from her eyes. "He's going to be all right? Please? I didn't know the others weren't family. I thought I'd been found." Her voice wobbled with the weight of her tears.

Slow breaths moved the ribs of the animal before them, slow and steady, but apparently unaware, his head lying comfortably on the young girl's thigh. "I know, honey. He's going to be fine. You've had a long day. Let's go inside."

Sheridan held her arms open and Zoe slowly flowed into her embrace. She was long limbed and gangly, but Sheridan didn't seem to have any problems with her in her arms.

"Let me get her inside. Her parents probably think she's curled up somewhere in the house. We'll take him home in a minute."

"Him?" Kay croaked.

Sheridan nodded, her own eyes glittering with unshed tears. "I've never seen him this beat up." She swallowed, then seeming to remember the girl in her arms, tucked her against her shoulder and carried her inside without saying anything else.

"Rush?" Kay murmured, gaping in shock at the dark, coffee-brown pelt of the animal in front of her. Even in the absence of strong light, she could see the bite wounds that tore into its rich coat, blood thickening the fur in spots to matted clumps. Several centered on his back and his front shoulder, like the other animals had tried to take him down by sheer force.

It couldn't be. Whipping to look over her shoulder, she stared hard at the house, praying, waiting for Rush to come limping out, or at worst, out with help, but he never did. Should she follow Sheridan? Where was Rush? Confused, she reached forward to the animal before her. It lay there, doing nothing but breathing. Thick fur slid beneath her fingers. She leaped back when its breathing changed.

No. She was imagining this. He did not just sigh. None of what Sheridan had said on the drive over could be possible. It just couldn't. It wasn't logical. There was no such thing as shifters. But inarguably, a wolf lay before her, had been sleeping on Zoe's leg. And Sheridan had every intention that Kay could tell of taking it home with them.

"Rush?" she asked again, a little stronger, knowing there was not one thing sane in thinking this animal was him. A single eye dragged opened, a blue hazel eye. The world vanished, her entire being focused on the wolf in front of her as reality vacuumed on itself.

Somehow, he lifted his head, fighting to rise to his feet. Kay froze, watching the struggle, every inch of the animal before her trembling with the effort.

"No," she whispered sharply, stopping his progress. He did, looking at her questioningly. "Oh my, God, Rush." Hands that shook wildly lifted and palmed the furred face of the beast in front of her. As if that was all he'd been waiting for, his blue eyes closed and his entire length went slack, collapsing to the bed of the truck. Kay didn't know how she stayed standing until Sheridan came out to find her staring in shock. When Rush collapsed, he'd wound a paw over one of the hands she'd held him with, tying them together even when he couldn't be aware of the touch.

Once home, Sheridan carried him easily from the pickup to his room and laid him on his bed. "It's one of the benefits. We're a bit stronger than most," she explained. Even beneath the bruises, Kay was positive she was pale, watching and living this.

"It's really him, isn't it?" Breathing was a torture.

"It is," Sheridan answered. "He will heal, but it'll take some time."

"How?" She licked her lips, fighting to grasp reality, which was a fleeting memory at the moment.

"It's what I was doing such a bad job of explaining earlier. We're born this way. The gene is male dominant, but any child born of a paternal wolf can shift. Both our parents were shifters." Sheridan stroked the fur on his head in comfort as she spoke. Kay stood next to the bed, still in shock. He had a fair-sized bed, but the breadth and width of his slack body dwarfed it.

Sheridan caught her gaze. "I know this is a shock. I'm positive it's not how he wanted you to find out."

Kay nodded, dazed. "Everyone called him Alpha." *Just like in the dream.* It hadn't been a dream after all, if she was to believe the woman standing on the other side of the bed. Believing that the animal laying on Rush's bed was actually him, Kay was dealing with it a moment at a time.

Sheridan's fingers never stopped furrowing through the thick pelt. "Because he is. In the human world, he is a man like any other, but within the pack, he is our leader, our judge and jury. He has earned the right to be Alpha, though he has his doubts."

"You don't doubt him." Kay was positive of it, watching his sister's adoring expressions.

"Never have." Her smile was indulgent.

Kay watched them both. The wolf lay as still as death on the bed, though the rise and fall of his ribs proved he was only unconscious. They lived with this secret their whole lives. And somehow she'd been tossed in the middle of their world.

"What can I do?" she asked, her voice paper thin.

Sheridan's thoughtful face lifted, piercing the space separating the two women. "Do you mean it?"

Kay met her intense gaze, the hurt and worry of a sister in the almost identical hazel eyes of the man—wolf—on the bed. "I do."

"You are his, and his healing will be faster if he doesn't have to worry about your safety. Stay with him."

"His...what?"

The indulgent smile was back. "Now that is one I know I can't take from my brother. He'll tell you when he's ready."

Kay straightened her shoulders, becoming aware she'd been staring at the furred lump on the bed. She made up her mind, watching the slow rise and fall of his breathing. "If I give you a list and my keys, can you go to my place?"

"I'd be happy to."

"Then let's make sure he heals."

Sheridan's smile was only outshined by the thankful tears in her eyes.

Chapter Eleven

Rush stretched, his fingers digging into blanket and a warm woman.

Warm woman? His eyes snapped open. There right beneath his chin in the darkened room was a full head of espresso brown hair.

It smelled like summer sunshine.

"Kaisha?" He swallowed when he croaked her name. Her thinly covered breasts pressed into his bare stomach like she'd always been there. Her arms were snug around his torso, his hand resting easily on her hip. Hot breath warmed the base of his throat.

She tilted her chin and he caught his breath at her sweet smile. Threading her fingers through his hair, she whispered sleepily, "Hi there."

He didn't know where to start, with the fact that she'd removed most of her bandage, or just how good she looked to him. A lot of the swelling in her face was gone and the bruising had improved dramatically.

A low, needy groan rose from within as he buried his nose into her neck and shoulder, holding her flush against him, so glad to be with her, to be skin to skin. Exactly how he'd wanted to be, how he'd imagined her next to him. Her body warmed his beneath the covers, sending heat to dispel any chill he may have felt.

Slowly, it returned to him. The wolves he'd fought to regain Zoe, the damage and wounds he couldn't avoid for the effort.

Rush couldn't even remember how he'd made it home. Or have any idea of how long he'd been laying in bed with this sweet woman holding him within her arms.

He jerked up to see for himself what shouldn't be. *A lot* of the damage had healed.

The pit of his stomach felt frozen solid. "How long?"

"Not quite four days. You were really hurt when Tanner brought you back. You almost lost a leg in the fight." Her fingers slipped through his hair, drifting over his shoulders to return.

Rush rolled his shoulder, more memories returning in snips and flashes. "Yeah," he mumbled. Then what she said registered. "What did you say?" He was almost scared to breathe, staring at her with unblinking eyes. How could she know what shape he'd been in? How long had she been there? The weekend he'd met her was a vague sleep-ridden blur at the moment, but hadn't that just been yesterday? A day more, maybe? She had to be wrong. He couldn't have been out for that long. Panic was settling in. Because that meant...

She leaned up and pressed a warm kiss to the bottom of his jaw. "It's okay, Rush. I know." Her uncovered eye was sparkling up at him. "Although I've never slept with anything furrier than a bear, it wasn't all that bad. At least you don't dig in your sleep." Her teasing laughter was beautiful.

"You...slept...?" He wasn't sure if he should shout with joy or pray in thankfulness.

"The whole time."

She said that with such sweet, relaxed assurance that he couldn't help the smile from pouring free. With gentle hands, he rolled her onto her back until he stretched over her. Her small frame was almost engulfed beneath his. "How much longer do you have the patch?"

"I was supposed to go earlier today, but I didn't want to leave you."

"So it can come off?"

"Mm hm. Doctor Aimes said with the way things have progressed, it's safe."

"Then why didn't you?" he asked her, mildly confused.

Her chest rose and fell beneath him, her breasts lightly meeting the wall of his body, a hint of uncertainty in her gaze. "Because I wanted you to be the one I see when I remove it."

All he could do was look in humbled awe at her, his eyes touching her where his hands wanted to be next. "You're perfect," he breathed. Emotions belted him one after another, and none were stronger than the love he felt for her. "Can I?" he asked, trembling with everything he was feeling.

When she nodded her agreement, he lifted a hand. She caught him before he could touch her. The determined strength behind her slight hand around his wrist was surprising. "I better warn you. It's not going to be pretty. I've seen it once already. I still look like road kill."

"Oh, honey. Kay," he groaned. "There's no one as beautiful, anywhere." He lowered himself and pressed a tender kiss to her mouth. He didn't demand more, exacting his own type of torture, enraptured with her scent as he drifted down her jaw. The fragrant silk of her skin sent jolts of need through his body.

He almost vibrated with the growing hunger, with the emotional overload. He whispered into her ear. "You really slept in this bed with my wolf?"

The answer he got was a breathy moan. Impatient fingers stroked at his shoulders. "For two days solid. You didn't shift until the second night." And there wasn't a hint of fear anywhere on her, or in her voice.

He couldn't help himself. He had to touch and kiss her, the hunger for her so deep, he felt like he was drowning. Trailing hot kisses down her neck until he reached her shoulder, he clamped down with his teeth. He wasn't sure who needed it more, him or his wolf, to mark her, to claim her. Her whole body arched like a bow, a keening cry slipping from her body. Her arousal was instant as her body flooded in preparation of the ecstasy to be received. Every sense was tuned to her body. Her scent between them, the taste of her on his tongue, the sound of her voice imbedded in his brain. There was nothing but Kay.

"Mine," he growled thickly, licking at the tender spot. "Now and forever."

Her answer was a mumbled purr. The teasing drag of her foot up his thigh made his synapses pop. Her hips rose and rubbed against his shaft to further tempt him. Sweeping a hand up her body, he captured her hands from their seductive meandering to hold them over her head beneath one palm.

"Patience. This first," he told her. Gently, he pried the tape from the side of her face, lifting the large circle of gauze covering her left eye. She lay perfectly still for him, only small quivers exposing her anticipation. "Now, let me see. Slowly."

Like the rise of a curtain, the excruciating wait to see her, for her to see him again, was over.

"I told you. There's still a lot of damage."

His shoulders tightened with surprise as he focused on her expression and not just the woman he couldn't seem to get enough of, then the corner of his mouth lifted. "I didn't even notice it. I was captured by the most gorgeous gray eyes I've ever seen."

A rose blush filled her cheeks, and those inky lashes, just like he remembered, lowered to hide her thunderhead eyes. It was a perfect color for her. She'd stolen into his life like a silent storm, only to blow him away with everything that was Kay.

With her pinned beneath him, everything else vanished. "You smell so good." The raw edge of his voice was only an echo of the raging hunger of his body. He dipped again and nuzzled beneath her ear. She turned easily, allowing him access to anything and everything. "Perfect," he crooned. Then he began to lick and sip at the most delicious treat—her body.

He knew she was two years older than he was because he'd filled out most of her paperwork at the hospital, but her body still carried the supple, limber ability of her years in gymnastics, as he soon found out when she lifted a leg over his hip, wrapping over his waist like a pole and hanging on. Holding fragile wrists in his palm, he slid his hand down her length, caressing every curve, every dip and valley.

"I can't say this enough. You are perfect."

Her moans were breathy, her eyes closed as he swept her down a river of pleasure. He learned her body with a leisurely hand, adoring her, holding her flesh in firm then gentle fingers, each discovery sending his blood pounding harder through his body. His cock strained as it filled, emphasizing his desires with a quickening throb.

It took little effort to pull the shirt she wore over her head. Peaked nipples taunted him with their rouge rose color, and he knew they'd taste as good as they looked. She fit perfectly within his hand when he covered her breast, rolling the hardened tip beneath his palm. Her breath caught with low growled sobs that deepened when he gave each tip a light pinched twist.

"Not too hard?" he asked, when her moan turned guttural.

"No," she gasped, shuddering beneath his weight. Rush wasn't a rough lover, but when he made love to a woman, he pleasured her before anything else. He wanted to find out everything about Kay. What she liked, what made her moan, what would make her orgasm in ecstasy. Tonight, he wanted a piece of her soul as well as her pleasure. There was no doubt that Kay would own a little of his by morning as well. He wanted no one else's.

Still holding her, he licked at the peak to soothe the treatment he'd given her and she arched, silently begging for more. With each inhale, he could smell her arousal, making his mouth water. Her body undulated and molded to his, fitting and sliding over his chest and rubbing against him. She fit so well against him, he knew he could eat her in just one bite, like the big bad wolf and Red.

The thought of her lying next to him, holding his wolf, maybe soothing him or caressing him in his sleep, made his dick solid as steel. The veracity that she wasn't screaming in terror, but was still with him, in the same bed knowing the truth about his closest secret was almost more than he could comprehend. Rush had wallowed in his doubts about how to tell her. In order to have her completely, she had to know the truth, and she did.

And she was still in his bed. Somewhere in the back of his brain, he knew there was something else he should tell her, but if there was a coherent thought to be found anywhere, he didn't have it. The sweet essence of her hunger, of her body, embraced him, blocking out all other interruptions. Even those by his conscience.

Lingering over her nipple, he wrapped his tongue around the taut point, his hand drifting in languid patterns up and down her body. She bowed off the bed, seeking, following when he lifted, moaning again when he licked his way to the other delicious playground of her body.

She tasted even better on his tongue, warm flesh and sweet breasts. "I could play with this," he lipped her nipple, surrounding it with light tugs, "all day."

Her head thrashed to the side when he drew her into his mouth with a slow pull. It thrilled him that she was so sensitive.

Dropping kisses upward to her collarbone, his hand slid down to her hip, cradling her, feeling her softer body along his. Without missing a beat, he shifted again, stroking her waist with his thumb, teasing the edge of her panties. "These have got to go," he told her. With a twist and a pop, he ripped the waistband and flung them from her body, nothing but a scrap of worthless lace now.

Her eyes snapped open, startled.

"You should never hide this luscious body from me," he told her, nipping the underside of her breast in punctuation with sharp teeth.

"Clothes are kind of necessary," she replied in a husky whisper.

"Everywhere but here," he told her. If he had his way, she would never wear a strip of anything in his bed again. Why ruin the perfection of her body with something as ordinary as clothing? He would be too inclined to remove it as soon as she was next to him anyway.

Whatever would have been said was forgotten when he flicked at the damp curls between her legs. Her body shivered in reaction. Holding her hands over her head kept her stretched out beneath his weight, his hand and mouth able to reach and caress at will, a veritable physical playground of aroused Kay.

Using a flat palm, he opened her thighs for his exploration. Lying down fully, he stretched out along her side. He suckled at her breast with tender licks and pulls, letting his fingers play and tease with her sweet pussy. Smooth skin pressed against his from his chest to his thigh. Bending a leg at the knee, he arched it over the nearest of hers, locking her down, capturing her under his weight.

Nuzzling her ear, he taunted her with his desires, the entire time slipping his fingers closer and closer through the tight curls that covered her core. "I want to lick every inch of your body, taste the sweet heat of your juice when you come." A harsh gasp slipped from her quaking lips. "Does it turn you on, knowing how much I want you?"

She licked her bottom lip, leaving a glistening shine behind. "Yes," she managed in an aching voice.

He lowered himself to taste her lips. At the instant of contact, he caressed the hard bundle of nerves beneath his fingertips. She cried out, his kiss swallowing her pleasure. Delving between her lips with his tongue, he stroked the folds beneath his fingers, lost in the slick heat of her desire, invading her on two levels. Sliding against her tongue, he mimicked the action with his fingers, gliding over her clit in perfect harmony.

Rush tried to keep the kiss gentle, but her whimpers, the way she lifted seeking him, battered his efforts until he claimed her completely. Thrusting his tongue deep into the heated crevice of her mouth, dueling with her tongue, he found the silken sheath of her body and thrust inside her channel. Her body stiffened with bliss.

"Let me feel it, baby," he murmured above her lips.

She gasped, her body arching, fighting to be free, enraptured with the pleasure. Stroking her with his fingers, he felt her walls tighten, plump and heated with the need to be fulfilled.

Releasing her mouth, he licked her flesh, traveling with teasing twirls down her neck for the tip of her breast. His hand holding her loosened, and she didn't try to move, letting him control the moment, every touch. Holding her prisoner beneath his larger size, he continued to thrust into her pussy with hard even strokes, flicking with teasing nails over her clit and tempting her, bringing her pleasure higher. The trembles started at her shoulders and he bit with commanding pressure at the tempting nub beneath his lips, building her orgasm into an explosive burst.

He wanted to feast on her body, but he couldn't wait any longer to feel her surrounding him. He would please them both endlessly, but the need that fired his veins went deeper, feral and primal, demanding he claim and satisfy his mate. The scent of her in the room wrapped around him, engulfing his senses with the mix that was only her. With the heat of her body calling his, he reached for his nightstand before he lost all ability to think beyond the wonder of her laying there, so tempting and gorgeous. Quickly searching, he found a condom packet, thankful. Covering himself, shuddering beneath wicked fingers that now trailed down his chest, he fit himself between her thighs.

The pounding of his heart was deep, racing, as he became captured by her eyes again, darkened with her lust and desire. He throbbed painfully, holding on with the last ounce of sanity. Lowering to her lips, their soft shape welcomed him, calmed him within the maelstrom of need circling him. Breathy bursts slipped between them with him seated right at her entrance, so close to what he desperately needed. The strain bunched his muscles to not take her, his natural desires leading him. The very last thread of his control was quickly being stretched to its limits.

"Tell me now. I won't let you go after this," he said, his only warning, because it was the truth. Once he entered her body, there was no going back. A bonded mating was permanent, more binding than any super glue invented. He waited, his pulse ripping through him like a hurricane.

"Please," she mewled, her fingers riding into his hair and gripping like he was a lifeline.

With one thrust, he claimed her body, feeling her claim his soul in the same instant. A fire like nothing in his lifetime flooded him and he held on, muffling his gasp against her body as lightning stole his sanity for a heartbeat, tearing through him. Like a piece of him had been missing his whole life, she filled him more than he filled her. Gradually, the sensation of her fingers reawakened him to her within his embrace, demanding yet gentle.

"Perfect," he managed through a single growl as his body took over, sinking into the pleasure that was Kay, thrusting into her heat like he wanted to crawl into her very soul and stay there, safe and warm and loved.

Slender hips rose, and he sank deeper, lights exploding as air rushed from him. Her pussy clenched down on his shaft and he shuddered. "Oh, shit, Kay." He couldn't help it. He was going to tear right down the middle with each stroke, bringing him closer to the edge.

"Yes," she cried, pressing her lips to his throat, licking and sucking between bursts of gulped air. He tipped his chin, and she raked his throat with her teeth. His wolf snapped his head up and howled within.

Rush exploded, pounding into her welcoming body like it was his home, taking her with him when the ecstasy overpowered him. The universe as he knew it, vanished.

CHAPTER TWELVE

KAY nuzzled the warm arm beneath her cheek. The sun was beginning to streak the sky outside the window of Rush's room, making her blink as the gray brightened. It would likely take a few more days for her vision to completely square itself. She really needed to call Mr. Savrenson and let him know how she was doing. He'd told her to take all the time she needed, considering the attack she'd suffered. Her work was commission and cost, anyway. If she missed a week, it wouldn't kill her or his store.

Rush's easy breathing rustled the strands of her hair over her ear. He was completely healed now. After watching over him for four days with Sheridan, watching in awe as he healed from the wounds on his body, she knew it was time for her to get back to her life. Their fun was over, if she could call what had happened to her having fun. He didn't need her now, and she needed to go home before she allowed herself to feel anything more for the man.

She liked him, and hadn't been able to stop herself from wanting him last night, a clear sign to evacuate and quickly. Liking him was okay, sleeping with him was even better, but at the same time? She couldn't do it. She didn't use men the way her mother did. She had no idea what her mother was looking for or even needed when it came to men. Kay knew to keep any sex separate from any feelings, friendly or otherwise, that she may feel toward them.

The problem was she was scared. She felt too much for Rush already, a clear sign to end this before it spiraled out of control. She could like him, and did, but she couldn't love him. She refused to let her heart fall into the same patterns as her mother. Falling in and out of love as often as the rise and fall of the sun. With a sneer of distaste, Kay knew her mother went through men and boyfriends faster than Brittany Spears appeared in gossip rags.

With the press of his chest to her back, she indulged in a few more minutes before facing the inevitable. Her one luxury was to not hurry through this last morning.

She sighed softly, snuggled in his embrace. His hand splayed across her stomach in sleep, holding her close, her back flush to his chest. He hadn't let her go all night, keeping her pressed to his body like a warmer.

Carful to not wake him, she lifted a hand and ran it over her face. She'd hardly looked at herself while caring for Rush, but the pain was gone and except for soreness around her eye, she was back to normal. Even the split in her lip had healed. She knew the bruises were still there, but they'd begun to discolor, breaking down to disappear.

Gliding up her side, his hand captured her fluttering one. "Stop," he mumbled. "You're beautiful."

"I look like a science experiment gone wrong," she replied.

"It's already fading, baby." He pressed a kiss to the top of her head. He surged forward, pressing his groin into her ass, molding them together like two peas in a pod. The man was *not* lacking, she mused. She still ached with pleasurable memories. And he was definitely a morning person. Kay grinned, tucking into his curved elbow to try to hide her smile.

He sighed, dropping kisses to her shoulder. "I need to call work, find out what Sheridan told them and get my time straightened out."

"I think she told him you had a family emergency."

Rush didn't reply, only nodding. "She hates lying," he said quietly a few minutes later.

"Well, it was an emergency, and you are *her* family," she offered, trying to find a way to validate his emergency.

He chuckled. "You probably signed your own absence slips at school."

"I'll never tell."

His laughter was deeper, richer, rocking her within his embrace.

"I need to get back, too," she told him as the silence filled the room comfortably. She rubbed against him again, loathe to really get up and leave, not after the night they'd shared.

She'd been with Rush for almost a full week now. Not that anyone would miss her if she wasn't at home, but she needed to get back to her life. Stacee was probably tapping her toes right now, impatient to let her know how things were since last Saturday, and with Rush's condition. Kay hadn't told her how he'd been hurt, only that he had been and she was staying with him because he'd done the same for her.

"When are you coming back?"

Light as feathers, Rush's lips danced along her shoulder, his tongue flicking out to hit her pulse every few seconds. She was pretty sure he'd given her a hickey. She tingled every time his lips or touch came close to it. She didn't mind. What was one more bruise among the mess she already wore?

"Coming back?" she asked. Kay really hadn't thought that far ahead. She hadn't considered it an option.

"I'd ask you to just move in, but I know that's pushing it," he said in a cajoling, low rumble.

"What?" she whispered with a shocked gulp. "Move in?" She hadn't been expecting that.

"Mm hm," he purred. His lips were still flitting all along her neck and shoulders and his hand was beginning to get ideas too. "You are perfect for me, my little precious."

"Um..." She corralled his hand, halting his wandering progress. "What is that supposed to mean?"

"We'll take this slow, I promise, but I need you. You are mine to love and cherish."

Shit! Love? Is he out of his mind? This was just what she'd wanted to avoid. Too late. She saw the train barreling right for her. She'd had no idea Rush thought he was falling for her. He'd been unconscious for more than three days! He couldn't love her. He was mistaken.

"Look, Rush..." she said nervous now, ready to flee, the moment spent in his embrace shattered. Licking her lips, Kay tried to reason with him. "It's because we've been together non-stop since Steven's attack on me. You don't mean that."

She tried to sit up, but his arms caged her within their unbreakable strength. "I do mean it. I claimed you last night."

"Claim?" She almost snickered a laugh, but he sounded so serious. "What the hell does that mean?"

"You're my other half. I didn't know it, and when I realized it, I didn't want to admit it." He sipped lightly at the skin beneath her ear. "When you told me you slept with my wolf, held him, cared for him, I knew I couldn't let you go." His voice was low, raking her nerves like hot coals.

"What are you talking about?" she demanded, fighting to keep her voice down, because he wasn't making sense. His wolf? What did he have to do with this?

"You're my mate," he stated as a simple fact. She felt the flick of his tongue on her ear, and her mind and body both dared to short circuit, for two different reasons.

"Your what?" She was *not* a wolf's mate!

"My other half, my mate, my soul." He said each with slow purpose, punctuating each with tender kisses.

She rolled her eyes. *Oh, God, he's waxing poetic. He must still be feeling ill, or feverish, or something.* She felt trapped and her heart started to pound. She pulled his hands loose. He didn't fight, but watched her carefully as she sat up.

"Rush, I'm none of that. We connected. I was hurt, and then you were hurt." She stood, going to the dresser where her suitcase full of spare clothes lay open. "It's time I got back to what I do."

She noticed when his eyes narrowed. "You accepted me, all of me, my wolf and me," he stressed, no longer cajoling, but flat, with a hardness she hadn't heard from him before.

"I don't know what..." Her thoughts brought back snatches of the night before. *"I'll never let you go."* She stood slowly, clothes clutched in her bloodless fist, staring blankly at the wall in front of her. Her lungs emptied as though she'd been kicked. She whirled to face him. "What did you do?" she bit out. His mouth opened, but she flung up a hand. "Wait!" She drew a breath, feeling dizzy, very dizzy. Blinking to steady the room, she asked, "First, what is a fem-alpha?"

He sat on the edge of the bed watching her, the sheets draped over his thigh like a toga tail. The rest of his chest and torso were bared and so easy to linger on with her gaze. She wrenched herself upward when he started to explain.

"The fem-alpha is the feminine leader of our pack, the other alpha. This pack did not have one because I wasn't mated. Until last night."

Her throat hurt because she was trying to breathe and swallow at the same time. "I can't believe this." The shirt in her hand swayed as she raked her fingers through her clothes, searching for what she didn't know. She couldn't look at him. Her heart and body did things she wasn't familiar with. Okay, lust she knew, and desire, but there was more, and more she just didn't have time for.

"You know I'm a shifter. That doesn't bother you."

"I do know, and no it doesn't," she replied cautiously, not ready to admit to more, least of all that she'd somehow bonded with Rush. She'd had days to deal with and accept that the wolf and the man were one and same. Just because a week ago it was inconceivable didn't mean it wasn't true. She'd never seen a million dollars in cash, but apparently for many, it existed. No, she had accepted his wolf.

The rest was just insane. *That doesn't really happen; it can't, can it? With just sex?* She mentally shook a finger at herself for calling something so wonderful, so all-consuming as what they'd shared as mere sex. What had happened between them the night before had been shattering. But it did not tie them together.

"Kay...Kaisha. We need to talk about this," he told her, standing.

She blinked to not look. The man was a specimen of perfection. Solid shoulders, a lightly hair-dusted chest that veed down to his navel with a hint of temptation further. And that hint didn't lie. Even now, his length drew her, thickening under her gaze. Breaking away was hard to do. Then there were his legs and thighs that were strong and looked it. He was walking muscle, a wall of iron. He made her heart stutter with renewed hunger. That was why she knew she needed to leave. Rush made her want, more than any other man had in her life, and wanting only led to disappointment and pain. She refused to cause this man, or herself, pain. Kay could not, would not, love. She was *not* her mother!

"When a wolf finds his true mate, the woman he's meant to share his life with, shifter or otherwise, when they make love it cements their souls. We are more than just two people who slept together, regardless of how we ended up in that bed." He reached out, his fingers drifting down her arm. "You are more to me than that. You have been since the moment I met you."

She bit her tongue, not wanting to speak, afraid she'd tell him she understood. Because she did. She just couldn't believe she'd somehow tied herself to him by sleeping with him. That *couldn't* happen. Underneath everything, wolf or not, he was still a man. And she was a woman.

Yet, because he was a wolf, she feared something had happened between them. There was a suspicion that he was right. She'd never felt so consumed, so swept away by a lover in her life. And it shocked her that she wanted him, now, again. Wanted him touching her, pleasing her, kissing her.

Gripping the clothes in her fist, she drew air into tight lungs. "Rush," she managed, her mouth feeling dry, while her body almost hummed with a renewed need. She had to push him away. She couldn't look into those eyes and be cruel to him. He stopped her before she could speak.

Slowly, so slowly, his hand cupped her fist, covering her. "Kay, give it a chance." She caught the cock of his grin when he told her, "This is new to me too, you know. This only happens once, if we're lucky."

Her eyes widened with disbelief and surprise. "No one divorces? Or dies?"

"Divorces? No." He drew her hand closer, pinning her to his chest. "If one dies, the other can find a companion if they can, but there's never a second mate. There's only one shot at this." His voice had dropped to a husky whisper, and she felt his breath as he tipped, caressing her knuckle with his lip, the way he had before, in thought. What was going through his mind then? What was causing the dark clouds and shadows? No! She couldn't do it. She could not let this continue.

The hoarse echo of his voice filled her ears when he told her, "I never thought I wanted this. I wasn't even remotely looking, but now that I have you, I would split the earth to keep you."

She swallowed to hide the burning lump in her throat. Here she was a walking wreck and he was spouting eternal love. He was feeling pity, compassion, trust, and mistaking it all for more than attraction. She knew because she was having the same problem. She didn't ever let anyone this close. It wasn't safe.

Closing her eyes, she did the only thing she could do. She denied everything, and him. "Look, I can't tell you how grateful I am for how much you helped me."

He froze next to her. "Grateful? I don't want your gratitude."

She yanked on her hand, but he held firm. "What happened here is no more than a step out of time." Now in the light of day, there was a very surreal feeling to the days she'd spent on that bed, wrapped around his lupine body, or tucked into his human one. She shook her head to clear the images. How many people slept with wolves? *Kevin Costner, eat your heart out.*

"You're kidding?"

"Do I look like a woman who's kidding?" she shot back, glaring up at him. "You weren't looking, or expecting anything out of this. Neither was I. There is no bond. We had a connection of commonality, nothing more."

A hiss broke through his teeth, like he'd been hit or worse, hurt. She turned a deaf ear to it. She had to get out of that house. She had to get away from him before she succumbed to the pull of his gaze, the sexy taunt of his lips. Something she knew she could never do.

"You are the fem-alpha of this pack," he said, the tone direct and decisive. "You can run all you want, Kaisha, but that will never change or disappear."

She huffed impatiently. "I don't even know what that is! I can't turn wolf!" He needed to just stop! He wasn't doing himself any favors.

"It's not necessary." The words were firm, yet trying to be comforting and supportive.

She stopped herself from rolling her eyes. She was not like them, what "they" were. Kay was willing to bet her grandmother's emerald on how well a non-shifter fem would go over. She saw the way Zoe's family protected her, how they circled Sheridan when she'd told them she was bringing Rush home to heal. No one cared then that Kay was around, and they won't care now that she was gone. They wouldn't miss the dime-sized fem-alpha who never existed for them.

"I can't love you, Rush. It's time I went home." She couldn't make it any clearer than that.

Coldly, he released her hand, and stepped back. "Then go," he snapped, a diamond-hard, forbidding light in his eyes that she'd never seen. It sent a shiver screaming down her spine.

Surprised he didn't fight harder and confused as to why she wanted him to, she whirled for the bathroom to hide the tears she felt building. She knew it was for the best. This couldn't continue. They hardly knew each other. They'd hardly spoken in all the time they'd shared the same bed, the same room. For the duration, at least one had been incapable. Until last night.

Bracing herself on the sink, she sagged, sucking air in taut gasps, fighting the pain. It would end. *This is not real.* People don't meet and fall in love like this. *People nothing!* He wasn't even human in the real world.

Just one more reason she couldn't stay. She didn't belong with him. It would never work. She knew that from experience.

Swiping her eyes with a palm, she cleared the blur of her tears and landed on her reflection. *How could he fall in love with this?* The grimace of pain was more than her face fighting back, but she refused to say it was her heart.

CHAPTER THIRTEEN

SHERIDAN frowned at Rush. "How long are you going to stew over this?"

Couldn't she just quit asking? He ignored her looks, eating his dinner with quiet patience. It had been three weeks since he'd let Kay walk away from him. Three long, painful weeks of calling himself everything in the book.

"It's not me," he told her coolly. Spearing another piece of meat, he slowly chewed, refusing to let her see the deep agony he'd been living with since the slam of the front door the day Kay had turned her back on him. He wondered if she was fairing any better.

Snarling inwardly, he knew he shouldn't be thinking of her at all. Late at night though, when he was alone and felt the hunger of his soul, he did think of her. Couldn't avoid it. She'd grown into a specter that he couldn't shake.

"And you're going to let it stay like this?" she asked bluntly.

He tossed his fork down, leaning away from the table, and not bothering to hide his glare of annoyance at her prodding. "What am I supposed to do?"

Sheridan's eyes shone with sisterly love. "Rush, she wanted to help you. No one forced her to stay. She's the one who needs to learn how to be an alpha, not you. You're doing just fine on your own."

He swallowed the snort out of habit. He wasn't so sure. He'd let his woman walk out of his life with hardly a growl or

166

argument. "She doesn't want to have anything to do with being alpha." *Or with me*, but he left that unsaid.

"Are you feeling it?" she asked gently.

God damn it, he hated when she sounded like their mother, sympathetic and understanding, because that wasn't sympathy in her eyes. He didn't have to ask what she meant. Long term separation wasn't easy to handle, typically for either, but Rush guessed if Kay hadn't complained, who was he to start?

He stabbed at his eyes with stiff fingers and rubbed. It didn't help.

"Go see her. Convince her. Court her. That's what you would have done if she'd stayed. Ease her into being the fem-alpha, let her find her way with you at her side and protecting her back. Nothing says you can't win her because she didn't stay. Usually that's the way it's done anyway, the courting *and then* the pissing off." She smirked at him knowingly.

He crossed his arms over his chest. "I know I sprung it on her, but I didn't see the problem with it."

"Of course you didn't. You weren't the one having to completely uproot your life and create a new one with a shifter that she'd never known existed until you." That was a definite rebuke in her gaze now. He didn't wince, but he wanted to. How did his sister, his *younger* sister, manage to make him feel like he was the baby? Rush wasn't the one living in the land of denial, not now. Maybe in the beginning, but after what they'd shared? No, he knew what she was and knew he needed her. The problem was, she didn't need him.

Sheridan cleared her throat. "I've been putting this off because I was hoping..." She picked at the table with a fingernail. "Anyway, I'm moving out."

"What?" He shot straight in his chair. "Why?"

"Well, because you don't need me here anymore. I'm not leaving the pack, but you need your own place. Especially when Kay comes back."

He snarled under his breath. "She's not coming back."

"Uh huh," she murmured, her lips twitching with suppressed laughter. Rush refused to answer her. She left him at the table, glowering after her. Thinking. And wanting.

"Damn you, Sheridan," he whispered, dropping his head into his braced palms. Rubbing his eyes with the heels of stiff hands, the slowly building groans turned into impatient growls. By the time he rose from the table, there was only one choice to be made. If she wouldn't come to the mountain, the mountain would go to her. Even if he had to do it with her kicking and screaming, she was coming back with him. Where she belonged.

If Kaisha thought she was going to brush him off like a layer of dust, then she had another thing coming.

KAY stood in the kitchen with Stacee, rinsing off the dinner dishes. Jonas had wandered into the living room to give the girls a couple minutes of privacy, which wasn't easy considering the living room, dining and kitchen were essentially one room.

"How are you holding up?" Stacee asked, toweling off an item or two.

Kay ran water methodically over a bowl in her hand then slid it into the dishwasher. "Fine," she answered. "Why?"

Stacee cut her a glance. "Because you've changed since your incident."

Kay's hands paused, her gaze glued to the water sluicing over her fingers. "What do you mean, changed?"

"You hardly smile. You don't laugh. It's like you're depressed, when usually nothing ever gets you down." Stacee rested a hip against the counter, her longer legs giving her quite the height advantage over Kay. "So, what is it? Are you worried about Steven?"

Kay shook her head. "No, since he was arrested again, his probation was broken." He was completely out of the picture. "I just never found out what the big deal was about me."

"Was he ever here with you?" she asked Kay, coming closer to keep her answer in confidence.

"Once or twice, picking me up for a date, but not overnight." Kay slid the upper shelf into the dishwasher and closed the door. She'd run it before bed.

"What about Rush? Have you heard from him?"

Kay blinked at Stacee's hopeful note. "No." Kay had made sure of that.

She ignored the apologetic sigh from her best friend. Stacee hadn't stopped beating herself up over having to leave her in the hands of a stranger. "He sounded more trustworthy on the phone. I'm sorry I left you there to stay with him. If I'd known—"

"No," Kay cut her off. "It wasn't like that. He was a perfect gentleman." The most patient, understanding, compassionate man she'd ever known.

He just also happened to be a wolf shifter.

Kay bit her cheek to not say those words. She wasn't entirely sure she could, to be honest.

Gathering her courage, she whispered, "What if I told you he was an important person? Like a leader?"

"Really? Like politically?" Kay saw the way Stacee's eyes focused inward. "I could have sworn he told me he worked at the South Lake precinct as a detective."

Kay nodded, stilted. "He does, but that's not what I mean."

Stacee set the towel down, and Kay purposely shut off the water.

"What do you mean?"

"I mean—" A knock interrupted her before she could let her mouth cause her trouble, which was probably a good thing. It would sound insane anyway. Sucking in a breath, she asked, "Jonas, could you get that? It's probably a newspaper salesman." They'd been canvassing again, pitching sales almost every weekend that month.

"Sure."

"Look," Kay said, focusing on Stacee again. "It just didn't work out, not that surprising. I was a victim that he took pity on."

"Honey, that wasn't pity in his voice when he all but begged me to take care of you himself. He had a reason."

Kay's chin dropped. Yeah, he had a reason all right.

The front door opened, and the one voice she hadn't heard, yet had craved for weeks, sharp and snarled, carried all through the apartment.

"You have exactly ten seconds to tell me what the fuck you're doing in my woman's den!"

Kay whirled and gasped. "Rush!"

Oh, God, he looked good. Good and pissed. And good enough to eat.

Stacee hopped out of the kitchen to stand with Jonas. That was when Kay noticed how tense both men were. Rush had a fist already curling, and Jonas looked ready to receive and return the volley. Angry heat glittered in Rush's eyes. She had to do something to diffuse this. She'd never seen Rush or Jonas behave like this.

She took a step on the linoleum. "Rush? What are you doing here?"

His gaze flashed, flickering over to her. "Who is he?" he coldly demanded with a stony glare.

"Jonas," Stacee said, with a hand on his shoulder. "Calm down, honey." Kay watched as Stacee not only laid claim to the man at her side, but he seemed to relax and calm under her gentle touch.

He turned and pressed a kiss to her cheek. "Sorry. It's reaction."

"I know," she purred with a smile that could melt even the most hardened heart. She turned and smiled at Rush. "Hi. You must be Rush. I'd offer to shake your hand, but until you're both calm, let's just not go there."

Kay was following this and trying like hell to not get lost between the three in her own apartment. Why was she talking like that? What did she mean?

"You're...?" Rush's gaze flicked over them. "Stacee?"

"Yes, and this is Jonas."

Dawning reality had him looking around at everything else for several seconds, until he scrubbed a hand down his face.

"Damn it," he muttered. "It was just a shock."

"Come in," Stacee said, not even bothering to ask if Kay was okay with it. Rush stepped in and Stacee closed the door. Jonas took a step back as well.

Kay's chin came up, stung by his curtness. "What? I'm not allowed to have friends over?"

"It's not that." He hadn't come near her yet, and her whole body ached. After so long without him, he was too far away. "Having the door opened... Finding him..."

His voice trailed off, and he looked uncomfortable, like he knew he was digging himself deeper.

Kay swallowed. "Look, Rush, whatever you have to say—"

His blue hazel eyes glistened, making her heart pound. "Stop. You got to do all the talking last time. My turn." He cleared the distance between them, a long jean-covered stride that ate up the steps in nothing flat. "You could have told me your best friend is mated to a shifter, baby."

"What?" Kay's eyes popped wide. Whipping around to look at them, there was no difference that she could see. They looked the same, for as long as she'd known them.

"She didn't know, Rush," Stacee informed him. Both looked toward the other couple and saw that Jonas had wrapped a hand around Stacee's waist, her head on his shoulder. A complete couple.

Kay rubbed her eyes. "Wait. A. Damn. Minute." She blew out a breath. "Jonas?"

"Yeah?"

"Whose pack?" she asked, determined to get to the bottom of this.

"Cougar Nall's."

Rush nodded his head. "He was a friend of my dad's when he was alive."

"Are you Rush Donovan? Alpha Donovan?" Jonas asked with a new respect.

"Yes." Rush's voice had calmed, smoothed, but still held a rough edge, like something darker, stronger lay just underneath the cool exterior. His chin was up, his back straight even though he was relaxed; he was prepared for anything. Kay was seeing his alpha side in person. Her next indrawn breath was staggered with a mix of emotions.

He stood like a man in charge, like the man she'd seen at the coffee shop who had faced down Steven with nothing more than a few words and a stare. Like a man who would spend an entire night tracking a missing girl and risk his life for any of his pack, for any of his family.

There was strength, patience and so much loving tenderness. She wanted to sink into the floor as she acknowledged she'd been a royal bitch. And not the regal kind, either. Running scared, overwhelmed and insecure with so much to try to understand. She still didn't, but she knew he deserved an apology. Being scared didn't give her the right to be cruel.

"God, Rush, I'm so sorry."

"No, shh. Let me." He pressed a tender finger to her lips, his gaze once more on her. "I didn't do one thing right. You make me feel out of control, wild in ways that scared the shit out of me."

Kay saw the other couple move, but stopped them. "Don't go," she asked quietly.

"If you're sure?" Jonas asked, looking at her and Rush both.

"Stay," he added. "I don't want to take her away from her friends because of this."

Jonas nodded, and he and Stacee stood to the side in silent support of her. The breadth of Rush's shoulders rose and rolled as he faced her again.

Rush lifted her chin with a finger. "Kay, I love you. I don't want to lose you. You won't be alone as the fem-alpha."

"But I'm not like you," she whispered, feeling whipped and shredded, her emotions scattered and difficult to define. With him there, standing in front of her again... Her heart raced like a horse on the run. All the wanting she'd denied reared up and stared her in the eye.

"You don't have to be." Glancing up, he turned toward Jonas. "Stacee, you're human."

"Completely."

"Was finding out the truth a shock?"

Jonas smirked, and the glance he shared with Stacee filled with a memory they'll never forget. "She fainted."

Kay gasped, stunned. "She doesn't faint."

"I did," she confirmed, giggling behind her hand.

"Kay." Rush's voice caressed her ears. "I should have let you decide. I took that away from you, and I didn't mean to. Every time I came to grips with something, I just moved on, never thinking about how it would affect you or if it would even matter." Leaning down, he touched his forehead to hers. "It was a lot to take in. I'm sorry. I was the inconsiderate jerk in this."

"You were only helping me. I was a wreck the whole week. How?"

He lifted a hand and wound her hair over her ear, leaving a tingling trail beneath his fingertips. "Because to me you're simply perfect. There's no explanation that could really describe it," he replied softly.

Subconsciously, she lifted a hand to her face. "But..."

He fisted over her hand, stopping her, twining his fingers through hers. "I knew you before that happened, and you were beautiful to me. You are beautiful." He brought her hand to his mouth, brushing a tender kiss to her skin. "And I think you're wrong. You are the perfect mate for an alpha. What you did and faced, with nothing but near-strangers with you at the time, took courage. Kaisha Noelles is an alpha, a strong one that I would be proud to know stood at my side."

Hanging on his every word, his declaration brought a burst of heat to her cheeks.

"Give us, this, a chance," he whispered, nuzzling with his lip against the hand he held. "I'll be more patient. I promise. I need you Kay."

Kay barely blinked, completely captured by his gaze and his words. The soft tap of the front door closing dragged her focus to the living room. They were alone.

"They left." The sound of her voice sounded loud in the quiet of the apartment. Even the beating of her heart seemed to echo with a heavy, nervous tattoo.

"Do you want me to?" he asked her, his gaze and voice utterly serious.

She drew a breath, trying to still her trembling legs. "No." His touch was sending shooting heat up her arms.

Studying his face, she wondered if they were putting it all on the table. Was this the deciding moment to their future? She lowered her eyes, watching the tender slide of his lip over her hand, his breath warming her and making her heart race and leap inside her chest. At the least, she owed him a full apology and explanation to her behavior.

It was just going to be one of the hardest apologies of her life.

CHAPTER FOURTEEN

"RUSH?" She whispered his name, mesmerized by the back and forth of his mouth hovering over her hand. "It wasn't just you. I'm sorry."

"I tried to push you into something, rush you into it, even."

Steeling herself, preparing to expose her darkest secret, she told him, "Do you know why I wasn't hurt when Steven broke up with me?"

He froze, but he was listening. "Why?"

"Because I wouldn't let myself care for him. I haven't been in a long-term relationship since I was twenty-three. At most, I dated for six months then moved on. The guys I met weren't looking for anything deeper, either. We all knew it. Someone to go to movies, to hit a club or two. I rarely saw any guy more than three times," she admitted. Not sleeping with them usually precluded a lot of interest on their part. She couldn't look up, didn't want to see the disappointment in his eyes as she bared her soul to him.

"Since I was nine, maybe younger to be honest, my mother would leave me in the care of her friends and sisters while she went out, and I don't mean it was just for a few hours or even overnight. Sometimes it was for days." Kay was surprised she was able to tell him about her childhood without breaking down, without letting the years of pain leak through. "I didn't suffer through a lifetime of 'uncles', but I did have to accept my mother's selfish nature and her incapability of loving long term. Me included."

"Kay," he whispered.

She fought the tender understanding in his gaze, in his touch. She needed to say this, just once. "No, this is important." He threaded his free hand through her hair comforting her, massaging her, but didn't say another word.

"In many ways, I'm like her except I don't have a child, and I never lead my flavor of the month falsely, dropping them unexpectedly when I felt I wasn't receiving something I felt I needed or thought I could do better with the next man to cross my path. I don't go out of my way looking for affection or love. I go out of my way to avoid it. When you said we'd bonded, I felt trapped. Utterly and irrevocably. I don't understand it," she said, her voice thickening as she got to the really hard truths. "But I've been miserable without you. I think if you hadn't shown up tonight, Stacee would have either suggested I find you or she was going to do it for us."

Rush's jaw flexed just above her line of sight, and she was sure that sexy quirk of his lips had appeared. She couldn't raise her vision any higher than the joined hands in front of her, her shame keeping her from looking into the eyes that she knew saw right through her. Swallowing, she finished. "I don't understand any of this."

"That is my fault. I haven't been fair to you. Every time I came to terms with something, I became distracted and by the time I had the chance to think clearly enough to talk to you about it, the moment was gone and something else had moved into its place."

The scent of his skin filled her senses when he leaned down to rest against her forehead again. Husky and deep, his voice reached out to her. "I've been miserable, too. It's been hell without you."

Her gaze flew to his eyes, drawn like a moth to a flame, wanting the truth and it was there, bared for her. She saw the tiredness in the dull gleam of his blue eyes, the lines in the corners that hadn't been there before. His skin was warm when she lifted her fingers to caress those tell-tale signs. "You haven't been sleeping."

"Have you?" he asked right back.

"Not well." A giddy sensation blossomed in her chest, warm and small, just a nugget, but it was there.

"I won't lie to you, Kay. The bond is there. It's unbreakable in our world." Leaning closer until his cheek fit next to hers and she could feel each breath on her skin, he said, "I can't, I wouldn't, take it back. You may not believe it yet, but I love you. I have since I woke up with you in my arms and knew you had been there all along with me. You accepted me when I've never wanted anyone else to even try. No, it's not how I would have had it happen between us, but it did." He brushed a feathery finger across her lips, ramming at her barriers with gentle persuasion. "And I'm not going to let someone else watch over the greatest treasure I've ever received. Don't live with that fear between us. I need you too much."

Glancing away, she blinked to hide the fresh dampness in her eyes. "You've got a way with words," she teased, trying to hide the depth of her reaction from him. It all sounded so wonderful; it was just taking time for her heart and mind to both agree to believe in them.

"Let go," he breathed. "Let go and love me." Then his lips touched her temple and her eyes fluttered shut.

A light tug brought her flush to his body, and she couldn't stop herself from melting straight through. The lean length of him pressed to hers, his thighs solid against hers. With her free hand, she braced herself on his chest, surprised to feel the ripple of skin and muscle beneath her fingertips. He sighed.

"Yes, princess. Touch me. God, I missed you."

The nickname sent a shot of hunger clear down to her toes. The princess she'd envisioned had been a protection, an untouchable wall to separate herself from the world and the hurt surrounding her life. A barrier that kept the world at bay because princesses weren't approachable, were detached from reality. The way he said it though, the husky rumble, made the nickname sound precious, treasured. Protected.

The gentle pressure of his hand on her back guided her closer, and her hand slid upward, caressing his shoulder. The cotton of his shirt smelled like him and she couldn't resist rubbing her cheek over him to absorb all of him at once. She'd missed him so much. The scent of his skin, the heat of his body, the tenderness in his touch. She sighed quietly, too content to move for several minutes.

With the hand in her hair, he tipped her up to him. The depth of longing and wanting in his gaze stole her breath. He hid nothing from her. Not how much he desired her or needed her, or how much he craved her physically. The steel hardness of his length jutted into her through his jeans in an adamant statement of longing.

"I want you, Kay, but I won't ask for more unless you can honestly tell me you can give me a chance. I can give you the time you need to understand this, but it won't stop me from wanting you."

Gazing up at him into the flecked blue of his eyes, she felt a chink against her heart. A large crack was the result. "You mean it?"

A gentle kiss to her mouth had her sighing. "Completely. I want to court you the way I should have from the beginning. Circumstances being what they were, I never got to really show you much. We kind of jumped right to the middle and the end." He teased her with that smile of his, warm and heady. He slipped from her mouth to lick at the corner of her lips. "You taste so good. I've dreamed of kissing you."

Aches were spiraling, slowly coiling her body tighter with need and desire.

Tucked against her neck, he drew a slow breath, his tongue flicking against her pulse, and she shivered. "Did I ever tell you a wolf has a heightened sense of smell?"

"N-No." She gasped as he continued to tease the one spot that had remained sensitive even when everything else had healed.

"I can smell how much you want me, princess," he told her, his rich voice slipping into her blood stream. "I can find your arousal on your skin, taste it, and it's driving me insane with wanting you."

The thickened roll of his voice sent shivers down her body in a constant shower, increasing her own desire with every kiss, touch, breath. A dampness she couldn't control built and her pussy clenched. Her body thrummed like a taut wire being plucked as his fingers caressed and danced up and down her spine.

Something between a growl and a groan grew between them as he shuddered against her body. Slowly, as though she was fragile and he feared breaking her, he straightened.

"Kay."

She followed the slow movement of his throat as he swallowed. The dull tiredness she'd seen in his eyes was gone. Now they almost burned with his desire. Tension radiated outward. Control hardened his entire length. "I need to leave. I won't force you back into my bed, and right now the only thing keeping me from ravishing that body for hours is a very thin thread of control."

Her fingers dug into his waist, her legs having turned to water ages ago. "Rush," she whimpered, "I've never felt this before." She closed her eyes as another wave made her body hum harder.

"Does it scare you?" Something softened in his expression, his tone washing over her with a blanket of understanding.

"A little, but I want it. I want you." Her eyes widened at the open admittance of her own needs. A heat that had nothing to do with wanting flooded her cheeks.

"Baby," he breathed, dipping to capture another kiss. "This is normal." He moved to whisper into her ear. "This *hunger*," he growled. Reaching for a hand, he cupped her and slid her palm over his pulsating cock. She licked her lips, unable to deny what he was doing to her. "This is only for you. No one else, ever again."

Her eyes sank shut and dots rose up in a swarm in front of her vision. Heat and scents flooded her, sweat coated her body and somewhere inside, a part of her cried out for him. Stubbornly refusing to put a voice to it out of fear made the dots glow and spin. She swayed, and he caught her.

With a single movement, he scooped her up and cradled her. He buried his nose against her throat as though unable to get enough of any part of her. Gently, he stretched her on her bed then stood. "Better?" he asked. She hardly recognized his voice. She couldn't find hers to answer him.

She didn't know how long she lay there, her world completely distorted as her body and her mind collided. One was filled with a gnawing need that cried for fulfillment, the other screaming with dire terror at what was happening and fearing every step of it.

At some point, she felt his hand holding hers, his thumb brushing over her as he'd done so many times in the past. Time flickered through her mind, knowing it was passing, but no concept of how long.

Eventually she whispered his name without opening her eyes, frightened that she would be alone now. She never wanted to be alone again.

"I'm here, princess." His weight moved on the bed and she turned toward that voice. Opening her eyes to the shadowy quiet of her bedroom, she found him laying along her length beside her, not touching, merely holding himself up with a palm to watch over her. Protecting her. Loving her.

Finding him there, that crack in her heart shattered completely apart.

The wrenched cry she made was soul shattering. Without an ounce of restraint, she threw herself into his hard body. He caught her, rolling beneath her. "Don't ever leave me. Don't ever let me be stupid like this again."

"Never baby," he agreed, nuzzling her, his arms wrapped around her body, cradling her into his chest. "You can do anything, think anything, but this will never end. I love you."

He dropped butterfly kisses over her face and down her neck, his breath sweeping through her hair in hot bursts with every caress.

Lying across his broad chest, one leg draped between his thighs, the hard press of his erection thickened beneath her weight. The solid pound of his heart thudded against her breast where she pressed into him.

"Rush?"

"Hm?" he answered, apparently very engrossed in his current mission of kissing every exposed inch within reach.

"I can. I want this. I want us," she whispered, tilting to feel the spark of his lips strike against her skin.

The kisses stopped, and he dropped back down to the pillow. "Do you love me?" he asked.

She blinked into the shadowy stillness of her bedroom, taking her time to really think about his question, to not lie, which was her first reflex, and not push him away. He deserved the truth, and an honest answer was the only way. The clock on her bedside table said it was just after midnight. Lowering her eyes, she picked at the hem of his sleeve between her fingers.

Did she love him? She thought she could, felt herself longing for something that she'd never come close to experiencing or wanting. Rolling to look into his eyes, her worries seemed lighter, maybe even easier to handle because she wouldn't be doing any of this alone. Lifting a hand, she traced his mouth with a finger. He gently kissed the tip, not demanding more, though she could see the lingering desire in his eyes, just waiting for the moment to flare to life again.

"I think I do," she whispered. "It still scares me."

Another kiss to her fingers. "I know it does, princess. I'll do whatever it takes to be here for you."

She let her lashes drop, lost in the sea of tossed emotions crashing over her. "Rush?"

"Yes?"

"Love me." Two words, so achingly quiet, and her own heartbeat drowned them out of her ears.

CHAPTER FIFTEEN

"KAISHA," he whispered, a groan that flitted like a sparrow between them. The lightest pressure of his fingers lifted her when he twisted his fingers into her hair to play with the length. "Never hide from me. If you want something, tell me. If you're mad at me, scream then tell me why, but please, never hide from me." He caressed her lips with his own with aching slowness, seducing her with his tongue.

"I don't know how to do this, Rush," she admitted. He kept her from turning away again.

"We'll both find our way."

His body heat enveloped her, and she felt truly, entirely safe.

Kay rose over him on her palms to see him better. The banked desire in his eyes was only a hint of what she knew he felt, and he was studying her as closely as she was him. The shadows that played around the room liked his features, the broader cheekbones and thick hair, giving him a mysterious aura. It was a stark reminder that there was more to him, to any person, than she'd given him credit for. Replaying the week they'd spent together in forced seclusion and mutual care, she knew she'd done more than shortchanged him. She'd been so intent on running first, far and fast that she'd blinded herself to what was really between them.

God help her, she was falling for him. Stroking his cheek with her palm, the rough bite of his beard shocked her nerves, making her tremble. Holding herself above him, she found his lips, kissing him the way she'd craved since he walked in the door. The sizzle of his fingers in her hair made her nerves stand on end. The masculine strength of his kiss was gentle, accepting, letting her find her way.

Allowing her go at her own pace, she traced his lip, sipping lightly on the full bottom one, loving their heat. A hot burst bathed her lips when she found his flesh between small teeth and nipped down on him.

An appreciative sound filled his throat, urging her for more. Holding his head between her hands, chest to chest, she covered his mouth, claiming him with her kiss, thrusting and dueling with lustful energy against his tongue. The entire length of his body beneath her grew taut, his cock pulsing through two layers of denim to burn her flesh. Instinctively, she rubbed up and down his body, purring with pleasure as her body heated and longing filled her.

The fingers in her hair massaged her while his other slid south to cup her ass. A firm squeeze made her groan. She loved the feeling of his hand cupping her body. Lava began to fill her veins.

Breaking away from her, he dropped kisses along her jaw, licking with abandon. "Sexy," he breathed.

With the strength of his hand on her ass, he guided her to straddle his hips, seating her directly over his cock.

"Oh." He groaned, his eyes closing in bliss. "Shit, Kay."

Harsh breaths made his chest rise and fall in quick patterns.

Trailing her hands down his chest, she purposely dragged her nails over his nipples, feeling the way they formed into hard little bullets. The hand in her hair slipped loose. He was at her mercy.

"I want you to strip for me," she told him.

Like he was drugged his eyes opened slowly. "And then what?"

"Guess you'll just have to find out," she said with a coquettish tilt of her chin and a smile. To tease him, she rocked back and forth over the bulge between her thighs and his head snapped back again. He was completely turned on and letting her run the show. It was a heady feeling. This was more than sex. More than anything she'd ever experienced.

Leaning forward, she flicked his ear. "Or you can just stay like this and I can leave you hurting."

"N-No," he gasped, shuddering beneath her weight because she'd captured one of his earlobes and given it a solid tug.

Sliding off his body, he rolled to the side of the bed. She removed her sandals, jeans and blouse, leaving on her underwear and bra, watching him strip with teasing slowness in front of her.

Skin peeked at her, first his abdomen, solid and lightly tan, with the hinted trail of hair diving for his bellybutton and further. Not a lot, just enough hair to lure her body, fingers and tongue. She licked her lips, wanting to taste him.

The t-shirt fell to the floor then he undid his jeans, a button at a time. Her pulse ticked harder. The slow pace was killing her, but she was loving it too much to make him hurry.

Denim dropped with a quiet whoosh and he kicked them off with his sneakers, his socks disappearing at the same time. Unbidden, or maybe uncontrollably, her gaze rose and stuck on the cock before her. She hadn't really taken the time to appreciate him fully before. The smooth head topped a thick, reddened shaft, a drop of moisture sitting on the tip. Deep black curls covered his balls, and as she watched him, they twitched and tightened, the length of his arousal bobbing as though trying to get her attention. She licked her lips again. He had her attention. All of it.

That is mine, she thought with a giddiness that took her by surprise. She'd never once thought of any guy she'd slept with as hers, had never wanted one like this. She wanted all of Rush. Glancing up, she found his eyes darkened by lowered lids and knew he was thinking the same thing. It was written like large print all over his face. He wanted her and only her.

"Lay down on your back, like you were."

Leaning over, he dropped a single kiss on her mouth then complied, no argument, no demanding to know why.

His absolute trust in her actions stole into her heart, mending another wound that had been long buried.

Lying like a sacrifice on top of her bed, he was gorgeous. "I'm all yours, baby."

Kay glided to the end of the bed, one hand curving over his leg. Rough hair slid under her palm as she worked her way upward. Kneeling between his legs, she alternated licking, kissing and caressing up his body. His body hardened and shuddered in intervals, especially as she got closer and closer to the shaft standing proud and hungry for her.

"Remember what you said about taste?" she asked him on a throaty sigh. A single-syllable groan was his answer. "You taste like the outdoors on the wind." Heated leaves and sweet earth. A musk that was all his. Licking his inner thigh, she decided she couldn't get enough of it.

Fists bunched the blankets at his waist. "Kay," he moaned. Leg muscles clenched and loosened with each lap of her tongue.

"What?" she asked him innocently, not lifting from her purpose.

"Want you," he gasped. She blew her breath across his groin, and he pulsed in answer. He was beautiful, thick and slick as satin with a steel center that created a heated vortex of need, making her pussy flutter with want.

She nipped at his thigh, her teeth grasping but not bruising. "What do I have to do to mark you?" she asked him. It was a leap to assume it went both ways, or that as a non-shifter, she would have the ability. It was also a leap into the unknown, a step of permanency that she hadn't thought she would want, but when speaking the words, she realized she wanted it all.

When he didn't answer for a long stretched minute, she wasn't so confident when she said, "Do I get to?"

He sat up, his expression unreadable. "Kaisha? That's a big step. I shouldn't have mark—"

"Never mind," she mumbled, sorry she'd brought it up. Spontaneity sucked.

"Baby, no. Don't do that." He lifted her by the chin to peer into her eyes. "I didn't mean it like that. I rushed you. I want your mark." He slashed stiff fingers through his hair. "Fuck, you don't know how much I want it."

"Is it something I can do?" She couldn't meet his gaze, fighting to hide the trembling she felt building. *Bad idea; it was just a bad idea.*

"Yes," he said, holding her face in his palm. Leaning forward, he captured her mouth. "Yes, Kay, I want your mark. Find a pressure point and bite down. You don't have to break the skin, just teeth marks. The rest happens between us naturally." Cautiously, she met his gaze. "But remember, once you do, you've given yourself to me. Right now it's only half done, giving us both time."

"What happens if I complete it?" She swallowed, listening.

"We are permanent. You remember how miserable you were without me?" She nodded into his palm. "Multiply it by about twenty. Long separations are next to impossible. I would need at least your voice."

"So, if I complete it, now, tonight, I have to move in with you?" Her heart stuttered then jolted back to life. The idea terrified her stiff, but the promise of what could come between them gave her just a smidge of strength to not turn away from the idea completely.

He nodded. "Think long and hard on it, baby. I can wait." Then with the sweetest kiss, he covered her lips, seducing her down to a molten molecule. "Now, please, finish what you started. I'm dying."

She giggled, the tension of her outburst suggestion dissipating with his wicked grin, showing her how much he desired her.

RUSH blinked to stop the swirling stars over his eyes. His body was on fire. His heart was racing, pounding to escape his ribs.

Kay wanted to finish the bonding, wanted to mark him. It was killing him to be rational about it. He wanted to scream to the rooftops, *Yes!* He was in shock that she'd come to the conclusion herself that it was a shared intimacy. The urge to push her into it, to have what was his, was blinding. Fighting it was killing him, but he wouldn't force her. He'd made a promise to her. He was thankful that she'd come this far. The fear that he'd lost her forever had been stone cold real until he'd come here tonight.

The finger-light stroke of her against his thigh snapped his head back and slammed his thoughts to a dead stop. Every inch of his body ached for her, burned for her touch. Warm breath surrounded his cock, and his spine shot straight. Her tongue twirled over the head like an ice cream cone, and he knew his eyes crossed.

Taking a deep breath, he cracked open his eyes and lifted his head to see her, to watch that succulent mouth devour him. "Oh, God, Kay." He moaned and hefted himself up on his elbows, clutching at the blanket to restrain his hands. Slim fingers wrapped around him, and his neck went slack with blissful pleasure. Low grunts were all he was capable of as she squeezed and sucked on him in rhythm.

Just as good as he imagined and so much more. Her tongue was a wicked tool, sliding around and over his flesh. He pulsed and thrust with little bumps of his hips, unable not to try to reach for more. When she pulled her hair out of her way, he almost lost it. The way her mouth captured him was erotic as hell.

There was a tentative stroke then her fingers fondled his sac, and he collapsed to the bed, boneless but harder than he'd ever been in his life. "Kay! I'm going to come!"

That seemed to only excite her more, and she doubled the pace of her driving mouth, sliding up and down his shaft like an overheated piston. He couldn't stop her, and he was helpless, so deliciously helpless.

The burn built, starting at the base of his skull. His body found her rhythm, meeting her with solid thrusts into the cavern of her mouth. Pleasure grew like a fireball, spinning wildly, rolling down his spine for her mouth. Ecstasy he'd never experienced set his nerves ablaze. All he could do was take her sweet punishment.

With a roar, the fireball hit his groin, exploding with bursts of pleasure that stole his breath as he pulsed his seed into her mouth. She took every thrust, every throbbing spurt until she'd licked him clean.

Gasping, he lay like a depleted balloon, empty and limp. Harsh breathing was the only sound in the room as tingles surged then faded down his limbs. With lithe movements, she shimmied up his body, dropping a light kiss on his chest then his cheek.

Turning, he found her mouth and kissed her hard. Thrusting his tongue into her sweetness, finding a hint of salt from his own orgasm, he didn't care. The only thing he wanted was her.

"Amazing," he told her, his hand finding the will to wrap over her side as she snuggled into him. He nuzzled against her, completely content.

"Don't worry, baby," he told her a few moments later when he could formulate complete sentences again. "That is only the beginning. You're not even naked yet."

"Oh?" she asked sweetly, turning that coy grin up to him. "You gonna do something about that?"

"Sooner than you think," he warned. Before she saw it coming, he tossed her off his shoulder and pinned her to the bed. Showing his teeth in a feral grin, he told her, "My turn."

"Oh, no! The big bad wolf is going to eat me," she cried in woeful theatrics.

"I think eating you is only going to be the first course," he replied, heat surging through his frame like an electrical current gone crazy. "Sexy as sin in lace." He knew he was going to enjoy unwrapping her over and over.

Lowering for a kiss, he said, "I love you, Kay."

She cupped his face holding him above her. He could see it in her eyes. It was there, but instead of pushing for it, he simply kissed her and loved her. All night long.

EPILOGUE

RUSH walked from the bathroom with a towel slung over his hips, finding the petite beauty waiting for him on the bed. Three months. He didn't know how he lasted through the waiting without exploding with impatience, but he had and now Kay sat on his bed, completely moved in and taking her place as the fem-alpha. Knowing she had expected contention from the pack because she wasn't a shifter, her ease of stepping into the roll was amplified when several of the couples welcomed her with open arms.

Sheridan had been her staunchest supporter, paving the way to introduce Kay. She had won over Rush's sister hands down when she'd stayed by his side while he healed. He had no idea what the two women talked about during those four days, and didn't want to know how many childhood secrets were divulged. Sheridan had found a new home of her own closer to the college last month, but was still close enough to harass her brother. Having her remain as his second, close, meant the world to him. The tight community of the pack was doing good things for Kay, too. He'd always known their support and always had family on some level. Kay's experiences had made her wary, but that was slowly changing, for the better, for the both of them.

She hadn't mentioned the marking again, and he wasn't going to push her. It wasn't a small gift or a returnable piece of clothing. The mark was forever. Leaning on his shoulder on the door, he believed he understood his mother better now, too. He'd never connected the strain of loss to the reasoning behind her death. More than likely, her passing hadn't even been a real choice. He promised to do better with Kay, and with Sheridan in the future, now that he had a better understanding after living through some of this himself. He wouldn't trade a minute of it, either.

"What are you smiling at?" she asked him, those gray eyes of hers teasing him from beneath a wealth of lashes.

"Just the most beautiful woman in the world," he replied, meaning it.

"Really?" She whirled on the bed. "Where is she? Maybe I can get some fashion tips."

He launched from the door and pinned her to the bed amid a cacophony of giggles.

Burying his nose into the creamy softness of her shoulder, he wrapped his arms around her and hung on tight. Rolling, they stopped on their sides facing each other.

"Rush," she said, with the sound of his name tugging his engrossed gaze up rather than following his meandering fingers on the tips of her breasts. Her nipples poked like pebbles beneath her nightshirt. Tight little pebbles that he wanted to suck and nibble like hard candy.

"Hm?"

"I want to complete it."

His hand froze as he locked on her gaze. He didn't pretend that he misunderstood. This was too important for those kinds of games.

"Now?"

Ducking her chin, she answered, "Well, tonight."

"You're positive?" His heart had lodged itself in his throat.

Nodding, she said, "I love you, Rush. It's time I stepped up, too." She smiled, her heartbreaking smile that made him feel like he was ten feet tall and bulletproof.

He blinked. "Wait. Did you say—"

Pressing light fingers to his lips and with laughter in her voice, she said, "Yes, I love you. I've known for a while, I think, but until I made up my mind about the mark, the significance wasn't concrete. It wasn't easy for me."

With a hand tucked through her hair, he drew her forward until her forehead touched his. "I know, baby. I believed in us, and I'm glad to know you do, too. If you're ready then, God, yes. Please."

A flicker of unease dampened her gaze. "I guess this means we're essentially married, then?" Her tongue sneaked out, trailing her lips. It was impossible to miss the hesitation and worry. It was written all over her face. Deep inside, he wanted to take her back to her childhood and remove all the scars she carried. Unable to do that for her, he promised from that day forward to love her in ways she'd always been denied. To love her the way she was meant to be, adored and cherished for the wonderful, beautiful soul that was Kaisha.

"It will be all right. You don't have to do it yet. I want you to be perfectly okay, perfectly comfortable with what it means, sweetheart." He stroked her with his thumb, waiting. When she didn't retreat, he explained with a soothing burred rumble, "If we do complete it then yes, all we need is the legal paper for everyone else, but for you and me and any of our kind, you are taken."

She nodded, a comfortable silence filling the room. A dark eyebrow arched a moment later. "How do they know the difference? Stacee isn't a shifter, but she knew immediately."

Rush chuckled, having wondered when she'd remember that. "It's because she's bonded with Jonas. As easily as they can tell she's taken, she can recognize any of us."

"Wow," she murmured in quiet awe.

"Do you want a big wedding?" Knowing how she felt about the idea of matrimony, he didn't want anything left unspoken between them. He caressed her jaw with a thumb. He'd give her anything she wanted to keep her happy.

"No. Just Stacee and Jonas and your sister are fine."

"Not your mom?" He wasn't going to push. It was her choice. Kay hadn't gone out of her way to introduce them yet, but she had told her mother she was in a serious relationship. The reaction had been less than ecstatic. A little part of him wanted to cry for the neglect she'd lived through and still had to deal with. Though his parents were gone, he'd never been without the knowledge that they'd loved him and Sheridan endlessly.

She let out a sigh. "Honestly, I don't know. I'll think about it."

"Okay." He sipped at her lips. With a hand on her hip, he tugged her flush to his frame. "You know, it would be a shame to waste that."

"That what?" she asked, confused.

"This," he growled, palming her ass to let his erection nestle between her thighs. He thrust in even motions, sliding up and down the barrier of her panties.

"Ooh, that," she crooned, her come-and-get-me grin returning. "I had no intention of wasting that." She winked. Then Rush's head snapped back on his neck because she had wrapped her fingers around the base of his shaft beneath the towel. "Ditch the towel, if you dare."

He dared. The towel was gone in nothing flat, leaving his body exposed for her pleasure, and his.

Seconds later she was as naked as he was, her pert breasts peaked with beautifully rosy nipples. He loved her body, loved everything about her. Trailing her trim length with his fingers, he stopped when he reached the heated essence of her pussy.

"Did you do something different?" The full nest of hair that he enjoyed playing with felt...shorter.

"I trimmed. Do you like it?" She bit her bottom lip, waiting for his answer.

Inching down her body, she spread her thighs, his fingers drifting over the edges of her labia so he could explore. "I love it."

"I almost decided on a full wax, but wanted to do a test first."

His breath hitched hard. He'd die if she did a wax. There was little left to say about how much he liked the new style when licking her juice off her skin seemed to say so much more.

She groaned, her hips rising to find more of him as he dipped and suckled at sensitive skin. Playing and stabbing at her clit made her writhe and moan wildly, her scent soaking into his senses with each inhale. He couldn't picture anything better than her lost in the pleasure he gave her. Thrusting deep with his tongue, Rush stroked her into her orgasm, continually amazed at how sensitive her body was to his touch. Licking her with slow swipes to feel her quiver beneath him, he then covered her smaller frame, resting for her to catch her breath.

"Rush," she moaned, pulling him closer. Gently, he speared her body, filling her inch by delicious inch. In moments, they'd found that perfect rhythm, her heat enveloping his cock as he drove her closer and closer to the edge.

Following the urging of her fingers, he wrapped his hands beneath her body and drove into her harder, deeper.

Her whimpers turned into full-throttle cries of ecstasy in seconds. His own orgasm was quickly barreling down on him. Heat and electricity swarmed through his blood like a lightning storm, striking with random explosions of ecstasy. Then, without warning, pain and pleasure ignited on his shoulder and he arched, stiffening as Kay completed the bonding. For a split second, his world went red then black as their souls merged completely. Nothing prepared him for the euphoria of knowing she was his, of her claiming him as her own. Driving into her softness, into her embrace, the nova that swept over him melted him from the inside out with love for her. Together, they shared his orgasmic high, carrying her with him as they both tumbled over the edge.

His heart screamed, ready to burst from his chest, and he finally remembered to breathe, shudders rocking his body as she clenched around him, around his shoulders, trying to absorb him in every way imaginable.

"I love you," she whispered, her lips caressing the shell of his ear, sending another shocked shudder down his body. He'd never tire of hearing those words in her voice.

"I love you too, princess." A contented sigh flowed over his flushed skin, and she snuggled in tighter beneath his shoulder. Wrapped in her arms, he drew her sweetness into his body, looking forward to doing the exact same thing for the rest of his life.

The End

Love's
Learning Curves

To Se, Mi, and Mina. To my awesome editor, DTJ.
To Traci, and her crazy blonde moments.
Sometimes they turn out better than you could ever dream.

CHAPTER ONE

DARIO slammed his desk drawer shut, annoyance thinning his patience. The doors to his office opened, and his uncle Antonio walked in. *Great.* He didn't bother to look up, fully aware of the reason for the visit.

"I'm not taking Muffy to the Spring Luncheon."

He yanked out another drawer, rifled through the contents and smacked it shut. *Still no damn keys. Where the hell did I leave them?*

Antonio's lips thinned. "She needs an escort."

"So? There's plenty of toys for her to choose from."

"That was crude," Antonio growled.

Dario shrugged. It was the truth. Antonio had been pushing him at Muffy for the better part of a year now. He wouldn't come out and say he hated her, but she sure as hell didn't do a damn thing for him.

Raking his hand stiffly through his hair, he said, "Look, Antonio, I know what you're doing, but it needs to stop."

"You're the heir," he ground out.

"Tell me something I don't know," Dario muttered without looking up at the other man. Louder, he snarled, "Where are my keys?"

A knock on his door snapped his attention to the front of his office. "Uh, D. I have your keys. Remember? I borrowed the car this morning."

Chance stood pensively at the front of the office, bouncing from one foot to the other, the missing key ring held aloft in his fingers.

"Shit, I'm sorry, Chance. I did forget. Did you get all your stuff done?"

"I did, but I need another favor."

Dario practically jumped for joy. Anything to get him out of his uncle's sight for the next five minutes. Standing, he leaned over and shut off his monitor, done for the day. Chance walked in. His younger cousin watched him with an apprehensive hopefulness. Dario, not his dad. *Go figure.* Dario adored Chance. Antonio, though a fair man, could be a bit brusque and cold, even toward his own son.

"Dad can't do it, but could you take me and Bethany to the State Fair this weekend? Her folks won't let her go unless we have an adult drive us." Chance grimaced, not that Dario didn't understand his angst. For seventeen, his cousin was a very level young man. He may have been considerably younger, but he respected Dario, looked up to him, so he made sure he did his best to treat him fairly.

"This weekend is the Luncheon," Antonio was quick to remind them both.

Somewhere in the ether of his imagination, Dario heard the hallelujah chorus and bells. "I'd be glad to, Chance. Have her folks come to my place to meet me and we'll leave from there. Good?"

"You rock!" Chance tossed him the keys and shot out of the office.

Antonio fumed. "Dario."

"Sorry. I have plans, Antonio." He managed not to grin like the Cheshire cat with that announcement. Just barely.

"If your father knew you were skirting your duty..."

Dario choked. "He doesn't expect me to dance to his tune, Antonio. Why can't you do the same?"

"Because at least one of us in this family, in this pride, has to take it seriously."

Dario narrowed his eyes at Antonio's clenched fist, his stormy features. "Be very careful how you malign Dad, Antonio. You know as well as I do, he's doing a damn fine job. Just because

I won't give your prize protégé the time of day doesn't mean I'm *not* doing *my* duty."

When his uncle would have said more, Dario stopped him with a sharp head shake. "Antonio, it's almost Friday. Dad and Mom will be back in time for the Luncheon Saturday. I'm not even needed. Muffy will be fine with whoever she chooses to attend with her."

"It would look better to the other prides if you were present, *and* with a respected date."

Dario stifled his groan. *Respected my ass. More like claws in waiting.* He didn't bother to reply; instead leaving his uncle standing in the office, knowing if he didn't, Antonio would only continue to needle him over the situation. The answer was clear.

He wasn't going to the Luncheon, and he wasn't going to court Muffy.

———

Shrieks and squeals of laughter filled the air. Hard packed dirt gave way to little tufts of grass along the edges of the causeways where the rock borders met the grounds. Music blared through the air as they passed another carnival ride going full speed, to the screamed enjoyment of the riders. Sheridan froze and rose up on her toes as an enthusiastic herd of kids ran past her, charging for their next adventure. Dropping to her feet, she laughed and shook her head, taking the near stampede in stride. It was all a person could do in the chaos that was the State Fair.

"Lose any toes?" Kay asked, grinning.

Sheridan wiggled them in her sandals. "Nope, all intact." Glancing at her brother, Rush, and Kay, his wife of five months, she asked them, "So what are you two up for now?" Stacee and Jonas caught up to them, sharing dyed sugar on a stick. Cotton candy sweetened the air.

"If it spins, I'll pass," Stacee offered. "I can't handle vertigo, especially loaded on sugar."

Jonas wrapped a hand around her waist. A very slight bulge showed the beginning signs of her pregnancy beneath her clothing. Sugar and baby. Sheridan didn't blame her for passing.

Up ahead, the line for the Ferris wheel wasn't too long. She motioned with a hand flip. "How about that?"

"I don't know," Stacee balked, looking a little green at the idea. The baby had been kicking her ass from the inside out. She hadn't handled a whole lot of the fair as of yet, but the day was young.

Jonas pressed a kiss to her forehead. "It's okay. We'll come again when Junior is old enough and you can show him how tough you really are." He was grinning while he said it, mischief painted clearly on his face.

"Her," she stated succinctly. "I'm telling you, her." Then she stuck her tongue out. It was blue.

"Well, I want to go," Sheridan said. When it looked like none of the four were going to team up with her to ride the wheel, she said, "This won't take long. Don't go far."

"We'll be over at the water guns," Rush said, pointing to a standalone booth. "You up for it?" He challenged Jonas with a show of teeth, not meaning anything, except maybe a test of pride. Considering the two's personalities, and their initial meeting, they got along really well.

"Men," Stacee mumbled.

"Alphas," Kay agreed, and then all three women giggled. "Don't worry. We won't leave you."

Sheridan sighed, the only sign of her exasperated frustration with their persistence. "I'm fine. Really."

"We know," Rush was quick to point out. "Just taking care of my sis." He jostled her toward the line. "Go. I don't want to beat him more than twice." He stated that with a definite evil gleam in his eyes, rolling a shoulder in Jonas's direction. Jonas snickered and said rude comment back.

Ignoring their byplay, she refrained from grumbling. Ever since Brant asked Mona to marry, everyone had been treating her like spun glass. Big deal. So they'd only dated for six weeks when he'd asked. So her ex chose someone else, after spending more than two years with Sheridan. Time to move on. It was just a large pill to swallow when Mona was also a classmate and only too willing to brag and rhapsodize over their wonderful relationship.

Turning on a heel, she left the four behind her. Standing in line, she drew a breath through her nose to calm her ire. She wasn't mad at *them*. Not really. She knew they had her best interests at heart. So what if Brant had practically begged her to set him up with Mona after they'd broken up? So what if it had worked out that well for them? It wasn't like he was ever around for her. He couldn't even find the time to come to Rush's wedding. It wasn't a huge event, just family at the Justice of the Peace. Brant simply couldn't be bothered to break his routine and schedule for one Saturday. Honestly, she hadn't expected he would to begin with, but it had been the last straw. After watching Kay and Rush, Sheridan knew she was ready for something more. Brant had taken the out rather than the commitment.

What did sting was the fact that Mona was a size six on her worst day. Perfect breasts, lush blonde hair, and robin egg blue eyes. Every man's Katherine Heigl fantasy. With blue eyes. The epitome of what Sheridan wasn't. That felt like a slap to the face, and her family's insistence on coddling her only made it harder to shake it all loose. She really didn't care that he'd chosen to marry Mona. What stung was the apparent differences between the two of them, because even in her dreams, Sheridan wasn't a six.

"The line is moving," a gruff voice murmured near her ear.

"Oh! Sorry." Coming out of her thoughts, she closed the distance.

"Are you riding alone?"

Sheridan blinked and looked over her shoulder. And almost gasped at the intense set of eyes she found. Melted brown sugar, or better yet, deep clover honey. Either way, they were stunning. "I am."

He grinned with a low chuckle. "Do you mind if I ride with you? I'm going up to see if I can spot my cousin, but I feel weird sitting alone." Tilting his head with an owl blink of realization, he added, "And that would be the lousiest pick-up line ever, if I weren't telling the truth."

"Really? Not a pick-up line?" She laughed when he actually glanced away, apparently with a hint of embarrassment.

With a short shrug, he asked, "Why are you riding alone?"

Sheridan waved down the fairgrounds. "One of our group is pregnant and not handling the rides too well. I don't mind doing this one alone. I love the views."

A long silence fell between them, his eyes staring into hers for breathless seconds.

"I agree."

Though the way he said it, an intense purr between them, made her think he wasn't talking about the viewable sights from the top of the wheel. That *did* sound like a pick-up line.

"In fact, I think I'd love to sit with you," he said. "If you're okay with it?" He waited expectantly.

Sheridan knew there were all kinds of warnings she should be heeding at the moment, but with those golden bronze eyes watching her, honest and open, it was hard to really listen, harder to care. And really, what could he do? He'd never escape, especially with her brother a scream away. The last thing she was feeling was threatened. Finally, she agreed.

He stood straight and handed over enough tickets for the both of them. "This one is on me." The attendant opened the swing gate and allowed them to enter the swaying bucket of the ride.

She wasn't uncomfortable, but she knew an alpha when she saw one. He wasn't wolf. That much she was positive of.

He inched closer, though he didn't crowd her on the seat. "I promise; I'm looking for my cousin. He came with his girlfriend, and he isn't answering his phone." The bucket pitched and jerked as the rotation paused and started for new riders.

"What does he look like?" She searched beneath them as they gradually made their circuit, rising higher.

"Brown hair, average height. He's wearing jeans, and a green t-shirt. Bethany is a willowy blonde. I think she was in shorts."

"Does he tuck in his shirts?" she asked, studying the grounds below them.

"Doubt it. He's seventeen."

"A hat? Is that him?"

Her ride partner shook his head. "No. No hat." He gave her a smile. "Great eye though." He leaned on his forearm on the edge of the cup's rim, his gaze sweeping the grounds that they could see. "What's your name?"

"Sheridan."

He offered a hand. "Dario." The flesh of his palm was smooth and warm, confident in her grasp. The sunlight streaked off his eyes like fireworks. He didn't rush to release her hand. "Don't I know you?"

She calmed her erratically beating heart with a slow drawn breath and a lot of effort. His palm held hers in an easy grip. She could pull free, if she wanted. It wasn't his hold that was making her blood race; it was the way he was looking at her. Like he wanted to lick her and then devour her, and then maybe lick her all over again.

It took two tries to find her voice. "I don't think so."

"No, I know I do. I've seen you somewhere."

Tilting her head, she examined his face. A twinge of recognition snaked over her spine. But from where, was the question. "Your eyes," she whispered. He nodded.

"I know. You had your hair up." Reaching carefully, he swept it behind her ear, watching the motion thoughtfully. "I'm positive of it."

She fought to remember where she could have been in the last year. Nowhere. With a shake of her head, she explained, "The last place I had a need to dress for the occasion was for Jonas's commendation banquet." The ginger-orange colored bucket swayed as the wheel stopped, leaving them at the very top.

"South Lake?"

She nodded.

"That's it!" He was nearly beaming. "Almost two years ago, right?"

Sheridan barely remembered seeing any particular face, since the whole evening had been a blur of jokes, teasing and tears for Stacee's husband. "He received honors for busting a federal case. That case was how he met Stacee."

"My parents were invited guests, so I went, too. You were at a full table, but there was a time or two..." Dario's voice drifted away, his attention focused on where he held her as though sifting through those memories. All she felt was the gentle stroke of his thumb on the top of her hand. Each unconscious motion sent tingles up her arm. "I saw you, and all I wanted was to know who you were. By the time I could get away, you were nowhere to be found." Rising, he captured her eyes in the golden halo of his own. "Are you married?"

She shook her head.

"Dating?"

A twinge of hurt snuck up on her, but she answered him honestly. "No. Why?"

"Because I wanted to ask you to go out with me tomorrow. You're here with friends, or I'd offer to make this an impromptu date. My cousin asked me to bring him and Bethany. He didn't mention how hard it would be to keep them close, or that they'd purposely ditch me not ten minutes inside the gates."

"Come with us," she offered, then blushed at her forwardness. She cleared her throat. "I'm usually not this impulsive."

"But..." he prodded. Humor made his eyes glow.

What she wanted to say took her by surprise. That she wanted to get to know him better, that he had amazing eyes, that her heart seemed to have developed an unnatural pace since he'd clasped her hand. Just staring at him, his eyes, his lips, was making her feel odd. She couldn't tell him any of it. Instead, she explained, "Because there's no fun in walking this place alone. Besides, who are you going to make faces at in the fun house?"

His smile broadened. "Promise me tomorrow, and I'll stay as long as you want the company today."

Suddenly the ride came to a stop, and the safety gate was unlatched, disrupting their conversation.

With a shared laugh, they both realized they'd completely forgotten to keep looking for Dario's cousin.

CHAPTER TWO

DARIO could barely contain his cougar. Twice the damn beast had head rammed his solar plexus since he'd walked up behind the curvy beauty. Black hair that sparkled like wet ink in the sunlight flowed in rich, heavy waves and curls down Sheridan's back. Then she'd turned around and flashed those blue-hazel eyes, and he began to understand the insistence. She had the most incredible eyes, the first thing to grab him completely when she looked at him. Dark blue, with slashes of honey brown and dove gray surrounded by thick onyx lashes. *Remarkable.*

Luscious and stunning, she had a sweet, rich voice and a slightly plumped bottom lip, giving her a natural pout. For a few seconds, when they'd stood talking, the only thing he could think, as his brain short-circuited, was how much he wanted to nibble on that lip and discover how she would taste. The temptation of her kiss was only the very beginning while she spoke. He wanted to devour that bewitching mouth. It was all too easy to picture her riding his cock, those sweet lips wrapped around him as he thrust between them. His heart pounded in answer to the rush of raw desire.

He kept his own lips closed with a forceful control, stifling the groan as he walked with her to meet whomever; he assumed the group she'd mentioned earlier. There was no way he was letting her out of his sight twice.

Holding her hand in his sent his blood pulsing wildly through his body. It wasn't a lie that he'd been looking for Chance and Bethany. The only small white lie was that it had to be at exactly that minute. Even with Chance ignoring his phone, Dario was their ride home. No way was that kid going to disappear and risk the wrath of his father while on a date.

Dario had spotted Sheridan getting into line and quickly fell in behind her, hoping for just a moment to talk to her. He was practically drooling, and he doubted she had any idea by how much.

As a male, he loved a woman with curves, with a body he could hold, touch and feel. She would fit perfectly against him, resting right under his chin if she'd only leaned back a few inches to meet his chest. His arms had twitched to reach around her and mold her to him.

Dario wanted a passionate woman, and knew from the fire and heat he'd fleetingly captured in her eyes, she was passion untapped. Cut-out females weren't in the least sexy, or the least appealing to him. A sheet of wood was more arousing. There was little doubt the woman walking at his side, curled within his finger's grasp, aroused himself *and* his cougar. Sheridan wore cute denim shorts, a summery yellow blouse and sandals that strapped over each foot. Modest was what came to mind. Devilishly enchanting for the right beholder.

She had sweet, delicate skin all along her jaw. He'd almost lost his control when he'd leaned in to whisper to her in line, her scent so intoxicating, so fresh; a clear mountain stream woven through the enticing allure. That single drawn scent had his cougar yowling. Even now, he was pacing back and forth within, impatient, but for what, Dario didn't know. It wasn't something he could take care of right at that second anyway.

The last thing he had expected was for her to be the woman he'd seen at the banquet. Now he could barely contain the rising heat and needs zinging through his blood. He'd *known* then she would be someone special, but he'd lost his chance that night. This was the best unexpected surprise he could have ever hoped for.

"There they are," she stated, gratefully bringing him back to the Fair and all its noise.

Looking ahead, he spotted two couples. Not surprisingly, both of the men were watching him with distrust and suspicion. With a light squeeze to her hand, he let hers slip away, settling a palm to her spine instead. He couldn't let her go completely.

He'd even face her two guard dogs to make sure he didn't lose her twice.

"Do they bite?" he asked, only half-joking. He feared they did.

"They're both in law enforcement."

He slowed. "Wait. Promise me tomorrow first. You didn't give me an answer."

"Worried they'll run you off?" she asked with a cheeky grin tipping the corners of her mouth.

He stopped walking and with a finger to her chin, lifted her face. "No, more worried I'll leave and never see you again. I saw you once before and it took two years for luck to be on my side again." He bit his cheek to shut his trap. He'd almost blurted how badly he wanted to kiss her. Watching the sun sparkle in her eyes, the gentle slope of her lips, it was all he could do *not* to kiss her.

He'd thought she'd been beautiful a room away. Standing in front of her, he was enchanted.

"You better have a good reason to be touching my sister," a voice threatened just beyond his shoulder.

"Rush," she interjected with a sharp exasperation. "Chill. Dario, my brother, Rush." She pursed her lips at the man behind him as she said it. Being intelligent, Dario let his hand fall, though he hated to have to do it.

He turned and faced the firing squad. Rush looked a lot like his sister. There was no doubting the family resemblance. "Dario Acardi," he said, offering his hand. Introductions continued until Sheridan intervened.

"I invited him since none of you are willing to hit the rides. He's not an ax murderer," she stated clearly for her brother's sake.

"D! Dario."

He swiveled on a hip and spotted Chance and Bethany jogging up to him. "What's up?"

"We're gonna do lunch, if that's okay?" Chance slid a glance around the group, but dismissed them when none of them were family.

"Do you need money?"

Chance looked insulted and Dario almost smacked himself. *"Dispiace. Ho dimenticato."*

"Grazie."

With a nod, Dario told them, "Go ahead. Just remember to keep your phone on." A final, stern reminder. He wasn't going to hunt through the grounds in a few hours because his cousin wanted space with his girlfriend.

"Will do." With a brief acknowledgment to those fanning around Dario, Chance turned and guided Bethany back to the concessions.

"What was all that about?" Sheridan asked.

"That's who I'm chaperoning. Sort of. Chance got a job last year, and I forgot he would have his own money. He still borrows my car. At least he puts gas in it when he does."

"So it wasn't a pick up line after all," she teased him. Mirth made the splashes of color in her eyes sparkle.

"Nope."

It seemed to be a tacit agreement when everyone turned to start walking, though they were obviously strolling to make it easy for them to keep up. She slipped a hand into his.

"Come on," she urged him with a quiet hint. "They're just protective."

He could easily see that. What made him happier was she didn't try to take her hand back as they walked with the other two couples. His cougar rolled over and basked, content for the first time since he'd walked up behind her.

Crazy cat, he thought.

"I think I do remember you," she murmured a few minutes later. "Someone at your table gave a speech."

"My dad." Even though she remembered his dad more than him, it still made him tingle that she'd placed him. "If I remember right, you wore a powder blue gown."

She twitched, looking up at him with wide eyes. "I think I did." She breathed a laugh. "I'm shocked you'd remember that."

"You were stunning. How could I not notice you?"

A warmed tint hued her cheeks. "Thank you."

Giving her hand a squeeze, he asked, "So what do I have to do for you to say yes?"

"Yes?"

"To tomorrow. I'm desperate for brownie points," he teased, liking the way she laughed. She bobbed a shoulder, giving him the signal to do his best. "Okay." Dario thought for a moment. "How about a gondola ride in Venice?"

She gasped. "You're kidding, right?"

"Yes." He reached and tapped her nose. "I'll save that for the second date."

Her laugh was robust and carefree, drawing curious peeks from those ahead of them.

"So what do you say? Don't you want to know what I have planned for the first date?"

She slipped him a glance from beneath her lashes. "Okay. You win. You've definitely made me curious."

"Wonderful," Dario whispered. His chest swelled, as he thought ahead to the evening he'd have this beautiful woman at his side, especially without the suspicious looks from her friends and brother. It's a good thing he did have a clean record. He had little doubt Rush would know his entire life's history by that same time tomorrow.

CHAPTER THREE

DARIO drew a deep breath. Sitting in his car outside her front door, he felt like a teenager picking up his date. The fun he'd had the day before with Sheridan had been unreal, and so unexpected. After anticipating watching over Chance and Bethany with only marginal enthusiasm, considering how quickly they'd vanished into the crowds, his day had improved dramatically as soon as he met Sheridan. Even Stacee and Jonas had warmed up as the afternoon had worn on, though Dario wasn't sure where he stood with her brother. He hadn't proved himself yet.

It was an afternoon of frustration and enjoyment. The enjoyment had definitely been due to her. The frustration was all about his cougar. If he strayed from her, the feline grew agitated. At one point, an operator had flirted with her at one of the booths to get her attention to play his ring games. Dario's cougar had gone berserk. He wouldn't be at all surprised to find needle-sized holes in his innards from the claws that had held on, just waiting for the chance to break free. When Dario had denied his cat the chance to filet the young man in question, his cat had hissed—the first time in his life that he'd ever hissed *at* Dario. Needless to say, he was at his wit's end over his cat's behavior.

What is your problem?

A single thud reverberated between Dario's ears when his cat rammed his solar plexus. *I let you run last night,* he groused with annoyance. *I can't let you out now. You need to behave, at least for tonight. I'll let you run more later, okay?* he cajoled. Begged was more like it.

At least this time there was no sharp spike of pain, rather an impatient pacing.

With a sigh, Dario got out of his car and walked to her front door. A lower floor apartment in a nice, secure community. The sound of locks on the inside reached him through the wood following his knock. She guarded herself. He found the knowledge actually relaxed him a little.

It didn't last.

Sheridan appeared before him, barefoot, in jeans and a blouse, with her hair down around her shoulders in a thick, onyx sheet of looping waves. Claws ripped at his ribs, and he sucked in a breath. *Please, stop,* he pleaded. His cougar was adamant. It wanted her.

"Are you okay?" She canted a hip, watching him with distress-shadowed eyes. "You look like you're in pain."

"Yeah." He forced a calmer expression, literally putting a palm to his cougar's face and shoving him down. *Let me do this or we're both going to lose.*

The seriousness wasn't lost on his cougar. He crouched, attentive, but silent.

"Phantom muscle pains," he said, winking. "You look adorable." Forcing air into his lungs to think, he admired her, taking in her full breasts and waist, curvy hips and long legs. Her top was a print floral pink something with a ribbon threaded down the front, an innocent appeal worn by a dark-haired siren. The things he wanted to do with that ribbon... His heart thudded into his ribs when the thought happened. The jeans she wore clung to her, leaving nothing to the imagination. He was practically salivating. She was heaven in denim. *Perfect.* For once, he and his cat were in perfect harmony.

"Come on in," she invited. "I just need to grab shoes."

"Take your time." Following the sway of her hips as she left him sent a jolt of lust soaring through him. If he could keep his hands off of her for the rest of the evening, it would be a miracle. He'd been a gentleman and hadn't even tried to kiss her yet. Watching her walk away, he decided that was something he was going to rectify by the end of the evening, multiple times.

Waiting, he took a moment to study her apartment, searching for anything to help take his mind off her lush shape. The woman had more peaks and valleys than the Alps, and he wanted to caress and taste every single one.

He had to admit, he loved the space and the location where she lived. New and still unblemished apartments, up-scale without seemingly being too trendy. Designed with thick, sandstone colored carpet and wood accents. She'd added a little to it to mark it as hers, but she'd let a lot of the natural design highlight the spaces with the high ceilings and molding.

It was large for a one-bedroom. There was a study where he noticed her computer. The bedroom was tucked around the corner where he could hear her moving around. With a searching glance, he was glad, rather selfishly, that she didn't seem to have a thing for pink, or laughably, kittens.

While he waited, he noticed she'd left a stack of mail on her kitchen break counter. Not meaning to snoop, a single envelope still caught his attention. Nearing, on the very top of the pile, was an embossed card. A wedding invitation, dated for the following weekend. Did she have a date? Was she going?

"Ready," she said, reappearing from the bedroom. She'd added stylish boots to her outfit and finished it with a thin-strapped purse she slipped over a shoulder. With a hand to her spine, he waited for her to lock her door then helped her get settled into the car. A final warning to his cougar and he rounded the car. For once, he prayed his cougar would listen; otherwise it was going to be a very tense evening.

* * *

SHERIDAN was going to have to talk to Rush, and soon. For some reason, her wolf was whining. A lot. She'd never had this problem before. She didn't even know what was causing the animal to rise into her subconscious. Most of the time she was quiet, a silent, strong-willed beast. She had to be with Rush as her Alpha. They'd fought plenty growing up, but no two were tighter, either.

Studying Dario, she remembered he hadn't once let her hand go the day before. Though, when he was talking with the others, she'd had a chance to breathe, which had become a difficult task. Every now and then, he'd bumped against her, thigh to thigh or hip to hip and her heart had leaped at the contact. The tingles she'd first encountered within his grip had never dissipated, even without the shocking punch of when he'd first shaken her hand. It had remained more like a pulsing current between them.

Her wolf seemed genuinely curious, though cautious about the man sitting in the car with her. She'd taken a minor interest in a few of her dates, though very little in Brant. She'd simply assumed that was the way it was. The gene was male dominant. Women shifters didn't have the capacity to share the gene. Sheridan knew it was to keep from creating a 'mule', in their terms. Rather than a horse-jackass hybrid, a wolf and God only knew what, because though they didn't cross paths often, the wolf packs weren't the only shifters around.

The constant whining ring between her ears, though? That was new.

Her attention was tugged from the scenery and her tumbling thoughts when he asked, "Do you have plans for next weekend?"

She drew a breath, stifling the sour wave that roiled through her stomach. "Unfortunately."

"Oh?" Dario arched an eyebrow, making a right turn into a restaurant parking lot. They'd agreed to keep it casual since the next day was a work day for him and a school day for her.

"I have a wedding I *should* go to."

"Should? Don't you want to go?"

Not really. Steeling herself, she admitted, "It's my ex-boyfriend's wedding."

"Damn," he breathed. "That's ballsy." The Mercedes hummed, sliding easily into a spot where he turned it off.

She chuckled. "He didn't invite me. The bride did. She's a classmate."

He blinked. "Wait." He paused, turning in his seat to see her better. "Okay, let me get this straight. Ex-boyfriend for how long?"

"We broke up right after the holidays."

"Dated?"

"For a little more than two years."

He snarled. "And he had the audacity to date a classmate of yours?"

Her laughter was lighter. "It gets better. He asked me to introduce them." She leaned on her shoulder, pleasantly warmed at his anger on her behalf.

Dario rubbed his eyes with stiff fingers. "Next weekend. Shit." He cursed lowly. "Just how long did they date before he asked her, if the wedding is next weekend?"

"Six weeks." She laughed fully when his mouth popped open. "It's okay. Really. I'm over him. I think I was expecting the end."

He curled one of her hands into his. "Why? You're beautiful, fun, ambitious, smart. What could he want that you didn't have? Because to me, he's a fool."

She froze, swept away by his declaration and compliments. Sheridan knew deep inside why. Granted, now that they'd separated, she'd realized she didn't love him, but part of it was she really wasn't what Brant had wanted in a woman. He was the second strike. Luc had been the first, but... She refused to dwell on him at all. In the end, they'd both found her lacking for the same reason, or maybe 'lacking' wasn't the right word. It was more an overabundance.

The warmth of his palm cupped her chin, bringing her focus to him. "Sheridan, you're amazing. If he couldn't see that, then it is his loss."

Her pulse pounded against her skin. The heat in his tawny gold eyes made them glimmer. He leaned forward, cresting the console between them. With both hands touching her, she felt electric, drawn to him like a moth to a flame.

"I'm going to kiss you, sweetheart," he murmured.

He stopped moving forward, a breath from her lips. She felt the rush of his exhale as he waited, gave her a chance to deny him, or stop him.

Sheridan didn't want to.

Her fingers tightened over his palm. Dario erased the distance between them. It was like she was reliving her very first kiss. He didn't plunder, he caressed. He didn't demand; he lingered. Gentle whips of his tongue sent desire curling through her. He purred when she dipped, wanting more.

A brush of his lips left her seeking for more when he rose from her. After opening her eyes, the banked hunger in his gaze made her shiver with need.

"Soon, lovely." He pressed his forehead to hers. "What I want shouldn't be done in a car, in front of a restaurant." Hot breath whisked over her ear when he slid against her to whisper, "What I want to do is devour you, one sweet kiss at a time. I want to hear you scream my name. I've wanted your kiss since that first look." Sheridan shivered at the underlying promise in those words.

With a kiss to the fingers of the hand he held, he let her go, releasing first her seatbelt then his own. "Don't move."

Dazed, she didn't. Hopping from the car, he strode to her door and opened it, helping her out with an offered hand. With an arm locked around her waist, Dario made it clear she was with him.

Chapter Four

THEY were waiting on the change from the check, when Dario made his offer.

"Let me take you to the wedding."

She absently waved her fingers in dismissal. "Oh, you don't have to."

He caught her hand, wrapping her snugly between both of his. "I know I don't have to. I want to." The idea had been taunting him all through dinner. He'd seen the hurt in her eyes earlier. It didn't matter that she was over him. There was something about it all that had wounded her. Whether it was the breakup, or knowing who the bride was, he wasn't sure. But he'd be damned before he'd let anyone hurt this woman ever again.

"Think of it as just desserts. He's apparently over you enough to marry this other woman barely months after having a long term relationship with you." Immediately, he could've kicked his own ass, as her eyes dimmed and she dropped her gaze to the tabletop. He hadn't meant to put the pressure on her that it was her fault that he'd jumped into this other relationship.

"Damn," he breathed. "I didn't mean—"

"It's okay. I know why he was willing to accept the split." She traced a tile on the table without looking up. "Believe it or not, I broke up with him. I was hoping for a deeper commitment, but he took the out instead." A shrug of nonchalance was a blatant smokescreen to her real emotions.

"Why? I meant what I said. You're one of the most amazing women I've ever run across."

A pleased blush deepened her cheeks even as she denied it. "I'm not. I'm too tall, too big. I'm heavy in the chest." She was speaking quietly, keeping the conversation private, and he had to lean across the table to catch the words. What he heard took him a second to digest.

"Wait. Are you saying you're fat?"

Her lips thinned. Her lashes kept her eyes completely hidden now.

"Bullshit," he bit out. Grabbing the purser packet, he ripped out a ten to toss on the table and took the rest, shoving it in a pocket unconcerned. He grasped a wrist with a firm circle of loose fingers to not hurt her, but he refused to sit there and let her talk about herself that way.

Careful to not rush her, he purposely kept her close, half afraid she might suddenly bolt. Stopped outside his car, he told her, "Let's finish this discussion at your apartment, okay?"

She made a sound, as if it didn't matter. *So she's the stubborn, quiet type, huh?* Lucky for her, she'd met her match.

It took them only twenty minutes to be standing outside her door. Her entry light illuminated her space in the breezeway. She unlocked it, but faced him instead of continuing through. "Look, Dario, I really appreciate the offer, and dinner—"

"Open the door. I'm not leaving until we've talked."

She groaned, then lifting her gaze, shoved the door inward. "Fine."

The door closed with a resounding note of determination. "Now then, let me make this clear." She dropped her purse on the kitchen break bar as if she couldn't run fast enough. There was limited space to run, though. He followed her and turned her around. She refused to meet his gaze. "You are not fat. You're beautiful. Is that why he left?"

Sheridan tried to play it off to be of no consequence with an evasive, dismissive tone. "I can assume so. Mona is everything I'm not."

Right there, he wanted to strangle her ex. "What? Is she smarter?"

She blinked, as though surprised that would be the first thing he'd pick on.

"Is she wittier?"

Her mouth popped open, but no sounds emerged.

"What then? Because I don't see the faults that apparently you think you have."

She glared at him. "Jesus! Do you want me to spell it out for you?"

She was even more stunning when she let her fire take over. The different colors in her blue hazel eyes almost danced as her heat rose, making them spark like roman candles. Dario moved up close enough to crowd her. He caged her front while the bar blocked her back.

"Tell me, and we'll see."

"I'll never be able to wear a bikini. I have hips the size of Mount Rushmore and a chest that makes Shamu look tiny. I'm a size sixteen. In other words, not perfect."

He did the only thing he could think of. Grabbing her forearms, he slammed his mouth down on hers to stop her. Sheridan would slap him unconscious if she had even an inkling of how much he wanted to take advantage of her cleavage. Sliding his cock between her lush mounds had been one of his best dreams last night. And don't even get him thinking about her mouth. Erotic inspiration started with just her lips. Every time he'd looked at her, he'd found himself drawn, like a bee to flower petals, to her lips.

Instead, he drove his tongue into sweet heaven, imagining her taste in all the places he wanted to explore. He reached deep and plied her tongue alongside his, making her mold tighter against his chest. His heart pounded as, this time, he took everything he'd wanted in the car, and then some.

Rising when he had no choice but to let them both breathe, he told her, "Let me tell you what I see. I see a woman a man can hold. One who won't break if loving turns into passion. I see curves and beauty. Do you have any idea how much sleep I got last night?"

She trembled beneath his hands, but managed to shake her head, wide eyes watching him without blinking.

"Two hours. It took that long to convince my body to come down from wanting you. I left the Fair with a hard-on and didn't lose it until after three this morning. And not because I took care of it. All I could think of was how much I wanted you." He'd had to take a nap just to function. He sucked air through a clenched jaw, calming the raging beast in his blood. "Damn, woman. You drove me insane yesterday and you never even knew it." Leaning into her softness, he showed her exactly how she affected him, rubbing the aching ridge of his cock against her stomach, wishing he could do more. Wishing he could drive into her welcoming body and stay there. "Tell me. Do you really think I could fake that?"

His voice evened out, the passion she'd stirred morphing into real desire instead of anger. "Sheridan, sweetheart. You are perfect. You're my kind of perfect. Never in my life has a skinny beanpole even made me look twice. A nice set of tits, okay. I'm a guy, but honey. You...are...beautiful." He leaned forward until his forehead rested on hers. "Being able to wear a bikini is a stupid bar to set. Have you seen what some women who wear them *really* look like? Most of them shouldn't be allowed outdoors, but they do it anyway, and it's not a sexy look."

She giggled, her eyes widening.

"So tell me again why I shouldn't escort you next weekend. Are you over him?"

"Completely."

"And you're friends with the bride?"

"Not best friends, but yeah, we spent a lot of time up until him on class work together."

He lowered and nipped at her bottom lip. When she arched to give him her mouth, he claimed her offering. Slipping an arm around her shoulders and the other around her waist, any space between them vanished, chest to chest, lifting her as close as he dared to his own body. Every part of him wanted to make love to her right there. His cougar was crying for more. His body was aching for release. His lungs burned as he tried to breathe around the onslaught of hungers.

It was with a will of steel that he controlled it all.

Panting heavily, he teased her lips, letting her go slowly as he tried to think above the screaming urges pummeling him.

"Then let me show him what he lost, that I'm so grateful for because there isn't a doubt I'm ever letting you go. He can't have you back, either." Grinning evilly, he even knew how he could make the other man eat crow for ever making Sheridan feel like she was less of a woman. Like she wasn't beautiful, or perfect.

Dario was going to treat her like a princess and love every minute of spoiling her rotten.

CHAPTER FIVE

DARIO picked up his phone on his desk Tuesday afternoon. "Acardi."

"I need you this weekend."

He rolled his eyes, straightening regretfully in his chair. "Hello, Muffy."

She purred. Sadly, her cougar only put his to sleep. Not that he could ever tell her that. She'd be insulted, and likely claw him to shreds. In fact, his cougar was actually turned off by Muffy. She thought she was the cat's meow, all blonde perfection. She'd be appalled to learn she did nothing for him. His cougar rolled over in utter disinterest with his thoughts on the blonde.

Giving the bid on his desk a lingering look, preferring it to the woman on the other end of the phone, he explained, "I already have plans this weekend." He wondered if he should go so far as to tell her he was seeing someone, but didn't want to put the cap on that bottle just yet.

His cougar wanted Sheridan like a kitten and his first bowl of cream. He'd eat her alive and go back for seconds, making her love it then scream for more. Dario just wanted to lose himself in her. The tattoo of his pulse against his ears made his skin tight just thinking about her.

Rolling his hips, he pressed the heel of his hand to his cock beneath his business slacks. *Down boy.*

"But you were busy last weekend too," she complained, trying to flirt with him and failing miserably. "I really do need you this weekend."

He almost asked her what for, and then clamped his jaws shut. *Don't give her an inch.* "And I'm sorry, Muffy. I can't."

"You're not even going to tell me what is so important that you can't come with me?"

He reached for a pencil and idly tapped the eraser on his desk. "Nope. I do have a life. Last I checked, it was mine to live."

Chilled silence was his answer. "You're avoiding me. Ever since the Christmas ball."

He pitched the pencil and scrubbed his hand down his face. "I'm sorry, Muffy. You got the wrong idea."

It had been an incredibly bad idea to escort her to that one. Everyone had exclaimed at their pairing. She was prime for him, and perfect for his status. She ate that up like a prom queen. Dario couldn't wait for the evening to end. From that night on, it had seemed to only be a matter of when they'd announce their engagement. It was enough to make him ill. Ever since, he'd avoided anything in the least public with the woman. The last thing he needed was more tongue wagging and people already seeing them with a house and kids. He shuddered. *God, no.*

"Dario." Her voice lowered, a sexy cajoling sound that probably worked on every other male on the planet, Uncle Antonio included, but it didn't work on him. "If you're not ready, I understand, but please. I need you for this weekend."

He shook his head. *How magnanimous of you.* "I'm sorry, Muffy. I really can't."

After hanging up with her, it took less than five minutes before both his uncle and his father stormed his office.

"What is so important that you can't take Muffy this weekend?"

Dario gave his dad a pleading look. By the indifferent expression he received in return, it appeared his dad was on the 'Muffy for a daughter-in-law' train as well.

"I already have plans."

"Break them. You managed to avoid the Luncheon last weekend. This weekend you are needed to make an appearance." He wasn't shocked to hear it. He *was* shocked to hear it come so flatly from his father. It was a borderline demand, and not like his dad in the least.

Dario studied his father. "Dad? What is going on? What is this weekend that is so damned important that you can't live without me being there?"

"The council is requiring a Taja presence for their next ascension. You're the heir coming into place behind me. It's time you began to do your duty."

Dario stood, his eyes narrowing at his uncle. "Duty? Now why does that sound familiar?" Antonio used to be his favorite uncle, but ever since Dario came into age, he'd been hounding him to marry, and his flavor for the pride matriarch had been the blonde he'd turned down less than ten minutes before.

"You're shirking your responsibility."

A growl was hard to swallow. He'd never hurt his uncle, but the man had been pushing buttons for months over Muffy. "The hell I am. Dad, you and I both know the presence is voluntary. There's no requirement in it. If they want a showing of the Taja pride, why?" He leaned on taut fists on his desks, not giving a single inch. "I'm sorry. I do. But I have plans for this weekend, and I can't back out of them."

That was when it hit him. It wasn't that he just *wouldn't* back out, but he sincerely *couldn't*. Sheridan's dewy gaze rose before his face, and he felt himself melt a little. His cougar purred with mild impatience, wanting. He knew the drill. Work had to be done. Both had a place in Dario's life, and he fought hard to keep his cougar happy, letting him run when he needed and as often as he could, which wasn't always easy. The feline part of him was inseparable in so many ways.

So why didn't he realize what it all meant sooner than now? It had been before him for two days. In fact, she'd been right before him and he'd never suspected.

Regarding the two standing in front of his desk, he almost blurted it out, so overwhelmed with the truth, he felt weightless.

Sheridan was his match. His cougar's mate. The snort he heard between his ears made him chuckle to himself. *Okay, so I'm a little slow.* At least now, he knew there was no way, ever, that Muffy would get her claws into him, no matter how appropriate the match seemed.

Focusing, he sat, clearly ending the discussion. "I'm sorry. I have this bid to finish." He wanted to roll and sunbathe in his newfound discovery.

"Dario."

He lifted a hand to silence his dad. "I'm sorry. Please, don't bring it up again. I will not court her, and from this point forward, I am off the block for her mate."

"Are you serious?" His uncle shared a wide eyed glare with Dario's dad. "You need to give her a chance, son."

"I can't." Leaning back in his chair, he felt like the cat that ate the canary, when he replied with a grin, "She's too late."

<hr />

AN HOUR later, his phone rang again. "Acardi."

"You are never going to believe this!" Sheridan was fuming about something.

"What, baby?" With much more anticipation than with the last phone call he'd received, he promptly dismissed the bid he was almost done researching for approval.

"Mona needs a bridesmaid. One of her friends is puking sick and won't be on her feet before Saturday."

He wanted to laugh, but hearing the confused pain in her voice, was able to keep it in his throat. "Don't tell me..." He left it hanging.

"You guessed it in one."

"Now *that* is ballsy."

She sighed then managed a weak laugh. "I'm flattered that she thought of me first as a friend, but I'm somewhere between shocked and dumbfounded."

"She does remember you're the ex, right?"

"I doubt she even thought about it that far. She's not the brightest light bulb in the room."

Dario snickered. *Cat fight.* He shushed his cougar when it perked up. "When did she ask?"

"At the end of class today. We're done early Thursday for this semester. One more to go," she murmured as an aside. "It means I have less than four days to get a gown fitted and pretend I give a damn."

Dario shook his head as he sat up in his chair. "You said you'd do it? Why?"

"I did think about saying no," she admitted. "Honestly, if I don't go, I'll look like the wounded ex. Now that she's done this, if I don't step up, it's going to look way too personal. It wasn't an ugly breakup, so there's no reason I can't still be friendly. Damn, but she did put me on a spot, didn't she?" He heard noises in the background. She must have come straight home and called him. The thud of her book bag, the smack of the refrigerator. It warmed him that he was the first person she came to with this landslide of thoughtlessness.

"Just tell me when you need to be picked up for the ceremony and I'll be there."

"Are you sure?"

"I was going to take you, right?" She made an affirmative sound. Instead of letting his dick get too happy about that particular vibration, he told her, "Then there's very little different about this."

"Do you have dinner plans?"

"No." Even if he had, he'd have cancelled in a heartbeat.

"Come over. I'll cook and we'll watch a movie. I doubt I'm going to have two seconds to myself from Thursday until this is over."

It was impossible to get his head back into work mode after talking with Sheridan. Images of her sitting next to him on the couch segued into non-stop hungry fantasies for the woman.

SHERIDAN opened the door for him a little after six-thirty. She waved in Dario, the phone still pinned to her ear. She rolled her eyes. Her sister-in-law had been going strong for ten minutes solid. Sheridan cut her off. "I know, Kay. Look, he just got here."

"Dinner?" she asked.

"Yes. Goodbye, Kay."

"Love you."

"You too, sis." With a sigh of relief that she didn't bother to restrain, she hit the 'enough already' button, also known as the end button. "Thank you." She leaned up and touched her lips to his. "My hero."

"Oh?" Dario grinned, wrapping his arms around her. "All I have to do is show up and I'm a hero?"

"No, all you have to do is get Kay off the phone. She's been reading me the riot act over the bridesmaid thing." She tucked against his chest, suddenly succumbing to the solid build of his chest and the strength of his arms around her. God, he felt good. He nuzzled the top of her head, letting her relax where she stood.

"She doesn't agree?"

"Yes and no. She's more ticked that Mona would consider it, without even taking my feelings into account. It's not going to be easy, but not in the 'I should've had him' sense."

His arms tightened and a palm began to stroke her spine. "What do you see?"

Closing her eyes, she drifted under his touch. "It's more a 'Why two years' question." He nudged her forward, walking her backward. She didn't care. She trusted him. When he slipped away, she opened her eyes and found him sitting on the couch. Tenderly, he tugged her down until she sat on his lap.

"Better," he breathed, resting his lips to her temple with a quiet sigh. "Okay, continue."

"We dated for two years—Are you sure you want to hear this?"

"Anything to help you, sweetheart." The low burn of his gaze told her he meant it. When he brought her closer to let her rest on his shoulder, she went willingly.

"Okay, two years." She drew a breath. "Honestly, we just didn't see that much of each other. He was always traveling. Kay hated that about him. He always had something more important, a client, an account. He's in marketing. He didn't make time to attend even their wedding, and I think that was the last straw for me." She played absently with a button on his shirt front. "It was comfortable, but after watching Rush and Kay, I knew I wanted more. He didn't."

"And when he asked to meet Mona?" he prodded her gently.

Sheridan shrugged. "I didn't care. I knew he was going to move on. It was the whole wham-bam-we're getting married bomb that got to me."

"I'm not surprised. It sounds more like a rebound than reality, but it's their choice."

She lifted and gave him a studious eye. "I thought the same thing, to be honest."

"And you think they're happy?"

Sheridan tilted her head, considering for a moment before she answered. "I think so. I'd like to think so."

A devilish light hit his gaze. "Want to show them that you've moved on too? I know a guy who can do it in style."

She thumped his chest with a harmless fist. He groaned through deep laughter, creating a ball of warmth in her stomach that infused her limbs and heart. "Just being with me will be all I need."

"Then, you have me," he purred. The words were sweet and low, but it was the heat in his eyes that created a lustful shimmy to slide down her spine. Her fingers flicked through the short ends of his hair at his nape, scraping her nails delicately over his skin. When he closed the distance to meet her lips with his, she sank into his embrace.

Chapter Six

UNABLE to do much to help her clean after dinner, he'd ambled to the living room for the couple minutes she needed, but his interest got the better of him after seeing drawings and sketches pinned to her walls. He hadn't taken a lot of time to look too closely, since he'd mostly been picking her up or dropping her off. Curious, he strolled to her workspace and felt his jaw slowly drop with shock and awe at the detailed artwork surrounding him.

When he heard her coming closer, he asked, "Is this for your classes?" Dario stood in front of Sheridan's computer. She'd tacked several large full frame images of dragons, lions, cars, scenes that could be for any of the latest movies, even people, to her work board. Some were dramatic, others were so life-like, he felt like he could reach out and touch them.

"Different stills that I wanted to put together for the demo reel I have to submit for my final this week." She came up beside him and he curled an arm around her.

"These are gorgeous. You're very talented."

She blushed, tucking against his arm. "The programs do a lot for us, but there are things that require an imagination and eye, and a bit of talent." He grinned with her when she smirked.

"Like?"

"Shading and lighting, texture, and putting together a final composite."

"What are you studying to do with it?"

"Matte painting and concept art." She named them each, showing him different images that showcased the skills she'd been learning and honing. "We also have to show that we can do motion, integration, corrective color on shade and lighting, and a ton of other stuff, then when it's all done, we send it to employers."

"What kind companies hire for this?"

"Gaming companies, movie production companies, advertisers. Almost everything created now for movie or TV has some level of computer art generated layering in it. Games are all computer generated."

"Where are these places?" he asked, feeling a little nauseous, fighting to keep it out of his voice. He was very interested in what she was doing, what it could do for her. She couldn't leave, but he couldn't hold her back from her dream job, either.

She curled into his side, both of them looking over her wall. Her desk was equally covered with papers, books, drawing tablets and more electronic technology than he could possibly name.

"A lot of them are in California, Hollywood. New York. I'm hoping to find something closer to home, though. The money is out there, but I don't want to be that far from Rush. Right now, I'm doing freelance work, and I have aid money to support myself. My parents had set aside some too, in case one of us went to college. Rush used a little to go to the academy, but he also qualified for grants because of our living status."

He pressed a kiss to the top of her head. "Your parents must have been wonderful people."

"They were."

"What happened to them?" he asked, studying her features. It seemed to be the only time she had a hard time answering him when she wouldn't look up at him, the hesitation in her answer pronounced. She'd only briefly mentioned them Sunday night over dinner.

"My dad was in a bad accident, and Mom couldn't take the grief. She died following him."

He felt her pain and curled her closer. "They must have loved each other very much."

She swallowed then nodded. "They did. High school sweethearts."

His gaze continued to sweep her wall. "If you found something close, that paid well enough, you'd be happy?"

"Thrilled. I don't need much. Just living expenses, for now anyway. I might need to update my programs as they improve, or my system, but that's not going to happen until I actually find work and learn what I need to do that job."

Pointing at a design that had grid work, he asked her what it was.

"That's 3D modeling. We start with a basic drawing, and then import the 2D concept into the 3D workspace and sculpt a polygon model, like a clay sculptor on a wheel, only drawn. From there you add textures, shading, lighting, and finally, render, which presses the layers into one finite image."

He nodded, amazed at her skills and her knowledge. He'd been a numbers whiz, without a creative bone in his body. From what he was looking at, she was truly talented. He brought her up for a slow kiss.

"This is really gorgeous work, Sheridan."

She wrapped her arms around his waist and followed the wall, the same as he. "I love doing it. I've been a drawing nut since I could hold a pencil. Used to fill my homework spirals with drawings rather than homework."

He chuckled, seeing the amused gleam in her eyes. He could see the mischievous child she had been in that playful light in her eyes. "You ready for that movie?"

"I'm ready if you are." Leading her to the couch, she scooted up beside him and that's where she'd been for the last half hour.

Dario held Sheridan tucked snug into his side. Dinner had been lighthearted, teasing and he'd never seen a more beautiful smile than hers. He wasn't even sure of the movie's name. Didn't really care. Just that he had her beside him. Her hand rested comfortably on his thigh, her head on his chest.

Relaxed now, she wore a loose yellow shirt that covered her to her hips and cream colored jeans that stopped below her knees. She looked like spring. He wound a length of hair over his fingers, back and forth, savoring the silken weight. Several times, he'd had to pull his attention to the front of the room to the TV. It was hard to not grasp for peeks of her breasts. Fleeting hints of flesh beneath the collar, and the occasional tease of rose pink satin.

He drew a breath, stretching a few muscles, trying to make his jeans fit a little less tightly. It didn't help. She made him hornier than a sixteen year old kid on his first date.

"You okay?" Her breath flowed over his shirt, skimming his skin, and his heart thudded in answer.

"Yeah." Though it was a bald-faced lie. She twisted to peer up into his face, leaning more against his body with a shoulder.

He wrapped an arm around her, supporting her as she snuggled into him. Her sigh of contentment made all his discomforts worthwhile. Thick lashes brushed over her cheeks as she found a position to rest. Watching her, he simply gave up on paying attention to the TV. It just couldn't compete with the woman in his arms.

His cougar batted at his sides, wanting out, wanting to meet her, but he knew he couldn't. One, it was too soon. Second, he had to give her a chance to understand. He knew she was his mate, but even with nature nudging him, her heart had taken a beating. There was no way he was going to jeopardize any part of this. Gazing at her, his vision stroked her from her eyelashes down her cute nose to her lips. The echo of his heart pulsed through his veins again.

There was no way around it. He loved her mouth. Sexy pink lips. This late at night, they were bare, pale and natural. Without an ounce of effort, the dream he'd awakened to floated over his memory. The gliding in and out of his cock between those very supple and succulent lips. Each teasing flick of her tongue. Heat, wet and torturous, enflamed his skin as she sucked him. In the dream, she'd taken him deep. He'd awakened when he'd almost climaxed. From a dream.

Shit.

He closed his eyes, trying to calm the slam of hunger that rose up out of nowhere to crash over him. Burying his nose in her hair, he thrashed inside to not fall off the precipice. He must have made a sound, or tensed. Sheridan straightened to look him square in the face.

"Dario?" Concern clouded her expressive eyes.

"I think I better go," he mumbled, fighting to stay where he was, to not let his real needs, or the depth, show. The alternative was to throw her to the floor and rip her clothes from her body, to claim her until neither had a breath left in their bodies. If he touched her, the thread of control that was pulled so tight it was strumming, would snap.

She quickly slid away from his side, her eyes sweeping to the floor. "Okay."

He froze, her backpedaling reaction sluicing ice water over his lust. "Sheridan."

"It's okay. It's getting late. Didn't mean to keep you so long," she rambled. He could fight the worry and win. It was the roiling self-doubt emanating from her that sliced him like a red-hot blade right out of the forge.

Fuck.

He practically fell from the couch, landing on his knees in front of her. "Baby, look at me." When she didn't, rather leaning away, he reached and fisted his hands gently in her hair, halting her retreat. It was painful watching her try to ball into herself, withdrawing deeper every second. "Don't do that." Searching her, he knew he was going to have to explain it.

"I under—"

He brought them close, shutting her up with punctuated kisses. "Shut. Up." He nibbled at her lips. "It isn't you. Never, *ever,* think that."

As though she were rising from behind the tempest of a receding storm, her lashes rose, exposing dark, glistening, questioning eyes. He stood, bringing her with him until he held her chest to chest, her feet on the floor. He refused to let her go until this was cleared, because he knew like a bad vine, this one doubt would continue to plague them until she began to believe in what he saw.

"My imagination got the better of me," he admitted. The tension in her shoulders slackened in minute hitches. "I'm trying to not push you into anything, Sheridan. I want you to want me as much as I want you." He snickered in a self-deprecating way. "Hell, I want you so much, I hurt." More tension eased out of her. She was listening. Holding her by her arms, he studied her, waiting.

"Tell me what it was then. What did I do wrong?"

He growled. "I swear; I'm going to kick his ass. Did he tell you, make you think you did things wrong? Make you feel like you weren't doing things good enough for him?"

She shrugged then hunched in on herself. *Son-of-a-bitch.* He sucked in a deep breath. Okay, this wasn't the time to deal with that. With a bent finger under her chin, he made her meet his gaze. "Sweetheart. Take your hand and put it over my zipper." She blinked in shock and he laughed. "Okay, no I don't mean it that way. I want to prove something to you."

Hesitantly, she did, gradually forming her entire palm over his cock. The explosion of lust and desire that assaulted him stole his sanity for a split second. God, to have her touch him skin to skin? He'd come unglued. Steeling himself with another drawn breath, he explained, "Do you feel that? Do you understand that it's you doing that to me?" His heart pounded fiercely, throbbing in tempo with the blood now rushing to fill his aching length. "Last night, I had dreams about you. At least one of them woke me up. Just because I got the hard-on to go away Sunday doesn't mean it kept its distance. The dream that woke me up was sexy as hell."

This was where it could get damned embarrassing. *Like it wasn't already?* he mocked himself. Rolling his head to loosen the muscles knotting across his neck, he continued, "Sitting on the couch just now, holding you, I remembered that dream. That's what happened," he mused, meaning the pulsating staff beneath her fingers. His voice was growing gravelly, the edge of his restraint slipping with her hand still cradling him. What was the bright idea again of having her do that? The pressure of her touch was excruciatingly delicious. "I was trying to protect you from how much I want you," he whispered, his frame trembling with desire beneath her touch.

He groaned, the subtle flex of her fingers taking his shape and molding to it. He dug deep for the strength to let her go before he lost his total sense of decency, but she shook her head, freezing him. In that instant, he was sure his heart stopped.

"What was the dream?"

Silence ticked by with hard pulses of his blood in his ears. Her lips parted, and he hungered.

He swallowed when he found he couldn't utter a single sound. A single spark of sanity inserted itself into his common sense. He shook his head and tried to create space between them. "No, Sheridan. Not like this."

She squeezed gently, enough to get his attention. His spine snapped straight. He'd have followed her through the gates of Hell in that instant.

"Tell me."

He shuddered at the throaty, seductive rawness in her voice. He lowered and kissed her, thrusting his tongue to touch her, to lick her, to taste her. She whimpered and her palm slid up and down his zipper. The groan slipped out before he knew he was even making it.

When he left the playground of her lips, the dream sliced into him with a carnal heat that scorched his insides with hunger. Panting, he zeroed in on her mouth. "I love your lips, your mouth. I love your mouth." He shuddered, desire raging to feel his length sliding into that wicked heat. He gulped when she deliberately raked her fingernails down denim, striking the teeth of his zipper in an erotic, teasing vibration. He hissed. "Sheridan."

Giving one last tenuous warning, he told her, "If I don't leave now, I won't be leaving until morning."

"I have coffee."

He growled, his cougar echoing the intense need boiling through his veins with a yowling scream. Dario's resistance crashed into a pile like a building imploding. One second, strong and sturdy, the next, a pile of dust and shattered willpower. With a quick glance to make sure all the blinds were drawn, he grasped the bottom of her blouse and ripped it free over her head.

His cock hardened painfully when he saw her body, indulging in the first view of her breasts, encased in rose colored satin. "Another fantasy of mine," he murmured.

"Oh?" she asked breathlessly.

Running a learning finger from the bottom of her chin, he slipped into the valley of her breasts, up and down with methodical slowness. "These luscious tits and my cock. God, you have an incredible body." Wrapping his arms around her, he licked her, savoring her flavor as he traveled down her shoulder to the top of her breast. She shivered in answer when he nipped with tender teeth at the plump skin held so delightfully in her bra.

She arched, thrusting into him. Dario didn't misread her need. She squirmed and panted as he laved over the hardened nub beneath the satin. Grasping it between his teeth, he suckled her, drawing the cloth-covered nipple into his mouth, swirling his tongue over her. Her fingers clawed into his waist as shudders rolled down her body.

Letting her stand straight, he pressed his face into her breasts, fucking the dark, silk valley of her body with his tongue. He purred, licking his lips, relishing her sweet taste. The sharp tug of her nails in his hair brought him up again. Desire made her eyes sparkle. "Beautiful." She shivered again. He claimed her mouth before she could think of any kind of rebuttal.

Impatiently, he unhooked the strap of her bra, gliding it down her body. Once free, the heavy mounds of flesh filled his hands. He squeezed them and she shivered. "Sensitive, sweetheart?"

She whimpered, nodding shakily. *Oh, sweet Jesus,* he silently moaned. Could she get any better? She trembled when he scraped the hardened tips with his nails. Before she crumpled completely, he inched her towards to the couch. Laying her down, he covered her, a thigh between her legs. The heat of her desire singed him through two layers of denim and underwear.

Shit! He tried to remember if he had any rubbers. Diving for a kiss, her fingers drilling through his hair, his brain made one last effort before it malfunctioned. "Baby, I don't have any condoms."

"Bedroom," she gasped.

When he rose up on his forearms, making sure he'd heard her right, she explained while she worked her way under his rumpled shirt, touching his stomach and abdomen with curious fingers. "I'm modern, not stupid."

In that moment, he knew he fell a little in love with her.

CHAPTER SEVEN

HEFTING off of her body, he lifted her to her feet with a single hand, scooping the other around her bare back until her breasts mashed into his chest. He groaned. "Fuck me." Then he swept in and kissed her. Blood pulsed like a roaring river, ramming through his body. He couldn't remember a single time when he'd ever felt this hot, this *hungry* for a woman. She was turning him into an inferno of need.

"I'm going to tell you every single fantasy I've ever had, baby." He licked at the seam of her lips and she melted into him. Rising on her toes, she pressed her body against his groin. Dario moaned through the sensation of her body rubbing over his.

"You didn't even tell me the first one," she replied, a laughing, teasing lilt in her voice.

Guiding her into the one room he hadn't visited yet, he didn't bother turning on the light. "Sweetheart, if I get that one fantasy tonight, my heart may not survive the shock."

Lashes fluttered. "Oh. Now that does sound like a challenge." The drag of her fingers snaked under his shirt again, and he chuckled. Then she was tugging it free of his jeans waist. With a little help, the pullover vanished beyond his shoulder.

Within minutes, they'd managed to strip each other bare, except for one little article that left Dario speechless.

"A thong?" His beautiful woman wore thongs? He couldn't believe it, but there it was. A silk triangle smaller than a handkerchief.

She giggled self-consciously. "They make me feel sexy."

"Sheridan, if you were any sexier, I'd incinerate."

Her eyes widened, her immediate answer being to shake her head. He gripped her between firm palms. "Never again. I mean that." Confusion dampened her excitement. "After. We'll talk later. I need you now, baby."

With his mouth devouring hers, he urged her backward until the edge of the bed stopped her. "Where are they? I'm not getting out of this bed for anything."

"Nightstand."

He grinned. "Hallelujah." Then laughing at her startled chirp, he toppled them both to the bed, catching her in his arms. Rolling her beneath him, he began to drop open-mouth kisses across her collarbone. When he reached the harried beat of her pulse in her neck, he suckled the erratic pounding between his lips, scraping his teeth over her before pulling hard on the skin. She arched and groaned like a winter wind, a low howl that made the hair on his arms stand up. He'd never heard that sound, never heard it come from a woman. He shuddered as the timbre faded.

The sound alone made his cock thicken more. Shaking his head as though to clear it, he bent, finding a puckered nipple. He didn't hesitate, drawing her deeply into his mouth. She mewled and clawed at the bed as raw passion spiked wildly.

Gliding his hand down over her hip and thigh, he stumbled yet again. *Waxed?* Waxed and thongs? He was so close to losing his control, he had to stop. Just for a second, or he was going ravage her, and he wanted their first time to be more than a rushed fuck.

Holding his lust in check, he licked, curving beneath the sweet flesh of her breast. She whimpered in answer, and it drove his cougar insane.

Mine. Ours, Dario corrected.

His cougar was anxious, wanting to mark her, to claim her, not that Dario could blame it. *Soon,* he soothed. *Trust first.* Delving under the miniscule excuse for underwear, the damp edges of her pussy waited for him. He moaned, sucking harder as his fingers investigated more of her body.

She cried through his name, arching off the bed. Releasing her breast, he licked his lips, her heady, sexy scent curling under his nose, enticing him. Inching down the bed and taking long, swiping licks of her skin on the way, he fingered the cream satin encircling her waist. Tracing the indent of her hip with his fingers, he grazed over her body until he stopped, hovering over the damp apex of material. Her body trembled with her reactions, her hands fisting into the blankets beneath her.

Bending at the waist, he pressed his lips to the satin and inhaled, licking the heady dampness onto his tongue. His cat clawed at his insides and he winced, snarling back. Retreating, knowing it had pushed its luck too hard, Dario was left in peace. With a sigh of relief, and praying Sheridan hadn't noticed the hiccup in his behavior, Dario hooked the strings of her thong under his thumbs and tugged, gliding it down her body.

He couldn't wait to drink from her well, to lap at the cream glistening on her plumped pussy edges. Tossing the underwear onto the closest surface, he used his shoulders to make room, spreading her thighs. They quivered in anticipation. With the delicate pressure of his thumbs, he spread her skin and inhaled, groaning as the scent slammed into his darkest recesses and bound him with a shackle he didn't want to ever break.

"I want to devour you," he managed, his voice raw with the rise and crest of his needs. A renewed shimmy sliced down her. He watched, entranced, as her body reacted, a fresh flush of dew slicking her core. "Do you like that, baby?" He lifted a few inches on his elbows to see her face. She'd captured her bottom lip between her teeth, her eyes closed as she panted. "Do you like hearing how sexy you are? How much I want to lick your pussy, how much you drive me insane?"

Jerkily, she nodded. She held the blankets so tightly, her fingers had turned white. *Fuck me. She likes the dirty talk.* With the friction of the bedding beneath him encouraging the throb of his cock, he had to take a deep breath for a whole new purpose. To try to calm his blood.

The woman was a smorgasbord of sexuality.

Getting as comfortable as he could with his shaft beating angrily at being ignored, Dario separated the slick folds and homed in on her clit. The swollen bead pulsed when he dared to tap it with his tongue. A cried mewl was her reply to his touches.

That would not do.

"What will it take to make you howl again, baby?" he mused, his breath flowing over her weeping sex.

"Dario," she pleaded. Her hips arched, enticing or begging, it mattered little.

"What if I did this?" he asked her, sucking her clit between his teeth then humming as he rolled his tongue over her. She cried out sharply.

No, that wasn't it either. Now, he was enjoying the challenge, taking his time with her pleasure. "Give me a pillow," he ordered.

With a shaking hand, one appeared before him. "Lift that beautiful ass, sweetness." She did and he smiled. With the pillow in place, he resumed his position. "I hope you're ready because I'm not quitting until I hear you howl."

She shivered, whimpering.

When he slowly slid his tongue over the pinked flesh of her pussy, she gasped and stiffened. Pausing for a heartbeat, he asked her, "Are you an oral virgin?" Her reactions were off the chart with the little he'd done so far.

A weak, breathy "Yes" floated to him.

Fuckers. I bet they fucked her and ran.

Rolling a shoulder, he told her, "Okay honey, just lay there and enjoy." *Because I know I am.*

With sure strokes, he strummed her flesh, slipping in and out of the tight center with his tongue. Quakes rocked her hips and she pushed into him, silently pleading for more. Her taste was divine, sweet and unique as he licked at her cream.

Damn, he wanted her to come. He wanted to have her so deep on his tongue, he'd be able to taste her for days. Gliding a finger along her labia, he slicked her skin then swirled to lap up the moisture. Then, without letting her know his next move, he dove to suckle her clit, gliding his stiff finger into her sheath. Heat and silk. She clamped down on him, and he shuddered in answer. His dick ached, starving for that delicious torture.

In and out he stroked, lapping at her flesh, sipping her flushed skin between his lips or nipping gently at her clit. Her body gyrated, her hips lifting. He increased the speed.

Her body was soaked with her juice, her head rocking back and forth as her pleasure climbed.

Dario went for the final assault, lapping hungrily at her slit. "Come for me, baby. Come hard."

Leaning on his elbows, he held her in his palm. He pressed his thumb to her ass, adding sensation to the muscles to tease her. Adding another finger to the one slamming in and out of her pussy seemed to light her fuse of no return.

She bucked followed by a howling shriek that filled the room with the sound of her release.

"That's my girl," he murmured, feeling the shudder of her channel as she soared over the edge of her climax. Yanking his hand out of the way, Dario drank, sucking then thrusting with his tongue until he'd caught every last drop of her pleasure. Purring, he let her float, licking his lips and cleaning his fingers as his heart rate eased.

Rising over her, flushed cheeks and swollen lips told him how high she'd flown. After removing the pillow, he dropped it to the side of the bed, He reached for the nightstand drawer. Finding the box, he tugged one out, quickly dispensing with the wrapper. He hissed rolling it on his engorged shaft. After her climax, he'd be lucky to last five seconds. Shudders still walked down his spine as he tasted her cream on his lips.

Glancing at the vixen at his side, slumberous eyes studied him. A trailing hand snaked up his thigh and raked lightly over his chest. "Dario?" she managed, a husky question.

He bent and settled a gentle kiss to her lips. "Shh," he breathed.

He aligned himself between her quivering thighs as her hands fluttered to find purchase. Slowly, savoring every sensation, he entered the warmth of her body. Sheridan gasped, moaning in short breaths.

Once seated, he stilled, letting everything about the moment soak into him. *Home.* She was perfect.

Setting an easy rhythm, he brought her with him, daring the edge of the cliff all over again, only this time, she wasn't going over alone. His jaw clenched when her hips lifted, meeting him, sending shots of electricity through his body. "Sheridan," he moaned. He tingled as desire snaked over nerves. She clenched down on his cock as he stroked, her thighs holding him close.

He grunted incoherently. Stiff fingers stole into his hair, then down his shoulders, caressing and kneading as their slick skin met over and over. Taut nipples raked over his chest, driving him mad. The liquid heat of her pussy grasped at him, sucked at him as her passion rose, and he groaned, feeling the strike of passion as hot as any lightning bolt flash down his frame. Her body, her passion was too much. Dario had finally found everything he wanted.

He lost himself in her softness, in her hunger. Thrusting deep, her channel slick with her earlier pleasure, he shouted, stiffening as he shot into the condom, the pulse so intense, he froze solid under the pleasurable explosion, sparks igniting across his vision.

Sheridan trembled beneath him, her body undulating, wrapped around his cock as her orgasm clasped him deep.

Gasping for any air, Dario nearly collapsed. He hadn't lasted at all. Her nails lightly flitted through his damp hair. The echoes of her orgasm massaged his cock, and he flexed at the sensation. "Next time, baby. I promise."

"What?" Her breath danced over his ear.

"I'll last longer. I'm sorry."

"Dario, that was..." She fell silent, her fingers stopped moving. Then they started again. "Dario, that was amazing. Better than amazing," she whispered.

Dario grinned, careful to keep it hidden. He'd found a national treasure. And she was all his.

Chapter Eight

"OH MY GOD! Come here!" Lucy was almost screaming as Sheridan walked into the dressing room where the rest of the girls were gathered at the church Saturday afternoon.

Gasps and sounds of breathless wonder were coming from all of them, gazing out the tiny corner window at the view of the tree-shaded parking lot.

"Whose is that?"

"Did you see who drove it?"

"See what?" Sheridan asked.

"That sweet car!" Lucy was gripping Belinda's elbow, with Mona standing on her toes to see over them. "Red foreign something. I can't make it out."

"You mean the Alfa Romeo?" Sheridan asked calmly. Three women gaped, spinning to face her.

"It's an *Alfa Romeo*?" Lucy gushed.

"I don't know anyone with that kind of money," Mona whispered, her eyes wide.

Sheridan didn't say anything, thinking, *No, but I do.* Dario was a Financial Director for his father's company, a leading aerospace solar panel design manufacturer, which worked closely with NASA. She knew the car had been a gift from one of their Italian contracts, *but* letting the girls think what they wanted was too delicious to not savor. Not that she hadn't drooled a bit herself when he'd pulled up at her door in it. *Revenge sure could be sweet,* she mused. When he'd said style, he knew what he was talking about.

A knock at the door gave them their warning. Belinda tugged on Mona's veil. "You ready?" With a last envious peek at the car out the window, Mona nodded.

Sheridan couldn't help the small smile of victory. Mona was going to flip when she realized she'd come in that 'sweet car'.

Dario was well behaved, at least outwardly. The entire time he sat on his pew, his eyes never left Sheridan. Taller than the others, and sinfully, exotically dark where they were blonde and pale, she stood out like a vibrant orchid amid hothouse roses.

He wasn't in the least interested in the sticks standing with her. He was salivating for the curves in the yellow chiffon and satin trim. His cougar had ceased its impatient yowling and whining at some point during the drive to the church, calming down to an attentive crouch, the whip of a tail on his subconscious his only sign of the cat's angst at being made to wait. He'd had to be on his best behavior since Tuesday, him and his cat. Dario hadn't seen her since their night together. His cat was less than pleased with the situation.

Dario wasn't exactly thrilled with it either, but what could he do? At least they'd had time to talk in the evenings. Sheridan hadn't been kidding when she'd said Mona wouldn't give her a moment to breathe between then and today. Between fittings, finals and rehearsals, Mona had been running his woman ragged. Thankfully, the semester was officially over and after this weekend, Dario wasn't letting the gorgeous woman out of his sight again.

Smooth skin, hued with a spring tan complimented thick waves of black, inky curls swept into a twist held in place with the pearls all the maids wore. Only hers were white to show in her hair, while the blondes wore them in deep golden hues.

The pale yellow dress she wore showed her curves in spectacular sculpted beauty. Her breasts were full, round and plump, pushing snugly into the neckline. Moving his tongue over his teeth, he craved licking the valley between her breasts, nibbling his way over their softness until he lapped hungrily at her beaded nipples. He wanted a repeat of Tuesday night, and then some, badly.

With a crooked finger, he tugged at his neckline. He wished it were a little cooler inside the church. He had no choice but to yank himself away from the visual temptation she made. Heat singed his chest as the image took hold before he completely blocked it, imagining the way she would feel, smooth as satin and liquid soft. He closed his eyes, focusing instead on the preacher's words. That helped derail the lust snaking through his veins. A few more slow breaths and he was, once again, under control.

With agonizing slowness, the minutes ticked past, the ceremony coming to its close. He'd only imagined her undressed a handful of times, dying to discover what she wore beneath that dress. He craved to undress and unwrap every delectable inch of her shapely form.

Applause erupted and he focused forward, standing to join the others to greet the newly married couple. The bridesmaids formed up, pairing off behind the new couple to leave the front of the church. Watching Sheridan put her hand on the groomsman's arm brought up a snarl that he had to cough to hide, surprised at the unbidden reaction in not only himself, but his cat. Neither liked her touching or being touched by another male.

When she crossed in front of him, she sought him beyond her escort's chest and smiled, warmly. The cougar itching to tear her escort apart, calmed. It amazed him how quickly his cat reacted, and equally how fast the knowledge that she was safe soothed the beast.

He trailed the guests leaving the church's interior, all congratulating and shaking hands with the wedding party. When he reached Sheridan, he purposely leaned close to her and nipped at her neck with his lips, subliminally marking her when he wanted to do so much more. "Lovely," he murmured. Her reaction was instantaneous. The hard exhale, the grip on his hand. He wasn't alone with his desire. The sudden flare of heat on her skin beneath his lips burned him.

He hated letting her go, only moving down the line because he had no choice. One of the others in yellow, the maid of honor, he thought, sounding congenially interested, asked him, "Who are you? Do you know Brant or Mona?"

Offering a devastating smile down to her, since she was at least a foot shorter, he replied, "Neither," then moved on, leaving it at that. He congratulated the couple, studying Mona, who could've been sisters with the other two. Shaking Brant's hand, he looked him in the eye. "Congratulations, and thank you." Dario doubted he'd ever understand why he'd said that, though he still wanted to beat the shit out of him for the way he'd treated Sheridan. He did have enough couth to not do it at the man's wedding. Studying Sheridan's ex, Dario guessed he was handsome enough, but considering the woman he'd actually chosen, he had to wonder just what the other man had been thinking. His opinion hadn't changed. Brant was a fool, and his loss was happily Dario's gain.

"Glad you could come," Brant replied automatically, his puzzled expression saying he was trying to place him, but the next person behind Dario interrupted and he was forgotten, nudged along and out of the way. Dario angled to the edge of the foyer, a palm to his chin as he continued to watch Sheridan charm the guests. His cat had begun pacing again, unhappy with the continued distance and all the attention she was drawing.

With a moment of quiet aloneness, he asked, *What is with you? You're driving me nuts.* The feline whined, butting against his cage to be out. *Out?* He flattened a hand to his chest when the answer was a head ram to the solar plexus. *Okay. I get it, but I can't do it here. You know that.*

A light laugh brought his focus to Sheridan and a young male. When he moved too close to her, as though whispering to her, Dario's skin rippled with the energy to shift and he had to fist his control with an iron will.

The huff of plain disgust at the forced block echoed between his ears louder than a gong. *Just because you want to screw her brains out and mark her, doesn't mean we can.*

He swallowed the 'ow' he almost blurted when claws tore at his innards. *Behave! Go to a corner somewhere or I'll torture us both and not even kiss her.*

That seemed to get the cat's attention. With his tail poised and a flat nose in the air, he slunk into Dario subconscious. "Beast," he muttered.

Finally, the last of the guests left. With a sigh and looking much more relieved when she spotted him, Sheridan cleared the distance between them. "Thank you for being here, for waiting."

He didn't think twice. He simply wrapped his arms around her waist and tugged her into his frame. Her hands lifted to spread across his chest, not pushing him away, more for balance. It didn't matter. He pulsed beneath the press of her palms. He'd have given anything in that moment to rip his suit off and let her touch him skin to skin.

"I'm all yours," he breathed. He knew she'd take it to mean for the evening.

He meant it forever. Time slipped away as he stared into her eyes. Dark orbs deepened, drawing him in, making him crave. The pulse in her neck beat harder, echoing his already racing heart rate and the pounding of his blood. Remembering her reaction when he'd suckled on that pounding point sent shards of sharp need slicing through him. He'd never wanted any woman more than he wanted Sheridan in that moment.

"Sheridan, you ready for the pictures?"

She drew a breath, as if shaking herself back into the now. "I guess."

"You do what you need to, love. I'm not leaving without you."

Mona tugged Brant to the spread church doors amid yards of white satin. "See it? Whose is it?"

Brant let out a low whistle. "I don't know, but color me green."

Meeting Sheridan's eyes as his grip loosened from around her, a shared grin of justice said it all. *Just wait,* he mouthed. Laughter vibrated her chest, and he tightened all over in reflex.

"Evil. You're plain evil."

"Never doubt it," Dario replied with a teasing boast.

Reluctantly, he let her go, taking a position out of the way to let them do the portraits of the wedding party. Sadly, he never could get his erection to go away.

How could he when he kept envisioning her spread across the hood of his car, screaming his name as he finally branded her as his?

CHAPTER NINE

"THANK God," Dario breathed, sweeping Sheridan into his arms to spin her to the dance floor. "I've been dying to hold you. The best man, Michael? Long winded bastard."

She laughed, giggling deeply into his shoulder. "That's Brant's brother. Lots of ammunition, if you know what I mean." She leaned into his strength, her arm around his waist while he held her to move them effortlessly to the waltz being played. She closed her eyes and floated with him as one song fed into another, wanting nothing more than his arms and the swaying grace of his body pressed to hers. She'd missed him. No sense in avoiding it.

"Who was it that walked with you?"

She followed his easy pace with half a mind, worn out and ready to unwind from the long afternoon. A lot of pomp and circumstance. Sheridan doubted Mona would remember anything that wasn't in a picture. "That was Leroy."

"He seemed very friendly," he mentioned with a stiff tone.

She peeked at him, noting his taut jaw. Was he jealous? Why?

"He's married. I don't think his wife would've appreciated it if he'd been *that* friendly."

When his entire body shuddered, relaxing within her embrace, she realized he *had been* jealous. The truth made her snuggle in closer. There were still a lot of things to work through, but right at the moment, all she wanted was his arms and quiet.

He'd been the perfect gentleman all week. He'd stayed all Tuesday night, waking her once more to make slow, sweet love to her. She'd never felt more treasured in her life. While in the shower Wednesday morning, he'd made the coffee, then they'd traded places. With a kiss and a good luck on her tests, he'd left her to go home and change for work. They'd talked every night she could get away from the wedding shenanigans. Then today, he'd arrived in the 8C and like Prince Charming to Cinderella, had escorted her to the wedding with a flattering amount of attention. She refused to think that he had an ulterior motive for all the attention. She desperately wanted to believe his interest was genuine. Because, no matter how she tried to protect her heart, she was losing it to him.

He tipped down when she sighed in contentment.

Desire flared in his bright golden eyes. A frisson of excitement stole through her, leaving a wake of needy desire. The heat in his touch sent her pulse racing. Though the way he looked at her, the way he held her, almost had her hoping.

"What, love?" he answered.

She swallowed. He lowered, whispering those two words. The rush of his breath skimmed her lips. Her heart tripped in answer. His thumb stroked her palm and the little thinking she'd managed evaporated.

"I..." Her brain put up the 'out to lunch' sign and she stumbled over her words.

"I'd love to," he said on a raw growl, closing the gap between his lips and hers. Distantly, she realized he'd stopped dancing, but somehow, she couldn't find it in her to care.

Then his lips were brushing over hers, teasing her, and she trembled. Clinging tighter, she held on to his taller, solid frame. Dario didn't rush one single caress. He took his time, plucking every sane thought out of her mind with each lingering taste of skin. He leaned into her and she formed to him, chest to knee. A rumbled purr rose from his chest, and she shivered at the wild sound.

Her fingers dug into the silken weave of his jacket, gripping to not melt to the floor. Dario tilted and claimed her fully, thrusting his tongue between her lips. Sheridan heard a whimper. It was her. He plied against her tongue, learning her, enticing her and when she followed, he sucked her into his mouth with slow, intoxicating pulls. They chased each other, back and forth, the heat of his mouth, the caress of his lips, eclipsing all thought for the moment. Her breasts ached as arousal poured into her bloodstream. The weight of his hand on her spine was tender though possessive. He held her closer. Her body swelled as desire flashed through her.

They were both breathing heavy when he released her. The man was a phenomenal kisser. She blinked and noticed the walls on two sides of her. What happened to the dance floor? "What? Where are we?"

A gentle finger under her chin raised her to his view. "I will never put you on display, Sheridan." The tender swipe of a thumb to her bottom lip made her breath hitch. "You ready to leave this circus?"

"Sure. Let me see if they've snuck out yet. I'm sure they have."

He captured her mouth for a quick, searing kiss. "Don't take long."

The heat in his eyes pleaded with her. *Don't make me wait,* they told her. After a kiss like that, she was just as ready to get out of there!

Slipping out of the alcove where he'd hidden them, she went in search of Belinda or Lucy, not expecting to find either the bride or groom at the later hour. She was right. A lot of the reception had already departed.

She found the other two women, chatting near the cake table, Lucy rubbing her calf with obvious relief. "I haven't danced this much since I was nineteen," she complained with wry humor.

"Hi there. I think I'm ready to call it a night." Sheridan brought over a cushion padded chair to sit with them.

"We wondered if you'd be saying goodbye." Belinda shared a catty look with Lucy, who shrugged.

"It was a wonderful wedding. I'm sure they'll be happy." Sheridan wasn't up to their mind games. She'd had enough of that during the days to the wedding and the rehearsal. Her inclusion hadn't gone over well with Belinda, not that Sheridan cared. It was as if the other woman had expected her to cause problems, when getting between Mona and Brant hadn't been anywhere on her radar. She was too happy to shove them on their way.

"Who is that guy you're with? I don't remember meeting him," Belinda asked in fake casualness.

"My date. You didn't think I came alone, did you?" Sheridan felt a small jolt of pleasure seeing both of the blondes blink. They honestly thought she wasn't over Brant? That she hadn't moved on? She rolled her eyes inside. How much more *over* could she get than watching him marry another woman, *with her blessing*?

"You're dating?" Belinda quit trying to be coy. Sheridan realized what this was about. She wanted to know if Dario was available. Whether she was over Brant wasn't even a concern. *Bitch*. Dario was with her.

A warm, tender hand curved over her shoulder. "Sorry, love. We better get going. Our reservation expires in fifteen."

Belinda's jaw dropped. "Reservations?" Her blue eyes gleamed with predatory interest at Dario.

"Dinner," Dario answered from above Sheridan, which was fine because she didn't know what he was talking about. He motioned a hand to the catering table. "This was a few hours ago." Really taking in a view of the room, she noted the reception hall was almost cleared. Sheridan realized it had to be after eight. No wonder she was dragging. He'd picked her up to be at the church by two.

He offered a palm and she gratefully took it, helping her stand from the chair.

"But you didn't answer my question." Belinda rose to walk with them, seemingly at *her* side, though her gaze continued to take stock of Dario.

No matter how little right she had to do it, she desperately wanted to throw an elbow into Belinda's side to get her away from him.

Once outside the hall, Dario made no bones about walking for the 8C.

"Wait! *You* came in the Alfa Romeo?" Belinda almost tripped in shock when her feet stopped moving.

"Excuse us." Dario smiled coolly then opened the door when he reached the side of the low-slung Italian dream. He took his time helping Sheridan into the car, being sure to make a show of buckling her in. Standing with slow purpose, he dropped a light kiss on her lips, making it apparent he was savoring the moment. She wondered if he was, or if he was simply goading Belinda.

Sheridan waved a hand as they left the gaping woman in the parking lot staring after them.

"How long do you think it'll be before they're calling to tell them who was in the car?" he asked her. He chuckled with the glee of a little boy, sharing in the joke.

"As long as it takes to grab a phone," Sheridan replied, feeling absolutely vindicated by Belinda's reaction. With her hands in her lap, she let her head sag to the buttery leather of the seat, ready to relax with a glass of wine and her comfy sweats. "Don't forget the suit. Silk blend Italian is sure to be mentioned."

"They noticed that, too?" he asked, surprise woven through the question.

"They were totally stalking you. Belinda wanted to know if we were dating."

"What did you tell her?" He flipped the turn signal on.

"I didn't answer her." No point in lying. In truth, Sheridan hadn't dared put a label to their relationship. She kept waiting for him to wake up and realize what she was, as in 'not skinny'. The same way Brant had. The same way Luc had.

He reached for her hand, his warmth seeping into her with a rare comfort. It wasn't lost on her how just his touch made the pain of Luc's cruelty diminish until it faded away. Sheridan knew he thought it had been Brant who'd made her gun shy. It hadn't been. Brant had actually been the first since Luc for her to want to try again. He hadn't been anywhere near as brutal in his judgment, but his emotional and physical apathy hadn't done her self-esteem any favors either. In hindsight, they'd simply been a convenience for each other.

A bare few moments later, she felt the car ease to a stop. The rush of his breath surrounded her fingers a second before his lips caressed her. His voice was close to her ear before she knew he'd moved. Her eyes snapped open.

"Sheridan, it's time you realized something."

Expecting a stop light, she gaped in shock taking in her surroundings. He'd parked in front of Le Pont. With the car idling, a valet scurried around to his side to open the door. His thumb stroked her hand beneath his on her thigh.

"We are most definitely dating." He leaned forward, capturing her lips. "And you are most definitely with me."

The possessive growl in his words sent a whip of desire coursing through her. She swallowed, nodding in silence. It was the most she could manage. He'd stolen her voice with the fire raging in his eyes for her.

"Wha—" She was interrupted when the door popped open. A valet in a crisp red vest and standard uniform stood at her side. "Huh?"

"Dinner, love. I wasn't kidding. I'm hungry." His grin had warmed his features into a little boy's infectious charm.

"But, I'm not dressed for dinner," she exclaimed, swinging to stare at the front of the restaurant then back to him. She was dolled-up like someone's poor excuse for a pineapple.

"Oh, believe me, you are," he replied right before he nibbled at her fingers. Somehow, she didn't think he meant the kind of 'dinner' you ate with a knife and fork. The thought sent a shiver coursing through her body. Releasing her, he exited the car. Sheridan was utterly lost.

"Ma'am?" A hand was waiting for her.

Grasping it lightly, she twisted on the seat and met Dario outside the vehicle.

"Be gentle, Kyle. This isn't the Mercedes."

Kyle nodded with a broad smile, and a youthful lusting gleam for the car. "Yes, Sir, Mr. Acardi!"

Sheridan's head was whirling. "They know you by name here?" With a hand to her lower back, she had no choice but to walk with him up the red fabric carpet through the glass and gold emblem doors. Le Pont was *the* exclusive reservation-only French restaurant in town, and he just walked in with a fifteen minute warning.

"I'll explain over dinner. It's not a family vaulted secret," he said, winking at her playfully. "I've waited all week to be with you again. Tonight is ours." The doors opened with a whooshed flourish of sound, and opulence spread before her.

Biting her tongue, she could only hope she didn't embarrass him.

CHAPTER TEN

"I HAVE to say, what you did today was very commendable. I'm not sure I would've done the same thing for an ex."

Sheridan sipped at her coffee, a quizzical tilt moving her chin. "Why do you say that?" The dishes had been cleared from their shared appetizer and dessert, neither wanting anything too filling that late at night. The calm of the restaurant and the barely discernible string music playing around them added to the intimacy of their table. The room was quieting, though they weren't the last ones remaining.

"Well, after the way he treated you, I think you took the whole situation with a great deal of aplomb."

She set the china cup down. "Treated me?"

Dario scooped up her hand. "I'm sorry." He paused. "Maybe I have the wrong idea." But he doubted it. Encasing her hand between his, he said what had been on his mind since that afternoon. "Did he emotionally abuse you?" Dario was positive she hadn't been physically abused. Everything he'd witnessed stemmed from her self-image.

Sheridan was quick to shake her head, her eyes widening in an instant. "No!" She lowered her voice, but continued. "He was quiet, to be honest. I always wondered if I was doing things right. He never showed encouragement, just..." She shrugged. "I guessed he was uninterested in sex in general. We were both comfortable with the status quo. The occasional weekend together and if things happened..." She let it trail off. "Especially with my focus on my classes." She lowered her gaze to her trapped hand. "It wasn't until Kay met Rush that I began to realize I was shortchanging myself, probably hiding as much as I was avoiding. When I wanted more, he wanted out. It happens."

"Sweetheart." He purred, lifting her hand to touch her to his lips. When her liquid gaze met his, he asked, "Who hurt you?"

She swallowed, her lips parting as she leaned back marginally. "Why do you think—"

He gave her an admonishing look. "I'm beginning to know you," he told her tenderly. "I want to know everything about you. And I don't want to hurt you. I know someone did. If it wasn't Brant, then who?" Because if he ever saw the bastard, Dario was going to rip him to shreds.

She firmed her fingers in his hand. "Why do you think someone hurt me? I wasn't abused, if that's what you're worried about."

"No, I don't think that in the least." He tapped his chin with their clutched hands. "If I told you right this second that I thought you were stunning, the most beautiful woman in the world, to me, would you believe me?"

She laughed shakily. Though she blushed prettily at the compliment, she shook her head. "Of course not."

"Why?" He scooted his chair closer, sitting side by side rather than face to face. "If I'm telling you, and I believe it, why don't you?"

"Because I know I'm not."

"Who told you you weren't?" he demanded gently.

Liquid and edged with a deep remembered pain, she blinked.

"Was it someone you dated? Someone you grew up with? Someone close to you?"

"Why does it matter?" Her voice was hoarse trying to control the tears. He ached seeing them, but he refused to let her carry this disillusionment another second, or let it continue to hurt her.

"Because it's hurting you, Sheridan. It's keeping you from me. I meant what I said in the car. I *want* to be with you." He forged forward, knowing it wouldn't be easy for her, or for him to hear it. "There's a part of me that I know is desperate to meet you, but until I know deep down that you trust me, I can't." It was the closest Dario had ever come to exposing his nature. He slid a gentle finger under her chin. "Sweetheart, I care for you. I want to take care of you. Let me help you with this."

Lowered lashes stole her soul away from him again, but she didn't physically withdraw. *Space, give her space.* So, he waited.

"Several years ago, I was in love. Luc. I've never been model perfect. I just don't have the physique. I thought he was okay with that, that he loved me, cared for me, and maybe he did. But the opinion of his friends mattered more. I overheard them telling him what time would do to my figure. If I had kids..." She swallowed, the bitter pain clear in every word. He stroked his thumb over her hand, letting her take her own time, but sharing his support. "It burned. I was humiliated. Then he began talking like them, demanding I do anything it took to make myself prettier in their eyes. Instead of supporting me for the person I am, he wanted me to fit into the mold his friends had set."

Dario hadn't realized he'd begun to growl until her eyes shot up. "Dario?"

Lowering his head, he rested his forehead on their joined hands, breathing deeply to hide his beast, and his anger. The urge to unsheathe his claws, to let his cougar free to destroy this Luc was beyond anything he'd ever experienced. He may not have physically laid a single hand on Sheridan, but what he'd done to her self-esteem was pure abuse.

Sucking air through his nose to calm himself, he was finally able to reply, "I hope to God I never meet him. I will kill him."

A sharp, short gasp was her reaction. "Why? It was a long time ago, Dario."

"Because his stupidity almost destroyed the most beautiful person I've ever known. The most beautiful soul and woman."

She glanced away, and he felt her will want to shut down. "Don't." Cupping her cheek, he brought her back to him. "He was a bigger fool than Brant, only he took his weaknesses out on you. Let me make this very clear." Uncaring of appropriateness for being in public, he brought her into his embrace to speak right into her ear. "I don't think you're beautiful. I know it. I don't think about what other people say, because I'm the only one allowed to make that decision for me. If you had any idea the number of impure thoughts I had in that church, I'd have to go to confession for a week, if I was Catholic." Brushing a single kiss to her cheek, he moved away, wanting to see her expressions on her face. "Sitting there today, I saw no other woman, I wanted no other woman." Holding her steady, he pressed his lips to hers. "I *want* no one else, Sheridan." He nudged closer again. "And if you want the honest truth, I love your breasts. They drive me fucking wild."

She giggled, startled by his statement and the underlying growl of lust that Dario didn't try to restrain.

"In fact, let's stop by your place for a change of clothes. I want you to come home with me tonight."

Sheridan sat straight in her chair. "Your place?"

"Is that okay?"

Fidgeting in her chair for a moment, indecision ripe in her posture, she finally calmed, and with a soft smile appearing, said, "Yes. I would like that."

With an arm around her waist, he guided her outside where the valet had his car already waiting. Helping her inside, he took the time to ensure she was buckled in, then straightening, paused on the way for a lingering kiss. "Sweet," he murmured. Then he popped the door closed and rounded the car, relieving the valet of the door with a handshake and a tip. "'Night, Kyle."

"Bye, Mr. Acardi."

With a grin, he buckled up and put the Alfa Romeo in drive. "Ready?"

"Completely."

With a smile he felt to his heart and soul, he drove to her apartment.

⁕⁕⁕⁕

SHERIDAN let Dario take the overnight bag from her shoulder, leading her through the garage. It was a large garage, but other than the 8C, the only other car was his Mercedes taking space. She'd expected more extravagance than she'd seen so far. Though the house was in a gated community, it wasn't exclusive to the rich. *Well, maybe the better off,* she mused.

"I hope you're not disappointed," he said, turning on the lights in the kitchen.

She swiveled to stare at him. "Why would I be disappointed?"

He grinned and rolled a shoulder. "The car isn't the real me. I usually have it stored, but brought it out earlier this week just for the weekend."

"You went to all that trouble for me?" She almost stumbled walking through the door, unprepared for his admission.

Setting her bag down on the kitchen table, he said, "Honey, I'd do anything for you." With a chaste kiss on her lips, he shucked his jacket to rest on a chair back. "Come on. Let me show you the *abode de Acardi*."

"That didn't sound Italian."

Reaching for her hand, he told her, "Because it wasn't." He smiled when she laughed at his antics. Threading her fingers through his, he started in the kitchen then led her through the dining room. The large table set for four was a beautiful pecan masterpiece, large enough to sit eight.

"Don't let the table fool you. My maid does that. I never eat there."

"Why not?"

"What? And disturb her wonderful efforts to make it look so good?" He winked with charming glee.

She continued to watch him. He was enjoying this, like showing his best friend his prized card collection as he gave her the tour of his house. "It's only one storey." He popped into the rooms, letting her see where things were placed. Each room had a purpose. One was his at-home office, another was a library, and another was a guest room fully decorated with a queen bed and set.

"Before I show you the master, let me show you the back." He tugged heavy curtains clear with the pull rope, and then eased the blinds partially open. With a flick of a light, she uttered a surprised, "Oh.".

"Amazing," she breathed.

A large brick deck with a railing stretched from the rear of the house. A covered hot tub sat in a corner and a multi-use barbecue station aligned the opposite side. What drew her attention even beyond that was the rolling expanse beyond the deck. Hills and trees as far as she could see into the darkness. It wasn't as deeply forested as the land Rush's house abutted, but it was still breathtaking. It even made her wolf stand up and take notice. "Beautiful."

With a cautious note in his explanation, he told her, "I like to run in the hills. Gives me time and space to think."

"I can see that," she agreed. Sheridan usually ran behind Rush's though she hadn't lately. Sadly, no matter how much her wolf side exercised, she'd never managed reaching more than a size fourteen. It was all on her human genetics, not her shifter side.

That was when she realized that her wolf had grown silent. Trying to find her inside, she wasn't hiding, or indifferent, she was simply calm. When had the whining stopped? She was grateful, but it confused her. Sheridan got the impression her wolf liked Dario. Which was saying something considering the other relationships and men she'd been around. *Safe.* Sheridan felt it all the way to her bones. Her wolf knew she was safe with Dario. Sheridan almost negated the inner voice; she didn't know enough about Dario, or what it all meant. They'd known each other a week, but it seemed to matter little to her soul shifter.

Was this normal? Why didn't she get more of a reaction? Rush had known. Why couldn't she? This was frustrating. It wasn't cheating, damn it, if the guys could do it, but she really couldn't tell by instinct if Dario, if any man, was meant to be hers.

Staring out into the green hills, she could see her wolf running wild there. The image, the idea, pleased her wolf and she brushed against Sheridan's insides, sharing the quiet hunger to run. *You like him, don't you?* Her wolf only nuzzled closer. It was the first time her wolf had ever shown an interest, or approval.

That realization also brought up the worry about telling him *about* her wolf. Would he fear her? Fear the wolf? Hate her? Despise her? Sheridan had never even felt the want to tell Brant, and Luc... She'd almost told him. Now she couldn't be more thankful she hadn't. Surprisingly, she wanted to tell Dario. Wanted him to know everything about her. He'd said he wanted to know about her, help her. The only way they could continue would be to explain the whole truth to him. But when?

"Where'd you go?" A single caress warmed her cheek, his finger halting beneath her chin.

Blinking, focusing on his concerned features, she said, "Just thinking."

His mouth quirked to the side. His next response told her he was worried about what direction her thoughts had been going in.

"Well, before you start thinking I'm Midas, I'm not. The company owns the land. It was the surest way to keep it natural. The community was built to protect it. This area will never be expanded and it's several hundred acres deep. No one person can decide to sell any part of it and none of the board will ever let it be commercialized. The house isn't even paid for, but I did have it built the way I wanted."

He'd dropped his gaze, paying a lot of attention to her hand lying in his palm as he traced the lines with a fingertip.

"Dario, I'm not disappointed. Your money only means that you're established and responsible. You work hard. There's no reason you shouldn't have a little something to show what that has gotten for you." So he had a mortgage and bills? It only further proved he was real, and not a dream, because to her, it seemed every moment with him was a wish come true.

Relief filled his body, a breath rolling his shoulders. The gleam in his eyes told her just how much her answer mattered.

With a hand cupping her neck, he drew her up to him. Gently, he sipped at her lips, making her heart flip. "Come on. Let's go change into something relaxing."

The raw edge of want was in his voice again, melting her from the inside out. When he deepened the kiss, shaping her body to his, Sheridan knew she was in trouble.

She was falling for him.

The bigger worry was she didn't think she wanted to fight it.

CHAPTER ELEVEN

DARIO purred. Nuzzling into the nape of the woman in his arms, he'd never felt more at peace. A peeked glance at the clock only confirmed what the shadows were telling him. The sun was on its way. He wished he could stop the sun and time. He didn't want her to wake, didn't want her to leave. Rousing next to her, her soft body against his every morning made his skin itch to tell her the truth. And it wasn't all his cougar's impatience.

The larger question was how to break it to her? How do you prepare someone for this kind of a secret?

He'd thought he'd been crafty the night before, hinting, but even in his own ears he knew he'd been too obscure, too vague. Dario had never thought he'd be exposing himself to someone not of his own pride, much less someone who may not accept at all. It was a sobering prospect, because now that he'd found her, he knew he couldn't lose her. Her head rested beneath his chin, both sharing the pillow, nestled together. His fingers flexed, curling around an unfettered breast. Sheridan twitched.

How hard would it be to convince her to stay in bed all day? He quietly chuckled. It wouldn't take anything to convince him. It had been years since he'd indulged in a day of nothing, and never with a woman at his side.

Sheridan didn't know it, but she was the first he'd brought home, the first woman he'd ever invited to stay over. Dario also knew that within hours of their arrival, and her lack of leaving, the entire community would be abuzz with questions about his guest.

Hard to avoid considering the majority of the Taja pride lived in this community, his parents among them. Hopefully, they'd leave him alone until he was ready to introduce her, if he got to. He wouldn't before he'd told her the truth. It would be shocking to learn their secrets from anyone other than him.

"Do you always do that?" she mused.

He tensed, unaware he'd been doing anything. "What, love?"

"That quiet purr. I can tell when you're thinking. It's like you're humming to yourself, but much deeper."

Dario chuckled. "No, I never even knew I did it." He lifted enough to nip at her ear. "I didn't mean to wake you."

Stretching, she formed along his length, and he brought her closer. His cock stiffened along her ass. Now, *that* almost made him purr for a totally different reason.

"You didn't." She jerked. "Is that clock right?" Horror filled her words.

"Yes, why?"

"School!" She tried to leap from bed.

He caught at her shoulders, holding her steady. "Sheridan, it's Sunday."

She froze, half in and half uncovered. "Oh." She giggled through an embarrassed sigh. "I remember. I was dreaming about our final, or actually, all the hours and practice I'd done to prepare it. I had this awful feeling I'd forgotten it."

He held her closer as she readjusted at his side under the comforter. "Nope. You turned it all in on Wednesday. You told me you did." *Poor baby. Too much stress this week. Definitely.*

She burrowed into the pillow. "I'm sorry; I don't know what got into me."

"Time to unwind, lovely." Gliding a foot over her calf, he enticed her. "Stay today. Stay in bed, stay in any way you want, just stay."

"Hm. Will you stay with me?"

"Of course," he replied, nipping at her shoulder. His cougar perked up. *Claim. Ours.* Dario ignored him. Who knew he had such a demanding feline? Though if he could get her to stay, he could work in the shifter explanation. He could make her see, understand, and hopefully, accept. Then he could claim her. All

Dario knew was his cougar hated plotting. That lack of patience was showing up again.

As he arched to mold to her shape, the full swell of her breast filled his palm again. The beaded tip hardened beneath the gentle flick of his touch.

"Mm," he breathed against her neck. "You feel so good." It was impossible to not tug and play with the sexy nub. It begged him for attention so prettily. Ignoring her body's request wasn't an option.

He stroked her side with his loose hand, roaming from her shoulder to her hip. She was so smooth, he glided over her skin. Her curves... He shivered as his desire flared to life. He hated holding a woman and feeling their bones through their skin. He loved Sheridan's breasts; that simply was a fact, but she had the sweetest hips and thighs. There was strength in her limbs.

She called herself fat, which he hated and refused to see. He saw lushness, a soft woman to come home too, to hold him when the world demanded too much. Brushing his nose against her neck, he inhaled her gentle scent. He let his hand drift over her ass, palming her shape. She shivered against his chest when he slipped his fingertip down the crease of her ass, following the curve of her body until he hit the moist, dewy flesh of her center. A low hiss escaped. "You're hot, babe."

She bowed outward, pressing her breast into his teasing hand, giving him even more to play with of her body.

"Keep that up, and I can promise you'll love what I do," he joked.

"That's what I'm hoping for," she replied, breathless.

Bending her leg to arch over his thigh, he ran his fingertips over the smooth edges of her pussy, teasing the sensitive skin until she shuddered. "This is sexy." Not increasing his pace, he worked his finger up and down her smooth slit. Almost immediately, she began to tremble with hunger. "You drive me insane, do you know that? I love the way you taste, sweet and hot." Keeping her close, he licked warmed skin in slow swipes with his tongue. "I go to sleep thinking about you, dream about you."

Sheridan inched closer, pushing against his touch. It didn't make him speed up; he moved with definite control. The scent of her need filled the air. His body throbbed in answer, and he was grateful they had all day to enjoy each other.

"I love how wet you get. This hot pussy is all mine." Tapping her clit with a stiff finger brought out a row of whimpers. Swirling along her edges, he felt the flushed warmth of her skin, enticing her arousal until her pussy lips were plump and begging for more. "One of these days I'm going to watch you make yourself come. I want to watch you play with this pussy until you scream. Do you ever do that? Do you ever play with yourself? Play with the wet jewel...right...here?" He rubbed over her clit hard and she gasped, her length shuddering. Drops of cream filled her channel to fall to his hand. He groaned. "Damn, baby. I could eat you out for days."

Sheridan clutched at the bed, rocking onto his hand, needing.

With her lying in the crook of his arm, the mound of her breast rested in his palm. As he rolled over her clit, he tugged lightly at her nipple at the same time. After slicking his thumb with her juice, he pressed the pad of his digit over her anus, plying all three sensations. She cried out as pleasure sang through them both.

"Like that, baby?" he asked, sounding rougher by the minute as his hungers rose to match hers. "Has anyone ever been with you here?" Dario hooked is thumb, scraping gently over skin.

"Ahhh!"

"I'll take that as a no." He chuckled. "I will. I want to love every inch of this sweet body of yours."

She whimpered through his name. It was music to his ears. She was so turned on. He wanted to play with her for hours, make her body quiver with desire, and weep with need. He wanted to watch her play with her pussy, could imagine how wet she would be. Stroking her, he shuddered. *Shit.* Next time. He had absolutely no control around Sheridan.

"Get me a condom, sweetheart. I can't wait any longer to have you."

Groping, she yanked on the drawer, handing over the square with trembling fingers. Fitting his cock with the condom, his vision blurred. Holding her hip, he braced himself behind her, gliding into her hot channel from behind in slow increments. A sharp exhalation hissed through his teeth. "So fucking tight," he growled. He stopped, grasping for any strength while held between convulsing walls. Pulling out, he knew what he wanted. Whispering, he told her, "Roll over to your stomach."

Kneeling behind her, he lifted her to her knees. "Oh, sweetheart," he groaned. She rested on her elbows, her ass presented like a gift. Her slicked pussy opened for him, glistening and pulsating. He'd never seen anything so fucking hot in his life.

Holding her tight, he lined himself up and thrust home to her delicious shout. "Yes! Howl for me, baby."

Gripping her hips, he pounded into her, the sound of his balls smacking into her wet body driving him crazy. The sharp tingle of each slap tightened his spine. Gritting his teeth, he held on. He refused to let his lust make him lose control.

"I'm going to make you come, sweetheart," he warned her. "I want you to cream all over my cock." His eyes crossed when she convulsed, gripping his length tight within her silken walls at his words. She was close. Leaning on his calves, he drew her up with him, straddling his body. With a hand on her hip, he thrust upward and she shuddered. "That's it, Sheridan. Come for me." She drove him wild as he hammered upward. "Touch yourself, baby. Come for me. I want you to." Dario was gasping, growling. *So close.*

His balls tightened hard into his body when she stroked over her clit, her pussy clenching down on him, capturing him deep inside. "Shit." He moaned through the word. He craved to feel her slickness over his balls. Her hot cream dripped down his cock, slipping over his tight skin, but he wanted more. When he reached around and pinched her nipple, she screamed, her head tossed back, the sound deepening to a howl that sent his blood pounding. He wanted to bite down on her so bad, wanted to mark her as his, her shoulder bared and *right there.* Closing his eyes, he focused on their heat, the wet proof of her pleasure soaking his groin.

"One more time, baby. Want to come," he groaned, his voice raw, his restraint to hold back slipping. "Play with your pussy. Please." Her body reacted as she glided over and tortured her clit. He lifted his hands, cupping both breasts, pinching and tweaking her nipples into diamond hard points. She whimpered and cried out, her body clenching down on his as rapture spun tighter between them.

Sparks ignited in his balls and he shouted, his orgasm racing like lava through his veins. He groaned long and deep as he pulsed, her body sucking at his as she came again, juicing his dick with hot cream. "Oh, God," he moaned. "I love that." The sensation blew his mind.

His throat was raw, his lungs ached, but he'd never felt more replete, never felt so pleasantly weak in his life. He almost blurted the words that were pounding through his heart.

Instead he looped his arms around his woman and held her, cradled in her into his chest as shudders rolled over them both, memories of their shared pleasure that he couldn't wait to relive.

CHAPTER TWELVE

RELAXING in the slow swirling heat of the hot tub after their nap and a late breakfast, he wrapped his arms around Sheridan, bringing her onto his lap. He swept her hair out of the way, the length thick and dripping from her playful antics in the bubbling water, exposing the silken length of her throat for exploration. "Ever have hot tub sex?" he asked, licking beneath her ear. A cool breeze rattled the leaves of the closest trees, but otherwise, it was a calm and quiet Sunday.

She laughed, bending to give him room. "No."

"Want to?"

Her laughter was belly deep. "You're insatiable."

He shrugged, not at all repentant. "What can I say?" He lifted her closer, letting her get comfortable over his thighs. Her arms looped lazily around his shoulders, her fingers toying with the short ends of his hair. Each touch sent a shiver down his spine. His erection nestled neatly against her cleft, making him ache all the harder. "You make me think sex." Proving it, he leaned forward and lipped at a nipple, toying and teasing her with light swipes of flesh.

Her lashes lowered, though her cheeks filled with a blush red that rivaled any rose he'd seen. Sunlight warmed her skin, making her glow. Water clung to her lashes like dewdrops, just waiting to be sipped away. The water dancing around them glittered like jewels in blues and reds as the sun climbed higher. Watching her, his chest trembled. Somewhere in the last week, he'd fallen head over heels for the beauty before him. Mates be damned. Instincts could be tossed out the window. He loved her.

He silently screamed on the inside to tell her how he felt.

Dario had to explain his cougar first. He refused to be one of those who used the mating to bind her before she was sure. It had been done, but he couldn't. He respected her choice. And considering the assholes she'd been involved with, he never wanted her to feel like she wasn't worthy, over anything.

"Remember when I said there was a part of me I wanted you to meet?"

Her blue hazel eyes glistened. Drops of water trailed down her cheeks to drip seductively over her shoulders and breasts. Cotton candy pink nipples brushed against his chest, making him crave to lap his tongue over them again. He swallowed, fighting to keep his mind on his purpose. It didn't help that he'd miscalculated her position over his lap. Blood pulsed hotly through his cock as the gentle sway of the water rocked her over his hips.

"I do. Last night." She drifted forward and touched her lips to his. "I trust you, Dario. I wouldn't have come this far if I didn't think I could."

Relief made his chest stagger as he exhaled a sigh. Her eyes were wide and clear when she straightened. "In fact," she drew a breath, "there's something I've been wanting to tell you, too." She caught her lower lip between her teeth, then, "I really care for you Dario. I hope you're not pressured to know that." Peering through her lashes, she seemed to be waiting.

Something light filled his soul, giving him that weightless feeling again. Shaking his head, he whispered, "No, not at all." Forgetting about his raging hard-on, he ran caressing fingers into her hair, holding her close. "I think there could be something very real here," he murmured, pressing his lips to hers.

Rubbing a hand over her arm in slow sweeps, he said, "This is important to me, what I want to—"

The doorbell interrupted.

He frowned. *What the hell?*

"Maybe they'll..." The bell pealed again. "...leave." He groaned a sigh, rolling his eyes. "Damn it. They couldn't give me one damn day?"

"Who?"

"My family." With a loving kiss to her mouth, he set her away from him to stand. "Don't go anywhere. I'm getting rid of them and then turning off the phone." Water sluiced from him as he hopped over the side and grabbed a towel to briskly dry off. Wrapping it secure over his hips, he gave her one last smile. Turning away from the nymph in the water, he marched toward the source of the repeated peal of his doorbell. "This better be fucking important," he muttered under his breath.

"Look, Dad—" Only he was stopped short when he opened the door. It wasn't his dad.

"Good, you're almost ready." Muffy walked in like she lived there, nodding and arranging her keys and handbag. "Go on, go finish getting dressed. We're going to be late."

"Late? What the hell? What are you doing here?" Dario felt his blood pressure rise as the woman stood eyeing him imperiously, impatience making her toes tap.

"The pride meeting, remember? We're supposed to be there in half an hour."

Antonio! "Fuck!" He raked stiff fingers through his hair. "Look, Muffy, I'm not going. Whatever Antonio said or did—"

Muffy approached and put her palm flat on his chest. Gazing up at him, she smiled. "If you'd rather take a few minutes before," she said with lusting enticement, licking at her lips as though she wanted to lick him. She eyed his bare chest like he was a delicious snack. "It's about time the pride heir took a mate, don't you think?" Golden hair rippled as she bent closer, though careful to not get her business suit damp. "I knew you were waiting for me. I'm ready. I've been waiting for you." Her voice had taken on the seductive growl he'd heard too many times to count.

"Muffy, I can't go, and I'm not mating with you."

"But you need a mate," she persisted. "Your ascension is coming. You can't take over the pride alone. We're perfect together." She closed a little more of the distance between them, her hand lowering to rest on his abdomen.

Dario flinched, trying to halt her progress with a firm hand on hers. *Shit! Last time I answer the door in a towel.*

He captured her arms, stilling her hand from daring to reach for more. Bending to make it clear, he bit out the words. "I found my mate, and she's here. Now get the hell out of my house!"

A gasp snapped him straight, his vision raking from the side entry of the front door toward that sound of shocked horror. The pain on Sheridan's face made his stomach plummet to his ankles. "Sheridan!" She whirled for the deck, the robe she wore flapping in her haste. Good, maybe he'd get a chance to explain it all. There was nowhere to go if she went outside again. He didn't even know how much she'd heard.

With a less than caring grip on Muffy, he opened the door and launched her through it. "Get out! I'm not going. I'm not your mate." Hell at the moment, he was ready to dust his hands of the whole fucking pride!

STRIPPING out of the robe as if it were on fire, Sheridan shot off the deck, running on four feet before she even thought it completely through. She just knew she had to get away. Damn it! She'd almost told him she loved him! Almost started to tell him the truth about her wolf!

We're perfect together.

Sheridan wanted to vomit. She hadn't meant to intrude, but she had to cross the hall to go to the bathroom. Then hearing a woman's voice, she'd peeked. Oh, how stupid had *that* been? They were practically on top of each other. Dario held the other woman close while she all but climbed him. It looked like he was on the verge of kissing her, they were so tight together. And her hand was *in* his damned towel! Sheridan closed her eyes, blocking the wave of pain, but the image remained.

She should have known better. How many times did she have to be taken to realize she would never be good enough? It didn't matter how sweet they talked, or what they promised, they all lied.

She hiccupped, refusing to let the tears blurring her vision make her stop running. Maybe if she was lucky, she'd actually run herself into exhaustion.

DARIO clutched the robe he'd found tossed on the deck in a shaking fist, confused and worried. The robe had been easy to spot, but there was no Sheridan. "Sheridan?" Searching the immediate shadows of the tree line, he couldn't see her, and she was nowhere outside. She hadn't come back in either. "Sheridan!" His voice carried, but there was no answer.

Where did she go? She couldn't have gone far. She was as naked as he was. Dressing in the robe, he tied it with a hard yank, pacing. Waiting. But when a half hour became an hour, and an hour, two and she hadn't returned, he began to fear for her.

She was vulnerable. Sheridan didn't know the land, and being naked... How far *could* she have gone? After an hour of pacing, he took a chance to let his cougar free in broad daylight and shifted, jogging to and fro, searching for any sign of her. Her clean scent literally disappeared only yards from his home, frustrating both his cougar and himself. If there wasn't even a faint trail, he could comb the entire forest and miss her by yards. She couldn't have done a 'Beam me up, Scotty'. So where did she go?

Should he call together a search party? What could he tell them? That they'd had a fight? He knew as the afternoon dragged on that it was going to become a matter of necessity, not choice, to find help to search for her. Creeping closer to the point when common sense had to be obeyed, he dressed in jeans and a t-shirt, silently praying for her to return.

Around four in the afternoon, the gate called his home. "There's a Mr. Rush Donovan here to see you."

Giving the okay, Dario continued to pace, unsure why her brother would be there, unless he was looking for her. Dario didn't want to be the one to tell the man he'd lost his sister.

The knock on his door was loud, almost a pounding. He'd barely opened it when pain exploded across his face. The next conscious moment he was blinking, staring at the vaulted ceiling, cold tile chilling his shoulders. Rolling jerkily to a knee, he cupped his nose. It didn't feel broken, but it throbbed until he was seeing stars. Shaking his head, he sought upward with a blurred gaze. "What the hell?"

"Get me Sheridan's things." A fierce scowl added weight to the demand.

"Where is she? Do you know where she is?" Dario stumbled trying to get to his feet. He reached for a wall to steady himself. A drop of blood on the back of his hand proved the man had cocked him a good one. Grasping the hem of his shirt, he stuffed it under his nose, uncaring of the shirt itself.

"Get me her things before I break your fucking neck!" Rush roared. He must have shut the door after he'd introduced Dario to his fist. He hadn't moved from in front of it.

Swallowing, Dario sucked air. "No. I have to know where she is." He didn't care how foolish it was to face off with her brother. If he knew where Sheridan was then he had to tell Dario.

Rush snarled and stomped past him with a cold shove.

"Wait!" Dario whirled, ignoring the queasy wrench of his stomach with the movement. Doors slammed against walls as Rush searched for her things. Dario found him in his room bent on a knee, stuffing her belongings into her overnight bag. "Please. Where did she go? Is she all right?" He sounded muffled, his voice jacked up with his sinuses closed solid. Stopping in the doorway to try to breathe through his mouth, he said, "Please, is she safe? I searched for over an hour and couldn't find a trace of her."

Rush slowed, but he didn't stop. "She's safe." Dropping her purse in the bag, he then stood. "Is this everything?"

Dario nodded. A headache was forming between his eyes. Not all that surprising, he supposed. "Yes, that's everything."

Rush stalked through the room. Before he could get past Dario, he blurted, "Rush. I love her. I don't know what happened, but I think I know what she thinks she saw. I need to fix it." He leaned on the doorframe, the pressure in his head feeling as though he'd been holding onto a jackhammer. He rested his hand protectively over his nose. "And a bag of ice. You hit like a bastard."

Rush frowned. "I don't know what she saw. She didn't tell me."

Dario wondered if he could get Rush on his side. Closing his eyes and sagging harder on the door, Dario doubted he had a chance. Whatever she'd seen had blown any trust he'd earned to smithereens. "How did she get to you? Don't you live on the other side of the college?"

"Doesn't matter."

Dario followed Sheridan's brother as he marched out of the bedroom for the front door again. He was right. At least she'd made it safe and was where she could be cared for. Dario's shoulders slumped as he trailed after the other man.

"Rush?" Dario was ready to beg. He had to find her. Had to tell her the truth, let her know she was wrong. He didn't give a shit about Muffy. He just didn't know if he'd get the chance to even begin to explain it.

The other man halted in front of the door, slinging the bag over a shoulder. He squarely met Dario's gaze. "Wait a few days. She's not going to hear anything you tell her until then. Don't make me regret letting you have a second chance. She's been hurt enough."

With a grim acceptance, Dario clung to that chance like a life preserver.

CHAPTER THIRTEEN

DARIO didn't go to work on Monday. Being able to breathe was kind of a necessity, and until his swollen sinuses loosened up, he was taking things easy. By Tuesday, he'd made up his mind as to what he was going to do.

He waited in the conference room where most of their meetings were held, strumming the table as he leaned back in the head chair. He waved a hand when his uncle and father walked in, offering them seats. They shared a bewildered look. Dario usually gave the head chair to his dad.

"What happened to you?" his dad asked, promptly sitting to study his son. Dario knew his left eye was seriously blackened, though it was healing.

"Nothing that hasn't been taken care of." Dario wasn't going to bother to explain that part of his weekend. He had a much larger purpose to this gathering.

A moment later, Muffy walked in.

"Shut the door," he ordered. After she did, she turned, smiling. He had little doubt she saw the meeting as the first steps to claiming her in front of the pride alpha. Fire filled his veins, an anger so intense he wanted to strangle every single one of the people in the room with him. "Sit." It was a barked demand, ice off his tongue.

Muffy blinked, but hurried to take a chair, primping her skirt high on her thigh. She had the gall to smile and wink at him. He wanted to throw her in a pigsty and let her play with the livestock, but refrained from being so rude as to say it. He'd never treat a woman that way, but after Sunday, she deserved what she got. It was her damn fault he was in this mess. Hers, and he was positive, his uncle's.

Dario stood, perusing each in turn. "Let me make this perfectly fucking clear. Do not *ever* make arrangements for me again. Do not presume to plan my life." He leaned on his knuckles, flat on the table, glaring at each in turn. "I don't know which one of you thought it would be okay to railroad me into attending the ascension meeting Sunday, and I don't care. Because of your fucking interference, my mate," Dario pinned his gaze on Muffy when she sniffed in utter dismissal, "yes, my *mate* thinks I'm cheating on her with this twit!"

Muffy gasped, her cheeks flooding with outrage.

"Now, wait—"

Dario roared. A literal, 'shut the fuck up' roar.

Antonio fell back into his chair, his jaw loose.

"I have found her, and I love her. If you—sorry to have to include you in this, Dad—if you interfering assholes can't get it through your heads then I'm going to withdraw from the pride."

"Dario!" His father, Pietro, finally interrupted, his stunned expression dissipating.

Dario shook his head. "I'm not done." What came next was entirely for his uncle. He turned to the man on his right, pinning him down with his words. "I know why you chose Muffy to be Matriarch, and honestly Antonio, I don't give a flying shit about what you consider a proper match. Sheridan *will* be Matriarch. If you cause even a hint of discourse, I will leave. I won't challenge you. I will just leave."

"You don't mean it," Pietro stuttered, shocked.

Turning to his dad, Dario said succinctly, "Try me. This is no game. Whoever encouraged Muffy to come to my house Sunday deserves my wrath." Pietro looked absolutely perplexed. It was as Dario figured. Antonio had gone against his wishes and sent her anyway. He stood and straightened his jacket with a firm tug to his sleeves. "And don't think holding my job over my head will make me crack. I have options."

"You won't be able to stay in the Taja community," Antonio pointed out, as though it held weight or mattered to Dario.

"In that, you're wrong," he smoothly overrode him. "But if it comes down to it, I will gladly leave behind all of this manipulative bullshit. The job, the house, all of it." Facing his uncle one last time, Dario gave him a toothy snarl. "Because I know exactly who to name in front of the council if I lose Sheridan completely. And driving a mate away from their match is a crime even you don't want to be charged with, Antonio."

Looking briefly at his father then his uncle, he ignored Muffy. "Think carefully about whose life you want to interfere with again. I can guarantee when I take over for Dad, if I hear a whisper about this kind of bullshit happening, everyone involved will be permanently banned from the pride, and that will only be the place I start. Do I make myself clear?"

"You can't threaten me!" Antonio started to leap from his chair, but Pietro met him halfway.

"*Basta!* My son has spoken." Pietro braced his frame on his palms, eye to eye with his brother. "As head of the Taja pride, I am saying it is enough," he intoned with rolling authority. "Dario has shown incredible tolerance, and I can't fault his decisions."

Drawing a calming breath, he stood before Dario, saying, "I, for one, am glad he found his mate to love." With a hand on his son's shoulder, he gripped him warmly. "If you need any help in clearing this," he gave a flat glance across the table, "let us know."

"Thanks, Dad. But I think I can handle this. She's no one's fool."

"Then I look forward to meeting her."

Glad for his father's support, both with Sheridan and as his successor, he nodded once then left the room to his next mission: claiming Sheridan for his own.

SHERIDAN sat on her couch, huddled under an afghan even though it was ninety-two degrees outside. She still felt frozen inside. She hadn't changed out of her thin sweats since the night before, when even she realized she needed a shower and couldn't stand the sight of herself in the mirror another day. An oversized t-shirt was the balance of her slumming it at home look. What did it matter? No one was going to see her. No one was going to give a damn one way or the other. She didn't have the energy to care yet, either.

A knock at her door should have surprised her, but it didn't. For the last four days she'd received—and rejected—a flower delivery.

"Go away! I don't want them!" She almost screamed it, yanking the afghan tighter around her shoulders.

The doorbell rang this time. Twice. Groaning, she tossed the afghan over the back of her couch. Her TV was off. She couldn't bear to look at it. The movie they'd watched that night sat on the console, lazily forgotten in the rush of the week, and then Mona and Brant's wedding. She couldn't deal with any of it.

The doorbell buzzed again.

"I said I don't want it! Give them away!"

"Sorry, ma'am. I can't do that."

She ground her teeth together. Fine, he wanted to send them, she'd throw them away. Sheridan yanked the door open, ready to lambast the person behind the largest bouquet of pink roses she'd ever seen in her life. All she could see was his hands on the vase. It wasn't all that surprising, she guessed. The deliveries had been growing by monstrous proportions daily.

"This is heavy. It might be a good idea if I set it down for you."

"Only if you can throw it in the trash," she retorted. When the delivery person didn't move, she stepped clear of the door. "Fine, put them down on the bar."

The crystal vase *was* gorgeous, she conceded. Maybe she'd keep that simply because it looked valuable. He held it carefully, positioning it just right. Then he turned.

"You!" She almost shrieked her outrage. "Get out!"

Dario cleared the distance between them, fighting the door from her pinched fingers to swing it shut. "Not until I've had a chance to explain. If you still want me to leave after, I will, but I deserve a chance to clearly explain what it was you saw."

His lips thinned and he crossed his arms. The man wasn't budging.

"I know what I saw! She had her damned hand down your front. Did you enjoy the free feel-up? Or was she next on your list of women to sleep with?" she bit out tightly. The image of him bent down to kiss the woman burned her eyelids. She clenched them, refusing to cry over him.

He raked a hand down his face. "She didn't, but I'm not saying it didn't look that way. My uncle Antonio has been throwing Muffy at me for almost a year, since my dad announced he was ready to step down and let me take his place as head of the Taja pride." Spinning slowly on a heel, he walked the other way. He couldn't go far. He dug his hands into his slacks pockets.

"Sheridan, I realized it over the weekend. I love you. I want to be with you. Muffy has been chasing me, prodded by my uncle. I thought their bullshit would cease when I found my mate, but my uncle chose to ignore it. He's been grooming Muffy to stand with me, and she is just as convinced that she's the next pride Matriarch." Rolling a shoulder, he let out a breath. "In the prides, if a feline doesn't find their mate by a certain age, they're encouraged to take a spouse to keep the prides inclusive, even if they never have children." Lowering his voice, he added, "Even if they don't love each other. I'm not nearly old enough to even have to begin to worry about it, but Muffy was willing to marry me simply because she'd gain the status."

Sheridan shook her head. "Pride?" She couldn't be hearing him the way he meant it.

He turned marginally, and she spotted the circles under his eyes for the first time. They were impossible to miss. He looked exhausted. His hair was mussed and his shirt was wrinkled. He always looked so put together. This wasn't the man she knew. He looked like he hadn't slept in a week.

"Yes, Sheridan. I'm a cat shifter. My shifter is a cougar."

Her legs felt wobbly. This couldn't be happening. She collapsed to the floor, a chair nowhere nearby to make it easier on her. "Are you serious?"

He barked a gruff laugh. "Yeah. I didn't think you'd believe me. I didn't explain that the way I wanted to, either." Covering his face in his palms, he scrubbed absently, his shoulders shuddering. Sucking in a deep breath, a moment later he let them drop, gazing at her. "Muffy was sent to the house on Sunday by Antonio for a meeting I'd already told them I wouldn't be attending. She's nothing to me, never has been. I've never even kissed her." A broad blanch of disgust made his jaw move, like he was tasting something bad. "Hell, I was trying to kick her out when you turned the corner. She was..." He smirked. "Well, you saw what she was trying to do." With a forlorn sound, he added, "She was trying. Believe me when I say I didn't want her to, and wasn't encouraging her."

She couldn't formulate a single coherent sentence. Shifter? He was a *cougar*?

He approached and squatted down on his haunches in front of her. "Sheridan, say something." He lifted a shaking hand, and with stuttered hesitation, touched her cheek. "I know it's a lot to take in, but know this, I love you. I don't want to live without you."

Looking up into his eyes, tawny eyes that were cloudy with his pain and fatigue, she blurted, "Wolf. I'm wolf."

He blinked, straightening an inch or two. "What?"

"It won't work," was her next realization, her thoughts whipping frantically as images of their future became unveiled. "You're cougar. I'm wolf. They'll never accept me."

"They will, or I'll leave," he stated emphatically, with an assuredness that stunned her.

"No! You can't."

He dropped to the floor with her. "I will. Nothing and no *one* is as important to me as you are, sweetheart." He brushed her cheek with the pad of his thumb. "You're really wolf?"

She swallowed, her heart thundering in her chest before she managed a weak nod. "You're not shocked?"

"Actually, I am. But not that you're wolf, that you're shifter at all." With a note of acknowledgement, he murmured, "That's how you disappeared. God, I was worried sick."

"You were?" *He'd cared enough to look?* That took a moment to process.

"Yes! I searched for over an hour and was convincing myself I had no choice but to call in a search party when Rush showed up."

The feather light glide of his hand caressed her arm as he traced her with a fingertip to reach her hand. Threading her fingers through his, she soaked up his physical warmth, beginning to feel the thaw of her soul.

"I had no idea," he mused, watching their clasped hands.

"Me either." Then she shook her head. "No." She tugged her hand away, curling into her body. Her heart was stuttering, torn between rejoicing and shattering over and over again.

"But, Sheridan—"

Before he could say more, she silenced him with a finger to his mouth. "It gets worse."

"How?" he mumbled around her digit.

"I'm Rush's second in the pack. He's our Alpha, *my* Alpha. I can't leave him. He's my only family." She knew she was pleading, but for what she didn't know.

Shackling her wrist gently to speak, he answered her. "I never would ask you to, Sheridan."

"I can't be two things at once," she denied. The truth made her throat convulse with tears she refused to let escape.

"Why not? People are heads of their prides, as well as work, have families, hobbies. Why can't you be the Taja Matriarch and Rush's second lieutenant? The odds of having a crisis happen for each side at the exact same time where you'd be split down the middle for loyalty are astronomical. We'll cross that bridge if and when we ever get to it." Leaning forward off his knees, he cradled her in his palms. "Listen to me, lovely. No matter what we do, I will *never* take you away from your family. Yes, I would give up everything for you, but I had made the decision as to which was more important before anything else. Even before I sent the first bouquet to try to get you just to talk to me. If my pride denies my ascension because of you, I will leave them. They are not my pride if they are that prejudiced. My father agrees with me."

Her chest staggered as her heart thumped painfully. "You would really do that?"

"In a heartbeat," he answered sincerely, without a flicker of remorse.

She lifted again, pressing her fingertips to his lips, this time not to silence him, but in awe of him. "You really do love me." His eyes softened, their warmth so deep, she felt utterly embraced in it.

"Heart and soul," he whispered.

Leaping forward, she launched herself into his embrace. "I love you!"

Wrapped into his crushing arms, held so tight she felt the knit of his shirt through her own, he fell over backward, taking her with him. "I love you, Sheridan." His breath twisted through the loose strands of her hair. "I missed you, baby." Sweeping it up and away, he searched her eyes, the dimness she'd seen gone. Now his eyes glowed. "Make me an honest man, sweetheart. Marry me."

Trembling against his chest, she choked, knowing she was seconds from sobbing uncontrollably. "Yes." She hid in the crook of his neck.

"Shh, sweetheart," he soothed her. "It'll be okay. You'll see." He stroked her hair and back until she calmed, then he continued to do it for a long time after.

EPILOGUE

DARIO walked in from the garage, setting his briefcase on the small breakfast nook table. Twisting his neck, he let out a sigh accompanied by three soft pops. As he was stripping his jacket, he noticed the standing folded card on the table, with his name in classic calligraphy to get his attention. After setting his suit jacket on a chair back, he lifted the card and read.

"Good for one *hot* fantasy." He chuckled. *What are you doing, sweetheart?* he mused. Glancing around the kitchen for any sign of her, he spotted another sheet on the counter with his name on it. Feeling a rush of adrenaline that swept away the fatigue of his day, he turned it over. It was Sheridan's grades for her final quarter and her artwork reel. Along with a note from her instructor:

Best work I've seen in four years of any student. I have three studios interested in your submission reel. Email me the okay to forward. Prof. E.

"Oh, hot damn," he breathed, letting out a whistle. Pride for his woman's skills filled him. He knew how hard she'd worked on that final reel. He'd gladly given up one of his rooms to let her have her own workspace. It was currently covered wall to wall with drawings, sketches and things he couldn't begin to name, but she knew it all inside and out. They balanced each other out. Sheridan didn't even argue over letting him pay the bills or handle the checking account.

Holding both card and page, he turned, aiming for the bedroom. He was stopped short at the formal dining table. Another bent card rested on the polished wood. Now, instead of four places, the table was permanently set for two, and they ate there together every night.

Laughing, he read the latest find. "If you don't hurry, you'll miss the final *climax.*" Air slammed out of his lungs. "Oh shit!"

Sprinting for their bedroom, he slid to a halt in the doorway. There, lying in the middle of the bed was Sheridan. Silken skin was wrapped in black lace draping from her shoulders to the tops of her thighs in a boudoir pose to rival the sexiest centerfold. The woman he'd met more than seven months ago had bloomed into a tempestuous vixen with a lingerie addiction. Not that he'd *ever* complain. He tugged at his necktie, feeling his smile and his cock both swell. "Hello, gorgeous."

Stretched out on her side, her head cupped in a lifted palm, she dragged a fingertip along her hip.

"I see you found them," she murmured, eyeing the papers in his hand.

Startled and forgetting he was holding anything, he chuckled, waving them between his fingers. "Congratulations. I knew you had a winner."

Lashes lowered for a second, a slight smile accompanied by a blush flitting over her features.

Loosening his tie, he yanked it free, popping buttons with a quick pace until his shirt was undone. Setting down the cards and page, he stalked to the bed, crawling up on his hands and knees. "So, what's the special occasion? Celebrating your grades?"

She shook her head, a knowing, teasing glimmer in her eyes.

"Um... It's Friday?" He moved forward a few inches.

Another grinning head shake. Peering at him through heavy lashes, she told him, "Do you realize since meeting you, how much I've accomplished?"

Dario paused, resting on his knees. Discovering the deep sparkle in her blue eyes, he realized this was important. "No. I just wanted what was best for you. I could see it..." She nodded, licking her bottom lip with a slow tongue. *Witch,* he lovingly accused.

"When I couldn't." She flipped the lace and silk robe length off her hip, exposing the high cut body sheath. She slipped a nail under the edge, along the indent of her hip and thigh. "You've also..." She blushed harder. "You've also helped me find my pride." It was a murmured breath. Her breasts rose and fell beneath the lace cups. Her nipples puckered as he stared and his cock answered her arousal, aching behind his slacks' zipper. "Looking at you, the way you're following my every motion right now, I feel powerful. I *feel* beautiful."

"Sweetheart. You are. Gorgeous." When he went to lean forward, she shook her head, and he paused, frowning.

Sheridan rolled to her back, her thick hair spilling around her shoulders on the white quilt. The contrast of black on white was stunning, showcasing her like a jewel. She lifted her free hand over her head, stretching her length. The fingers trailing her hip inched completely beneath the silk sheath. Her eyes grew heavy lidded as she neared her pussy. Dario shrugged out of his loose shirt, tossing it to the floor.

"Sexy," he rasped.

Then she widened her thighs and her lips parted on a gasp.

"Shit," he groaned. "Don't stop." Slipping from the bed, he tugged at his zipper, easing the pressure on his cock with a solid groan rising. Snatching one of the dressing chairs, he brought it closer and promptly collapsed into it, his hand already stroking his cock. He loved watching her pleasure herself. Sheridan was incredible, sexy and very willing to please her, him and them.

He understood what she was doing, and why, and loved her more for it every day. He'd watched her come out of her insecure shell a little at a time. She never cringed anymore, and she never doubted herself around other women. It didn't matter to him at all if anyone thought she wasn't worthy. Hers, then his opinions were the only ones that mattered, and he'd shown that to her every day.

Now, he had a sexy goddess on his bed inching toward an orgasm just to please and arouse him, making his heart pound.

"You're beautiful," he encouraged her. "I love watching you." She moaned in answer, a breathy sound that shot another wave of desire into his bloodstream.

Bringing her other hand between her legs, she tugged on the crotch of her negligee and it popped free, three little snaps. He swallowed, his eyes on her soaked slit. He hissed in answer, fighting to stay in the chair. Lifting his hips, he dropped his slacks, kicking them, his shoes and socks off as quickly as possible until he was in the chair naked.

Heat roared through his body following her motions. She played with her clit, moaning, her ass cheeks clenching and rising off the bed as her orgasm rushed down on her.

"Come for me, baby. Cream that hot pussy for me."

She whimpered, her breasts shaking as her efforts increased.

Rolling his hand over the top of his cock, he used the pearls to slicken the tightness of his shaft beneath his palm.

With a guttural cry, she arched, her pussy convulsing as her orgasm crashed over her. Dropping to his knees on the floor at the side of the bed, he yanked her close and dove into the heated silk of her climax, thrusting his tongue to lap at her. In a matter of seconds, she was crying out, clawing the bed as her pleasure crested again.

Standing, he eased between her thighs. With Sheridan on the pill, they didn't need condoms anymore, and Dario loved feeling her skin to skin. He dropped kisses to her soft belly, letting her catch her breath. Licking his way up her frame, he nipped at her ribs, then beneath her breast, until he finally found a hardened tip to suckle.

She groaned, pushing herself into him.

Holding her hip, he steadied his stance and with a single push, thrust deep into her welcoming body. His eyes slammed shut as sensations poured over him. "Oh, damn," he groaned. "So good."

Reaching, he stole a hard kiss from her lips, placing a palm near her shoulder to hold himself up.

"Wrap yourself around me, baby." She lifted her hips and he drove into her. She howled; the one sound that drove him out of his mind. His balls tightened up against his body.

Gripping her hips, he pounded into her, filling her as deep as he could reach. Her walls clenched down on him, shuddering with the pace.

"Harder," she gasped.

He gritted his teeth knowing he was going to shatter. Nails raked down his arms, drawing his primal needs closer to the surface. The pain and pleasure of their bite reached everywhere from his shoulders to his hips and across his chest. Focused on her, he loved every single sting, every single mark his woman gave him. She was so close, her body dripped with the sign of her impending climax.

"Do it, Sheridan," he growled. He couldn't get enough of her hot body as he fucked her, and she wanted it, needed more. Snapping his head back on his shoulders he roared, the rush of his orgasm flooding his veins, thickening his cock until he felt every inch of her clenched around him, each stroke as he filled her, pounded into her.

The steamy cream of her orgasm rushed over his skin and he shuddered, lights sparking and popping on his eyelids. Wave after wave flowed between them as he stiffened in spurts, driving into her softness, each pulse of his cock driving a new height of pleasure from her body to coat his flesh.

Gasping, he sagged, the steel in his spine turning into a noodle. His legs were water. Sheridan lay there, panting, her skin flushed with a rose pink and her lips swollen from biting them. Slowly, the room came back into view as the slight draft of the heater rolled over his shoulders.

With a flicked look outside the windows, he noticed it had started to snow.

Lucky for him, he had a reason to be inside for the entire weekend. Folding in half, he laid down beside her, cradling the woman he loved into his arms.

"Rest, lovely," he managed, sounding raw.

Nodding, she snuggled into his frame and together, they dozed their way into the weekend.

The End

ABOUT THE AUTHOR

DIANA DERICCI is the sexy, flirty pen name of Diana Castilleja. A romance author at heart, DeRicci's writing takes you into a saucier spectrum of sensuality and sexual adventure, where a happily-ever-after is still the key to any story. Diana lives in Central Texas with her husband, one son and a feisty little Chihuahua named Rascal. You can catch the latest news on all of Diana DeRicci's writing and books on her website. Feel free to drop Diana an email. She'd love to hear from you.

Visit her on the web at:
www.DianaDeRicci.com

PURPLE SWORD PUBLICATIONS
Romantic Speculative Fiction
www.purplesword.com